COURTING
MISFORTUNE

Books by Regina Jennings

THE JOPLIN
CHRONICLES
* 1 *

COURTING MISFORTUNE

REGINA JENNINGS

BETHANYHOUSE

a division of Baker Publishing Group
Minneapolis, Minnesota

Published by Bethany House Publishers
11400 Hampshire Avenue South
Bloomington, Minnesota 55438
www.bethanyhouse.com

Bethany House Publishers is a division of
Baker Publishing Group, Grand Rapids, Michigan

Printed in the United States of America

Library of Congress Cataloging-in-Publication Data
Names: Jennings, Regina (Regina Lea), author.
Title: Courting misfortune / Regina Jennings.
Description: Minneapolis, Minnesota : Bethany House, a division of Baker
    Publishing Group, [2020] | Series: The Joplin chronicles ; 1
Identifiers: LCCN 2020029205 | ISBN 9780764235344 (trade paperback) | ISBN
    9780764237898 (casebound) | ISBN 9781493428267 (ebook)
Subjects: GSAFD: Historical fiction.
Classification: LCC PS3610.F5614 C68 2020 | DDC 813/.6—dc23
LC record available at https://lccn.loc.gov/2020029205

Scripture quotations are from the King James Version of the Bible.

This is a work of historical reconstruction; the appearances of certain historical figures are therefore inevitable. All other characters, however, are products of the author's imagination, and any resemblance to actual persons, living or dead, is coincidental.

Cover design by Dan Thornberg, Design Source Creative Services

20 21 22 23 24 25 26   7 6 5 4 3 2 1

For Kristy, Ann, and N'Lisa.
I'll never forget how you made the fort feel like home.

For TREL.
I'll never forget how you turned our home into a fort.

The Kentworth Family

Albert & Laura Kentworth

Children
— Bill — m June
  - Finn   Amos   Maisie

— Oscar — m Myra
  - Willow   Olive

— Pauline (Polly) — m Richard York
  - Corban   Calista   Evangelina

Calbert Kentworth — m Gretchen
(Grandpa Albert's Twin Brother)
  - Hannah   Hilda   Hank

CHAPTER

1

1898
CHICAGO

"You want me to work for Jinxy Seaton?" Calista York dropped her handbag onto her desk and reached up to remove her hatpin from her heavy swirl of brown curls. "The last I heard, we had scruples against helping criminal gangsters who corrupt Chicago with their nefarious—"

She was interrupted by the clatter of a letter opener skittering across the desk and landing on the floor. Calista froze, hands above her head, gripping her hatpin in case it was needed for defense. One look showed her that her boss, Robert Pinkerton, was the offender, and it wasn't advisable to poke him with a hatpin, no matter the provocation.

"I'm talking about Mr. Jinxy Seaton," Mr. Pinkerton said, his voice a growled whisper. "The man who risked his life to double-cross the unions for this agency and who is now sitting in my office." With a jerk of his grayed head, he motioned to the open door.

Calista leaned to peer around the doorframe. While she couldn't exactly see Mr. Seaton, she did get the definite sense of a dark mass in the chair opposite Mr. Pinkerton's desk. She was paid to be observant, but she'd missed that?

Sorry, she mouthed as she lifted her hat off her bouffant and deposited it next to her bag.

"What I was telling you is that our good friend Mr. Seaton is requesting our help." This time Mr. Pinkerton's voice echoed through the office as if he were giving another speech to the Railroad Loss Prevention Board. "Why don't you join us in my office, Miss York?" He widened his eyes to emphasize the importance of her cooperation.

Bending, Calista swept her hand beneath the desk until her fingers hit cold metal. "You seem to have misplaced your letter opener," she said and dropped the utensil into his palm as she walked past him.

Jinxy stood when she entered. Two hundred and fifty pounds of sausage and cannelloni stuffed into a striped suit. She dipped her head to avoid a handshake and took a station in the corner behind Mr. Pinkerton's desk.

Calista had worked undercover for five months. When she applied for the job as a Pinkerton agent, she'd understood there would be danger and intrigue. She'd anticipated that there would be distasteful assignments, or at the very least, ones that required her to don a wardrobe that was particularly loathsome. If she was going to enter Jinxy's world, she had to prepare herself for even greater indignities. But seeing a wrong righted would always be worth it.

"Miss Calista York has joined our staff since your earlier association with our company." Mr. Pinkerton pushed his chair to one side so he could view both Calista and his client as Jinxy took a seat. "She is our youngest female operative and has just returned from Emporia, Kansas, where she helped bust a smuggling ring on Mr. Buchanan's railroad. Before that she was instrumental in obtaining a confession from an embezzler, but she has no experience with kidnappers."

Calista shot a sideways glance at Pinkerton. Despite her success in her last case, Pinkerton still expressed misgivings over her skills. He thought she was overconfident and naive. Her partners worried that she wasn't discreet enough. She had to convince them that she could do better if she wanted a permanent spot with the agency.

"I'm not interested in stopping any smuggling or embezzlement," Jinxy said. "A man's got to earn a living. All I'm interested in is finding Lila. Just knowing she's alive . . ." He pulled out a crisp handkerchief and blew into it like a foghorn. "Ever since Florence was killed, we've kept an eye on Lila. Somehow even that wasn't enough."

"Remind us about Florence. Was your daughter's killer ever found?" Pinkerton asked.

"No, but my gut tells me the same people took Lila. I didn't think we'd ever see her again, but now, eight months after she disappeared, someone spotted her six hundred miles away." Jinxy wadded his handkerchief and shoved it into his vest's inner pocket. "But who has her? What are they doing with her? She was at a place . . . a place she shouldn't be. My own flesh and blood being exploited. I can't bear it."

Mr. Pinkerton rubbed his brow. "I wish you would reconsider and use one of our male operatives. Mr. Sampson is available, and he's got a strong record of—"

"Absolutely not. Lila's barely twenty years old, and just think what she's been through in the last eight months. The thought of a man going after her . . . absolutely not." His jowls quivered, and he swung his arm in Calista's direction. "This gal will do. She looks like a reassuring sort."

Pinkerton looked anything but reassured. "You say we have a witness who saw her, and with that information, we have every hope that this case will be resolved speedily and your daughter will be returned to you soon, even without the assistance of Mr. Sampson."

"I sincerely hope so." Jinxy leaned over the desk, his fists clenched. "Those goons with the union know I helped you. My life and my business have been wrecked since then. At the very least, you can do this for me. If I don't get my daughter back, I don't know what I'll do."

Beneath the veiled threat, Calista sensed a father genuinely concerned about his daughter. She leaned against the wall and studied him. If knowledge of his double-crossing the union had gotten out, that was incentive enough to murder his family. Florence was already one innocent casualty, but it sounded like Lila's suffering had just begun.

"Do you have a photo?" she asked.

Mr. Pinkerton raised an eyebrow at her interruption but remained silent as Jinxy shoved his hand into his vest and produced a bent photograph. Calista stepped up to the desk as he dropped it in front of them.

"That's her a year ago. Her mother had that dress made special for the Spring Ball. I couldn't believe how grown-up she looked."

Lila was striking, posed as she looked over her shoulder, her thick dark hair pulled back from her high forehead and arranged like a cloud. And although one had to ignore the hand-tinting on the photograph, the rosy cheeks didn't seem out of place with her porcelain complexion. *Beautiful* wasn't the right word . . . maybe *haunting*. Haunted. Calista leaned forward for a better look. Yes, there was fear in her eyes.

"Someone saw her?" Calista asked. "They're sure it was her?"

"Yes, ma'am." His nose wrinkled as he spat out the words. "It was a brothel in Joplin, Missouri. The House of Lords."

At the name of the city, Calista's attention snapped to Mr. Pinkerton. Her Granny Laura lived outside Joplin. Joplin was practically Calista's second home. Mr. Pinkerton knew that, but his ever-so-slight movement toward his letter opener warned her to keep that information to herself.

Calista backed away from the desk until she felt the wall behind her. Work in Joplin? Was it possible? She'd assumed that secrecy was required with all cases. Although she'd grown up in Kansas City, which was one hundred and fifty miles from Joplin, her family's presence would make it impossible for her to work there incognito. On the other hand, she'd have connections available that she'd never had before. Working in Joplin would change the game.

As Mr. Seaton elaborated on the events that led him to them, Calista couldn't tear her eyes from the picture of Lila. According to her father, Miss Seaton had gone on a shopping excursion with her mother and an aunt. One minute she was trying on hats in a crowded haberdashery, the next she'd vanished. For weeks the Chicago police had taken notes, patrolled neighborhoods, and questioned Jinxy's foes, but they hadn't found anything. It wasn't until a business associate—Calista knew not to inquire as to what kind of business—told Jinxy that he'd seen Lila inside a Joplin brothel that they knew she'd survived and was still in danger.

"Who was this witness?" Mr. Pinkerton leaned back in his chair and steepled his fingers over his chest. "Can we interview him?"

"He's not keen on talking to detectives. Besides, he's currently unavailable." Jinxy lowered his eyes.

Calista shot a glance at her boss before asking, "If she's alive, why doesn't she contact you?"

"She's kept captive," Jinxy replied. "What else?"

"In Joplin, Missouri?" Pinkerton raised an eyebrow. "Compared to Chicago, that seems as wholesome—"

"You don't know Joplin," Calista interrupted. Joplin was a mining town that had sprung up out of the dirt. The quick money had attracted the most unsavory of characters and industries, creating a wild reputation in the region. Now, decades after the first zinc was discovered, the newly wealthy were trying to create a society out of rough parts, yet many of the homes considered respectable were funded by others' miseries.

As a child, Calista had spent every summer at Granny Laura's ranch, but when they went to town, Granny Laura guarded them like a mother hen marching her chicks through a snake pit. Calista would admit that her head got turned by the luxurious clothing the fancy women wore as they paraded right down Main Street, but she would never forget the girls tucked away in darker alleys. No one would voluntarily submit to the anguish she saw on their faces. If someone was going to profit from Lila's capture, Joplin was the logical place to take her.

"You know it will take time," Mr. Pinkerton said. "Our operatives have to create their characters. They have to integrate into society. Miss York won't walk into town, announce that she's a detective, and pass your daughter's photo around. Our methods yield results, but you must be patient."

"When I think of what she's enduring . . ." Mr. Seaton reached for the photo but stopped short, resting his hand on the desk. "I'll be as patient as I'm able. I just want her to know that no matter what she's done, or what's been done to her, we love her and want her to come home."

An admirable sentiment from a despicable character. But Lila was no gangster. She was an innocent girl, and she needed help.

And despite Mr. Pinkerton's misgivings, Calista considered herself the perfect person to rescue her.

JOPLIN, MISSOURI

If a young lady had been forced into a life of depravity and bondage, she wouldn't be staying at the Keystone Hotel. The six-story luxury hotel at Fourth and Main was respectable, which meant

Calista had to get away from her apartment to search for Lila. But she didn't have to go far.

In the shadow of the great hotel was the most notorious establishment in town. The House of Lords purported to be a café. That was what was on the ground floor, but everyone knew what went on upstairs. Calista had only arrived yesterday, but she was ready to storm the castle. She'd never heard of a case where they'd gotten such specific information about a missing person. If Lila was being held at the House of Lords, that was where Calista would start looking, albeit carefully. If the people holding her got spooked, the girl could disappear again, never to be found.

Calista cruised by the brothel's building again, wondering how to proceed. Before she'd left Chicago, Pinkerton had extracted a promise from her that she wouldn't pose as a soiled dove to get inside, that she wouldn't overestimate her skills, and that she would tell no one about her mission. If she didn't succeed within the month, he would insist that Jinxy replace Calista with a more experienced operative. In fact, Pinkerton was already making arrangements for her failure.

One month. If she couldn't find Lila Seaton by then, Calista would be recalled in disgrace, and her probation period with the agency would come to an end. She held her head high as she passed the shoeshine boy for the third time. Perhaps she should have thought up a strategy before leaving her apartment that morning.

Since this was only her third case and her first as the primary operative, her briefing with Pinkerton had been thorough. Together they pondered the inconsistencies of Jinxy's story. How could Lila be held in plain sight? Why hadn't she asked anyone for help? The kidnappers must hold some power over her. Maybe they'd drugged her until she was reliant on them, or perhaps mere threats against her family were enough to keep her compliant—her sister's recent murder made such threats believable. Whatever the situation, Calista would be dealing with dangerous men, but she had faith. God had called her on this path. Whatever she faced, it was better than her pointless existence as a debutante in Kansas City.

She needed to do the job and find Lila before Pinkerton talked Jinxy Seaton into replacing her.

But she couldn't bring herself to cross the threshold of that demon's lair. Once, when she was young, she'd asked to eat at the restaurant, and Granny Laura had said she'd rather Calista eat cold beans out of a tin can than give Rahn's House of Lords a dime of her honest money. Now that she understood, Calista wholeheartedly agreed with Granny Laura, but her personal preferences had to be set aside for the greater good. If she wanted to keep her job, she had to swallow her disgust and play the role.

On her sixth pass, Calista had started for the door of the café when she saw a small bag fall to the ground. It looked like a money sack—wrinkled and mostly empty, but valuable to someone, and that someone was probably the miner sauntering by.

"Excuse me," she called. She stood over the bag. "Sir, you dropped this."

He turned, but before he could react, a woman swooped down, snatched the bag off the ground, and made to flee.

"Hold up, sister." Calista grabbed a handful of tattered skirt, stopping the woman's escape.

"It's mine. I found it." The woman tried to tuck the money bag into the bosom of her dress, but as it was already full, there wasn't room.

The miner patted his empty pockets. "That's my money," he said. "It's all I have left until Saturday."

Calista tried to wrestle the bag from the woman's hand. "It isn't yours. I saw it fall, and you were nowhere near it." If she'd meant to stay inconspicuous in Joplin, she was failing, but she couldn't help herself. "Give it back to him."

With timely intervention, the miner pried the money bag free with blackened hands. "I did an honest day's work," he said to the bedraggled woman. "Go on and earn your own."

"If I had honest work available, I would," she huffed. Then, with a sneer toward Calista, she stalked away.

The miner paused only for a grateful nod before ambling off in the other direction.

Calista dusted off her white gloves. That had been gratifying. Equally gratifying was that her dress hadn't been mussed in the unexpected tussle, but she couldn't delay any longer. It was time to confront the House of Lords.

Through the windows, a shiny soda bar was visible along one wall, with electric lights reflecting in the mirrors behind it. Ladies and gentlemen crowded around the square tables, and it looked as proper as the Harvey House restaurant her cousin Willow had worked in. If one didn't know the owner's association with the activity upstairs, they wouldn't find anything untoward with the café.

Calista reached for the long brass door handle, but a hand appeared from behind her, pressing the door closed and blocking her path.

"I beg your pardon!" She fumed at the young man who positioned himself between her and the door. "I did not request your assistance."

He stood coiled, shoulders tense like he was prepared for battle. "You don't belong in this restaurant. It'd be better for you if you kept on moving."

She did a quick assessment of his plain workman's clothing. His eyes were clear, and his jaw was thrust forward as if expecting a strike. A glance from him to the three suit-clad men waiting to enter showed that he wasn't likely to be a customer. What, then? Some kind of tough hired to watch for trouble?

Excusing himself, he allowed the men to pass but didn't offer Calista the same courtesy.

"Don't be concerned for me," she said. "I was deciding whether to shop first and eat second, or eat first and shop second. Picking out a button hook for my boots is a serious matter. I wouldn't want to do it when I'm hungry, and I've heard the chicken salad at this restaurant is superb. On the other hand, a full meal often makes me drowsy, and making such an important decision should only be done when one is alert." According to Calista's experience, talking about shopping was guaranteed to lull the masculine mind into a stupor. She could only hope the stupor would be deep enough that he would forget about her.

Sliding his hand beneath his broad-brimmed hat, he brushed his sandy-brown hair out of his eyes. His glance did a swift sweep from the top of her plumed bonnet to the double-ribboned hem of her skirt. "Whatever instinct is keeping you away from this place, you should heed it."

Was that a threat? Calista's eyes glinted. Thus far, her youth had served her well in her profession. She'd never been challenged this early in an investigation. People found it easy to believe she was a feckless young girl who had stumbled unintentionally into whatever trouble they caught her in. She'd have to play it out, especially if this man was connected to the House of Lords.

"I'm very hungry, and being hungry makes me cantankerous, I'm afraid. Now, I'm determined to eat here, especially since you're teasing me like this." She braved a generous smile at the unsmiling man. "So if you'd excuse me . . ."

He tilted his head as if listening for a signal, then grimaced like he'd been stabbed in the gut. "I reckon I have to go in with you."

"What?" Calista felt a zap of anxiety rush through her. What had she done wrong? Did they know she was coming? Had someone followed her from Chicago? She gripped her handbag. Was this how Lila Seaton had felt when someone approached her at the haberdashery before she disappeared? "I'm not accustomed to eating with strangers," she said.

16

"If you're entering this establishment, I'm going to insist that you do so under my watch."

Part of her wanted to turn and run—this was a dangerous and unexpected complication—but she would hold to her role of a young lady coming to Joplin to look for work. Not a particularly wise young lady, nor a particularly respectable young lady. A young lady who might just think it an adventure to eat with a good-looking stranger, no matter how stern his expression.

Calista tried another smile. "If you insist, although you shouldn't think this gives you leave to be familiar."

If she'd thought her flirtation would win him over, she was mistaken. He dipped his chin and gave her a dour look that would be more at home on the face of a bloodhound.

She pulled the door open, surprised when he followed her in silence. The maître d' showed them to a table. Calista noticed that the café host was careful not to acknowledge any connection to the stranger.

She picked up a menu and hid her face behind it while trying to think how a normal, sane woman would act in this circumstance. Flattered? Annoyed? Shocked? She'd set the gauge at eighty percent annoyed and fifteen percent inconvenienced. She might as well leave five percent available for *flattered*, just in case she found a weakness to exploit in him.

Calista perused the listings of soups and beef cuts before remembering that she'd already committed to chicken salad. At least she hadn't previously expressed a preference for dessert. That would allow her some choice. She lowered the menu as the waiter approached and turned to her fuming companion for their order.

"I'm not buying anything," he said. "Only the lady will be eating."

"Yes, sir. And what will she be having?" Every stitch of the waiter's uniform was perfection, showing that the management here let no detail go unchallenged.

This rube hadn't been to many fine dining establishments, because he should've known that the gentleman always ordered for the lady. He squirmed in his seat as Calista and the waiter both stared at him. "How would I know what she wants to eat?" he said.

Calista cleared her throat. "I'll have the chicken salad plate and an iced tea, please. That's all for now."

The waiter smiled in sympathy as he took the menus and carried her order to the kitchen. Calista folded her hands in her lap. The situation wasn't a total loss. If she was searching for unusual activity that might point to criminality, she'd certainly found it. This man might be the first string to unravel in the mystery. It was up to her to do some picking if she wanted to find a loose end.

"We haven't been properly introduced," she said. "My name is Calista York."

He grunted. His eyes never stopped roving the room. "Matthew Cook."

"You've already had dinner, Mr. Cook?" She spread her napkin on her lap and tipped her face up to look at him.

"No, but I'm not going to eat right now. Not while I'm working."

"What exactly is your purpose at the House of Lords?"

"That depends on you." His gaze landed sharply on hers.

She chuckled lightly, but beneath the table she gripped the side of her chair. "I don't understand how my actions could influence your job." Taking stock of the ladies next to them, Calista decided they were respectable, wealthy, and unconcerned with the implications of where they were. More than likely, they had just concluded their charity meeting and were coming to eat. The fact that this establishment profited off the exploitation of girls didn't seem to bother them in the least. God forgive them. And Calista had to pretend to be just like them.

"You aren't here for the chicken salad," Mr. Cook said.

"What other possible reason could I have for sitting down to dinner?" she asked, wondering why he had to be so insightful.

"I don't know, and that's why I'm keeping an eye on you."

Prying her fingers off her chair, she touched the dark curls that had been caught in an upsweep. Since her eyelashes shared the same abundance as her hair, she performed a copious amount of fluttering as she lowered her eyes to her plate. He was demanding an explanation.

"It seems you are correct," she said at last. "I have another purpose for being here. I'm looking for employment, and I thought this place might need my services."

He flopped back in his chair as if the distance gave him a better view of her. "Exactly what kind of services do you offer?"

She wouldn't disappear like Lila. Robert Pinkerton knew where she was and expected her to check in regularly. She had the security of the Pinkerton Agency behind her. And if they failed, the entire Kentworth family would come to her aid. But she still felt chilled by his tone.

"I'm a designer," she said, surprised, as always, how easy it was to slip into character once she determined it was necessary. "I've heard that the rooms upstairs are in need of updating, and I'd like to offer my services."

If she'd thought he looked stern before, his face was a thundercloud now. "What exactly do you know about what goes on upstairs?"

"I'm no prude, I assure you. But my interest is in providing for myself, not in passing judgment on anyone." A bigger lie she'd never told. Calista was intensely judging all the customers in the café as a trio of ladies walked into the building and toward the staircase in the back. If it weren't for the addition of rouge and ostrich-plumed hats, they wouldn't have looked any different from the society ladies at the next table. Calista searched each face, looking for the missing girl, but found nothing.

Mr. Cook's demeanor toward her had changed. He didn't look as threatening—just sad. He took his hat from the table. "I misjudged the situation," he said. "You aren't who I thought you were."

Why was he disappointed? And how dare he make her feel guilty? His own conscience had to be as black as coal. "Who exactly were you looking for?" she asked.

"Someone I could help." He stood, pulled his hat low over his sorrowful eyes, and strode away, leaving Calista unsettled and wary.

CHAPTER

2

It had seemed so simple back home in Pine Gap. Matthew Cook had heard the call of God since he was young. It wasn't until he was fifteen and watched his uncle waste away from a poisoned liver that his calling had taken a specific bent. It was then that he discovered where he wanted to serve.

Matthew stopped at the corner and marveled at the busy street as he waited to cross. Main Street was as wide as the auction barn in Pine Gap. No narrow paths through the forest here. The only trees left standing downtown were the naked telephone poles bearing thick black lines in tangled masses at their tops. Instead of a squirrel scurrying across the road, Matthew saw horses, streetcars, and numerous liquor wagons making their deliveries to the saloons and whiskey dens on Main Street.

From the altar of his country church, Matthew had promised God to go to the darkest, most desperate place on earth. There were Mohammedans in the desert, witch doctors in deepest Africa, and idolaters in the Orient. Surely God wanted him in one of those places. And that was what he'd thought, until family matters alerted him to another place darker and more desperate than anywhere else.

Joplin.

Finding a gap in the parade of vehicles, Matthew jogged across the street and continued toward his apartment behind the flower shop. Grandpa Cook would be leaving in a few hours, now that Matthew was settled in, but Matthew could tell he was loath to go. Grandpa Cook had already watched Joplin destroy his son, and he had misgivings about leaving a member of the next generation. Truth be told, Matthew had half a mind to go back home with him. What if he hadn't heard God clearly? He'd thought he was supposed to come to Joplin, but he'd also thought he was supposed to intervene with that Calista York.

He'd wanted to warn Miss York that the House of Lords was no place for a lady, but instead he'd learned that she was looking to join their godless endeavors. He had to stop her. He had to stop her and the other pampered, rich people profiting from selling women. He had to interfere with the businesses that traded the miners' wages for whiskey instead of vittles. But if he was going to accomplish anything, he had to toughen up.

If he couldn't stand up to a thoughtless woman like Miss York, how was he going to preach in this town? He might not have another chance to set her straight, but he should be better prepared when he ran into her kind.

On the other hand, the battle-weary miner stumbling down the road needed his help more than the likes of Miss York. Matthew paused as the miner passed him on sore joints, barely able to keep the bottle from slipping from his hand and breaking on the sidewalk.

Out here was where Matthew needed to be, but not just out here on the street. He needed to be in the ore fields. That was where the spiritually hungry were. In the two days since he'd arrived in town, he'd learned that the well-off denizens of Joplin weren't looking for help. Like Miss York, they'd found that crime *did* pay, and they were willing to sell their souls for the sparkle of ore that the dirt-covered miners could bring them.

Matthew opened the door to Trochet's Flowers and was surrounded by the smell of . . . well, he couldn't name all these flowers, but they sure smelled pretty, and there were more colors than he'd known existed. He waved at Mr. Trochet as he passed through the shop toward the back. The tall, narrow back door stuck at the corner. With an extra shove, Matthew got it open and stepped into Mr. Trochet's garden. This courtyard connected the shop to the greenhouse, and tucked between the two buildings was a small gardener's cabin, where Mr. Trochet's father had spent his last years. Now that the senior Mr. Trochet had passed on, the flower-seller had been pleased to have a young preacher lease the cabin. Matthew, in turn, was pleased to have a spot of green amid the brick walls and piles of gray chat that littered the mine fields.

Matthew went into the one-room cabin and dropped his hat on the wooden table, his eyes alighting on the faded hydrangea in the vase. That would have to be remedied immediately. Besides keeping a live bloom, the cabin didn't require any maintenance. Matthew hadn't used the little stove yet, but the kitchen table was adequate for meeting with people if they were willing to ignore the rumpled bed in the corner. If only Mr. Trochet would get his father's things out of the wardrobe. Matthew felt like he was imposing every time he pushed the aged outfits aside to reach for his own clothes.

He tossed the wilted bloom into the bin and picked up a pair of shears on his way to the garden to await his grandfather's return. The best part of his new little home was this spot of green. Although just a few hours of train travel away, this city seemed far removed from the forests of his Ozark Mountains. He couldn't amble undiscovered for hours. He couldn't lose himself in leafy branches. But at least he'd found a spot where green things grew, even if it was in the shadow of the Keystone Hotel.

He walked the paving stones through the rosebushes and the lilies and knelt at the hydrangea. This one was blue. He snipped the stem and stood.

"If you keep at that, you're going to put Mr. Trochet out of business." Isaiah Cook could be a formidable man, but Matthew only knew him as his grandfather.

"Mr. Trochet's father always kept a live bloom in that vase for his wife," Matthew replied. "Just because they're both gone is no reason to let the tradition die."

"It's no wonder you were always your grandma's favorite."

Matthew brushed his hand over the petals and let them tickle his palm. "She's the reason I'm here," he said.

Grandpa popped his cane against his leg. "You can't bring her back. Or your uncle, either," he said, "but you have a purpose. It's a good purpose. And you aren't going it alone."

"I know."

"All of us back home are praying for you. It's not going to be easy, starting new in a place like this, but you'll do fine. You have your grandma's determination and spunk. Just be prepared for a rocky start. She'd tell you the same."

It was nearly time to take his grandpa to the train. Matthew didn't want him worrying on his account. He motioned about them. "You say a rocky start, but it seems I've landed in clover. You tell Ma and Pa that after years of cleaning out their stinky barn, I've found somewhere sweeter."

"I'll tell them, boy. I'll tell them. But don't you forget that those stinky smells have a purpose. Without the barnyard, there'd be no bacon. Without the fertilizer . . ." He waved his hand over the garden before turning again to Matthew. "Don't be afraid to deal with the mess, son. The sweetest moments come from the most offensive fertilizer."

If that was so, Joplin had the potential to be a virtual Eden, because Matthew had never known a place as rotten.

Now that the bothersome man had fled, Calista could survey her prospects and choose her strategy.

Her end goal was to question the women working at the House of Lords and see if Lila was there, but she didn't expect her presence would be tolerated without a pretense. So, how to proceed?

Calista requested her bill, then eavesdropped on the table of matrons next to her. Did any of them know her aunt Myra? How about Granny? Calista's presence in Joplin wouldn't long go undiscovered, but she had a few things working in her favor. One was that Aunt Myra was an invalid. She wouldn't be about town. Of her two daughters, Willow had just married and was on her honeymoon, while Olive generally stayed home to care for her mother. The rest of the family lived on the ranch west of town. Granny Laura was well-known, but she didn't waste her time in town. And since Calista's parents and siblings lived in Kansas City, they didn't have many connections in the area.

On Pinkerton's desk in Chicago were forged papers from the finishing school she was supposedly attending, ready to be mailed to her family if she was spotted in town. The excuse of a semester credit for research was a flimsy one, but it would buy her enough time to finish this case. If she could find Lila, then maybe her job would become permanent, and she could proudly tell her family what she'd accomplished. Calista's lips twitched as she imagined their amazement that their cosseted daughter had answered a Help Wanted ad in the newspaper and actually secured an intriguing job, all of her own initiative. But until she could tell them, the deception had to continue.

"Here's your change, ma'am." The waiter eased the hand-sized silver tray onto the table. "Is there anything else I may help you with?"

It was time to make a move. Calista lifted her chin. "Yes, sir. I'd like to meet the manager of your hotel to offer my skills as a designer and decorator." This was why she'd worn her newest gown today. Even a waiter would try to find some hole in her story, and a shabby wardrobe would be a most obvious inconsistency.

Evidently she passed the first test.

"If you'll follow me," he said. He ducked his head as they paraded through the busy dining room to the reception area.

Calista followed him around the maître d's podium to an office door that was inset with frosted glass. From the shadows moving inside, it appeared the House of Lords had a busy staff. The waiter pushed through and held the door open for Calista to enter. The hair on the back of her neck stood up, and she braced herself. Strangers appearing uninvited in dens of iniquity often received less than warm welcomes.

This was not the case, however.

As Calista entered, a couple came through a back door, the woman laughing garishly while the man ogled her ample bosom. Both carried heavy bags with the seams nearly bursting.

"We emptied the slots, Malcolm." She tried to raise the bags to present them, but failed to lift them above the countertop. Her companion bumped her with his elbow and held the gate to the desk area open with his foot for her to pass through.

A ringing telephone was answered by a middle-aged man. After a few mumbled words, he returned the receiver to the hook switch. "Mr. Olson requests a room tonight at eight o'clock with entertainment," he said to a neatly dressed woman who sat at a desk. "He's going to have five gentlemen in attendance."

"You got it, Carrots." She jotted down some notes, then ripped the paper out of her notebook. "Constance, take this up to Mrs. Wilds when you go. She'll know who to recruit for tonight."

Calista's head was spinning. If this was illegal activity, it was the least furtive operation she'd ever encountered. No one hung their head in shame. No one shuffled papers out of sight at her entrance. No one seemed bothered that a stranger was in their midst.

After passing the paper to the courier going up the staircase, the woman at the desk motioned Calista over. With a straight back and perfect precision, she pecked at a typewriter.

"Have a seat," she said, her fingers never slowing as the waiter departed. Calista sat primly in the sturdy chair. If she was looking for a hint of the opulence that supposedly decked the third floor, it was nowhere to be seen. This office, with its polished wooden floors and spacious windows, was as clean and respectable as Mr. Buchanan's railroad offices.

The secretary rolled the paper out of the typewriter and held it to the side of her desk. Immediately another courier appeared. "Take this liquor license to city hall," she said, "and make sure you get a receipt that it was received. Thank you." Then she spun her chair toward Calista. "How may I help you?"

If anyone in this room felt guilty for what they were doing, it was Calista. But she was here for Lila Seaton. No matter how cheerful these employees were, they were part of an operation that was holding a girl hostage.

"I'm recently arrived from St. Louis and am looking for work. I have experience with a designer, Madame DuBois. I have a letter of reference from her, recommending me for the remodeling of your entertaining areas." Whether the letter was legitimate or a forgery done by Pinkerton, Calista couldn't say.

The secretary barely gave her a glance. "You're from the Clarketon Hotel, aren't you? Want to get a look at our rooms? No, thank you. If our staff wasn't doing an admirable job, there wouldn't be so many competitors trying to imitate us. Have a nice day." She turned back to her typewriter and pulled another paper off a stack.

"Or maybe I could tour the place?" Calista persisted, "I think I have a relative who works here. I'd like to say hello to her before I leave, if that's possible." She knew she wouldn't persuade the secretary, but she was buying time. First and foremost, she was watching every face for Lila Seaton, but beyond that, you never knew when a crossed path would prove fortuitous.

One young lady in particular caught her eye. Wearing a stern black skirt and tan blouse, she was dressed too somberly for her age and too modestly for a woman employed at this business. Her thick bangs were cut so low as to nearly brush against her spectacles. She stood at a respectable distance, waiting for Calista to finish.

Her wait would be short. The dragoon at the receptionist table ripped the page from her typewriter and held it out to another courier. "Barney, tell Mrs. Wilds that Dr. Stevenson has scheduled ten of our girls for their checkups tomorrow. Here's a list of who needs to attend this time. And please get security to escort this woman out of my office."

"Me?" Calista pressed her hand against her fitted jacket. "I don't mean any harm."

But the woman at the typewriter only rolled her eyes before addressing the prudish woman next to Calista. "How can I help you?"

With a nervous glance at Calista, the woman stepped forward. "I'm Mrs. Bowman from the Children's Home," she said. "I've brought news for Fredericka. Her child has recovered from her illness. We thought she'd like to know."

The secretary grabbed a pencil and jotted a few words on a pad. "I'll get the message to her," she said.

A burly man entered, scanned the room, then started toward Calista.

Calista didn't need to be warned again. Besides, she'd acquired an interesting piece of information—employees of the Children's Home had interactions with the women at the House of Lords. Calista knew of a Children's Home on the road leading to Granny's ranch, but she'd never considered what children resided there. And if Mrs. Bowman was a courier between the ladies of the night and the Children's Home, she could be a wealth of information. She followed the prim woman from the orphanage out the door.

"You're from the Children's Home?" Calista said once she and Mrs. Bowman had reached the sidewalk. "Do you know many of the girls who work here at the House of Lords?"

Mrs. Bowman bit her lip, then looked over her shoulder at the imposing building behind them. "Our records are confidential. Only our staff and volunteers know where the children come from."

The copy of Lila Seaton's photo was in Calista's pocket, but this wasn't the right place or time. "Perhaps I'll find time to volunteer, then," she said. "I've always pitied children from unsavory—"

"Excuse me, ma'am," Mrs. Bowman interrupted. "You wouldn't be welcome, so better not to waste your time." Then, as if embarrassed by her candor, she gave Calista's wrist a friendly squeeze before trotting away.

Calista tilted her head in puzzlement. "I wasn't expecting that," she mused.

But neither was she expecting her cousin to round the corner.

"Calista York?" Olive Kentworth crushed a paper bag of groceries against her side and ran to hug Calista. Her small frame felt as fragile as the fuzzy blond curls pushing against the brim of her hat. "What are you doing in town?"

Calista turned her face away to keep from getting poked in the eyes with celery leaves. "It's so good to see you," she said as she took the groceries from Olive. "How's Aunt Myra?"

"Not well," Olive said. "The treatments don't help like they used to. The doctors don't give her much hope. We take each day as a gift."

Olive was a saint. Her mother had been unwell her entire life. Because of her illness, the family had never had any money, and the two daughters had sacrificed much of their young adulthood nursing her. Life was unfair. Calista's uncle Oscar had fallen in love and married sweet Aunt Myra, and they'd barely made ends meet since. On the other hand, Calista's mother, Pauline Kentworth, had fallen in love with a land developer. True, they'd had to move to Kansas City to pursue opportunity, but the rewards had been great. Calista and her siblings, Corban and Evangelina, had never wanted for anything. Except maybe purpose.

"Well, I hope you have an afternoon free this week," Calista said. "We could visit a tearoom. My treat."

"A tearoom? Aren't you going to stay at Granny Laura's?"

Calista wrinkled her nose. "Granny doesn't know I'm in town. In fact, no one does besides you. I'd like to keep it that way as long as possible."

"I can guarantee someone saw you at the depot when you came in and has already informed Granny that one of her Kansas City grandchildren is in the vicinity."

"I'm hoping for some time without all the family interference."

"Time for what?"

Calista's gut clenched. She hated lying to her family, but it was for Lila. Olive wouldn't be harmed by not knowing the full truth.

"I'm looking for a job." Calista winced, because it sounded false even to her.

"You? A job? And you left Kansas City and came to Joplin to find one?" Olive took her groceries out of Calista's hands. "That's hogwash, Calista York. You'd better not tell Granny that, or she's like to take a strap to you for lying to her. Besides, last I heard, you were nursing a sick classmate back to health in Emporia. Now I'm wondering if that had any truth to it either."

Calista blinked her round eyes wide, hoping to look innocent enough to kill suspicion. "Getting a job here is part of my education. The last stage in my finishing school is to collect a menagerie of experiences from different walks of life. I thought Joplin would be a natural place to start."

Olive narrowed her eyes. "Is that the story you're telling me? Are you sure about that?"

Calista shrugged. "That's the story," she said at last.

Olive's mouth pursed in disapproval. "Well then, I guess I'm duty bound to help. Father might be able to get you on at the mine, if there's an opening among his bookkeepers, although something tells me you won't be interested."

"That's very kind, but I don't think the mining industry is my goal."

"Then where . . ." Olive's gaze traveled past Calista to the building she'd just exited. "Not the House of Lords, Calista. How could you even entertain such a thought? Granny would grab you by the hair and drag you to the woodshed before you knew what hit you."

"Regardless of my reasons or my future punishment at Granny's hands, why don't we have a nice tea while I still have my freedom?"

Olive could be as stubborn as Missouri mules, and there was a chance Calista's attempt to find Lila was over before it had begun. Olive didn't like the change of subject, but with a shrug of her shoulders, she signaled defeat. "I don't have time to argue," she said, "but Mother can't eat at the restaurant—not with her illness—and Friday is my baking day. Tomorrow when we return from Dr. Stevenson's, I'll bake my dinner rolls and would be glad to share them."

There was nothing to observe in her aunt's sickroom, yet Calista dearly loved Aunt Myra, and her mother would expect her to call on her sister-in-law . . . if her mother knew Calista was in Joplin. Which she would shortly.

"I accept your invitation," Calista said. Then inspiration hit. "Did you say Dr. Stevenson?"

"Most of the other doctors are too expensive. He's the only one we can afford."

"Two birds with one stone." Calista took the bag of groceries back again. "I'll accompany you and your mother to the doctor tomorrow. How does that sound?"

"Visits to the doctor are rarely any cause for celebration, Calista. If you're looking for diverting entertainment, it's not the place."

"Actually I've been very interested in the medical field lately. In fact, after caring for my roommate, I've found that I have quite a knack for rehabilitating patients. Perhaps Dr. Stevenson needs an assistant? I'd be willing to work free of charge, if he'd only give me a chance. Plus, it would help with my class requirements."

"You, work for a doctor? You faint at the first sign of blood."

"I've overcome that failing. Working with my classmate has bolstered my resistance." No wonder Mr. Pinkerton had hired her with no references. Calista excelled at constructing fictions from thin air.

"If you're serious, I'd recommend asking Dr. Cortez or Dr. Hooper. You'd be more comfortable with their upscale clientele. Dr. Stevenson . . . well, don't tell Mother that I told you, but if it weren't for our finances, Mother wouldn't see him. There are rumors that he isn't particular about his patients. Maisie told me that she heard from Hank that Dr. Stevenson treats the entertainment. You know what I mean . . ." Olive jutted her chin toward Main Street and its saloons. "The women who work there."

Of course Calista knew what she meant. She also knew that somewhere in one of these houses, there was a girl who'd been enticed, seduced, or kidnapped against her will. And Calista would do whatever it took to save her.

CHAPTER
3

When staying in a hotel, it was better to get an upper room. A lady staying alone was safer if her room was a fair distance from the entrance. Pinkerton had taught Calista that thieves preferred to get in and out of a building quickly. So did kidnappers. Sometimes space was the best defense. So when Calista had requested a room on an upper level, she hadn't considered that the Keystone Hotel had six floors, but it had turned out to be an unexpected boon. She poured herself a goblet of mint-flavored water from a crystal carafe and returned to her post at the window.

Below, she could see the street in front of the House of Lords. A constant flow of people came and went, with no indication whether they were visiting the diner, the gambling hall, or the bordello. But from her vantage point, she didn't see many young ladies leaving through the front doors.

Calista ran her hand down the blue toile draperies, noticing the print for the first time. The women harvesting fruit in the pastoral scene looked charmingly disheveled, not at all like she and her cousins looked working in Granny's garden. She'd always marveled at how the dirt stuck to sweaty skin, something she didn't have much experience with back in Kansas City. The one thing she and her cousins did have in common with the laboring youth on the fabric was the smiles. Working with her cousins was always fun. No matter what the task had been, they'd enjoyed each other's company. After all, even if you had a tiff with one cousin, there were ample alternatives for companionship.

For some reason, when Calista thought about her rough-and-tumble male cousins—Finn, Amos, and Hank—it brought to mind the man who had pestered her at the diner. What was it? The chip on his shoulder? The way he bristled when she teased him? Just another Missouri country boy come to town, but there was something more to him. Her kin wouldn't appreciate being compared to someone as morally corrupt as Matthew Cook, but maybe he was redeemable. Maybe God had plans for him.

Calista continued to scan the roofs of the various buildings beneath her. Joplin wasn't an old city. It had expanded as quickly as they could dig the ore from the ground, which was about 180,000 tons a year. She remembered when the intersection of Main Street and Fourth Street was a duck pond. Joplin was infinitely more exciting now, but with that excitement came danger.

A cable car glided up the street toward the hotel. An ice wagon swerved as its horses startled at the car. A woman dragged two children along to catch the car before it left. A man stepped out of a shop with his arms full of flowers. Calista rubbed the corner of her mouth. That was a lot of flowers. More than one would give to a sweetheart. He had to be buying them for a business.

She watched as he jaunted along the sidewalk. What kind of business needed that amount of flowers? A funeral parlor, hotel lobbies. But he had a target in mind. His steps took him directly to the den of iniquity she was surveilling. Perhaps places like that relied on a sense of opulence to dull the consciences of their clients. And they had their flowers delivered. If the girls rarely came out, this might get her inside.

Flower delivery went on Calista's mental list along with the Children's Home and the doctor. Could she convince the flower shop that they should hire her to arrange and deliver their flowers? From her bird's-eye view, the shop looked respectable. It was separated from the hotel property by an alleyway, and she could see a postage stamp garden dwarfed by the large greenhouse behind it. As she'd expect a garden at the florist to look, it was filled with greenery, splashes of color in the bushes. Dozens of flowers crowded the green space, and a man knelt surrounded by them. She leaned her forehead against the glass and watched as he worked among the bushes. He cut a few blooms, then stood, seemingly as taken by the moment as she was.

Gripping the laughing-peasant draperies, Calista remembered the feel of cool dirt. She appreciated the snap of the stem when a bloom needed pruning. How relaxing it would be to spend an afternoon with flowers and not have to evaluate what she said, not have to calculate her every move, not have to lie to her family. Just her and the gardener, working silently.

And within an hour, she'd be bored. If she'd wanted to work in flowerbeds, she could've helped her parents' gardeners back home. Instead, she wanted a life of purpose. She wanted to make a difference in the world.

Someone knocked on the door. Regretfully, Calista turned away from the window and stepped across the blue-and-white rug to reach the brass knob.

"Miss York?" The bellboy politely refrained from looking over her shoulder into the room. "You have a caller waiting on the telephone in the office."

Mr. Pinkerton already? Calista picked up the tasseled key to her room and exited, carefully locking the door behind her. She followed the bellboy to the elevator and counted each floor as it passed, knowing that the busy director of the Pinkerton Agency had better things to do than wait for her.

When they reached the office, she thanked the bellboy and waited for him to exit before picking up the receiver.

"Miss York speaking."

"It's your father, from Chicago." Pinkerton would never disclose his identity on the phone. His name was too recognizable to the operator, who was undoubtedly listening in on the line. "How's my favorite daughter?"

"Doing well, thank you. The arrangements you've made are superb."

"Not too superb, I hope."

"Only the best for your daughter."

In his pause, Calista could see him weighing his letter opener as he looked for a target. "Glad to hear it," he said finally. "Have you made any new friends?"

This was her chance to give her report. "No, but I do have some job prospects that might open doors."

"Is there any way I can help in your quest?"

She mentally reviewed the contents of her travel case in her room. In it she had a variety of letters of introduction. In one letter she had three years of teaching experience, in another she was an excellent seamstress. She'd prepared the designer's letter, but she hadn't thought of creating a letter for nursing. "I'm going to apply at a doctor's office on account of the work I did at the Home of Mercy in Chicago."

"As luck would have it, I'm paying a visit there tomorrow. I'll tell them you send your regards."

And he'd arrange for them to say that she'd worked there if they were asked. "Send particular greetings to the patients in the women's ward. I miss them the most."

"I understand." He cleared his throat. "It shouldn't be long before you have some guests. As soon as loose ends are tied up—"

"Already?" she gasped. "I've only just arrived."

"But you should know soon if you're going to have a suc-cessf—er, enjoyable visit."

"Call me Monday," she said. "I've got some ideas that I'm pur-suing."

"Monday, then. Be careful, and your mother says hello. Good-bye . . . dear."

But the feeling of impending judgment was anything but en-dearing.

"If you've got steady work, then why don't you have any money?" Matthew took another bite of his sandwich while keep-ing an eye on the wiry miner sitting next to him on the steps of the Joplin Carnegie Library. In the miner's dirt-lined face, Mat-thew recognized his Uncle Manuel. Including, unfortunately, his bloodshot eyes.

Irvin's gaze lingered on the remaining slab of turkey between the bread. He wiped his stained fingers against his loose-fitting shirt. "Everything is so expensive. The money is gone before I know it."

"But you have enough money for whiskey?" Matthew asked.

Irvin snorted. "Do you know how much whiskey it takes to make my back stop aching? Do you know how much whiskey I have to drink before I can face the next day of digging, digging, and more digging?"

"It can't be that bad," Matthew said. "You're just not used to hard work."

The wizened miner raised a gray eyebrow.

Matthew's confidence wavered, and he handed Irvin the rest of his sandwich. "Next time you hit ore and have a payout, I hope you think ahead."

Irvin grunted around his mouthful of food. "I have the best intentions on Saturday when they weigh up the ore and settle up with us, but those intentions don't make it through the week." He sucked on his fingers one by one, getting the last of the turkey juice off them. "I thank you, sir. With some food in my belly, I'm perked up enough to give it another go. If there's ever anything I could do for you . . ."

"Actually, I would like to meet—have prayer, read the Bible. If you're sober."

"Welp, I remember you mentioning that last time, but my schedule didn't allow . . ."

"I never told you what time we were going to meet."

"Oh? I thought you did. When is your meeting?"

"Sunday morning, of course."

Irvin laughed. "Sunday morning ain't going to work for anyone. We're all sleeping off Saturday night."

Meet on a day besides Sunday? Was Matthew going to start compromising already? Yes, he was. "Whenever, then," he said. "If you know where Trochet's Flowers is, my apartment—"

"After a day of digging, I don't much feel like walking into town. Why don't you come to my place?"

Matthew hesitated. Was he wasting his time with Irvin? He wasn't exactly the most promising prospect out there. If Matthew had his druthers, he'd host his meetings at Silas Marsh's place—another miner who was younger, sharper, and cleaner than Irvin.

But this was just to see Irvin. It didn't mean he had to ask anyone else to come to the wastrel's home. "I'll come to your claim," Matthew said at last. "After dark would be best for you, right? You can't see what you're digging after dark. I'll bring some food. And tell your buddies. Everyone is welcome."

Irvin sucked the last of the turkey juice off his thumb. "Okay, then. Tonight after dark. My claim is on Wolstead's land, just past the Imperial Mine. I'll see you there."

Matthew's stomach still felt empty, but it was worth it. Now that Grandpa Cook had gone home, Matthew had no one to entertain, no one to plan with. Finally, he had an appointment, somewhere to be. But it was just a start, and from reading all the missionary books he could get his hands on, Matthew knew that many leads would fizzle out before one spark caught and grew. There was hope, though.

With a strong handshake, Irvin took out to his claim, leaving Matthew to set his feet toward his next project, which was to see what charities were in place in the city. He knew about the Elks, the Odd Fellows, and the Women's Benevolence League. There had to be more. Thankfully, he was in the right place to get information.

Passing beneath the massive columns of the Carnegie Library, Matthew shuffled to a stop right inside the doors. His head tipped back as he followed the bookcases up to the pressed tin ceiling high overhead. It took him a second to realize he was seeing two stories of bookcases before him, for they looked like long continuous shelves stacked to the sky.

Back in Pine Gap, he couldn't have imagined a building so fine, much less one built solely for holding books. While eccentric Betsy Puckett had a few shelves of books, there wasn't a public library they could call their own. Then again, neither were there seventy-six saloons in Pine Gap. Unlike Joplin, it also didn't have one hundred and seventeen whiskey shops. Before arriving earlier that week, his country mind couldn't fathom a town with that many businesses, much less ones dedicated to debauchery. But they did have a nice library.

Wishing he'd worn his Sunday best, Matthew headed toward the paneled desk that curved in the center of the room. Light from the six windows behind the desk streamed in and lit up the ladies like they were members of the heavenly host. He was so distracted, he nearly tripped over a lady with a squeaky shoe pushing a heavy cart of volumes past him.

"May I help you?" The librarian's rosy cheeks shone like they'd been polished. She'd probably already raised a passel of children, causing her permanently flustered appearance.

"Yes, ma'am. My name is Matthew Cook. I'm new to the area, and I wanted to inquire about the various charities in town."

She did a quick appraisal of him before smiling with compassion. "Certainly. What manner of help are you seeking?"

"No, not me. I'm a . . . well, I've come to help, and I thought I could give a hand . . ." He was talking in circles. Why couldn't he just say it? Because it didn't seem like he was worthy of the title. But he had to start somewhere. "I'm a missionary. I want to volunteer my services."

"A missionary? Where's your church?"

"I don't have one, but I've met one man—"

"Irvin? Yes, I saw you on the steps. You'll run out of food before you finish your sermon with that one. But why do you think Joplin needs a missionary? We have churches." Her fingers drummed against the cart. "You've been reading the Carthage newspaper, haven't you? The one that calls Joplin a naughty, wide-open town? Jealousy, that's what ails them. We don't need help. We have charities, but most of our poor are rich on Saturday and poor by Tuesday."

He'd wanted information, and he'd gotten a big portion of it. "What do you mean, rich on Saturday and poor by Tuesday?"

"On Saturday the miners, property owners, and foundries settle up their accounts. Even the banks open on Saturday in the evening, because those starving miners can't wait until Monday to get their cash. And then they hit the streets—or the whiskey dens, more likely. The whole town comes out and celebrates. And by Monday morning, most of them are broke again and counting the days until Saturday."

"What an awful way to live." In his young life, Matthew had been surrounded by disciplined, frugal people. The thought of such waste was horrendous to him.

"You should see the miners' wives and children. It's no wonder so many of the kids end up in the Children's Home. Even those who have proper fathers can't always be fed. But Joplin is doing its best to help."

A Children's Home? That sounded promising. Even if they didn't need a chaplain, they probably had maintenance he could help with. Or keeping the grounds. Although he aimed to be a man of the Word, he knew the value of working with his hands. He wasn't one to sit in his apartment when there were things to accomplish.

"And where is the Children's Home?" he asked.

She gave him directions. It would be a healthy walk to the outskirts of town, but he enjoyed stretching his legs. Matthew took up his hat, laid down his thanks, and left.

What kind of women would he meet at the Children's Home? Women who had chosen the wide path of destruction? That made him a speck nervous. Matthew was pretty green about women and had only heard tales about some who misused their beauty. He hoped he'd be strong enough to resist when he heard the sirens' calls. He knew some pretty girls back home, but none who would compare to the great beauties that lured men to their destruction.

As he walked along, the paved streets of Joplin turned to gravel, and the shade went from the solid blocks of tall buildings to the mottled coverage of dancing light coming down through the trees. Where the trees parted, farmhouses could be seen on green fields, making Matthew long for home. And then a home appeared that was grander than any he'd seen outside of the Murphysburg District of Joplin. It was the Children's Home, he suspected, and according to the librarian, the next fork would lead him to the front door.

"Stop it, you ignorant snot-bucket of a steer."

It was a woman's voice coming from a washout down beneath the road. A horse nickered from where it was tied to a tree alongside another. Matthew heard a man's laugh, and it wasn't a particularly nice laugh.

"Don't be such a killjoy. I've got it coming to me."

Matthew's teeth were set on edge. He was supposed to be a man of peace, but he wasn't a coward, and judging from the protests of the lady, she needed help. He looked both ways on the road and saw no one. No matter. He'd grown up with Bald Knobbers and bushwhackers infesting the woods around his farm. He'd learned to take care of himself and others from a young age. He could handle this.

He hopped down into the washout beneath the bridge. The man had the lady by the arm and was dragging her forward. Matthew couldn't believe it. It was the woman he'd seen at the House of Lords earlier that week. No, she just shared a resemblance, but she was also in trouble.

"I wouldn't be doing this, but it's owed me." The man's amusement sickened Matthew.

"Unhand her." Matthew had been waiting his whole life to say those words.

The man spun around. His eyes tightened as he sized Matthew up. He was shorter than Matthew but built like a regular rounder. "This here ain't none of your business," he said.

Finally, Matthew was on footing he understood. "If you're harassing that lady, it is."

The man looked like he could wrestle a wildcat. He also looked like he couldn't quite believe he was being challenged. He jerked the girl closer. "You better just move on."

The girl twisted her arm free, but Matthew had already committed to action. He swung for the stubborn jaw, but the man ducked so quickly that his blow swished harmlessly through the air. Thrown off balance, Matthew reached out to steady himself on the bank, but the girl lunged toward him. With a sweep of her foot, she hooked his calf and jerked it forward. The next thing

Matthew knew, both of his feet were pointing toward the sky and his spine was crashing into the gravel waterway beneath him.

His sight turned all white and sparkly as he tried to rise, but dizziness and a weight kept him on his back. When his eyes refocused, he saw the girl with her boot squarely on his chest and her hands on her hips. Her turned-up nose was wrinkled in merriment.

"What have we got here, Amos?" she said. "A regular Robin Hood to save me and Old Man Tormand's watermelons."

"Why do you always have to butt in, Maisie? I had him dead to rights. I can't hardly sock him now when he's lying there helpless as a newborn lamb."

"I'm not helpless," Matthew protested, but the fact that he'd prefer to stay on his back meant that their assessment was fair.

"You miners need to learn not to mess with the countryfolk." The lady stepped off him but kept her hands forward, as if ready to defend herself again.

"I'm not a miner." Matthew rolled to his side while keeping a leery eye on the couple. "I'm a preacher."

The girl's eyes widened. She covered her mouth with her hands, but not before a throaty laugh escaped.

The man extended a hand and hauled Matthew to his feet. "Good gravy, Maisie. You done took down a preacher." He would've turned Matthew around and dusted off his backside had Matthew not pushed away.

"You haven't accounted for your treatment of the lady." Matthew picked up his hat and tried to look stern.

"She ain't no lady. She's my sister. I had a hankering for a watermelon, and Tormand's patch is along this creek. He owes me for when I helped him with his runaway pigs, but he's never paid up. I thought to collect—"

"He wanted me to play lookout for him," the lady interrupted, "but I'm done with that. I'm always caught, and my brother sneaks away scot-free."

Her brother? Matthew rotated his shoulders to shake out the bruises. Knowing they were siblings made his presumptions ridiculous. Now that he understood the circumstances, he recognized them for what they were—farm folk coming to town. Just like him.

"Matthew Cook," he said and extended his hand to the man.

"Amos Kentworth, and this is my sister, Maisie." They had to speak up to be heard over the wagon crossing the bridge above them.

Matthew waited until it passed before asking, "Are you'uns from around here?"

"Yep. Our ranch starts a few miles back that way. What brings you to Joplin?"

"Ever heard of Pine Gap?"

"Nope."

"Not surprising, but I've certainly heard of Joplin. I figured that if I wanted to do any good with this life, I might as well go where I'm needed. They didn't need me in Pine Gap."

The girl grinned. "But Joplin is a different critter. Yessir, our folks don't usually let us come to town without one of our elders. It's a modern-day Sodom and Gomorrah. If it weren't for our cousin needing looking after . . ."

"What's wrong with your cousin?" Matthew wanted to make himself useful. Considering that these two had nearly knocked him unconscious, he was feeling right warmly toward them.

"She's up to no good. Always been the unruly sort. Another cousin of ours saw her in town this week, and believe me, if no one knew she was coming, then it's mischief she's after." Amos delivered his judgment with a twist of his mouth that could be taken as a sign of jealousy.

"She's a caution," Maisie said. "If everyone wasn't so busy with planting, they would've never sent us to bring her in. As it is, we're on our way to ambush her at our aunt's doctor's visit."

"I'd say the two of you could round up a whole herd of ne'er-do-wells," Matthew said.

The siblings grinned at each other. Amos winked. "They're afeared that when we find out what she's about, we might up and join her."

Matthew laughed. "Something tells me that you know better."

"Oh, we know the fear of the Lord, but there's lots of ways to have fun that the Lord hasn't thought to expressly prohibit," Amos said. "Finding those things is our specialty."

"Let's hope you don't find more than you bargained for, but if you do, you can find me out back of Trochet's flower store. I'm new to town, so I'm eager for company."

"We might do that," Amos said. "We just might. Now, if you'd like to share a watermelon, I still need a lookout."

His sister landed a solid punch on his arm. "Even if he don't look like it, he's a preacher, Amos. You can't ask him to help you steal from Mr. Tormand."

"I told you, it ain't stealing. He owes me money, so I've put a lien on his watermelon patch. With interest, we should be able to take—"

"Ill-gotten gains bring nothing but misery," Matthew said. "Good luck." He climbed out of the culvert and back onto the road.

Amos and Maisie. Since arriving in the metropolis of Joplin, they were the first people he'd met who felt familiar. Sure, they were spirited, but they had a code they would follow, and heaven help this cousin of theirs who was trying to break that code.

CHAPTER 4

She'd packed a severe ebony gown in case she needed to pretend to be in mourning. She'd packed a scandalous, gaudy day gown that looked more like evening wear in case she was invited to an event that wasn't quite proper. She had a whole wardrobe of clothes in between, but nothing that resembled a nurse's uniform.

Calista buckled a narrow leather belt around her camel-colored skirt. A white shirtwaist and a modest hat would have to suffice. She wouldn't look like a Parisian-trained decorator, but today her aim was to look like a responsible, efficient working girl who needed a job. If she didn't make progress on this case quickly, she would be looking for a job in earnest.

But it wasn't about her job. It was about a girl who'd been separated from her family. Calista couldn't dwell on the probable particulars of Lila's treatment at the hands of her captors. Such thinking would make her fearful and distract her from the task before her. Instead, she would focus on the satisfaction of solving another case.

The first time Calista had ever considered what a detective did was when a ruby necklace of her mother's went missing. It had likely been gone for weeks before her mother sent Mrs. Herman to fetch it for the Christmas ball and the case was discovered to be empty. When her father hired the Pinkerton Agency, they told the operative, one Mrs. Kate Warne, that they suspected a lady's maid who had recently left the position. What happened next fueled Calista's imagination for years.

After researching the situation and locating the suspect, Mrs. Warne adopted a disguise as L. L. Lucille, a fortune-teller, and set up a room nearby. It wasn't long before the superstitious maid found herself in Madame Lucille's crystal-bedecked den for a reading. Knowing the maid's fascination with the afterlife and that she'd lost a brother three years earlier, Detective Warne launched into a series of warnings that supposedly came straight from the maid's concerned brother.

Calista had sat on a tufted footstool with a plate of bonbons on her knee, listening wide-eyed as her father relayed the story. *"You are cursed,"* the Pinkerton agent posing as Madame Lucille posing as the dead brother had intoned. *"Give back the necklace or you will suffer with me for eternity."*

Although Calista's mother did not approve of fortune-telling— *"But it was a farce,"* her father had protested. *"Isn't it all a farce?"* her mother had replied—Pauline York was happy when the sparkling rubies were back in her hands. And in Mrs. Warne, Calista had a sparkling example of a woman taking her future into her own hands.

But to solve the world's problems, one had to leave the safety of her hotel room.

Calista slid her retractable baton into her pocket. In the two cases she had worked before, there hadn't been a deadline. Establishing herself as a new member of a community took weeks. Working her way into the confidence of an embezzling suspect's wife had taken a couple of months. Caution was valued over speed. But this case was different.

Lila Seaton might not be any younger than Calista, but she

was no match for whatever deviousness she'd fallen prey to. Every access that Calista was denied meant more chances that Lila was being harmed. Every failed attempt to get inside the underbelly of Joplin's seedy world meant more of a chance that Lila would be spirited away and they'd lose the trail once again.

Calista paused at the hotel lobby to ask directions to Dr. Stevenson's office. Working with family nearby presented unique challenges. In smaller towns, where ladies were always trying to determine who *your people* were, it took time to be accepted, but even though she'd grown up in Kansas City, Calista would have no problem establishing herself in Joplin. The Kentworth name would give her instant respect. The difficulty arose in that she didn't want respect. She wanted to get behind walls where respectable people wouldn't go. It would be a fine line to walk with Olive and Aunt Myra observing.

Slowing in front of the flower store on the other side of the alley, Calista bent over the tubs of blooms. The dainty tea roses gave off a strong scent for their size. Ever so gently, she let her palm skim over the buds. If she couldn't get a position at the doctor's office, the flower shop would be her next move, and then she'd try at the Children's Home, although that Mrs. Bowman had done her best to discourage her.

Calista found the doctor's home at the edge of a respectable neighborhood. A nicely lettered sign pointed the way for carriages to arrive at the back. Taking the footpath, Calista followed the brick walkway through a dense, overgrown garden around to the side of the house, noting that a buggy could easily come to the office door without any of the neighbors being able to see the passengers before they were inside.

A bell rang when she opened the door. She stepped into a waiting area.

"*Ahhh-choo!*" A sneeze exploded from a man as he lurched forward on a bench. Calista wished she could shut her nostrils up as tightly as she was closing her eyelids. She turned her face away, reminding herself that a nurse would be used to sloppy outbursts. If she wanted to interact with the girls at the brothel, this might be the only way.

Mustering her resolve, she pried her eyes open, ready to smile at whoever was hacking with the nasty, phlegmy cough at her left.

It was Aunt Myra.

Calista's heart sank. Her mother had always pitied Uncle Oscar and his wife. Ever proud, they wouldn't accept charity from the family, and Aunt Myra thought it poor taste for her daughters to wear Calista's hand-me-downs, as they would look presumptuous on girls of their limited means. Calista had always felt sorry for Willow and Olive because of the things they lacked, but now, faced with her aunt's painful condition, she realized the dresses weren't the girls' biggest concern.

Growing up had its disadvantages.

"Aunt Myra!" Calista knelt by her aunt's feet. Taking her hand, she squeezed it carefully. "You don't sound well."

Aunt Myra still had a strong grip. "Regardless, I'm happy to see my darling niece. What are you doing in town?"

"I'm working on a project for school. The professor wants us to prove that we're capable of managing in an unknown environment, so I came here." She moved aside to take a seat next to her aunt.

"You didn't say that part last time." Olive's mouth twisted up on one side. "Calling Joplin an unknown environment is cheating, Calista."

"Not really. Granny Laura never let me come to town." She started to grab the armrests of her chair, then remembered the condition of the people in the room and decided she'd rather not touch them.

"When Olive told me you might visit, I was tickled. You're just the diversion I need. But why in the world aren't you staying at the ranch?"

"I'm required to be in town, but also to work with some people who are underappreciated by Granny. If I limit my work to people whose company she enjoys, then I'd have no work at all."

Aunt Myra and Olive nodded their understanding. Granny didn't suffer fools gladly, and it turned out that she had crossed paths with a lot of fools. Most she'd be glad to give a hand up and set them on the right path, but those who either didn't need her help or who disregarded it weren't to be bothered with.

"Mrs. Kentworth?" A lady with thin hair pulled back into a puny bun made a mark on her clipboard. "Dr. Stevenson is ready for you."

Calista got to her feet and fell in behind her family as they moved toward the office, but Aunt Myra stopped her.

"There's no reason for you to go in. You might as well wait out here."

"I came to see you . . ." But Calista knew better than to argue. Her aunt wouldn't waste her breath saying it if she didn't mean it.

Dejected, Calista returned to the seats they'd vacated and tried not to think of all the sick people who'd sat there before. The only ones who interested her weren't here yet, but being a nurse at this office would give her opportunity to interview each of them. If it wasn't for her aversion to sick people, it was the perfect plan.

When the door from the examination room opened, Calista jumped up so quickly that the nurse startled.

"Hello. I'm Calista York, and I wanted to talk to you about employment," Calista blurted. "I'm a nurse, just moved to town, and I'm looking for a position at a small establishment. This place seems clean, efficient, and has reliable clientele."

"Reliable?" The nurse shot Calista a sidelong glance. "Are you suggesting we can count on them to remain sickly?" She shook her head. "Mr. Johnson, here's your prescription. Come back if it doesn't do the trick."

The sneezer stood, took the slip of paper from the nurse's hand, then exited the building, leaving Calista alone with her.

"That's not what I meant," Calista said. "It's just that I've looked at some of the more dignified practitioners in town, and those aren't the patients I want to work with. Women who lack nothing but attention, bothering us with phantom ailments. Men thinking they can bribe time into delaying their decay. Your clientele . . . well, at least we can be reasonably sure they're sick, or they wouldn't be here. And I can't imagine that it's easy to find nurses willing to work with them." She lowered her voice and leaned toward the nurse. "Especially the girls who are coming in today. I'm from Chicago, and I've seen it all. I might look young, but I've lived a life that's prepared me for just about anything. Nothing you face would shock me."

The nurse took a step back and surveyed Calista from head to toe. What a boon that she'd packed these scuffed boots to go with her working wardrobe. In Calista's opinion, they added an authenticity to her modest dress. But the nurse hadn't focused on the boots. Instead, she seemed fixated on Calista's hairline.

"The widow's peak," she said. "I probably wouldn't have thought twice about it, but you were in here talking to Mrs. Kentworth, and there's no denying the family resemblance. And if you are Mrs. Kentworth's niece, then more than likely you're Pauline's daughter. Last I heard, she'd married some wealthy businessman in Kansas City, not Chicago. As far as living a rough life . . . well, that's just another big story you're trying to get me to believe. I don't know what you're up to, miss, but if you think Dr. Stevenson is going to hire one of Laura Kentworth's granddaughters and put her to work with . . ." Her raised eyebrow finished the statement.

"Aunt Myra comes to you for treatment, so she couldn't object," Calista countered, "and Granny Laura doesn't even know I'm in town. Besides, she's a busy lady. She doesn't have time to keep track of all her grandchildren."

As fate would have it, the door burst open, and two people stumbled inside. Calista felt the air whoosh out of her lungs. What were Amos and Maisie doing here?

This could only mean one thing.

"Granny Laura wants to know what you're doing in town and why you didn't tell her." Maisie's skirt had twisted around her waist so that the buttons ran crookedly down the side. Her braids looked childish on a lady of her age—only a year younger than Calista—and even from across the office, Calista could see that her hands were sticky.

The cool appraisal of the nurse rankled. "Miss York, I think my point has been proven."

"I've never seen these people before in my life!" But even Calista knew that her disavowal was futile.

"Welp, I reckon you've seen me ever since you opened your eyes and saw the light of day," Amos drawled.

"You're interrupting a conversation," Calista said. "I'm trying to find employment—"

"You? Work?" The siblings looked at each other and burst out laughing.

"Can't you wait outside?" Calista pleaded, but her time was running out.

The door opened, and Aunt Myra and Olive came out of the office with Dr. Stevenson at their heels.

Stepping around her aunt, who didn't seem at all surprised to see two more family members in the reception area, Calista approached the doctor. "Hello, sir. I was wondering how my aunt's health is faring."

The doctor's face scrunched up. "Why don't you ask your aunt?"

She wouldn't normally have dared to use her aunt's condition to further her investigation, but she had no other choice. "I have some medical training, and I thought there might be some information you'd be willing to share with me that a civilian wouldn't be able to understand."

"Calista York!" Aunt Myra lowered her ever-present handkerchief from her mouth. "What could you possibly understand that I don't? I've suffered from this ailment for years. And when did you get medical training?"

"Medical training?" Amos laughed. "If she so much as sees a paper cut, she'll fall into a dead faint."

"What about the experiment you're doing?" Olive asked. "Is this part of your finishing school?"

"Finishing school? I thought you were looking for work at a doctor's office." In Calista's opinion, the nurse didn't need to look so satisfied at sharing that piece of information.

"Boy-howdy," Maisie exclaimed. "You've got more stories than the Carnegie Library. This is the most fun I've had since—"

"Since you stole that watermelon?" Calista was tired of everyone looking at her. She wasn't the only person getting into trouble. "Amos, you dripped juice on your cuff, but at least you bothered to wash your hands."

"He owed me," Amos protested. "I took the watermelon as payment."

"You took a watermelon from Mr. Tormand?" Olive slammed her bag into a chair with a *thud*. "He'll pay you when he can. You don't know what it's like to have money trouble." Usually the sweetest, most patient of the cousins, Olive had the hottest temper when riled.

"Calista is the one misbehaving," Maisie said. "I don't know how you've come around to talking about us."

The family hadn't had a row this public since Uncle Bill's Fourth of July fireworks prank. Only when Aunt Myra began her painful, thundering cough did the bickering stop. They watched helplessly as Aunt Myra dropped into a chair and heaved with all the strength she had remaining.

Amos elbowed Maisie. She dug her toe into the soft pine flooring. "Sorry, Aunt Myra. We didn't mean to cause a scene."

"She's too weak to walk home," Olive said, "and they won't want her on the streetcar when she sounds this bad."

"I have my horse," Amos said. "I'll see her home."

"You can take mine and ride along with him," Maisie offered to Olive. "I'll walk to your house."

Again Calista felt the unfamiliar unease of being with someone who was so awfully ill. What was one to do? It was like an ongoing funeral. She didn't know how Olive and Uncle Oscar managed.

They trooped out of the doctor's office as a group. Aunt Myra, Olive, and Amos mounted and took out toward their home in a more modest neighborhood. Calista took her remaining cousin by the arm and strolled beneath the young trees lining the street.

"What do you mean, scolding me?" Calista asked Maisie. "You should know that once cousins start tattling on each other, there's no telling what will be unearthed."

"I didn't tell Granny Laura anything. Neither did Olive. Uncle Oscar is the one who let the cat out of the bag, talking about your plans to meet Aunt Myra for lunch."

Of all the people who might be suspicious of Calista's activities, Granny would be the worst. She was the one person with the fortitude and the means to stop Calista, and the one most likely to either disapprove of or disbelieve Calista's claims about her schooling. Calista had hoped to have solved the case before her family interfered. She'd underestimated them.

A transport wagon with three rows of seats came rumbling down the street. It was unusual for a conveyance that large to come into a residential part of town. The wagon slowed as it passed them. Calista watched over her shoulder as it turned into Dr. Stevenson's hidden drive.

She slapped Maisie on the arm. "C'mon, we gotta run." Grabbing her skirt at the knees, Calista lifted it as she ran back toward the doctor's yard.

To Maisie's credit, she didn't need any inducement besides curiosity to follow. She would have outrun Calista if she'd known where they were going. When they reached the overgrown path beside the doctor's house, Calista squatted down. Motioning Maisie down as well, she crept forward.

"Who are we looking for?" Maisie whispered.

"I'll know when I see her."

The girls crawled forward as they peered through the hedge. The large coach had barely stopped rolling when the door opened. Maisie pried a gap in the hedge with her strong, tanned hands. It turned out Calista's untamed cousin could be an asset on an assignment like this. Years of rough-and-tumble summers full of pranks and plots had honed all of the family's senses to expect the unexpected and to improvise when necessary, but if word got back to Calista's parents that she was undertaking such a dangerous profession, that would be the end of it.

Willow, Olive's sister, had kept Calista's secret when she'd encountered her on the railroad case. Then again, Willow was married and traveling the country with her rich husband. Maisie didn't possess Willow's quiet reserve.

"Are those fancy women?" Maisie leaned into the bushes as she gaped at Calista. "Are we hiding in the bushes just so you can stare at fancy women?"

Calista was so busy searching faces that she hadn't noticed what they were wearing. On closer inspection, the women weren't dressed much differently than the wife or daughter of a moderately successful miner. They were going to the doctor, after all, and had the same resigned expression that typically accompanied that ordeal.

"What makes you think they're fancy women?" Calista whispered.

"You never see that many women traveling without a man unless they're fancy women, suffragettes, or temperance ladies. Those ain't no temperance ladies." Maisie pulled a branch down, making the gap bigger. "Look there. See that red scarf? And the lining of that one's hat is red too. Yep. They might be taking the day off, but they are what they are."

The finality of Maisie's judgment annoyed Calista. She thought of the haunted girl in her photograph. Many of those girls probably had similar stories—they'd run off looking for adventure or, even worse, had been kidnapped from their families. But Calista was here to find just one of them. The wagon had parked close to the office door, but everyone couldn't fit into the small reception area at the same time. From her hiding spot, Calista worked through the dozen milling women, waiting until each turned her face and she could eliminate her as a match.

Maisie stirred. "If you want to see them, what are we hiding for? Might as well go over and say howdy."

Calista caught her cousin by the arm. "How did you know that about the red clothing? I have a crimson dress. There's nothing sinful about a color." There were two women who hadn't turned toward her yet. One of them looked thicker and older than Lila would be. The other . . .

"There's something wrong with it in Joplin. I had my eye on a winter coat last year—black wool with red lining. Ma had a fit. Said there was no way her daughter would wear red. Maybe it's not like that everywhere, but here it's the same as handing out a calling card with your profession on it."

"Consider me warned," Calista said. And here she thought she'd prepared for this assignment. The last girl turned. Calista sighed. It wasn't Lila, but it was someone just as young and vulnerable-looking. "Come on," she said. "You're going to pretend you have a bellyache."

"I don't have a bellyache."

"Sure you do. You just ate half a watermelon." Calista turned to give Maisie her full attention. "Think about all that liquid sloshing in your stomach. It tasted good going down, but now you wish you had held back."

Maisie's mouth twitched. "Now that you mention it . . ." She wrapped her arms around her waist and let her shoulders droop. "Oww . . . my belly. It's ailing me."

"Shh! Not until we get out of the shrubbery." Calista stumbled toward the bricked walkway, kicking to release a vine from her boot.

Maisie took the more direct path, trampling a hosta in her suffering. "The pain is fierce. I'm gonna die."

"You're supposed to have a stomachache," Calista grunted, "not a gutshot."

They had attracted the attention of the women, although no one stepped forward to help. Regardless, Calista had her target in sight. "She needs to see the doctor." She spoke with an urgency that was hard to ignore and addressed the matronly woman whose job was probably to look after the young girls.

"The doctor is busy," she replied, "but if it's an emergency, you could go before us." Up close, Calista could see cosmetics smeared on her jaw where the washcloth had missed them.

"If one of these girls could help . . ." Calista pointed at her target, the young girl with the charming gap between her front teeth. "You, please. Could you take her other arm?"

On cue, Maisie's legs buckled. The frightened girl that Calista had indicated rushed forward to grab Maisie by the arm.

"To the office," Calista said. "Let's get her inside." She groaned at her cousin's sudden weight as they dragged Maisie through the doctor's door. "You have a bellyache, not two broken legs," she whispered.

"I always give my best effort," Maisie retorted between groans.

"How long have you been in Joplin?" Calista asked the girl over Maisie's head.

"What?" The girl's confusion was understandable, but Calista didn't have time to waste. The reception area was empty, but it wouldn't be for long.

Letting go of Maisie, Calista pulled the picture of Lila out of her handbag. "Have you ever seen this girl? She's new to Joplin, as well. Less than a year."

"It's you again?" The nurse was making a beeline toward them.

"I don't feel good." Maisie stumbled toward the nurse. "Help me."

"This is ridiculous," the nurse said. "You have to leave."

"I don't know her," the girl told Calista after glancing at the picture.

"You've never seen her?" Calista bent to gauge her reaction. "Do you know all the girls at the House of Lords?"

"Yes, ma'am, I do, but I don't know her." The girl lowered her eyes. "Does her family want her to come home?" The wistfulness was hard to miss, even with Maisie's increasingly frantic demands echoing in the room.

This girl wasn't Lila, but she was still worth saving. "Yes, they do." Calista took the girl's hand. "So does your family. Or someone does. Someone cares about you. You can leave."

"Doctor, there's a disturbance out here!" the nurse yelled.

"I have to go," said Calista, "but if you see this girl, please tell me. You can find me at the Keystone Hotel. Or if you need help, find me. Calista York. That's my name." She kept her eye on the door, wanting to keep her exit free.

"You're not going anywhere." The nurse came toward her. "Not until you give a full accounting for your behavior."

At first, Calista thought Maisie was overplaying her hand, but then she heard the *splat*. By instinct, Calista lifted her skirt and jumped back. Everyone did, but the nurse had walked right into the eruption. Calista stared at the pink mess drenching the nurse's white skirt. What had just happened? Where had the vomit come from?

Maisie stood upright and wiped her mouth with the back of her hand. "I feel better now." She blinked as innocently as one of her cows. "I wanna go home."

Calista squeezed the arm of the girl. "Remember what I told you."

Then she turned on her heel and hurried out the door before the smell could catch her. Keeping their heads down, she and Maisie sped through the group of women waiting outside, then down the hidden walkway to the street.

"I don't know what you were doing, but I hope you helped that girl," Maisie said. "She looked so sad."

"What about you?" Calista asked. "Are you really sick?"

Maisie shrugged. "The more I said I was sick, the more I thought that I might could actually be sick. But don't worry. Once I got it out of my system, I recovered."

Never underestimate Maisie's commitment to seeing a job through.

"Then you'll be fine to go on to Aunt Myra's on your own? As much as I'd love to visit with all of you, I find that my time is precious today."

"No, sirree. You aren't sending me back to Granny Laura without some kind of explanation."

"I did explain. I'm here doing a class assignment. Tell Granny that I'll come see her before I leave town, but that I'm just too busy to make the trip to the ranch."

"What did you show that girl?" Maisie asked. "Who was in that picture?"

"That's none of your business."

"You're family. Everything you do is my business."

"Like stealing Mr. Tormand's watermelon? Is that my business?"

Maisie plopped a hand over her stomach. "That preacher was right—ill-gotten gains bring nothing but misery. Fine, I'll tell Granny whatever you want me to tell her, but she won't be satisfied. You know that."

Calista did know. The clock was ticking on how long she could continue to work unencumbered by her relations, but Pinkerton might stop her before her family had a chance.

CHAPTER

5

The excitement had been building all day. Business owners carried their wares to the sidewalks to tempt buyers, restaurateurs crowded more tables into the dining rooms, and grocers' wagons hurried along, making deliveries of bushels of fruits and vegetables, wrapped cuts of beef, and bags of flour so that all shelves would be stocked. As the afternoon wore on, every head seemed cocked, listening for the mines' whistles that would signal the end of the workday and the release of the men and their funds.

Knowing that she might work until late, Calista had napped during the heat of the day, then woken refreshed, ready to see if Saturday night in Joplin was all that had been promised. Fairly certain that Lila was no longer at the House of Lords, Calista needed to broaden her search, and Saturday was her best opportunity for leads.

In the Keystone Hotel elevator, the well-to-do women plotted their expenditures as they rode down from their penthouses. Calista knew these weren't miners' wives. Their husbands might own the mines, or the foundries, or the smelters, but Saturday was payday from the top down. Their husbands would write the checks, and then they would make a claim on whatever was left over.

"I've had my eye on that fabric for weeks. I'm going to be in line at Temple's store, waiting for Jeffrey to balance the books. He'll come there first so no one buys it before me." The woman adjusted her hat like a major embarking on a mission.

Her friend nodded her approval. "I'm buying faucets for our kitchen. The house should be completed this month. After living in this hotel for a year, I'm more than ready. . . ."

The doors opened, and Calista stepped off the elevator into a lobby that was packed full of men. The small gilt tables that anchored every sitting area were each claimed by a check registry, an adding machine, and a line of men waiting their turn. She worked her way around the room, picking up what bits of conversation she could catch.

"Your load brought in two hundred and twenty-five dollars from your lease this week. After taking my twenty percent, that's one hundred and eighty dollars."

"Ore has gone up this week. Pay will be better, but set some aside."

"If it weren't for that ailment that beset me this week, I would've got more. Would you advance me a sum until next week?"

Calista had been warned that Saturday night in Joplin was unlike anywhere else in the world. The landowners settled their accounts with the operators who bought the ore. The operators paid the landowners, and they in turn paid the men leasing their stakes, minus their commission. Those were the independent miners who had leased land. Those who worked in the mines would not get rich, but they had steady income. They were also paid on Saturday night. It was payday for everyone, the money trickling down from owner to miners to storekeepers and grocers. Like a holiday once a week.

If Calista had thought Joplin completely debased itself on weeknights, she'd underestimated its abilities.

"I've got money in my pocket, sweetheart, but no company. How about you join me tonight?" The miner might have washed up and put on his best clothes, but he'd left his manners back at the tent on his claim.

Calista walked on through the lobby without answering. She didn't have time to address every inappropriate remark tonight. Her task was to look for Lila when women were most likely to be on the sidewalks.

In her hotel, the ratio of men to women made it easy to quickly discern that Lila wasn't among the females congratulating the men as they received their money. Some were wives and girlfriends, but others seemed the ambitious type who weren't going to wait for the men to stumble into their lairs. They were going hunting.

Calista focused her eyes ahead. She'd better be ready for anything. Pushing through the hotel doors, she found the sidewalks no less crowded. Whether the randy behavior on display was from intoxicated men or from men who planned to be intoxicated soon, she couldn't guess. When a family with children passed, the mother excitedly looking in shop windows while the father zealously kept his brood together, Calista stepped in behind them. Her passage would be easier if the miners assumed she was under the protection of this family. She looked into the face of every woman she passed while averting her gaze from the men. She craned her neck to look down dark alleys as they passed. Clearly there was activity in the shadows, but she was no fool. Pinkerton had made it clear that she was to avoid dangerous situations until she had more experience.

The open doors of a whiskey shop drew her interest. The piano music skipped along, and electric lamps flickered. Two girls stood at the entrance, calling out to passersby with promises of cold drink and hot food. A man with a gun belt slung low on his hips marched up and put his hands around one of the women's waists. She laughed, then pulled him to her for a sloppy kiss. Calista looked for her family escort, but they had moved on. When she looked at the whiskey shop again, the woman had pulled the man inside, and another girl had come to the doorstep to take her place.

While Calista wanted to gird up her armor and storm the place, she had to remember her disguise. She was a reckless young lady looking for excitement. That was the only way she'd be allowed to snoop through this cold world. She hoped no one mistook her recklessness for vulnerability. If they did, all she had for protection was a covering of prayer and a retractable baton. The coiled strip of metal hid easily in her palm, and with the flick of a button, it shot out to form a metal stick about two feet in length. It wasn't a sure option, but it was better than nothing.

With a deep breath, she prayed that God would honor her intentions and look after her safety, even as she put herself in harm's way.

Then she entered the den.

Matthew had been warned about Saturday night. During the week he'd been in Joplin, he'd made a few friends among the miners, and the further into the week they got, the more they sought out his company. On Tuesday, they would suffer a conversation with him if he provided a hot meal. On Wednesday, they'd let him pray for them for a piece of pie. By Friday, they were willing to open a Bible if he'd only give them a cup of coffee.

But tonight they'd get a second chance. With a week's worth of wages, they could finally break the habits that had enslaved them.

Even on market day, the streets of Pine Gap had never been this crowded. People jostled against each other, sometimes laughing, sometimes threatening. When Matthew saw a man leering at a group of girls, he went to intervene.

"Is this man acting unseemly?" he asked the girl, no older than his little sister.

She fell against him, her hand curled around the strap of his suspender. "As a matter of fact, I was waiting for you to step up and show me how a real man is supposed to act." Even by the weak streetlight, he could see the green tint of an old bruise beneath her eye and the gap where she was missing a tooth.

Oh, Lord. How long had he gone, thinking that these women were professional seducers, living a life of unrepentant luxury? Instead, he saw in the face of this girl all the children he'd served lunch to the day before. Had she grown up there at the Children's Home? Or had she left home to pursue excitement, only to be trapped?

With more patience than he'd thought he'd be capable of under the circumstances, he removed her hand. "I don't want anything from you, but I want something for you. Peace and freedom."

She searched his face. "You got nothing that can help me," she said at last, then disappeared into the crowd.

Shaken by the hopelessness he'd encountered, Matthew continued down the sidewalk. He felt like the shepherd looking for one lost lamb among wolves, but it would be easy to get distracted when the wolves were doing their dead level best to entice him away from the God he loved. The words of his mother about avoiding the path of the unrighteous had him wishing for escape, but he was called to walk this path for a time. At least for tonight.

And maybe this was why. Ahead, he saw Irvin hurrying down the street with his hand deep in his pocket.

"Irvin!" Matthew bounded through the crowd as he caught up with the miner. "Irvin, did you get your pay?"

Irvin turned, and Matthew saw the bottle in his hand.

"Why, Preacher, it's a fine thing, seeing you today, but I don't have time for a prayer. Come calling after work on Monday. I'll have time then."

Matthew wrinkled his nose at the smell of alcohol. "By Monday you'll be broke again and wallowing in your misery." And before too long, the drink would do irreversible damage to his constitution. Matthew had seen it with Uncle Manuel. "Better quit while you're ahead."

"I won't be broke. I'm going to double my money tonight. Just see if I don't." Irvin swayed along with the billiards advertisement over his head.

What could Matthew do short of kidnapping? Then he had an inspiration. If the dealers in the gambling dens could convince Irvin in his diminished state, why couldn't Matthew persuade him?

He pulled Irvin against the window of the saloon. "I've got a guaranteed deal for you, Irvin. It might not make you rich—"

"I'm going to get rich tonight."

"Okay, but first you're going to share some of that wealth with me, and I'm going to put it down on a prize for you. You'll win food for the whole week if we're lucky."

"And if we're not lucky?"

Matthew held out his hand. "I'll pay you back if I lose it. Guaranteed."

With a word of protest, Irvin pulled out his roll of bills from the bank and peeled off four of them. Matthew shook his head and took two more. "That leaves you with more than half to play with tonight. That's more than enough to lose. You come see me when you're hungry next week. I'll have this set aside."

"We'll see who has the best luck," Irvin said and laughed. "You don't know the first thing . . ." He was still laughing at Matthew when he disappeared into the mouth of the gambling hall.

Matthew stuffed the bills in his pocket with a small amount of satisfaction. He'd rather that Irvin had made the decision on his own, but any money kept out of the hands of the predatory businesses on a Saturday night was a victory.

"I saw what you did there." A miner no older than Matthew pushed off the wall to stand before him. Despite his youth, he was weathered beyond his years. "Dan Campbell," he said as he held out his hand.

"You're a neighbor of Irvin's," Matthew said.

"Yep. Seen you around his place."

Matthew held up both hands. "I wouldn't say I'm a friend of his, you understand. I don't approve of his choices."

"It's alright. No reason to be defensive. I *am* a friend of Irvin's, but I can offer friendship without condoning everything he does." Dan paused, like he was giving Matthew time to repent of something, and maybe he should have. "If I'm not mistaken, Irvin is going to eat better this week than he has in a long time, thanks to you." He studied Matthew for a moment before adding, "You're a preacher?"

"That's right. I don't have a church, but if anyone wants to get together . . ."

"If you're coming back to Irvin's on Monday, would you mind if my wife and I joined you?"

Matthew nearly fell over. "Please do! And it doesn't have to be at his place, or on Monday. Whenever you're free . . ." He was rambling, and Dan was laughing at him.

"Hold up there, Preacher. You're raring to go." Dan stepped aside to get them off the busy street. A rat darted from beneath a pile of newspapers in the alley and out onto the sidewalk, where a man pulled a pistol and shot it dead. Miners cheered and hooted, but Dan didn't bat an eye. "How long have you been in town?" he asked.

"A week. Now that I'm getting my bearings, I'm going to set about getting a job. Looking at one of the mines."

"Most people with a hankering to mine get themselves a lease first. Why not try your luck that way?" Dan asked.

"If I wanted to find my fortune in mining, I would, but that's not my aim," Matthew said.

"Be careful," Dan said. "If something goes wrong two hundred feet below, you might never see the sky again."

To a man accustomed to the sun, the wind, and the mountains, the thought of being under dirt was unsettling. But it was what Matthew needed to do. A fisherman had to go where the fish were.

"Where should I start?"

"You could do worse than talking to Oscar Kentworth at the Fox-Berry Mine. He does the hiring there." Cheers erupted on the street again, this time without an accompanying gunshot. Dan pulled his hat down tighter over his thick black hair. "I'd better get home, or Loretta is going to get concerned. She doesn't appreciate me staying in town on Saturday night, and she has her reasons. See you Monday."

Matthew watched him walk away through the spots of light on the sidewalk. He limped slightly, but his gait still showed power.

Just when Matthew had thought he'd never make any progress, God sent him some encouragement. It was sorely needed, because Matthew had never been in a situation that felt as dark as this night did. True, there were individuals hurrying through, perhaps to shield themselves until they could get their funds safely home, but for the most part, the unholy merriment was being enjoyed by all. And what really upset him were the respectable-looking citizens who didn't seem to mind that their fellow Joplinites were being fleeced. They had enough money to gamble and carouse on a Saturday night without their children going hungry. What did they care? And what was worse, many of them owned the buildings and businesses that were preying on the impulses of these impulsive men.

Dapper young men mocking the drunkards, proper young ladies gawking at their fallen sisters, peering into the dark dens for a salacious view. Matthew stopped. He knew very few people in Joplin, but he could hardly forget Miss Calista York. And here she was, unescorted after dark on a public street crowded with men at their worst. She might be more cosmopolitan than he was, and she might know the city, but he understood the attention she was drawing, and going inside that whiskey shop wasn't in her best interest.

He looked up at the span over the door, as if he expected it to have fangs and snap closed the second he crossed the threshold. Was this how Uncle Manuel got started? Did he also have innocent intentions but fell prey to temptation? And one drink led to another, which led to another. . . .

Matthew said a quick prayer that God would protect him and that he'd have the sense to know when to flee, and then he plowed forward. It was just a door in a building. He could walk out when he was ready, fight his way out if necessary.

Slipping past the two women at the door, Matthew scanned the room. Every table seemed full, most with businessmen doling out handshakes and checks like crooked politicians. The piano player's hands sped over the keys while his foot stomped the rhythm. Next to the piano, a woman who couldn't keep up with the quick beat fell laughing and swearing into the arms of a man whose beer splashed over both of them. This didn't look like anyplace that would hire a decorator of Miss York's taste. It was a far cry from the café of the House of Lords—but then again, she had mentioned that she wanted to decorate the upstairs. Who knew how low she was willing to go?

Thinking again of the young woman in the street made his stomach turn. How could Miss York have any part in that?

A man, probably a mine owner, lingered at the side of the room. With a point of his finger, he directed his clerk to gather up the account books and put them in a briefcase, and then, with his hands drumming the brim of the hat he was carrying, he headed toward the piano.

Perhaps it was intuition, but Matthew knew who the man had in mind even before he saw him approaching Miss York.

Although she was dressed modestly for the company she was keeping, it was no wonder that she'd caught the man's eye. Her brown curls tumbled down her back, stopping just shy of her slender waist. Why was Matthew here? What if someone recognized him in this place? Would he lose credibility? Especially when the lady in question seemed to be courting misfortune.

Matthew stepped closer and heard her speak over the piano music.

"I was just talking to my friends, here," she said to the man. "I'm not thirsty."

"Hans, do you know this lady?" The businessman called to someone behind the bar.

Hans leaned against the bar to support his weight as he made his way closer. "I've never seen her before. Are you one of those temperance women?"

When she covered her mouth to giggle, Matthew wanted to break something. "I enjoy a good time as much as the next girl. I was just asking Matilda the name of her perfume. It's got an original scent."

Hans didn't look happy with her answer. "Matilda is working and shouldn't be talking to people who aren't paying customers. I'm willing to overlook your rudeness if you'll sit down with my friend here for a visit. Bernard, I'll bring you two shots of whiskey."

Of all the naive, idiotic . . . Matthew's victory with Irvin faded. How could he be content in a world where girls didn't know any better? And yet, for all Miss York's bravado, there was a whiff of inconsistency—a split second when he felt rather than saw a flash of something more genuine than her actions.

Matthew often prayed that God would open his eyes to see the truth. Was this such a moment? Had something been revealed that he couldn't have recognized on his own?

Hans plopped two shot glasses before them. Miss York smiled at her companion as she took up her drink, then looked up at the mirror that ran the length of the bar. Her eyes focused as she searched for something in the reflection, and her gaze met Matthew's. Their eyes locked, and his chest thumped like he'd pulled the trigger on his shotgun. He stepped forward just as she lifted the shot glass and tossed the contents over her shoulder, all over his shirt.

He'd grabbed her by the arm before he had time to think. Her shock was evident as she blinked at him with wide brown eyes. Only then did it occur to him that she might not have meant to drench him. But if she wasn't throwing her drink on him, then why . . . ?

"I'm so glad you found me, Matthew," she said. "I'd lost track of time."

And then she threw herself against him, covering the wet splotch on his shirt. As her arms went around his neck, the drenched shirt offered little protection from the softness pressed against him. Matthew caught her by the waist, but before he could push her away, he felt a single word breathed against his neck.

"Please."

His hands tightened. He should free himself, but again he was making a decision that inched closer to that gray line. Yes, if he was like Uncle Manuel, this could definitely be his undoing. Flee or fight, he had to make a decision.

Matthew would fight, and fight for her if it would save her.

"Calista." Her heart-shaped face, glowing in the dim light, was shining up at him. Her smile was beguiling, but he saw in her eyes a flicker of fear. Matthew's courage grew. He could handle this. "Dinner is waiting. I have a table," he said.

Her hands lingered on his chest as she turned to the brute named Bernard. "Thank you for the drink," she said, "but I have a prior engagement."

How the businessman took the news, Matthew would never know, because he couldn't take his eyes off his companion. He noticed that she was content to be escorted by him. He also noticed that her dress had dampened from being pressed against him.

"Watch where you're going," the girl at the door said as Matthew bumped into her.

"Sorry." He stumbled down the stairs and into the bustling crowd. Instinctively, he turned toward the outskirts of town, away from the chaos. In this case, the darkness was residing in the lights. He wanted to get away from all of it.

"What were you doing there?" she asked. "Spying on the competition?"

He'd never thought to call those establishments competition, but he figured it was close enough. "Can I guess why you threw your drink on me?"

She bit her lip as she looked at his shirt. "Thank you for playing along. I didn't want to outright refuse his drink."

"You're going to face worse than that if you're working at the House of Lords."

"Are they offering me a job?" Her hand tightened on his arm. "What changed their mind?"

"How am I supposed to know? They don't consult me with their employment decisions." He'd heard that a life of sin led to a reprobate mind, but he hadn't thought it could muddle the thinking this much.

"I thought you worked there," she said.

His shocked look made her laugh.

"Calm down," she said. "I wish I worked there, remember? I'm not judging you, whether you do or don't."

"Anyone with ties to that establishment should be ashamed of themselves. Real suffering goes on there. God won't hold them that contribute blameless."

Her steps slowed beneath the streetlight. Releasing his arm, she turned to face him. The electric light buzzed above their heads. Blue flickers danced across her serious gaze.

"God? Did you say God?" Her eyes narrowed. "If you don't work at the House of Lords, where do you work?"

He regretted the embarrassment his answer would cause her. Not that he was ashamed, but he figured that a woman like her would feel judged. But there was nothing to do besides tell the truth.

"I work for the Lord. I'm a pastor," he said.

The immediate effect was . . . nothing. Her face was as smooth as cream in an undisturbed jar. Seconds ticked by. Matthew had to step out of the way of some carousers, but after they passed, he waved his hand in front of her face.

"Hello," he said. "Are you having a spell?"

She blinked, then looked down to the side. "When you invited yourself to my lunch table, you were thinking . . . ?"

"That I could convince you to leave. I saw what you did for that miner, giving his money back. I figured you were a decent sort."

"A pastor?" she repeated. "I didn't expect that. It could be useful."

His chest swelled with importance. "Of course I could be useful. I haven't been in town long, but if you're looking for employment, maybe I could introduce you to some less controversial jobs. And eventually I'd like to have a gathering. It wouldn't be appropriate for us to meet alone, but—"

"I can't be seen with you," she said, even as her eyes roved his face like she was seeing him for the first time.

His mouth went dry. If he wasn't being misled by vanity, he'd say she liked what she saw. "I promised you a dinner," he said. "If we can find a restaurant that isn't too busy—"

"I said I can't be seen with you."

"And I decided to ignore that statement. Don't say it again." He took her arm. "Whatever ridicule you fear from associating with me is nothing compared to what could happen to you alone on the street."

"Take me back to my hotel, then. At least we can limit the damage."

Matthew couldn't help but be amused by her resignation. "Which hotel is that?"

"The Keystone."

Right next to the flower shop. No wonder he kept running into her. And he hoped their paths would keep crossing. "What's wrong with being seen with me?" he asked. "I haven't submitted you to any hellfire and brimstone homilies."

"Yet." Her teeth gleamed with her grin. "I'm here to have fun and experience life. Not to belabor the obvious, Parson, but you're a hindrance to both."

"It's Matthew, and there's nothing wrong with having fun. I'm having fun right now, in fact." Although he had to remember not to barge down the street too quickly. Her dainty steps deserved consideration. Besides, he didn't want to cut their time short.

"What else did you do today that was fun?" she asked. He caught glimpses of her face as they walked side by side.

"Not much today, but earlier this week was noteworthy. I was attacked by a couple on the road, for starters."

She pouted. "Were you hurt?"

He kinda wished he had been. "It was a misunderstanding. After that I visited the Joplin Children's Home. It might not be the type of fun you're seeking, but I enjoyed it."

She tilted her head so that she could view him from beneath thick lashes. "Tell me more about this Children's Home. It sounds interesting."

She'd known he was a threat from the time she laid eyes on him. Sensible, direct, and too green to take anything for granted—those were the marks that exposed your game. The jaded man-about-town was easier to fool than the country boy who was analyzing everything about his new situation. And on top of that, he was a God-fearing man.

The moment he'd told her he was a parson was the closest she'd ever come to dropping her disguise with a stranger. From the beginning at the House of Lords, she'd found his direct honesty appealing. He was handsome, capable, bold, and everything she'd ever thought she'd want in a man, except for his morals. As long as she'd thought he was working for a brothel, she wasn't interested. True, she couldn't believe her luck when she had turned to find him at the saloon, and it was possible that she could have found a way to escape besides throwing herself into his arms, but it had seemed the most agreeable solution at the time.

And here he was with a connection to the very Children's Home that she was attempting to infiltrate.

"This Children's Home," she said. "Is there much need for it?"

His handsome face settled into more somber lines. "With all the solicitation in this city? Those babies aren't going to be raised in a house of entertainment."

It wasn't likely that Lila Seaton would have a child already, not unless she left home to hide a pregnancy, but it was worth checking out. Anywhere that the girls were likely to frequent was a place she could ask questions. Even more interesting was the possibility that she could accompany Mrs. Bowman on her rounds of the brothels. That would be the safest way for Calista to get a look behind the screens.

"What about the mothers? Are there any records of them?" Mrs. Bowman had said that volunteers had access.

"From what I understand, there are, unless the child is abandoned on the doorstep. They do have a maternity room for confinements . . ." He cleared his throat. "Pardon me. I'm not accustomed to discussing such things with a lady. I'd be better off talking about breeding animals."

He was so sweet, and she had to act jaded. She took a deep breath and prayed that God would never let her be as flippant as she was pretending to be. "You'll get over it. It's the way of the world. Anyway, I might be interested in lending a hand there. My job prospects don't amount to much. Might as well do something."

They'd reached the flower shop next to her hotel. His eyes flickered up to the green and gold sign above them. "You can't," he said.

Calista stopped. "What do you mean *I can't*? You said they need help." She turned and looked over her shoulder at the sign. What was he seeing?

"I'm going off my gut, but my gut says you aren't in the right state of mind to be there."

Pretending to be immature was no stretch at the moment. "Who are you to judge my state of mind? You don't know me. You don't know me at all."

But he wasn't moved. "I know your lackadaisical attitude toward their predicament."

"I don't have any attitude about them."

"You should. You should pity them. Instead you're trying to profit from the same men who are exploiting them."

While she regretted that his opinion of her was so low, at least he believed her disguise. "I need a job," she said. "If your church is hiring a decorator, I'd be glad to work for it."

His eye roll wasn't very chivalrous. "When I have a church of my own, I don't know that gilt mirrors will be called for."

"I've worked for years developing my own personal style," she said. "Perhaps we have a difference of tastes."

"Regardless, you have no business at the Children's Home. Many of these women visit, just for a glimpse of the children they've been separated from. How would it look to them if the same organization that claims to offer a safe, respectable place for their children to grow up also allows someone tainted by her associations to work there?"

Calista had been glad to learn he had morals. Now she wasn't so sure.

"It's a pity. When I think of all the help I could've been to those

76

poor girls . . ." This situation was spinning out of control. Matthew was a complication she hadn't bargained for. Better to end the conversation before she slipped up any further. "Thank you, Matthew, for providing me with an escape tonight. Hopefully your services won't be needed again. There's my hotel. Good evening, and good luck with your church."

Had things been different, she would have liked to hear his plans, but she could hardly tell him they were fighting on the same team. Dropping his arm with a huff, Calista stomped inside the hotel and hoped that her show of frustration disguised her wistfulness over what could have been a nice conversation under different circumstances.

CHAPTER

6

"Can you read?" the man asked as he handed Matthew a typed sheet of paper.

"Yes, sir." Although in the dark office of the Fox-Berry Mine, it wouldn't be easy. Matthew held the page up to catch the light flickering from the weak bulb above his head. He reckoned miners used to working underground didn't notice when the lighting was puny.

He licked the tip of his pencil before setting it to the form. The address of Trochet's Flowers was a mystery to him, but surely the name of the business would serve just as well. References? There he was at a loss. He should have asked Dan Campbell if he could use his name, but without permission, it seemed like an imposition.

The light bulb swung as the ground trembled beneath his feet. Matthew looked up and caught the eye of the bull of a man behind the desk.

"We gotta get that ore out of there somehow," he said. "I just wish the explosions didn't shake the office so." He snatched the completed form from Matthew and glanced over it. "You got a nice hand. What's an educated man want with going below?"

"I'm not educated," Matthew said. "Just took to learning on

my own after school." Especially stories about missionaries. Those were his favorite. "But I aim to be a pastor. What better way to do that than work side by side with the men?"

"This job is for a powder monkey, not a pastor."

What was a powder monkey? Matthew guessed he'd figure it out soon enough. "I know how to do a full day's work," he said. "I'll save my preaching for when I'm off the clock."

"Just the same, I'll bet the boss man will want to visit. Wait here."

Matthew shifted his feet beneath the chair and settled in for a wait. Despite his plans for Monday, it hadn't gone as planned. He'd started out after the final bell, invigorated by the thought of Bible study at Irvin's claim. The breeze whipping over the piles of chat had never been more refreshing as he passed by the tents and shanties of the miners returning from their workday.

If only Irvin had been home. He must have had some luck gambling over the weekend, because he still had money to spend on Monday. Instead of coming home to meet with Matthew, he'd found somewhere to stay in town.

If it hadn't been for Dan and Loretta Campbell, Matthew's day would have been miserable indeed.

The hiring man came back and, with a wave of his massive paw, motioned for Matthew to follow him.

"Matthew Cook." The man at the desk peered over the application form at him. His blond hair was slicked up and back off his forehead like a steep riverbank. "I'm Oscar Kentworth, and I'm looking for someone with intelligence."

Kentworth? Matthew wouldn't be surprised to learn that Amos and Maisie were kin of his, but someone with intelligence didn't mention street brawls they'd fought in.

"I hope you've found him," Matthew said.

"Have you had any experience with explosives?"

Not a question he'd ever been asked before. "No, sir."

"Too bad. We need a powder monkey, and someone who's as precise as you were filling out this form might fit the bill. Alas, without experience, I'll have to start you as a jack shoveler. You look strong enough."

Even Matthew knew that a jack shoveler was the lowest of the low. It didn't take skill or aptitude to work a shovel. It was mind-numbing, backbreaking work, but he prayed it would bring him in contact with the people he needed to meet.

"I'll take any work you have," he said. "When can I start?"

"Beginning of next week, how about? Show up at the doghouse out there at eight, and we'll get you outfitted." Mr. Kentworth rose and held out his hand. "And Godspeed your efforts on preaching, but if a preacher doesn't work as hard as the next man, he's set no example I'd be proud of."

"I understand."

With a firm shake of his hand, Mr. Kentworth said, "See you next Monday."

And just like that, Matthew was a miner.

He'd have to go through his clothes and see if he needed to purchase anything. He had canvas britches that would take wear, and a denim shirt. What about tools? Would the Fox-Berry provide them?

He returned to Trochet's and was on his way through the shop when he heard a voice that was becoming familiar. Pausing by a vase of lilies, Matthew spotted Calista in a stern white shirtwaist and a rich mahogany skirt. Looking at her today, he'd never guess she was adrift with no guidance.

"Our biggest accounts are the hotels and restaurants downtown, if that's what you're asking." Mr. Trochet was behind the counter with his spectacles perched on the end of his nose so he could see her better. Matthew didn't blame him. She warranted looking at.

Calista smoothed a wisp of hair behind her ear. "What I'm

proposing is that I'd make deliveries for you. I'm trained in flower arrangements, and I could add that to my service for no extra charge. Your customers will be forever loyal if your business not only delivers the flowers but arranges them throughout the premises as well."

"I already have Bennie. He has a horse and wagon. Bennie has worked with me for years."

"I could go with Bennie and put fresh flowers in each room instead of delivering them to the door, then leaving. Please, let me try it for a week, for free. If your customers don't appreciate the added service, then I'll give it up, no harassing you."

A flower arranger? Matthew supposed that flower arranging could be learned alongside decorating, but she hadn't mentioned it before. And while he'd prefer that she work for Mr. Trochet than at one of the bawdy houses, he regretted that Mr. Trochet's business was also tainted by the unrighteous trades. Was nothing in this city set apart? Matthew made his way through the rows of blooms to the cash register.

"No, thank you, ma'am. I have all the help I need." Mr. Trochet spotted Matthew approaching. "If Bennie needed more help with deliveries, I would send Matthew."

"Matthew?" Her face scrunched up in an adorable scowl. "I don't know Matthew, but I doubt he has my talent."

"Hello, Calista," Matthew said.

At her name, Calista spun around, one hand reaching for the countertop to steady herself, the other outstretched, as if defending herself was a concern. Her eyes flashed to his, scanned the room behind him, then did a complete sweep of his body.

He'd give his copy of David Brainerd's biography to know what she was looking for.

"You're the Matthew?" she asked.

"There's bound to be more than one, but as far as you're concerned, yes, I'm the Matthew."

"You know each other?" Mr. Trochet pushed his glasses up his nose. "That doesn't change my answer, but you're welcome to stay and look around. Matthew, don't let her leave without a rose, you hear?"

Calista dropped her gaze to the ground and fidgeted with the narrow strip of trim on her cuff as Mr. Trochet went back to his office. "You work here?" she asked.

"I live here," Matthew said. "In the gardener's cabin." He couldn't help but think the picture she made was a particularly attractive one, in her crisp white blouse surrounded by flowers and framed by every color of the rainbow. "Now you're a flower arranger?"

"Why wouldn't I be?" She smoothed her hair behind her ear again, and he noticed that her hat didn't fit her. For someone as fashionable as she was, you would think she'd only buy hats that fit.

"You never mentioned it before."

"There's a lot you don't know about me, but what you do know about me is consistent. I'm an artist of a sort. I make beauty, whether by decorating with fabrics or flowers. While I've been unsuccessful in obtaining employment, I'm persistent. I haven't given up."

She also sounded like a snake-oil salesman listing off the benefits of his brew.

"Congratulations, then." When had her cheeks pinked? It wasn't hot in here. "I commend your persistence and will do my best to match it. Come with me on Saturday night."

Her lips puckered in shocked disapproval. "Saturday night? Why?"

"Instead of fighting the crowds and the debauchery, I'm going to see if anyone wants to have a simple gathering. We can celebrate payday with food instead of spirits. Games instead of gambling. It'll be fun." It was an idea he'd been mulling over since he'd seen what Saturday nights were like. She just happened to be his first invitee.

If it weren't for the phone call from Pinkerton yesterday, Calista would have thrown caution to the wind and accepted Matthew's offer. She hadn't expected her job to be so lonely. Being a stranger in town, befriending people of questionable character, always hiding your true motives and personality—Calista yearned to let her guard down with Matthew.

But Pinkerton wanted results. After Matthew had escorted Calista back to her hotel on Saturday night, she'd skipped out the back door and headed in the opposite direction. She'd done her best, asking about Lila Seaton and showing her picture around, but Joplin had many places a girl could disappear into. While all her interviews corroborated that Lila was no longer at the House of Lords, as the gap-toothed girl at the doctor's office had said, Calista had a lot more places to check before she could say that Lila wasn't in Joplin.

And on Saturday nights, the brothels turned inside out. The women who normally stayed hidden away paraded down Main Street. Calista couldn't spend the evening enjoying herself in a cozy cabin with Matthew, as much as she wished she could. Not when Lila was somewhere out there.

"I'm sorry." She allowed a sliver of her yearning to show through. "I can't come on Saturday."

"Why? You aren't working."

"It's not a good time for me."

"You were out last Saturday."

"I said no." She crossed her arms. "You aren't supposed to question a lady when she declines your invitation."

"We agreed that we admire persistence. I'm practicing what I preach."

The bell on the front door rang as a customer walked in. Calista couldn't take her eyes off Matthew, even as she heard the clicking heels behind her. Of all the times to meet the man who could turn her head, why did it have to be now, when her every action would disgust him?

"I'm here to pick up flowers," the customer said, "for Dr. Stevenson's office."

Calista turned, then chomped on the inside of her cheek when she realized her mistake.

The nurse's eyebrow rose. "Miss York, what a surprise. You turn up like a bad penny, don't you? So tell me, did you manage to find work at another doctor's office that needed a nurse?"

"A nurse?" Matthew leaned forward so he didn't miss a word.

Calista waved her hand. "I've decided to change careers. I'm no longer in the nursing field."

"After that fiasco with that sick cousin of yours . . ." The nurse wrinkled her nose. "We cleaned the reception area, but in my mind, it still stinks. I'm hoping some flowers will help me forget it."

"You're a nurse?" Matthew's skepticism was impossible to miss. "Did you go to nursing school before or after design school? And how old are you, anyway?"

"I should be going," Calista said, glad that the nurse had summoned Mr. Trochet and was too busy to question her further. Calista went to the glass front doors, conflicted about leaving so soon, but there was no remedy.

She turned the knob and swung the door open . . . right into the path of Amos and Maisie. They gawked at each other, and quick as a wink, Calista pulled the door closed in their faces.

Striding past the nurse, she marched up to Matthew. "You have an apartment here? I'd very much like to see it. Take me." She grabbed his wrist.

His face broke into a lopsided smile. "I knew the women in Joplin were forward, but—"

The front door to the shop flew open.

"Calista York, where do you think you're going?" Amos's voice made the petals on the lilies shiver.

She'd been caught.

"You know him?" Matthew asked.

"Stay away from me," the nurse cried at Maisie. "I've yet to get my uniform clean from last time."

"Stop your bellyaching," Maisie shot back. "You work in a doctor's office. You're gonna encounter puke occasionally."

"The watermelon patch," Matthew said. "You two attacked me."

Amos grinned. "I thought you'd put that behind you, brother. It's not like a man of the cloth to hold a little tussle against a fella."

"My head . . . the heat . . . I really need to retire for a moment." Calista pressed the back of her hand against her forehead. "Is there a quiet place I might lie down?"

But Matthew was having none of it. He waited until the nurse had left the shop before asking, "How do you know these people?"

"She's the cousin you heard tell of," Maisie said. "The one who's shaming her family with her scandalous behavior."

Calista's head turned from Maisie to Matthew. "You know each other?"

"I told you I was attacked by two people, remember?" Matthew said. "It looks like they're family of yours."

Calista wasn't surprised. Amos could be volatile if he thought he'd been disrespected. And Maisie wasn't one to miss out on a fight if there was one in the vicinity.

"What exactly did you tell him?" Calista whispered to Maisie.

Ignoring Calista's discreet tone, Maisie chirped, "We told him the truth—that you are plumb out of your mind. That you're going against your raisings, and we're here to hold you to account."

Amos nodded toward Matthew. "If you're looking for a way-ward lamb to bring back into the fold, Preacher, this one here needs bidding."

Calista had to frame this new encounter in such a way as to further her work. Unexpectedly, Amos and Maisie's claims strengthened her disguise of being a person of low character. Their concern was authentic, even if misguided, and might get her out of explaining about the finishing school.

Matthew was studying her as Amos recited a laundry list of complaints from Granny Laura about the dangers of the town and how Calista shouldn't be there alone. Matthew's gaze was steady, thoughtful, and appraising. He'd left home out of his concern for others, lived simply, worked hard. As far as he knew, she was causing her family grief just because she wanted some excitement. In his eyes, she was less considerate than the felons she'd helped catch.

And there was no remedy until she found the girl she was looking for.

Matthew laid a hand on Amos's shoulder, stopping his recitation of all of Calista's misbehaviors. He was looking at her, making a connection that made her feel somewhat giddy. Would pretending to be besotted with him further her progress? Was she pretending?

"Tell your grandmother that Calista is attending a Bible study with a group of believers on Wednesday night," Matthew said. "That she has someone holding her accountable."

"You?" Maisie flung her braid over her shoulder. "What makes you think you're up to snuff?"

"If she warrants family intervention, I'll send word," Matthew said. "And by all means, hold her to account yourselves. Far be it from me to try to replace family concern."

Amos scratched his head. "It's not that I'd cast aspersions on your intentions, Matthew, but you're no older than the rest of us. It doesn't stand to reason that you'd be the best chaperone."

"I intervened when I thought you were harassing Miss Kentworth, didn't I?"

"And I whupped you good for it," Maisie said.

Calista rubbed her brow. Why hadn't she asked to be assigned to Wyoming or somewhere less complicated?

Matthew arched his back as if still feeling the soreness. "My point is—"

"His point is that I'm an adult," Calista interrupted. "I'm not doing anything illegal, but if it will settle my family's concerns to know that I'm keeping the company of a preacher, then they can rest easy." She hadn't decided yet if she would go through with the offer. Keeping his company didn't feel like a safe strategy, but someone with her poor character would make the promise without qualms just to end this discussion.

"So you aren't going to come with us to the ranch?" Amos asked.

"I have a room at the Keystone. It's very respectable," Calista answered.

"Where is this Bible study?" Maisie's eyes darted from Calista to Matthew, then back again.

"Tomorrow in the ore fields," Matthew answered. "I'll escort her there myself."

Amos winced. "Granny would be better off not knowing that she's going anywhere near the ore fields."

"Pastor Dixon is married and not nearly as handsome," Maisie whispered to Calista loudly enough for everyone to hear. "Are you sure it wouldn't be better to go there? As it is, you're kinda like Eve climbing an apple tree to get away from temptation."

Calista shot a startled look at Matthew, but he was immovable, not acknowledging the implications of Maisie's tactless observation. "I'm going to the ore fields with Matthew," she said. "What you tell Granny is your business."

Maisie dropped her braid, and Amos took his hands out of his pockets. "Welp," Amos drawled, "we said our piece. Thank you for your assistance, Mr. Cook."

Matthew dipped his head in acknowledgment. With one last look at Calista, Amos and Maisie walked out the door.

All the words that had been spoken seemed to take their time settling around the room. It took a minute before either of them felt like stirring them up again.

"Thank you," Calista said. "I'm glad they believed you."

"It's true," he replied. "You are coming. Bible study Wednesday, and then the party on Saturday. That wasn't an excuse to rescue you from your family."

"They love me." She could allow herself this one moment of honesty, couldn't she? She reached for a long-stemmed carnation and spun it between her fingers. "If they didn't care about me, they wouldn't be such a bother."

"And I intend to be every bit as big of a bother as they are," he said.

"I know why my family would do that, but why would you?"

His eyes were the color of her walnut desk when it was freshly polished. Why would she notice that now? Because neither of them could look away. Who was he? What was he thinking? Why would Matthew Cook, a good, upright man, bother to care about the likes of her?

Mr. Trochet walked out of his office. "I told you to give that girl a rose," he reminded Matthew. "You can do better than a carnation."

Matthew's jaw moved forward, and he inhaled a deep breath. The tips of Calista's fingers tingled as he looked her over. Then, with a sigh, he turned on his heel.

"I'll see you tomorrow night," he said over his shoulder as he strode out the back door.

CHAPTER

7

How did one tell if he was playing with fire? When his justifications were so weak, not even he believed them. Matthew was wearing a path bare as he argued both sides of the quandary.

With a family that good, Calista couldn't be all bad. With a family that good, she must be an awful person to cause them grief. She'd been raised right, so she had a good foundation. She'd been raised right and had turned her back on God. Despite her scandalous behavior, she seemed decent and charming. She used her charm to deceive and excuse her scandalous behavior.

"Amen," he heard himself say as eleven-year-old Toddie finished praying.

Calista also made his mind wander while leading a Bible study at an orphanage. Another charge against her character.

"Thank you, Toddie." Matthew rose off the cot they'd gathered around in the children's dorm. "That was a mighty fine prayer. You'uns listened good."

"Will you come outside with us and play ball?" Dolly asked.

"Maybe next time," he said.

They groaned just enough to be politely disappointed before stampeding outside to the fenced yard.

Matthew gathered the printed Sunday School readers they were using. As sad as it was for the kids to be here with no parents, it was better than the future many of them faced once they got out. Whenever the home ran short on funds, the older children were the first place they economized. The charitable leaders of Joplin were meeting at the orphanage today, and Matthew hoped they had come up with a good strategy to raise the needed money.

He reached the office just as a door opened down the hall on a boisterous gathering. From the jovial voices, the meeting had been a success. Graying mustaches spread over grinning mouths. A cane tip was bounced against the floor in satisfied approval. Matthew saw Clydell Blount, the wealthy owner of the Fox-Berry Mine, president of the Elks Club, and the most recognizable man in Joplin, exit the room. Every miner in town made way for him when he walked down the sidewalk, and he in return greeted them heartily, one and all.

"I take it the meeting was a success," Matthew said.

Mr. Blount's chest expanded. "We've come up with a plan that will address several needs at once." His story was interrupted by a racking cough that frequently waylaid him. He held up a finger until the fit passed, then continued. "The Elks Club is going to hold a baby raffle."

"A baby raffle? What are you going to raffle off to raise money for the babies?"

The man who sold the streetcars to the city stepped forward to explain. "We're going to raffle a baby. The winner gets a baby from right here at the home." He ran his hand over the gold braid running along the seam of his black suit.

Matthew wasn't hearing them right. That was the problem. Before he could ask for clarification, Mr. Blount spoke again.

"It's genius. We expect there'll be a lot of interest—hundreds of tickets sold. Most people either can't afford adoption, or they don't have the patience to wait for the proceedings. Or maybe they've never thought of it. This will make them more aware of the option, find a family for one of the kids, and raise some money. Can't put rocks in the kids' bellies, after all. They gotta have food."

"You're giving away a baby?" Matthew finally managed. "It's barbaric. A child isn't a prize to be won, like a suckling pig."

"Don't moralize on it," the streetcar man said. "It's novel, but not wrong."

"We'd make sure the winner is acceptable," said Mr. Blount. "The police department would let us know if the new parents were criminals, and the Children's Home already has a baby chosen. Cute little fellow, ten months old. He'll be on display at the Carnegie Library every weekday until all the tickets are sold."

Was Matthew being too idealistic? To barter with a human life denigrated its worth. He wondered what his pastor back home would say. No, Matthew didn't have to wonder. At the first news of a baby being displayed as a prize in Pine Gap, his mother would crash all the way through their mountain forests until she reached the child and took it to safety. His mother wasn't here, but he was.

"I ask you to reconsider," Matthew said. "Have we gone back to selling people?"

"Calm down, young man." Mr. Blount's large head settled and tilted to the side. "Why would someone pay money for a child if they didn't want it? It's just another form of adoption."

But something in Matthew's gut told him differently. It was dehumanizing, using a human life as a commodity. He didn't like it a bit, but he wasn't sure what he could do to stop it.

He waited inside the door of the Children's Home, not wanting to walk back to town in the company of the self-congratulating group. How was it that in Joplin even the good deeds were tainted?

As he let the community leaders clear out, he recognized someone coming across the grounds that he'd yet to introduce himself to. The tall, thin man in a loose-fitting suit stepped inside with a heavy portfolio beneath his arm.

Matthew extended his hand. "Reverend Dixon? My name is Matthew Cook. I'm here from Pine Gap—"

"Yes, yes, yes." The reverend nodded, making his gray curls swing against his neck. "Mrs. Fairfield told me about you and your work here. Very generous of you."

Some of the weight of Matthew's morning seemed to shift. "I'm familiar with your church too. It's quite impressive."

"It's not my church," Reverend Dixon said and laughed. "It's God's church. I'm just tending it for a few years. So, tell me, how has your stay been in Joplin? I'm very interested in hearing how your ministry is progressing."

His ministry? Besides the Campbells, the only people willing to talk to Matthew were under the bribery of food or the threat of family discipline. "It's been a slow start, sir. I'm learning my way around."

"Well, if you need any help, please call on me. We're on the same team. You may sow, and I water, but the harvest belongs to the Lord."

Matthew hadn't been a pastor very long. He'd yet to learn how to stretch a few words into a lengthy speech. To the point was more his style.

"There's something you could help me with," Matthew said. "I just spoke to the Elks Club—Mr. Blount in particular—"

"Mr. Blount is a member of my church. A very charitable individual." Reverend Dixon switched the portfolio to his other arm and shifted his weight.

Matthew swallowed hard. "Is he? That's surprising. In case you weren't aware, he's just proposed something outrageous. He's advocating raffling off one of the children from this home to raise funds. He's convinced the Elks Club and the Joplin Provident Society to go along with it."

"Mr. Blount can be unorthodox, but he's very effective. If you just look at what he's accomplished in this city—"

"I'm not talking about his professional résumé. I'm talking about auctioning off a baby. How can he have a heart—"

"Don't be hasty. You don't know the man."

"I know enough to determine he's wrong-minded." Matthew wished his voice wasn't rising, but he had a hard time staying calm when discussing weighty matters.

No matter how the reverend's smile was meant, Matthew felt it to be condescending. "I'm not going to stand in this lobby and slander someone who seeks my guidance, young man," Reverend Dixon said. "I'll speak to him, but in the meantime, I ask you to reserve judgment on him and the others. God uses rough vessels too."

When Matthew didn't answer, Reverend Dixon checked his watch. "I must go, but my door is always open to you. Please come and see me. I'm grateful there's another man with a conscience in town."

Was there? As far as Matthew could tell, he was fighting the good fight all alone.

"No, Father, I haven't seen my classmate since I've been here. I haven't found a job either, which has handicapped me in my search." Another call from Mr. Pinkerton, and Calista was forced to admit that she hadn't accomplished anything besides eliminating some possible scenarios. It was also a chance for her to hear how impatient Jinxy was to have some progress.

"Your brother wants to come visit. Would it be helpful if he came to town?" Pinkerton was offering to send another agent, but under the disguise of her brother? That wouldn't work. Calista had a brother, and her cousins would be quick to point out that Sampson wasn't him.

"I think it'd be better for him to stay in . . . Kansas City." She grimaced. She couldn't be sure who was listening in on the line, but it was possible they might know that she and her family hailed from Kansas City. Pinkerton was intimately acquainted with her file. Surely he would understand why she hadn't mentioned Chicago. "Thank you for the offer, though. Tell Mother I said hello."

She came out of the hotel's office more than discouraged. The calm gurgling of the fountain in the center of the lobby drew her toward it. Sparkling water rushed out of the granite spigot and splashed into the pool. Plump, lazy orange fish glided over the tiny blue tiles without a care in the world. She was getting nowhere. The only thing she was accomplishing was outraging her family.

And family was what compelled her. Jinxy Seaton might be a criminal, but a missing daughter affected more than one person. Every family in the neighborhood would be burdened with fear until Lila was returned. And the Seaton family had already lost one daughter. How could they survive another?

Calista would sacrifice much if it meant rescuing the haunted figure in that photograph, but so far her efforts had been in vain.

A man stepped into her light. Calista's shoulders relaxed. Instead of wariness, she felt peace in his shadow, as if she could glide through it as effortlessly as the goldfish.

"Why are there coins in the fountain?" Matthew asked. "Do they have something to do with the fish?"

He was so amusing. Calista unhooked the fastener on her bag and pulled out a coin. Although he wasn't in a suit like most of the men in the lobby, there was nothing shabby about his wardrobe. Homemade, perhaps, but sized for him from quality cloth. A good, honest cut that emphasized his wide shoulders and strong chest. When she held out the coin, his expression turned curious, but he lifted his hand and allowed her to press a bright penny into his palm. Maybe because he already thought the worst of her and wouldn't be surprised at coquetry, or maybe because she was discouraged and wanted the contact, she closed his fingers over the penny and wrapped her hands around his fist.

"Now close your eyes," she said over the tinkling of the water fountain, "and make a wish."

His eyes darkened as he gazed at her, and for a heartbeat she saw something in them she knew she hadn't seen before. Something he would have rather kept hidden. A thrill ran through her at what it could mean. Was he interested in her for more than her soul? If so, the guilt must have hit him immediately, for his eyes lowered, then shut. He remained motionless as they stood together, her hands around his.

"You're taking a long time," she said. "Surely you've made a wish by now."

"I reckon it's more like praying." He shot her a wary glance. "And with you around, I can't do too much of that."

She released his hand and moistened her suddenly dry lips. "In order for your wish to come true, you toss the coin into the fountain."

He looked at the penny. "I could skip it across the top and see if it'll bounce out the other side."

"Just a simple toss. No fuss, please."

Shrugging, he bounced the coin out of his hand. One fish startled at the splash, but the rest maintained their composed gliding. No matter how the surface was disturbed, they weren't ruffled.

And neither should she be. Calista closed her handbag. "You're here for me?"

"We promised your grandma."

"Then let's go."

He motioned for her to precede him out of the hotel lobby. Gentlemanly, but he failed to offer his arm. The sidewalk wasn't full of carousing drunkards this time, so maybe he didn't think it necessary. Despite her protestations, he paid for the streetcar and stood guard over her so no one entering or exiting would crowd her seat.

Calista looked out the window as the ornate buildings of Joplin passed. So much misery hidden behind those facades. The space that had been empty rolling fields when she was young was now renowned for its vice and corruption, all because someone had scratched through the surface of the ground and found ore. The financial gain that looked like a blessing had brought a curse to hundreds.

Poor Matthew. He was trying to compete with the glimmering allure of sin. If she thought he was the type to become frustrated and wash his hands of Joplin's residents, she wouldn't worry about him, but she knew better. He cared. He mourned for their weaknesses.

And she was giving him even more to worry about.

The sun flashed between the buildings as the streetcar clanged down the road. At least tonight she could be with believers. She could hear God's Word and be refreshed. Even if she had to pretend to be indifferent, her heart would know the truth.

The bell clanged. Matthew offered his hand. She took it and let him escort her off the streetcar. They were on the outskirts of town. After one more block, they'd passed the Joplin Gas Company's office and had reached the beginnings of the mines. To the north stood the Jack Rose Mine. Tall, utilitarian buildings of odd sizes and angles marred the spotless sky. Conveyor belts connected loaders over railroad tracks that were full of heavy cars waiting to start their trek to the smelters and then on to the factories of the world. The chat piles were gray mountains of shards of rock, discarded once the ore had been removed. This spot in the tri-state area was the world's leading producer of zinc and lead, but that success hadn't been shared by all.

At the edge of the works stood rows of shabby houses built for the miners. Made of rough boards and clumsy tin roofs, they didn't look comfortable, but the miners who lived there were guaranteed a paycheck and steady work. She and Matthew walked around the settlement to the prospectors' leases. Here the shelters depended solely on the luck of the prospector. Stained and ripped tents flapped in the wind. A tidy frame house showed that the man leasing that plot possessed both luck and determination. And then there were those who'd struck enough ore that they could move into town. In fact, quite a few of the mansions in the rich Murphysburg section of town belonged to men who had lived in tents like these just a few years ago.

"It's so capricious," Calista said, noting the differences in the homes they were passing. "What distinguishes the man who draws an ore-poor plot from one who hits a bonanza?"

"It's a field of opportunity, wide open to anyone, and most of them make something. It's what they do with their first earnings that often sets the stage for either success or failure. A wise man sets aside some for the weeks when his pocket of ore runs dry. A foolish man squanders what he makes, thinking that tomorrow he'll make the same or even more. One bad decision leads to more bad decisions, and there are plenty around who aim to ease them away from their money.

"This is Irvin's place." Matthew stopped and hooked his thumbs in his belt loops. "As you can tell from the tent, he hasn't gotten off to a good start, but I have hopes for him." He eyed her with confidence. "I have hopes for a lot of people."

Calista returned the smile, but inside, her spirits were sagging. This looked like an unlikely place to find Lila. No entertainment this far out of town. Nothing of interest to draw a troubled young girl out of the city. The sooner Calista could solve the case, the sooner she could stop misleading Matthew. Would she ever tell him the whole truth? Probably not, but it would be a relief to be able to show her true colors instead of pretending to be a reprehensible young lady. How pleased he'd be at the suddenness and completeness of her conversion.

"Hello, Pastor!" Irvin stepped out of his tent, squatted next to a bucket, and splashed water on his arms as he scrubbed at the dirt. "Dan and Loretta are bringing chairs. They'll be back in a jiffy." The dirt on his arms turned to mud and ran down his skin in rivulets.

"What do you say we meet out here?" Matthew asked.

Irvin scrunched up his face. "Probably best if we did. I don't want the ladies to lay eyes on my dirty sundries."

"That's enough reason. Dry off, and I'll introduce you to our guest."

Calista stepped forward once Irvin had dried his hands on his pant legs. "Thank you for inviting us to your property," she said. "It's nice to get away from the city." Mixing with people of all classes was necessary for her job, and doing it well was the mark of being truly educated.

Besides Irvin, another man appeared, a young, buoyant fellow named Silas Marsh. He swaggered like a parade of admirers was following in his wake and smiled like it was the dearest gift he could bestow on a person. Yet somehow Calista still found herself hoping he was as good as his opinion of himself. She accepted his introduction with warmth.

The woman coming around the piles of chat had an eager, pleasant face. From her narrow shoulders and quick, graceful movements, Calista guessed her to be in her midtwenties. She set down the chair she was carrying and turned smoothly to Calista.

"Welcome to our gathering. I'm Loretta Campbell, and I'm plumb tickled to have another gal here." Her dress was neat but faded and covered by a patched apron. She wore a bracelet made from a leather strap and pieces of mother-of-pearl, readily available from clams in the local rivers.

Her husband removed his hat and leaned forward to shake Calista's hand, marking him as someone who didn't know it was impolite to request a handshake from a lady. Not that she was offended. Not at all. She merely found it useful to be observant.

Another miner, introduced as Cokey John, completed the gathering. Cokey sat with his arms hanging listlessly at his sides as if they were too heavy to stow away properly. From his nearly absent response to Matthew's greeting, Calista got the impression he wasn't pleased to be there. Matthew seemed unaware of his skepticism.

Matthew moved the chairs around so they were in a circle, nearly knee-to-knee. Calista sat next to Loretta, but that put her directly opposite of Matthew. Every time she looked up, their eyes met, which was unsettling. She guessed it was unsettling to him too, because he stuttered as he asked to borrow the Campbells' Bible. Matthew turned to Galatians, chapter six, and they passed the book around, each reading a verse or two—all except for Irvin, who demurred, saying his eyesight wasn't good enough.

Calista looked about the circle and felt the sharp jab of wistfulness. These friends hadn't been together for long, but with the exception of Cokey, they'd already begun to face the future together. She could see it in the way Irvin deferred to Loretta, the way Dan punched Silas on the arm like a brother, and the way they all fussed over Matthew. This community was something she would never have as a Pink. Instead, she'd have a new identity for every case, and a different personality for each location. And if she did manage to make friends while working, those ties would wither when she up and left town one day without any explanation or good-bye. Even Matthew would disappear from her life and couldn't know why.

"Verse nine," Loretta said as she passed the Bible onto Calista's lap.

Calista moistened her lips, then read, "'And let us not be weary in well doing: for in due season we shall reap, if we faint not.'" Her eyes blurred. She *was* weary. While she believed that she was doing good, she wondered at the sacrifice. Was it worth it? And if she didn't have success, if she couldn't find Lila, would she have the strength to move on to another case?

Loretta patted her on the back. Calista cleared her throat and continued, "'As we have therefore opportunity, let us do good unto all men, especially unto them who are of the household of faith.'"

A household of faith—that was a good description for this fledgling group. Something she wanted to belong to again. She blinked away tears before looking up. Why did Matthew have to look so kind and understanding? He didn't understand anything. And she had to make sure she kept it that way.

Something in the passage had softened Calista's heart. It never ceased to amaze Matthew how Scripture could mean so many different things to different people. Take this chapter, for example. While it was meant as encouragement to the saints, somehow it had struck a chord with Calista. Or maybe he was presuming too much. Whatever was happening, he knew it was for the best.

The sun warmed his neck as he bent forward in his seat. He talked about the struggles of persevering, the monotony of making good decisions day after day, the resistance one met when taking that first step. Dan Campbell reached over and took his wife's hand, while Loretta patted Calista's back with her other hand. Silas fanned himself with his hat, and though he was listening, he couldn't keep his eyes from straying to Calista. With elbows resting on his knees, Irvin rubbed his hands together, only interrupted by the sudden jerks he made as he fought to stay comfortable on the stool he'd produced from his tent. Cokey dozed fitfully.

"It's easy to get overwhelmed in a society like ours," Matthew said. "Wealth beckons from every quarter, yet remains just out of reach for most of us. It's easy to get distracted, to allow our material concerns to shadow what's really important."

Cokey snorted. "What do you know about it, Reverend?"

So he hadn't been asleep the whole time? Matthew brushed

away the pride he felt at the title and addressed the question. "What do I know about money? I know that we should seek first the kingdom of God—"

"It's easy for you to say, but you aren't breaking your back in the mines every day. I don't know where you get your funds, but if you had to dig in the bowels of the earth for every penny, you'd have a better understanding of what we're up against."

Matthew glanced around the group. Silas hid a smile, while Dan kept his head down, cleaning his fingernails. Irvin's face was tilted up toward the sky as if he were weighing the fairness of Cokey's claim. Matthew closed the Bible. He didn't need to read it in print to know that Cokey was right.

"That's a fine suggestion," he said. "And I've already acted on it. I start at the Fox-Berry on Monday."

"The Fox-Berry?" Calista grimaced. "Did you meet Oscar Kentworth?"

One glance at her was all he needed to know this was another member of her invasive family. "Yes, I did. A very *respectable* man, he was."

Calista dropped her gaze and refolded her gloves on her lap.

"When I first came to town, I worked at the Quaker," Dan said. "I hadn't been there six months when the powder monkeys let a charge go off before we were clear. The blast messed me up. I was luckier than some, but it broke my leg. Couldn't work at the mine with a broken leg, and they wouldn't hire me back once I'd been injured. No one wanted to hire me."

The memory was too much for Loretta. She crumpled, her hands over her face. Calista patted Loretta's knee and looked up, meeting Matthew's gaze. In that raw moment, a solidarity was communicated.

"We had no income, and just a little money set by." Dan cast a worried glance at his wife but plowed ahead. "Once I was healed, we used that money to lease our claim, and since then we've met nothing but misery. It hasn't paid out enough to make ends meet. We've been in a bad way. Pray for us, if you're of a mind to."

"All the time," Matthew said, moved by Dan's simple report and Loretta's sorrow. Even Cokey nodded, no longer pouting over his own grief.

After they'd prayed and ended the service, Calista continued to comfort Loretta, while the men talked over each other, trying to supply Matthew with new terms and techniques he'd need as a miner. Matthew knew Calista was dishonest, but this moment was authentic. Perhaps he'd misjudged her. Was Calista York someone who had been led astray? Whatever the case, he wanted to believe her destined for redemption. He wanted her on his side.

The sun was going down, and these men didn't get enough rest as it was. Tomorrow was Thursday, and they'd be back at work, so he decided to end the meeting. After they sang a closing song—Calista knew all the words, he noticed—everyone said their good-byes.

"What are you doing in Joplin?" Silas asked Calista.

Although Matthew was very interested in her answer, Irvin caught him by the arm.

"Matthew, I need to ask you for the last of my money." He wiped the back of his hand over his forehead and disturbed a scraggly eyebrow. "I'm running low on vittles, but Saturday is just around the corner."

"Sure, here it is." Matthew yanked the money pouch out of his vest pocket and nearly tossed it at Irvin, then turned his head to catch Calista's reply.

But Irvin wasn't done. "This week was more tolerable than the last," he said. "Thank you for having good common sense when I had none."

"My pleasure," Matthew replied.

"Are all the girls in Kansas City as pretty as you?" Silas was asking.

Matthew liked Silas. He was good-humored and quick-witted. Actually, Matthew didn't like Silas, come to think of it.

"It was a help," Irvin said, "and I learned my lesson. This Saturday, I'll keep my money tight to my chest. We won't be quickly parted, so I won't need your help."

". . . my grandmother, aunts, uncles, and cousins, so I'm not completely alone." Did she sound too friendly? Was she humoring Silas, or did she find him that amusing?

Matthew forced his attention back to Irvin. "You say you've eaten better this week than any week in the past, and then you say that you want to go back to doing it the way you were? Where's the logic in that?"

"I know better than to gamble or drink it all away now. I'll spend a few dollars to wet my whistle, and I won't wager a buck unless I'm feeling particularly lucky, but if that's the case, then I'll come home with more money than you can imagine."

Let us not grow weary, let us not grow weary.

"Saturday is payday." Silas was looking at Calista with that aw-shucks grin he'd no doubt perfected at barn dances. "If you aren't doing anything, I'd be honored—"

"Saturday night we're going to have a party," Matthew blurted.

Irvin's eyes narrowed. Silas stepped back with a nervous chuckle, but Calista merely tilted her head.

"That's right," Matthew continued. "I'd forgotten to tell you. Why shouldn't we get together and celebrate weekly wages? There's nothing wrong with that. Come to my house behind Trochet's Flowers. Irvin knows where it is." He felt ashamed by how long he paused before adding, "Even you, Silas. What do you say?"

Irvin's mouth went slack, showing a few gaps where teeth should've been. "I don't know . . ."

"I'll be there," Silas said. "I, for one, will be happy to avoid the debauchery on the streets."

Matthew looked at Calista. He held his breath, waiting for her answer.

"I suppose I'll be there," she said. "After all, it's just next door, but I really thought you'd meant for us to be there alone." She winked at him as she started off on the road toward town.

Matthew gawked and then had to hide a smug smile when he realized that, once again, she'd used him as a decoy to get her out of a conversation with an overzealous man. He was pleased to be of assistance—whatever he could do to protect her—but he couldn't help but wish that her flirting wasn't part of some act.

CHAPTER

8

Calista closed her book and rose off the sofa in the sitting room of her apartment at the Keystone. The stark contrast of the white woodwork against the blue walls gave the room a crisp air. The pattern on the sofa's upholstery was as clear and sharp as Delft Blue pottery, but she was drawn to the window. The sun rising behind her hotel lit the windows of the buildings across the street and turned them into a burnished liquid gold—a color that hadn't been reproduced by the most talented jeweler or painter.

Ladies of the night weren't out and about this time of the morning, but from this height, Calista could watch the streetcars disappearing behind buildings and then reappearing in the gaps as they skimmed down their tracks. The wagons, horses, and automobiles moved more deliberately, stopping in clumps, then going forward as they picked their way ahead. In the distance, over the tops of the roof gardens and water tanks, the sharp points of the mines' conveyor belts jutted up into the sky. She couldn't see it from there, but she guessed they were already running, processing the ore that the miners had dug up that morning.

It was a busy, bustling town, full of buoyant optimism. The

poor could become rich. The rich could get even richer. From the sixth floor of a fine hotel, there was much to admire.

But more than the expanding town, the progress of modern conveniences, the jovial spirit that accompanied every Saturday payday—she admired what she saw in the tiny garden behind the flower store.

He'd been there since she'd woken up, sitting in a wrought-iron chair at the small round table with his Bible open. The table was too small to hold his notebook too, so he kept it on his lap until he found something that brooked noting, then balanced it on the edge of the table. It was adorable how he crammed his broad shoulders over the table as he bent over the notebook. How he tugged at his left eyebrow while trying to think of what to write. How every few minutes he bowed his head and clasped his hands together. She couldn't see his face, but she'd bet he was praying. Possibly even praying for her.

Since she'd gone with Matthew to the ore fields, he'd become more comfortable around her. It was clear she was earning his trust, but she hadn't decided if this was beneficial. Her plan of integrating into the seedier side of the business world hadn't panned out as she'd hoped. Perhaps membership in such a scandalous world was more difficult to obtain than she'd bargained for. Or perhaps there was nothing hidden, and Lila Seaton was nowhere near Joplin. While that might be the case, Calista couldn't assume anything. Finding Lila was too important to leave up to chance. If she wasn't getting results, then she'd have to attack from a new angle. And that was where Matthew came into play.

She picked up her shoe from the floor, pulled it on, and then propped her foot on the windowsill. Tugging at the shoelaces, she kept an eye on Matthew as he left off studying and began to patrol the flower garden. Calista had no remorse for posing as an out-of-work decorator, or nurse, or florist. Her cause was

just, and if the good, decent people knew why she was misleading them, they wouldn't have minded. And she had no care for
what those who *did* oppose her quest thought. But what about
her plans today? She didn't have to pretend to be a Christian. She
was one. She didn't have to pretend to care about the fate of the
young mothers and children at the Children's Home. Yet this felt
different. Not disclosing her story felt dishonest when it came to
Matthew. Volunteering for charity work when she had ulterior
motives felt hypocritical.

She'd laced both shoes. He'd gone to pinching off dead blooms,
methodically working over one stand of lilies at a time. He bent
and twisted off a dead rose bud next to the gate of the garden, then
headed inside his cabin, only pausing to gather his study materials.
Her view was superior, but she envied him his greenery and the
quiet, rooted peacefulness of the garden. Perhaps she'd get to see
it that night when they had their party.

Until then, she was headed to the Children's Home. After much
haranguing, Matthew had written a letter of recommendation for
her, and the home had requested her help for the morning. Their
workers were clearing out an old vegetable garden that had fallen
into disuse, and they needed extra hands to tend to the kids while
they cleared out last year's patch. She was glad for the chance. If
all went as planned, she could get another opportunity to befriend
Mrs. Bowman and perhaps be allowed to visit the mothers on
behalf of the Children's Home. It was worth the attempt.

By the time Calista stood at the front desk at the Children's
Home, it was nearing ten o'clock, but her spirits rose when Mrs.
Bowman herself came to show Calista the playroom.

"I'm surprised you were approved," said Mrs. Bowman with the
direct innocence of a child. "I didn't know what to think when you
asked all those questions about the girls at the House of Lords,
but we're excited for your help today. Just think what all we could
plant next year if we get that garden producing."

"I'm available to help in other ways too." Calista eyed the dark-haired beauty behind the thick spectacles. "For instance, running errands or making visits."

Mrs. Bowman beamed at the suggestion. "I'll talk to Mrs. Fairfield. It would be wonderful if you could purchase the bulk dry goods for the larder. That would allow me more time for my visits."

Before Calista could make another helpful suggestion, Mrs. Bowman opened a half door, and a score of serious toddler eyes turned their way. A bald-headed fellow lowered a tin rattle, stringing a web of slobber from it to his mouth. A thin little girl dropped her wooden doll and crawled toward Calista's feet. Another baby—boy or girl Calista couldn't guess in its white gown—took advantage of the distraction to steal a ball from a neighbor.

Mrs. Bowman knelt and, using the hem of her apron, wiped slobber off the face of one of the kids. "Miss Provone, you're free to go, if you'd like."

Miss Provone disentangled a baby's fingers from her curly blond hair and set the baby on the ground. "Thank you, miss," she said to Calista. "I love these wee ones, but after a full week, working in the garden will be a welcome change of pace."

Calista felt like a giant looking down on all the babies. "What am I supposed to do?"

"Keep them from hurting each other or eating something that will kill them," Mrs. Bowman said. "Someone will be at the desk right outside the door if you need anything. Oh, and if it stinks, change it."

How could Calista do any investigating while responsible for a dozen babies? She stalled. "How long have you worked here, Mrs. Bowman?" Mrs. Bowman didn't look much older than Calista, but she was infinitely more at ease with the children.

"Nearly a year. My husband and I thought it would be a good

place for me to practice my mothering skills before we had a little one of our own."

Habit sent Calista's gaze to the other woman's waistline, but there was no evidence of a happy event on the horizon.

"How about you?" Mrs. Bowman asked. "Why are you volunteering here? Let me guess—you were the oldest in a big family, and now that you're away from home, you miss caring for children. You feel lost without a baby on your hip."

It took all of Calista's self-control not to snort. She hadn't raised her siblings. While her mother was loving and involved, a team of nurses and governesses had played a part in her raising as well. "I really don't know how to diaper a child. I have no experience at all. I'm here because when I heard Matthew talking about it . . ."

"Matthew? Are you talking about that handsome preacher who comes to teach the kids?" Mrs. Bowman's fine eyebrow lifted. "He's reason enough to get involved, isn't he?"

The woman who popped her head into the doorway wasn't wearing a uniform. She wore a man's shirt untucked over a skirt made of coarse cloth. With a hoe held over her shoulder, she said, "She's sweet on Matthew?" She clicked her tongue. "I'd hoped my Lilith would catch his eye, but I'm not surprised he'd find you more interesting. You've got that slim waist that men like. Lilith has lumps where girls shouldn't have lumps, and she's prone to lisping. On the other hand, she is better endowed than you. If you want that shirt to fit properly, you should buy something padded—"

"Frannie!" Mrs. Bowman giggled. "You'd better get to the garden."

Frannie waved her hoe and, with a salute, headed outdoors.

Mrs. Bowman rolled her eyes. "Sorry about her. She's well-meaning but tends to speak too plainly."

"I'd rather have blunt honesty than padded falsehood." Then, remembering the last use of the word *padded*, Calista adjusted her shirt.

"Her point was that we all admire Matthew and think he's a fine catch. If there's any way we can help—"

"No." Calista held up a hand, then realized her protests had no basis. "I . . . he doesn't know. I would be embarrassed. He's such an upright man, and I'm so . . . modest. Please, I don't want to seem forward."

"I can't promise for everyone," Mrs. Bowman said with a smile and opened the door to step out.

"Before you leave . . ." Calista shifted her weight and knocked over a toddler. The baby toppled onto another crawling toward her. Both broke into cries. Raising her voice, Calista decided to pry one more time. "Do you see many of the mothers? After they leave their kids here, do they ever visit?"

"That's the second time you've asked about the mothers." Mrs. Bowman's brows pinched together over the bridge of her spectacles.

Calista swallowed. "All these children must have mothers."

Mrs. Bowman was talking, but Calista couldn't hear her over the din. She leaned forward and cupped her hand behind her ear. Honestly, didn't these babies know that she was trying to have a conversation? Mrs. Bowman's mouth tightened. Whatever she had to say, it looked like she was regretting that she'd welcomed Calista after all.

Mrs. Bowman opened the half door and scooped up the crawler, then held the baby out to Calista. Calista took it beneath the arms and held it suspended. It was heavier than it looked. She watched as Mrs. Bowman settled a toddler on her hip, then mimicked her, jutting out her side to give herself enough hip for the baby to rest on. But with the crying that close to her ear, all hopes for a conversation were vanishing.

Mrs. Bowman handed her the second screaming child, and then, with a tiny wave of her fingers, left Calista to the nearly toothless wolves.

By the time the regular workers returned, Calista understood why they would welcome a day of hard labor in the garden. She had never felt more rumpled or dowdy. Her hair was a mess, her sleeve was soggy from being gummed while she was on the floor playing, and her back needed stretching. What was worse, it was already getting dark, and she was going to be late for Matthew's Saturday night party.

And she'd accomplished nothing on the case. Whenever the young but suspicious Mrs. Bowman was out of sight, Calista passed around the picture of Lila and asked the nursery workers if they remembered this girl visiting in the last few months. Of course, she would have looked different, not dressed for a formal occasion, but no one had, although several of them commented on how young and tragic she looked. If they only knew.

The ride back to town took twice as long. At every stop, passengers shoved through the rows of seats to exit the streetcar, fighting against the passengers trying to get on. Evidently, there was no prescribed limit to how many passengers a car could legally carry. If they paid the fare, they were allowed to stand anywhere, even balance on the edge, as they rode along. If Calista hadn't already been run roughshod by the babies, she probably would have taken offense to the jostling she got from the passengers. Everyone from the mines, the refineries, and the claims that surrounded Joplin and its neighboring communities had come to town to settle up and get their weekly pay. Knowing that money would be in good supply, farmers, traders, and tinkers had brought their wares as well. It was like market day, crossed with a carnival, crossed with Christmas—if your Christmas involved flowing alcohol, brawls, and gambling.

The streetcar reached her corner. Calista had to fight her way through the crowded aisle to get off before it started up again.

Once off, she looked wistfully up at the side of the hotel. In the coming darkness, she couldn't make out her room, but as much as she'd like to change her clothes, she didn't want to keep Matthew's friends waiting. Besides, it might do him some good to see her mussed and realize how hard she'd worked.

She took the steps to the flower shop, not surprised to see it lit up and busy. A man held the door open for his lady, then waited politely for Calista to enter before following the woman with a bouquet. Calista waved to Mr. Trochet as he rang up another purchase, then made her way to the back of the store.

The door outside was open, and a streetlamp shed its light over the fence. The garden was more beautiful up close than it was from six floors above. The greenhouse was dark, with the outline of plants pressed against the glass walls, and the little cabin was nestled against the fence with a gravel walkway winding its way to the yellow painted steps.

Calista had never been to Matthew's cabin before. She was surprised at her feeling of uncertainty. What did she have to be nervous about? She'd been presented to more important society before. Her heels clomped against the hollow wooden stairs as voices from inside reached her.

"Thank you, Matt. We'd like to stay longer, but Loretta wants to get home before the streets become too unruly."

"What am I going to do with all these sandwiches?" That was Matthew. She could hear the smile in his voice as he encouraged them to take some home.

"You have an icebox," Loretta answered. "You can—" She spotted Calista in the doorway. "Calista! Good. I hope you're hungry. Matthew has all this food, and we were just leaving."

"Calista." Matthew stood proud and welcoming, making it impossible for her attention to rest anywhere but on him. "You're here." Then his bottom lip bounced. "The Campbells are already leaving. I don't think Silas is going to show up."

Dan had settled Loretta's shawl on her shoulders, but he paused. Calista shifted her bag to her other hand. If they were going, it wouldn't be right for her to stay. Not by herself. Loretta turned her head to catch her husband's eye.

"We're not in that big of a hurry," Dan said and took Loretta's shawl.

Did Matthew feel as relieved as she did? He beamed as he strode toward her. "Welcome. It's not much beyond a cozy little hole-in-the-wall, but it's comfortable."

"It's perfect," she said, although she hadn't yet taken her eyes off him.

"The floral wallpaper is an affront, and the prissy sofa won't wear well with me falling onto it of an evening, but the apartment came furnished, and what should one expect when living behind a flower shop?"

Calista forced herself to take stock of the room. As he'd said, the furniture would have looked more at home in a formal parlor, which was where it probably had been a decade ago. Yet, besides the fussy decor, the room contained everything a bachelor would need, from the economy gas stove and icebox to the metal-framed bed.

"It's nicer than being hustled along the sidewalks tonight," she said.

"Is that what happened to you?" he asked as he grabbed a plate and loaded it with more sandwiches than she'd eat in a month.

"Matthew!" Loretta blinked in shock. "Don't you know not to make a negative comment about a lady's appearance?"

"He didn't say anything about her appearance," Dan replied.

"Yes, he did. Her hair's awry, her clothes are rumpled," Loretta said. "That's what he meant."

Matthew passed the plate of sandwiches to Calista. "But I didn't say anything negative."

Calista adjusted the heavy knot of hair that was sliding off its designated spot and toward her ear. "If I look unkempt, it's Matthew's fault. He's the one who got me a volunteer position at the Children's Home."

Loretta sat suddenly, Dan barely having time to arrange a chair beneath her. "What age of children did you mind?"

"The babies." Calista passed the plate to her. "I didn't see any newborns, mind you, but those that are crawling and bigger."

Loretta took a sandwich off Calista's plate and ripped off a bite. "Did any of them stand out to you?"

"What do you mean?"

"Make an impression. Catch at your heart. Endear themselves?"

Calista shrugged. "I was so busy keeping sundries out of their mouths and keeping their diapers dry that I didn't have time to favor any in particular. I'm sure they are all precious, but I wouldn't be a good judge."

Matthew was leaning against the table with his arms crossed, watching Loretta thoughtfully. There didn't seem to be anything amiss to Calista. Loretta looked like she was satisfying a healthy appetite, especially since she'd claimed to be full earlier. If anyone looked ill at ease, it was her husband, Dan.

Calista took a bite of her sandwich. The vinegary jolt surprised her. "Pickles and salami?" she choked out. "Savory."

"I don't do a lot of cooking," Matthew said, "so I've been experimenting with the different meats at the deli. Especially those that have been discounted." He poured her a glass of tea. She guessed before its coolness splashed down her throat that it would be sweetened.

"Since moving in at the hotel, I haven't cooked much either," Calista said. "My rooms are spacious enough for entertaining, but they prohibit cooking. That means I spend more time in restaurants than I'd like."

"That's so pricey," Loretta said. "The expense must be a strain on you."

Calista waved away her suggestion with a story already in place. "You have to spend money to make money. If I'm going to get a career that fits me, I have to spend time in those circles. It's just the way things are."

"And what kind of job is that?" Mr. Campbell asked.

Calista sat in a small wooden chair, testing its base before she launched into the meat of her story. "My talents lie in the arts—decorating, flower arranging, fabric selection." Had she covered everything that Matthew had heard about? "I've also done some nursing," she added. There. That should suffice.

"The Keystone is very fine. Do you expect you'll make enough decorating to afford your lodging?" Mr. Campbell asked.

Matthew's foot stopped tapping, and he leaned forward for her answer. Calista could already tell he wasn't going to believe it, no matter what she said.

"Matt-hew . . ." Irvin's voice wavered from the entrance. "I told ya I'd come, Matt-hew, and here I am." He stepped into the room, holding a bottle by the neck. He shuffled sideways until he found a wall to lean against, then put his hands on his knees and bent forward.

Saved from answering, Calista took another bite of her sandwich as Loretta got up and propelled Irvin by the shoulders to her seat.

"Sit down before you fall down," Loretta said while her husband took away the bottle.

"I think you've worked this one over." Dan passed the bottle to Matthew, who tilted it to see that it was empty before dropping it into the trash bin.

"Welcome to the party." Forgoing a plate, Matthew picked up a sandwich and dropped it into Irvin's lap. "Are you hungry?"

"I'm not hungry. They fed me well over at Black Jack's. I didn't even have to leave the poker table. Food and drink appeared magically at my side."

"At least he decided to leave and come here," Loretta said. "He wasn't out all night."

"Is that true?" Matthew asked. "Did you decide to leave?"

Irvin rubbed his forehead hard, pushing the skin from one side to the other. "If I'd won that one hand, I would've left a rich man. As it were, I was out of chips, and they were out of patience."

"It'll be a hungry week," Matthew said.

Irvin stuck the sandwich inside his shirt. "I'll save this for later."

Loretta covered her mouth to hide her smile. Calista looked at Matthew to gauge his response. To her surprise, he winked, then poured Irvin a cup of coffee off the stove.

"Now that you have another guest, we don't feel so bad leaving," Dan said. "Loretta was looking to get home."

"Go on," Matthew told him. "I'll deal with Irvin. If Calista wants to stay . . ."

She'd seen drunks before. When she was befriending that Louisiana embezzler in her first case, he'd taken to drinking his guilt away. Unfortunately for him, the more he drowned his conscience, the more the facts of the case floated up. She knew Irvin meant her no disrespect, and if he did, Matthew looked fully capable of intervening.

"I just got here," she said. "You all go ahead. Don't worry about us."

Looking confused, Irvin lurched out of his chair and followed Dan out the cabin door. Matthew chased after him.

"No you don't." He turned Irvin on his heel and led him back to the cabin. "You're our chaperone. If I have to feed you all week, you can at least do that."

Irvin straightened and tugged his vest down smooth. Or as smooth as it could go with a sandwich beneath it. "I'm honored you trust me with such an exalted position."

Walking behind Calista's chair, Matthew trailed his hand over her shoulders as he passed, sending shivers down her spine. "This might be a total disaster," he whispered. "My apologies in advance."

"I'm up for the adventure," she said. And she was. This was infinitely more interesting than watching a room full of infants.

Reading her thoughts, Matthew asked, "How was your day at the Children's Home?"

"I survived. Barely." Running her hand over her hair, she felt how truly disorganized it had become. "Sticky fingers don't make good pomade."

"No one watches a nursery to improve their looks," he said, "but you did a good thing for them. When I think of what lies ahead for one of those boys . . ." He cut his eyes to Irvin, who was dozing off in his chair. "Upsy-daisy. Let's get you somewhere else before you fall out of that chair."

Matthew wrapped an arm around the miner's shoulders and lifted him to his feet. He tried to steer him to the sofa, but Irvin demanded to lie in the bed.

"It'll mean sacrificing my clean sheets and half of tomorrow to beat creepy-crawlies out of my mattress," Matthew said.

He was such a good man. Calista would have burned the mattress before letting Irvin sleep on it, and that wasn't because of the callous disguise she was adopting.

"What's happening to the kids at the Children's Home?" She took a bite of her sandwich, trying not to appear too curious. And also trying not to look disgusted by the taste.

The sorrow on his face sobered her. "To raise money for the home, the Elks are selling tickets." He rubbed his hands together. "They are having a raffle, and the winner gets a baby."

Calista didn't mean to laugh so suddenly. She also didn't mean to inhale a bite of her sandwich. A pickle plastered itself on the back of her throat, and she tried to cough it out.

Matthew was at her side in a moment and pounding her back with more force than necessary. Honestly, what was he trying to prove? That he was stronger than Paul Bunyan?

She couldn't stop laughing. "Give me a moment, will you?"

"As long as you're not going to die in my cabin."

"Not from this," she said. Throwing her shoulders back, she took a deep breath and salvaged some composure before facing him. "Do you mean to tell me that they hope to earn money by a raffle, and the prize for their raffle is going to be one of those babies?" She didn't give him time to answer before blurting out, "Who in the world would want that? That's the worst prize in the history of contests. They won't raise a cent."

CHAPTER 9

In Matthew's opinion, if anyone was going to be outraged by the thought of using a baby as a prize, it should be a woman. The fairer sex possessed the gentler spirits and domestic tendencies that improved the baser impulses of men and helped refine society. Compassionate women needed to show these community leaders the error of their ways. Loretta had nearly collapsed when he'd told her about the plan. He'd only waited this long to present the idea to Calista because he feared another strong reaction and didn't want to be responsible for causing her distress.

He shouldn't have worried.

She picked at a stain on her shoulder. "Winning a baby? Prizes are supposed to be something beneficial, not something that will take all your time, ruin your clothes, and tie you down forever." How could she look so wholesome and joyful when spouting such heartless thoughts? "I have an idea. If you really want to make some money, have a contest where the only way you can guarantee *not* to be left with the baby is if you donate. Put all the wealthy women on notice that if they don't raise funds, you'll deliver a child to their house for them to raise. That will help collections."

"Are you serious? You don't care about the children?"

"Would I have spent my day the way I did if I didn't care? Of course I care. It's just a prize I wouldn't want to win. Now, if you're going to raffle off some kid gloves, or a beaded handbag, then I might buy a ticket." She twisted her mouth to the side. "If I wasn't opposed to gambling, that is."

She was so obviously trying to appease him that Matthew felt guilty for his outrage. He fought to loosen the muscles in his neck. She was being honest. She was telling him what she thought. If he responded poorly, she would learn to hide her opinion, perhaps even to say what she thought he wanted to hear. Nothing would be more pointless.

"That's understandable," he managed, "but my concerns aren't whether you're going to buy tickets. My concerns are over the indignity to the child. People aren't property. You shouldn't be able to win one in a raffle."

"I understand, but when you look at it, this solves several problems simultaneously. The home has children it must provide for. They lack funds. Growing up in an orphanage isn't ideal, so it'd be better if children could be placed in families. If there are families wanting children, and willing to give some money for a chance at a child . . ."

"Morals aren't just a matter of what's financially beneficial."

"And just because something is financially beneficial doesn't mean it's immoral."

The feeling of conflict was disagreeable to Matthew. Having spent his life surrounded by the family and friends who raised him, he wasn't used to such stark differences of opinions on moral issues. People either agreed, or they were determined to be difficult. His instinct was to say Calista didn't care, but what if she did? Could she disagree with him and still be right?

"I'm trying to dissuade them from this event. Whatever the end result is, I think this road leads to darker, more sinister places."

Calista set her plate on the table, leaving only the crust of her sandwich. "I won't get in your way, Matthew. You have to listen to your conscience. But I wouldn't cry any tears if the Elks go ahead with the fundraiser. The child will probably be better off, and it might encourage some people to adopt when they hadn't thought of it before." She scanned the table as if he'd hidden dessert somewhere and she couldn't locate it. "You said this was a party?"

Of all the invitees to stay, it had to be the one who didn't consider a plate of sandwiches adequate fare for entertaining. "I was thinking of sustenance for Irvin more than sweets."

"Games?"

"There are only two of us."

"I can think of games for two." Surely she hadn't meant anything improper, but she blushed all the same.

He cleared his throat. "I made some pantomime cards." He picked up the bowl containing the folded activities he'd written. He should be disappointed that he only had one coherent visitor, but he regretted nothing.

"Then let's play that," she said.

"But I know all the answers already."

"Then I'll make mine up. I can do that, can't I?"

He motioned her to the sofa. "Since there are only two of us, besides Sleeping Beauty over there, we might as well be comfortable."

She pushed her chair out of the way and joined him on the couch. He fished his hand through the slips of paper, not even caring which he drew—until he opened it. He could have pulled lassoing a calf, or splitting logs, or any number of other pantomimes that would put his manliness at its best advantage. Why had he even included this one?

Sticking the slip of paper into his breast pocket, he stood before her, rubbing his hands together.

"I can't tell if you're getting ready for your turn, or if this is part of the act," she laughed.

"In real life, this is preparation for the activity." He cupped

121

his hands around his mouth and blew, hamming it up if it meant keeping her attention.

Her eyebrows lifted. "Well?"

"I'm getting there." He rubbed his hands on his thighs, then squatted down. It would be easier if he had a stool. As it were, he'd have to keep his balance and not fall over. Holding his hands in front of him, he pantomimed pulling downward with alternating strokes. She might be a city girl, but everyone knew what milking a cow looked like, didn't they?

Evidently not.

"Hmm . . . shoeing a horse?" she asked.

His face scrunched up. Did she seriously think this was how you shoed a horse?

Keeping silent, he exaggerated his motions. One arm, then the other. He looked up to see if she was close to an answer, but her face was as blank as a new blackboard.

"Knitting?" she said.

Maybe her pretty face masked a dunce's intellect? Going even bigger, Matthew exaggerated his movements, being careful to get the roll of his hands right. Poor cow. If this were a real milking, she'd be sore tomorrow. He looked up, and it must have been too quickly, because he caught Calista trying to hide a smile. She was laughing at him.

"You know, don't you?" He straightened with fists against his waist. "Why didn't you say? I lost feeling in my feet."

"Your technique wasn't quite right. When I stayed at my granny's ranch, if I milked a cow like that, I'd get kicked in the head."

"Your granny sounds like a fearsome lady."

Calista laughed. "She wouldn't be the one kicking me in the head, but that doesn't change her fearsomeness."

"You've had your laugh. Let's see how you do."

"I can't do one of the cards you made." She stood and tapped her chin as she paced the room, thinking.

Matthew settled onto the sofa. "C'mon. This isn't supposed to be too difficult."

She tilted her head toward the ceiling, then gave a quick nod. "Okay. It's juvenile, but you deserve something easy."

Calista stood in the empty space between the table and sofa. Despite her rumpled clothing, she still looked too fine to be in his lodgings. When he'd decided to leave Pine Gap to come to Joplin, all he could think of was the sacrifices he was willing to make. Suddenly, the sacrifices didn't seem so great.

With a flourish, Calista extended one arm in front of her and made a loose fist, as if she were holding something upright. She widened her eyes and rubbed her stomach as she moved her empty hand just beneath her chin. Then, to Matthew's infinite amusement, she began licking the air.

With long motions of ducking her head, then drawing it up with her tongue out, she mimicked licking a lollipop. Was it a lollipop? No, she was leaving room for something bigger in her hand. An ice cream cone—that was what she was pretending to lick. The faces she was making—eyes wide, getting her neck into it. He couldn't decide if she looked enticing or ridiculous, but he did decide that he wasn't going to let her stop.

"Going to the doctor?" he managed to choke out.

She shook her head. "Mmm . . ." she moaned as she twisted her head to get that imaginary ice cream cone from every angle.

"Bobbing for apples?"

"I'm using my tongue, not my teeth," she whispered, then went back to her task.

"My mistake," he said. This really would be remembered as one of the most interesting moments of his life. "Give me one more try. I think I'm about to get it."

Her moans of satisfaction should have been considered cheating, but Matthew wasn't about to stop her. From the corner of his eye, he saw movement. It was Irvin turning over on the bed.

"I know what she's doing." Irvin sat up and fluffed the pillow beneath his head. "She's necking with her fella."

Calista's mouth hinged wide open. She looked at Irvin; she looked at Matthew. Deep down, Matthew knew he should be mature. He knew that chivalry required him to cover for Irvin's horrifying observation. But when the chips were down, he was still a twenty-three-year-old farm boy with a fine appreciation for the ribald.

He burst out laughing. His chest tightened and convulsed with his guffaws. He could feel his eyes watering, but he couldn't stop. When he thought back to her enthusiastic licking and moans of pleasure, the comparison was too funny.

Not surprisingly, Calista didn't share his opinion.

"That's not what I was doing," she said. "I was eating an ice cream cone."

"I know . . . I know . . ." he gasped.

"You knew? Then why didn't you say . . . ?" Her eyes narrowed. "This is payback for the milking, isn't it?"

"You were enjoying that ice cream so much, I hated to interrupt you." With a wipe of his eyes, he walked over to her and touched her lightly on the jaw. "Go ahead and smile. This is supposed to be a party, remember?"

She looked up at him with those brown eyes. The air around them seemed to crackle.

"It's getting late," she said. "I should go back to the hotel." But she didn't move.

"I'll walk you, but one thing first." He didn't move either.

"What?"

"Tell me that you'd rather be here with me than in a saloon, being harassed by the customers."

She bit her lip as she gauged his sincerity. Then, in a move that made his heart jump, she took his arm. "If I had no other goal but my own entertainment, I'd stay here with you indefinitely."

He escorted her out, knowing that he would spend all night on the inadequate sofa, pondering what she meant by that indecipherable statement.

Matthew walked her to her hotel. Even though it was only across the alley, the streets were boisterous enough that he claimed to be concerned. If only he'd seen the other places she'd been, hiding alone, haunting vacant depots at night, pretending to be someone she wasn't and protected solely by falsehoods.

But tonight her true identity was adequate. A rambunctious, well-off lady from Kansas City. That was what she was, and that was all he could know for the time. There was a difference in the way he escorted her. Usually men were formal, keeping their arm away from their body as they escorted a lady. Matthew kept her arm tucked against his side. When they were caught swimming upstream against a rush of people, he wrapped an arm around her shoulders and kept her protected against him. It was a cozy arrangement. She wished it didn't have to end, but the way he ran his hand down the length of her arm and brushed against her waist before taking an official escort position again made it all worth it. She glanced up as they passed beneath a light pole. The corner of his mouth was tucked tight with the hint of a satisfied grin. She ducked her head before he caught her looking.

The enormous double doors of the hotel were propped open. As they entered the lobby, Matthew greeted a shoeless boy selling boutonnieres at the entrance. Calista watched as he inquired about the boy's business for the night, then dug deep into his pocket to find some coins. The boy winced until he saw that Matthew intended to buy a boutonniere. With his pride preserved, the boy sold him a rose on a straight pin with a smile.

They stepped across the threshold and into the marble monstrosity that was the Keystone lobby.

"You live in a flower store," she said above the din of the crowded room. "What do you need a boutonniere for?"

"To give to you," he said. "I talk to Georgie every week while he's digging through the garbage can in the back of the shop. The flowers are a tad wilted, but by eleven o'clock on a Saturday night, who's going to notice?"

She raised an eyebrow. "That flower was in the garbage?"

"It smells just as . . ." He held it up to his nose. "Never mind. You should probably drop this in the trash."

She'd keep it anyway.

They came to the ornate doors of the elevator. A half dozen men stood waiting for it to reach the ground floor. Matthew looked back toward the street, then again at the crowd of men.

"Thanks for inviting me," Calista said. "It was nice." It was more than nice, but she wasn't one to be effusive with sentiment.

"It was more than nice," he said. He continued to eye the men waiting at the elevator. They'd taken notice of her. As was her custom, she'd picked out the one who looked the least threatening to stand beside, although that was the problem with elevators. One couldn't choose who would be left in the elevator after a few stops.

Matthew was having the same thoughts. "I'll see you to your room," he said.

What would her father think? Or her brother, if he knew?

She kept her eyes downcast in the elevator. Her hotel suite was spacious. Several families lived in similar suites while their new homes were being built. This wasn't any more personal than visiting someone's home, but having Matthew with her felt intimate. With each ding of the bell, with each person exiting the elevator, she felt a delicious tension rising. He was being gallant, seeing her to her door, and she was happy for more time together.

As the last man left, he asked, "How many more floors do we have to go?"

"To the top."

The doors closed. He didn't know what to do with his hands. Clearing his throat, he waited while the attendant pushed the button to the sixth floor again. She felt flustered as well, and with every stolen moment, a warning in her heart was growing harder to ignore. She wondered what her father would think about Matthew. The more important question was what Mr. Pinkerton would think.

The doors opened to the long hallway. Matthew stepped out with the clear intention of seeing her behind a locked door before he abandoned his duty. Calista loosened the strings on her handbag to find her key. No distractions. She had to solve this case before Pinkerton talked Jinxy into sending someone more experienced. She had to find Lila both for the girl's sake and her own. Calista had a mission and a desire to do more than wear ballgowns and the latest coifs. She wanted more.

Matthew couldn't interfere with that.

"I've never been in such a beautiful place," he said as he tilted his head back to gawk at the teardrop chandelier over their heads. They had a similar one in her dining room at home, but she'd never thought it remarkable.

They reached her door. The key worked as smoothly as a skater on ice. She swung the door open, then turned to him. "You really didn't have to walk me this far."

"It was my pleasure." He craned his neck to see inside her suite, then whistled. "That's something else," he said. "Tomorrow is Sunday. Do you want to do a Bible study at Irvin's again? We'll have some strong coffee for everyone."

Every part of her wanted to say yes, but she had a mission, and it wouldn't be furthered by another afternoon with the limited company that met at Irvin's tent. She had to get to work.

"I'm going to try one of the bigger churches tomorrow," she said. "There are several right here in town."

He nodded his acquiescence. "Selfishness has never been a

failing of mine until now. I don't want to share you." He watched as she pulled off her gloves, loosening one finger at a time. "I start work at the Fox-Berry on Monday, but if you're around in the evening . . ."

She held her bare hand out to him. As pleasant as the evening had been, her attention had turned back to her case. The sooner Matthew left, the sooner she could sneak outside and speak to more girls. "I'll see what I can do."

He hesitated before taking her hand, but instead of a quick handshake, he held it. They stood there motionless. She felt it was an honest moment on his part, but she couldn't afford honesty. She had too much to lose. Lila had too much to lose. Besides, if she were merely visiting Joplin as Calista York, Kansas City debutante, would she be giving this backwoods preacher-boy the time of day, or was it just part of her disguise?

It troubled her that she couldn't answer that question. Or maybe she didn't want to answer that question. All she wanted to think about was how nice it was standing there in the hallway, holding his hand.

CHAPTER
10

"I'll take the laundry to the line," Calista volunteered. It sounded like the perfect assignment. No one at the Children's Home would be inconvenienced if she disappeared for a while, and no children would be hurt if she abandoned her station. After another weekend without any sign of Lila, it was time to dive into the home's records. While the House of Lords was a notorious brothel, there had to be smaller, lesser-known places that were exploiting women. Calista would search through them all.

After securing permission from the director, Mrs. Fairfield, Calista balanced the basket of clean, wet linens on her hip and sashayed in through the front door of the home. In Calista's opinion, her carefree manner was one of her most effective tools. Even if someone stopped and corrected her behavior, they rarely attributed anything sinister to her mistake. For some reason, people thought it likely that she didn't know where she was supposed to be or what she was supposed to be doing. Unfortunately, even Mr. Pinkerton seemed to believe her ruse. Calista hummed and twirled her floral scarf as she walked past the nurseries. Finding Lila would prove her value to her boss more than any dour expression could.

What would Matthew think if he knew? If things had stayed as they were, he might be annoyed, or maybe even amused, that she wasn't a girl looking for a designing job, as she claimed. But now it was different. Saturday night, everything had changed. He wasn't a man she'd just met. He wasn't an acquaintance from whom she could withhold information. She owed him the truth, and the fact that she had to deceive him troubled her greatly.

Calista's humming dropped as she approached the reception area. Stopping before she came in view of the desk, she leaned her back against the door to the records office, slanting it open. Cooler air wafted out of the dark room. She readjusted the basket on her hip and peered inside the office. Empty. Looking once over her shoulder to make sure no one was watching, she bumped against the door and slipped inside as it shut behind her.

Situated in the middle of the building, the room was windowless. With a flick of a switch, the electric lights hummed to life. Dropping the basket of wet laundry, Calista turned the knob on the deadbolt lock, ensuring that no one would interrupt her until she'd had time to find what she was looking for.

Starting at her left, Calista methodically made her way through the desk drawers, then the files in the credenza. Some were licenses, some were expense books, some were applications for adoption, some were employees' files. None of those interested her. It wasn't until she opened a wooden file drawer on an upright cabinet that her heart sped up.

It was the records on the children. A quick scan revealed that they weren't arranged chronologically, as she'd hoped, but alphabetically. Was there a file for every child at the Children's Home? She bit her lip and glared at the cherry desk clock on the credenza. How long would this take? No matter. Every piece of information had the potential to be useful.

Yanking out the first file, she flipped it open. The top record was a listing of the child's measurements and shoe size. This child was nearly as tall as she was. She snapped the file closed and traded it for the next one. She needed newer files. Who cared where the children came from ten years ago? It didn't take more than a couple of files before Calista learned to open the file to the back and look at the first record for the information she sought. There she found the date the child had been left at the home, the parents' names if known, and the parents' locations.

She focused on the parents' locations first. Scattered among the records were mentions of some of the shanty towns surrounding the mines. Women, maybe even married, who couldn't afford their child. Those records weren't what she was looking for.

The ones that made her giddy were the listings of the hotels, the saloons, the seedy apartments on Maiden Lane. While she didn't expect to find Lila Seaton's name on the records, all of the places the mothers lived were good places to search for the missing girl.

Calista worked her way through half the files, committing to memory the places that fit the criteria she was searching for. While they didn't have pictures in the files, the ages of the babies made them easy to pair with the children she'd tended. Calista wondered which was the baby that would be given away in the raffle. Or would the winner have their pick? Would these mothers who lived at the Grosman's Inn, Delilah's Inn, or the Clarketon come to watch?

Footsteps were coming. Calista paused, holding her breath. Should she close the file cabinet and unlock the door? No. She still had work to do. Besides, this facility was managed by kindhearted women, not the Chicago mob. She wasn't at risk of anything except a stern talking-to and being forbidden from ever volunteering again.

To be honest, she might miss getting to come back.

The footsteps stopped in front of the records office door. Her focus burned on the doorknob, watching for movement. It turned, then the door jammed forward, but the deadbolt lock held firm.

Calista gripped her scarf and pressed it against her chest. The door rattled as the potential opener refused to believe it to be stuck.

"Mrs. Fairfield, this door is jammed." It was Mrs. Bowman. "Can you open it?"

Mrs. Fairfield either had the strength to fix it or thought she did, because in no time, a thud crashed into the door. But the deadbolt held firmly.

"That's puzzling." Mrs. Bowman's voice came through the door. "This has never happened before. I'm not even sure there's a key, but we must get it open."

Calista tidied up the files and slid the wooden drawer closed. She still had half the files to look through, but that would have to wait until next time. If there was a next time.

"Mr. Cook, just the man we need. The lock on this door is jammed. Could you open it for us?"

Calista rolled her eyes. Matthew? He was supposed to be at the mine. This couldn't get any worse. Her heart thrilled at the timbre of his voice, but less inspiring was the thought that his help made her discovery unavoidable.

"Is it locked from the inside? How'd that happen?"

She looked around the room. There was no escape. Hiding beneath the desk might buy her seconds, but what good would that do? Should she come out of her own accord, or hope that he would give up and she might have a chance to get out later?

After rattling the door a few times, he asked for a screwdriver. He wasn't giving up.

"This doorframe will be scratched up when I'm done," he said.

"We have to get in there sometime," Mrs. Fairfield said. "We don't have a choice."

Calista chewed her fingernail off, then spat it across the room. What would be the best diversion? Pretending to be a fluff-head worked in many situations, but no one was dumb enough to stand in an office and not notice while people broke through the wall.

With a practiced eye, she measured the floor space. Could she curl up and pretend to be waking from a nap? Because a lady might just get overcome with weariness on her way to hang wet laundry, and lie down for a morning nap? No, unbelievable. Amnesia? She rubbed her elbow, deep in thought. There was a bookshelf. Knock it off the wall, let a book hit her in the head, and then they could discover her unconscious on the floor. If she could convince them that her memory had been wiped clean, she wouldn't have to provide a reason that she'd locked the door in the first place.

From the sounds on the doorknob, Matthew was making progress. In no time, he would have that screwdriver rammed into the doorframe, and he'd wedge the deadbolt back. She went to the desk and pulled her knee up on the desktop. From there, she'd be able to reach the shelf of books. The tricky part would be pulling it down without causing a racket. For her plan to work, they needed to think she'd been unconscious since she'd left them. But what about her head? Shouldn't there be some evidence of her injury? A knot, at the very least?

Just as she was reaching for the shelf, the tone outside the door changed. Everyone standing around Matthew had silenced, and a raised voice could be heard from farther down the hall.

"We're on our way," Mrs. Fairfield said. "Hurry, ladies."

There was a general commotion as footsteps scrambled toward the east wing of the building, then silence. Calista eased herself off the desk, bending to pick up papers that she'd scattered. After tidying the desk, she hefted the basket of wet laundry onto her hip, tiptoed to the door, and pressed her ear against the varnished wood.

It was absolutely silent in the hallway. Sometimes the Lord worked miracles for people who didn't deserve them. Today was one of those days. Calista slid the deadbolt open, grimacing at each click of the mechanism that echoed down the empty hallway. With her nose to the opening, she slowly pushed against the door, seeing only the empty hall ahead of her. What sudden emergency had called them all away? Whatever it was, she hoped it gave her enough time to make it outside before anyone returned.

No sooner had she taken her first step into the hall than she heard a deep voice that stopped her in her tracks.

"Calista York." It was Matthew, arms crossed and eyebrows lowered. "What were you doing in there?"

Her mouth went dry. The closer she could keep to the truth, the more chance she had of keeping him close. "I shouldn't have gone in there," she said. "Just snooping, like I'm wont to do. Please don't tell on me."

"Snooping for what?"

She shrugged. "Curiosity?"

"What could a Children's Home possibly be hiding in their records that would interest you?"

For the time being, she'd rather study his tanned forearms than look him in the face. "I didn't know what was behind the door. I just stepped in, then—"

"Then locked the door behind you and refused to open it when a chorus of people were banging on it?" Those forearms flexed. "You might not credit me with much intelligence, but—"

The door at the end of the east wing burst open, and Mrs. Bowman ran in with her cap slipping off to the side of her head. "I'm off to summon Dr. Stevenson," she said as she brushed her bangs out of her eyes. "Do you have a horse saddled?"

"I'm afoot," Matthew said. Calista gasped as he grabbed her arm. "But Miss York here is a nurse."

"Praise be to God." Mrs. Bowman clapped her hands together. "Come on, then. Patty broke her arm. We don't know what to do." She turned and fled back down the hall.

Calista's knees weakened. She leaned against Matthew. "I'm a nurse?" The tremble in her voice should have told him that she was unsure, but he propelled her forward.

"Don't you dare doubt your training now."

Training? The closest thing Calista had ever experienced to medical work was watching a chicken lay an egg at Granny Laura's. On the ranch, she'd stayed clear of all the birthing, butchering, and doctoring. With a dozen rambunctious cousins underfoot in the summer, someone was always falling out of the hayloft, or getting stuck by a pitchfork, or scraping the dickens out of their knees. It was general knowledge that you had to get Calista out of the way before you helped the injured, or you'd have two patients to deal with.

From childhood to her dangerous profession, she'd never learned to manage seeing the human body in anything less than optimal form. Even Aunt Myra's illness made her queasy. The thought of an appendage going in an unnatural direction was enough to dim the lights.

Matthew didn't know this, and Matthew didn't care. Instead, he was dragging her outside toward a group of kids gathered in a tight circle, all looking at something she'd give everything not to see.

She twisted out of his grasp. "Give me a moment," she pleaded.

The bright sun gave her an excuse to pause so her eyes could adjust. Or perhaps she should look directly at the sun and blind herself so she wouldn't have to see the sight that awaited her. Calista pressed her hand against her forehead. She had to remember her persona. For this case she was using her real name, but she was still pretending to be someone else, and that Calista was competent and helpful. That Calista knew what to do to ease the pain of the child and to settle the nerves of the ladies at the home. Could she be that Calista long enough to do what needed to be done? She had no choice. Not only would it save her mission, but some little girl named Patty needed her too.

"Alright, I'm ready."

With a gentle hand at her back, Matthew steered her through the crowd. Pushing thoughts of the actual injury away, Calista focused on what else she could accomplish.

"Mrs. Bowman," she said, "send these children away. They aren't needed here. And send for the doctor. He'll need to . . ." What was it that a doctor would do that she couldn't do? She had no idea. "He'll need to bring some medicine," she finally said.

"Yes, ma'am. What kind of medicine?"

Calista nearly laughed. "Whatever medicine fixes broken arms. He'll know what to bring."

Over the heads of the children, Mrs. Fairfield looked at her skeptically. The temptation to throw herself against Matthew and bury her face in his chest was overwhelming, but Calista fought it valiantly.

Walking toward the cries, she kept her focus on the little girl's face. Tear-swept and contorting in pain, the girl's eyes flashed around like a frightened horse's.

"Patty?" Calista said. "I'm here to help." She put her hand on the girl's shoulder.

"Ouch! Don't touch it." Patty squirmed away.

"Sorry!" Calista pulled her hand away and, without meaning to, caught sight of an arm that had an extra bend to it. Her mouth went dry, and she felt the blood drain from her face. Calista could tell that Mrs. Fairfield was frowning at her, but then her ample face blurred.

"Hey." It was Matthew shaking her back to sensibility. "What can I do?" he asked as he knelt next to her.

Unless he could miraculously fix broken bones, Calista didn't know what help he could offer, but she needed him. She felt like she was going to gag. She unwrapped the scarf from around her neck to keep from choking and was surprised when Matthew took it from her.

"Should I bind her arm with this?"

All she could see in the spinning world were his deep brown eyes. She nodded, and the movement sent her toppling to the side with barely enough time to catch herself.

136

"I don't think Miss York is well," said Mrs. Fairfield.

"She's worried about the child," said Matthew.

Even with her compromised faculties, Calista could hear him soothing the girl.

"It'll feel better if we can hold it steady," he was saying to Patty. "Let me wrap this around like this, and then let's tie it behind your neck. Here, I'll hold it. Calista . . ."

Again, she was drawn back to his eyes. "Yes?"

"Tie it." Somehow, he'd managed to get the ends of the scarf over Patty's shoulders while holding her arm steady.

"Of course." She rolled from her backside to her knees and crawled to Patty, fighting through her tangled skirts. With shaking hands, she took up the ends of the scarf. Drawing a deep breath, Calista tried to make some knot that would hold, but her fingers fumbled the ends of the scarf. She had to do this. At least this much. She tried not to think of bones and breaks and misshapen appendages, but instead focused on Patty's thick dark braid.

Who braided her hair? Did the girls do it themselves, or did one of these teachers make rounds in the morning, fixing hair? Patty had no bow, only a piece of twine securing the end of the braid. This scarf would liven up her ensemble. Just a secure knot at the back of her neck, and then cover it with the braid.

"There." Calista leaned back, satisfied with the bow she'd fashioned in the silk. "That looks pretty."

"Pretty?" Matthew raised an eyebrow. "Will it keep her arm from further damage?"

Her arm? Calista could feel her stomach rolling over again. She couldn't keep the dreadful image at bay much longer. If she fainted, they would all know—

"Look who I found coming up the road." Mrs. Bowman ran through the courtyard with good old Dr. Stevenson right behind her. "He was headed out to the mines when I caught him."

"Let's see what we have here." Dr. Stevenson didn't pause but went directly to Patty. Pushing the scarf to the end of her elbow, he examined the offending portion of her arm. "Yes, you did yourself no favors today, sister," he said.

Calista stood, then leaned over her basket of wet clothes as she caught her breath.

"Thank you for doing what you could," Mrs. Fairfield said. "It was a comfort knowing she was in your capable hands."

"Now that the doctor's here, I'll go hang this laundry," Calista said. She grasped the handles of the wicker basket but found she had no strength to lift it.

"Allow me." Matthew swung the basket beneath his arm and against his side. "The laundry line is out back?" He didn't wait for her reply but started that direction.

Calista followed, barely able to put one foot in front of the other. With the responsibility lifted, all the disturbing thoughts that she'd repressed came running back at her. Memories of bloodied noses at Granny's, the cat that had been crushed by a wagon wheel, and the bubbly rash that Olive got from climbing the oak tree covered in vines. Too many horrible images for her to handle. She felt the cool shade that meant they'd rounded the corner of the building, and then she felt nothing but relief.

For someone with nurse training, Calista sure looked as green as a spring onion. The odd angle of Patty's arm had given Matthew goosebumps, but nothing like how it hit Calista. He was so surprised that he'd almost forgotten to ask why she'd locked herself into the records office.

He bounced the laundry basket against his side and turned to speak to his companion, but no sooner had he turned than her eyes slid closed and her legs crumpled beneath her.

"Calista!"

He dropped the basket and made a snatch for her arm but was

too late. She dropped like a sack of potatoes on the green lawn of the Children's Home. Kneeling, he took her by the shoulders and rolled her over. Her head lolled back, requiring him to cradle her in his arms. She wore perfume. He guessed he'd always known that, but with her rubbing all up against him, he could state it as a fact now.

"Wake up," he said. It felt like there should be some sort of endearment included. *Wake up, sweetheart? Dear? Honey?* But he didn't feel it fair to be applying endearments when a lady wasn't able to reject them. Instead, he tapped her on the cheek. "Stop making a scene. You don't want the kids to see you."

"Ohhh . . ." she groaned. Her eyes moved behind closed lids, but she didn't seem to be in a hurry to open them.

Another pop on the cheek seemed excessive. If he had water, that would bring her out of it. Or a kiss. Despite whatever malady had afflicted her, her lips looked one-hundred-percent kissable. Surely that would get her attention.

"I know what you're thinking, and you'd best not."

Matthew felt a twinge of panic at the words, but Calista's lips hadn't uttered them. He knew. He'd been watching.

The warning came from Calista's cousin Maisie, who'd appeared before him with her hands on her hips, ready to tangle. Amos stood behind her with a smirk on his face.

"I'm not thinking anything," Matthew fibbed.

"Good thing we ran into Dr. Stevenson and he told us she was here," Amos said. "Otherwise there's no telling what indignities you would've submitted our cousin to."

"I resent your implications," Matthew said. "I'm trying to revive her."

Maisie fished a wet cloth out of the laundry basket and dropped it on Calista's face. "This soggy diaper will help. I hope it's clean."

Calista sputtered, and Matthew hurried to pull the wet rag off her face. He admired the way she kept her eyes on him as she contemplated her predicament. He also admired that she didn't seem in any hurry to get up. Pulling his own handkerchief out of his pocket, he dabbed the moisture off her brow, working his way beneath her eyes. He could have spent the entire forenoon in this occupation, but her troublesome kin had other ideas.

"What's wrong with her?" Maisie asked.

Amos chuckled. "Let me guess. Someone got hurt, and she dropped at the first sign of blood?"

"I don't understand," Matthew said. "How can she be a nurse if she's so squeamish?"

"A nurse?" Maisie roared with laughter.

Matthew didn't miss the warning look from Amos that interrupted her outburst. "Are you saying that she's not a nurse?"

Amos shrugged. "Truth be told, she's looked after a sick classmate before, but she can't abide injuries."

"We were all atwitter when she disappeared from her school, and I never thought it likely that she'd gone to sit at a sickbed. It doesn't suit her, but to think that she'd turn to nursing when she goes limp at the thought of a broken limb or cut . . ."

Disappearing from school? Calista had her hand over her eyes as if shielding them from the light. Or was she hiding from the truth? Come to think of it, Calista's stories often seemed to diverge from the truth.

"It does stand to reason that she can't have worked as a nurse if she responds this way every time," Matthew said.

Ignoring his attempts at logic, Maisie picked up another wet rag. "Get up, Calista, or I'm going to slap you with another diaper. You're wasting our time."

When Calista stirred, Matthew offered a hand to help her sit up. He immediately felt the lack of her against him. Almost as strongly, he felt the lack of clarity on what she was doing. He knew she was fibbing to him, but why? That was even more bothersome.

"I apologize." Calista arranged her skirt over her knees like she was spreading a picnic blanket. "I don't know what ailed me."

"We'll take care of you," Amos said. "Granny sent us to fetch you. She's tired of waiting for you to come to the ranch."

"You don't know what ailed you?" Matthew couldn't sit still any longer. Standing, he dusted off his britches before continuing. "Did it have something to do with Patty and her broken arm?"

Calista's rosy cheeks paled again. Maisie and her brother exchanged worried looks. Amos took Calista by the arm and hauled her upright. "Ma wants to see you too. She's been asking about Corban and Evangelina. She also wants your opinion on what color to paint our parlor."

"Because Calista is a decorator?" Matthew asked. "Or is she a nurse? A florist? What are you all conspiring over? Why are you protecting her?"

"Excuse me, *sir*." How Maisie drawled out that last word to make it an insult was impressive. "If there was some conspiracy going on here, we'd hardly have a mind to tell you. We don't know you from sic 'em. As far as protecting her, of course we'd protect her. She's family. Now, we have orders to haul her errant hide back to the ranch. So if you're finished interrogating her . . ."

Calista's first steps were none too steady, and Matthew didn't know what bothered him more—her physical distress or his confusion. Either way, he wasn't done dealing with these people.

"You might have rights to protect her, but she has rights too. Calista, are you sure you want to go with them? I'll get you safely back to your room if that's what you prefer."

He'd tussled with these two before, but this time he was prepared, and this time it was over the lady he cared about.

She looked at her cousins, then gave a halfhearted shrug. "I'll go with them," she said. "It's inevitable."

"You don't have to." He moved into their path.

"You're so sweet. After all this mess . . ." She stepped forward.

He read the intent in her eyes, and by the time her hand was against his chest, there was no way she could miss the pounding of his heart. Rising on her tiptoes, she pressed her lips to his cheek.

Matthew closed his eyes as their shadows overlapped. She was lilac perfume, a gentle warmth, and a cloud of luxurious bronze hair. It really was unfair to butter him up like this when he hadn't decided whether or not she was a felon. He opened his eyes as she retreated.

"You weren't supposed to be here," she said.

"They gave me my equipment at the mine and went over the rules. My first day will be tomorrow. Do you want me to come with you? I could. That way you won't have to travel back to town by yourself."

"No." Her quick reply set him back. "I mean, it's nice of you to offer, but it's premature. My family is . . . well, you've met Amos and Maisie. There's no reason to submit you to that."

"She's our responsibility, not yours," Amos said with a dark look, and then he followed Calista and Maisie toward the road.

Matthew hoisted the basket of clothes beneath his arm. He had more important things to worry about. Calista would have to take care of herself, because when he tried to think of what he could do for her, he was at a loss.

CHAPTER

11

"You told Granny Laura you would come to the ranch and see her, and she got tired of waiting." Maisie's steps fell heavily on the steep decline as they made their way to the creek crossing.

"I'm here now, aren't I?" Being kidnapped by her family was inconvenient, but so was answering Matthew's questions. Calista supposed she was grateful for the interference.

"Not of your own free will," Amos said. "Pa told me to come along for muscle. He was afeared that Maisie couldn't bring you in on her own."

No wonder Calista had succeeded early as a detective. Kidnapping, strong-arm tactics, interrogations—her family dealt in such maneuvers as a matter of course. It was almost like they were wired to be suspicious and strategic. Evidently Matthew came from similar stock.

The lingering queasiness was fading as she stretched her legs and filled her lungs with air. Strength and wholeness, that was what she wanted around her. For some reason, seeing hurt turned her inside out. It was ridiculous. One of these days, it was going to affect her performance on a case. What if she or a partner were injured? What if she witnessed violence? She'd need to keep her wits about her. Falling over in a faint would leave her vulnerable. And yet she found it hard to imagine the next case.

Since she'd started training with the Pinkerton Agency, she'd looked forward to taking on disguises and characters, but here in Joplin, she got to be Calista. She couldn't think about her next assignment without a sense of dread, but that was nothing compared to the dread of seeing her grandmother.

From a golden childhood, her time at her grandma's ranch shone the brightest. Every summer the cousins had gathered at Granny Laura's, and Granny Laura had whipped them into shape with ranch chores and lectures. But between feeding the animals, fixing fences, and weeding the gardens, the cousins had plenty of time to create their own society of value and familial connections from which their parents, aunts, and uncles were excluded.

The cousins might cover for each other, but they'd also hold you accountable, and the price was sure to be higher than any judge would make you pay.

"I'm glad you came with us," Maisie said. "Otherwise Olive and I were going to up the ante."

"You didn't need to bring Olive into it," Calista said as they came out of the woods and across the back pasture. "She's got enough on her plate. Besides, what's she going to do that Granny wouldn't?"

"She was going to call Corban." Amos's eyes shifted to Calista with dark warning. "You know the last thing we want to do is snitch to your parents, but if you leave us no choice . . ."

How had Mr. Pinkerton thought she could work unencumbered this close to her family? He should have known better.

"First I have to face Granny."

Her grandmother's rock farmhouse came into view. With a chimney at each end, it was stuck in the top of the hill as if it had been planted there and had grown roots. The house was as solid and immovable as the widow woman who ran the place.

Maisie slowed as they reached the turnoff to her house. "I don't know what got into you, girl, but Granny Laura is going to work you over. Good luck."

"You're not coming with me?" Calista asked.

"Pa was none too happy with us taking out for town today," Amos said. "If it weren't for Granny insisting she needed us, we would've been repainting the barn. We gotta get back to work."

Sure enough, Uncle Bill was atop a ladder that leaned against the barn. He paused in his work to wave a paintbrush at Calista, then whistled for his kids to hurry up.

Calista's shoulders dropped as she turned to the larger house. "Pray for me."

Maisie slapped Calista on the shoulder. "Always."

Calista's feet felt heavy. She hadn't quite shaken off the shame of what Matthew had witnessed earlier that morning. He didn't believe her about being locked in the office, and he had his doubts about her nursing experience. As bad as that was, she was now about to step into the crucible. Shoring up her courage, Calista jogged up the porch steps of Granny Laura's house.

When she'd taken this job from Mr. Pinkerton, she'd looked forward to the day when she could tell her family exactly what she'd been up to, but Mr. Pinkerton was adamant that she not tell them while on this case. That knowledge had to stay hidden, or Calista's safety would be in jeopardy. But now it seemed she might be forced to reveal something just as she was in the most danger of losing her job.

All was not lost yet. If she were lucky, she might catch Granny on a bad day. Maybe Calista could bluff her way out of the encounter with her cover story still intact.

With a toss of her head, just in case Granny was looking out the window, she opened the front door and let herself inside.

A heavy blanket draped the back of Granny's rocking chair and hid the occupant from her. Was Granny dozing in that sunny spot? Calista crept up to the rocking chair.

"Granny?" she whispered.

The chair lurched as a raccoon leapt from the rocker, streaked across the room, and scampered out the door. Calista would have liked to have screamed, but no sound came from her. Had she really seen that, or was she imagining things? She pounded her fist against her chest as she flipped the blanket over. She was braced, ready for another wild animal to emerge from its folds, but it was empty. So where was Granny Laura?

"What do you mean, sneaking in here like that?"

Calista looked around. Where had that voice come from? A wisp of movement in the next room caught her attention, and she started forward.

"I didn't know if you were expecting me," she called as she crossed the spacious threshold.

"Nonsense. I sent Amos and Maisie to fetch you. Of course I was expecting you."

Calista followed the voice up, her concern growing the higher her gaze traveled. Her diminutive granny stood atop the upright piano with a dust rag in her hand. The fringe on her chaps tangled with the petals of a silk flower arrangement in a Chinese vase. Her boots crumpled the lace doily beneath her feet.

It was clear what Granny Laura was doing up there, so Calista didn't utter the rhetorical question. Granny didn't suffer superfluous conversating. Instead Calista asked, "Do you need help?"

"I'm done here." Her granny took another swipe at the cornice, then squatted at the edge of the piano, her legs folding easily for a woman of any age. She dropped her feet to the keyboard with a discordant crash of notes. "Should've closed the cover before I climbed up," she said as she took Calista's offered hand and reached the floor. "First love and kisses before we prod the sore spots." She turned her tanned cheek up for Calista's kiss.

It didn't matter that Granny was shorter than all her grandchildren. Calista still felt like she was reaching up to her whenever they met.

After a strong hug, Granny Laura held Calista at arm's length. "Well, let me get a look at you. Polly will be asking how her daughter's faring." Her sharp eyes did a quick sweep. Remembering her lost scarf, Calista touched her neck, and Granny's eyes narrowed. "Did you lose something?"

"Did you know you have a raccoon in your parlor?" Calista jabbed her thumb over her shoulder.

"My granddaughter is a greater concern. When is the last time you talked to your parents?"

"They aren't worried about me." They would have the forged letter from the school by now, and that would explain everything. "They know I'm here, or they'll know soon enough."

"Myra says you're looking for work as a nurse in Joplin. Amos says you're staying at the Keystone. Maisie says you've been working with the foundlings. What does Calista say?"

"All of that's true, to some extent. I need to take a job to finish my schooling. It's a new requirement, so I'm weighing my options."

"But coming to stay with me at the ranch wasn't one of your options? Last I heard, my grandchildren loved spending time here. It makes more sense than a woman staying alone in a city as wicked as Joplin."

Calista walked to the piano. Reaching up, she straightened the doily that hung halfway off the top. She was an adult. She could tell her grandmother that her activities were none of her business, but that wasn't how Calista's family worked. It *was* Granny's business. Her doings were Maisie's and Olive's and Amos's business too. Because they were family.

The difficulty came in explaining what her business was without losing her position. And yet there was no one she trusted more than Granny Laura.

"Granny, I have a job. It's a job that requires me to act the way I'm acting. It's for a very good cause, and it doesn't mean that I've changed my beliefs or who I am. I just have to pretend to be someone else for a time."

"You're not an actress, are you? If I find out that you've been on the stage at the Club Theater, I'll burn the place down."

"No." Calista smiled to assure her. "I'm not on the stage. No one is watching me perform. In fact, they don't know that I'm performing, and I'd like to keep it that way."

Granny crossed her arms. Her mouth twisted, stretching the skin over her cheeks like delicate paper. "You're going to have to do better than that. I won't have it on my conscience if something happens to you. I have to have an explanation that will justify my decision not to send for your mother. You know I can keep a secret."

Calista looked down the hall and through the parlor to the front door. They were alone, but she felt like Mr. Pinkerton was watching over her shoulder. Not telling was a condition of her employment, but in this case, not telling would mean the end of her mission, and if she didn't succeed at this mission, it would be her last. Her grandmother might be able to keep a secret, but if she disapproved, then it was *Katie, bar the door.*

"Do you remember when Mother lost that ruby necklace?" Calista asked.

"Why Polly ever had need for such an expensive bauble is beyond me," Granny said. "Do you know how much cattle those rocks would buy?"

"Well, they hired a detective agency to find it."

"I remember." Granny's ice-blue eyes narrowed. Her face twitched. "Are you pulling my leg?"

"I'm working as an operative," Calista said, watching for her grandmother's reaction. "A detective for an agency in Chicago."

The slight movement was Granny's jaw dropping. "Not the Pinkertons?" she asked.

"The same."

Granny bent at the waist, pushing her face forward. "My grand-daughter is a Pinkerton agent?" Her eyes widened as she clapped her hands together and pressed them against her mouth.

"I'm working with them, but it's not official. I'm still on probation."

"You're solving crimes? You're outsmarting villains?" Granny's smile emerged from behind her hands as she hummed a little tune. "I wish your grandpa were here to see this."

"My parents think I'm finishing some studies that are required for my degree. I've been able to work that into my story for this case. I plan to tell them everything once I've secured my spot with the agency."

"That friend of yours . . . the sick one?"

"Never happened. I was in training."

Granny clapped her weathered hands again. "I knew it. I knew there was no way you were in a sickroom. Ha! Polly will be livid that you fooled her, but she'll want to hear all about it."

Just like her grandmother, Calista's mother, Pauline, would have much preferred the adventure of being a detective to learning how to dance and serve tea. And while Calista was relieved that Granny Laura had taken the news so well, now she feared that Granny was so enchanted by the idea, she wouldn't be able to keep it hidden.

"I should've known," Granny said. "I told myself you weren't a lost cause. That you would settle down and find a purpose. Here you are, exceeding all my expectations."

"Maybe your expectations were too low," Calista said.

"Quite possible, but who could blame me? Now, who are you investigating? Do you need help? Is it Mr. Holly, the owner of the paint factory? I've heard he has no former employees in town. People just disappear when they're finished with their job." The leather on her chaps swished as she paced the room. "Or is it

Mr. Wolstead? His scales aren't balanced. Every Saturday his leasers get shorted."

"I can't tell you," Calista said. "All you need to know is that I'm in no danger and I have the resources of the whole agency at my disposal."

Her grandmother nodded as she paced. "So if I hear that you've taken up with some unsuitable companions, it's because you're investigating them. Is that right? Not because you've turned your back on your raisings?"

Calista beamed. "Exactly."

"And if I hear that you're frequenting unsuitable establishments, it's because you're trying to expose evil?"

"More or less."

"And if you put yourself in danger, I don't need to worry because you'll have your family right there to bail you out?"

At this, Calista cocked her head. "Well, you're here at the ranch. If I need anything—"

"If you need anything, it's going to be too late." Granny had turned fierce. "You need someone in town with you, and I don't mean Olive. She's too busy with your aunt Myra. If I weren't so busy with branding, I'd go myself."

Calista gripped the back of a nearby chair. "I couldn't ask you to leave your work here, Granny. That's too much. I'll be fine."

"Nonsense. Kentworths look after their own. You aren't going to do this alone. My decision is between Amos and Maisie. Amos would look more threatening, but when push comes to shove, Maisie might be a better one in a fight. Plus, it'd be easy for her to bunk down at your hotel with you. No one would question your cousin coming to town."

Panic, like a sharp bile, was climbing up Calista's throat. "I don't need a babysitter, and I definitely don't need Maisie. She's uncouth. She's uncontrollable. She's—"

"She's just the companion you need." Granny's level gaze

had returned. "I'm proud of you, Calista, but I'm no fool. You don't want to admit to your old granny that you could have some hardened men after you, but I know the truth. Besides, you need to keep your family's reputation in mind. You might skedaddle off to another case, but we have to live with the rumors of what you're doing. Having Maisie with you will give you more respectability."

Mr. Pinkerton would not approve, and neither did Calista. "Granny, the reason I'm so effective is because people don't expect a young girl to be good at her job. They underestimate me, just like you're doing now."

"Don't talk to me about being underestimated, child." Granny ran her fingers through her short silver hair. "When your grandpa died, I was saddled with three young children and a ranch no one thought I could handle. Everyone told me to sell out and move to town. When those men got tired of trying to convince me that my land wasn't worth anything, they tried to convince me to marry them to help me manage my property. The one decision that wasn't acceptable would be for me to reject them and take care of it myself.

"You should've seen the looks on their faces the first time I showed up at the railhead with a herd, two hired men, and your uncle Bill riding like a wrangler, though barely twelve years old. I was dressed like the rest of the ranchers—dressed to get the job done. Since that day, I haven't much cared what people said, as long as I'm staying true to the trail Christ has called me on. But that doesn't mean being a stumbling block without cause. So you go along and be the best detective that Chicago man has. If people don't understand why you're doing something, that's not your worry, but there's no purpose in leaving yourself open to attack. And if there's anyone who is good in a fight, it's your cousin Maisie."

Maisie was a force to be reckoned with, which meant Calista

would have a hard time dealing with her. "My boss won't agree to that. She's not on the payroll."

Granny tapped her chin. "I've never been to Chicago. Do you reckon that Mr. Pinkerton would allow me to make a visit? I could stop in Kansas City along the way and pick up your father."

Calista's family ties had been one of Mr. Pinkerton's greatest concerns. He preferred to hire orphans or people estranged from their families. Now Calista understood why.

"I suppose he doesn't need to know if I have a roommate," she grumbled.

"That's the spirit. Now, if you can't tell me who you're investigating, then I've got a story to tell you. It's about a rabbit snare and a raccoon and how I came to have a pet crawling around the parlor. Come to the kitchen. I'll get you some vittles before we go to your uncle Bill's house and tell them that Maisie is going to be staying in town with you."

When it came to Granny Laura, one could argue until the cows came home and be no better off. Calista might as well accept defeat. By agreeing to Maisie's company, she had her Granny's approval, and that counted for a lot.

CHAPTER

12

Another blast from the powder monkeys, and Matthew moved in with the other cokeys. He would never get used to his sunshine lamp—a solid mixture of lard oil and kerosene that sat on the brim of his cap. The sunshine lamps burned slowly and smoked horribly. It would have been tolerable except for its proximity to his eyes and the lack of fresh air in the mine. With the swirling dust from the explosion, it would be a half hour before he could see very far anyway. And another half an hour before the smoke from the gunpowder stopped burning his nose.

The men moved to their ore cans. When they filled their can, they dropped a marker in it so they could claim it as their own for payment. Matthew found his can, ashamed he wasn't filling it as fast as some of the others, but he'd get better. According to Cokey John, it would be a few weeks before his back stopped twinging with every shovelful, but one never got used to darkness and poor air.

This was what the men had to endure. This was what drove them to speculate on leases and lose their earnings. This was what drove them to drink themselves into oblivion every weekend. Between the backbreaking work, the deadly lung diseases, and the depressing environment, hope seemed a far-off dream. It hadn't been a full day yet, and already Matthew had a better understanding of what compelled them to make the choices they made. He also had a better understanding of how arrogant he'd acted around the men, assuming he had all the answers—he who had never been tested like they had.

Speaking of trials and testing, how was he supposed to respond to Calista's unpredictable behavior? He dug his shovel into the pile of rubble and tossed it into his bucket. Was she part and parcel of the corruption of Joplin, or was there a more logical explanation for her actions?

Between thinking about Calista, praying for his friends, and plotting to stop the baby raffle, Matthew had enough on his mind to make the day pass. He wasn't bored as he'd feared, but despite his gloves, his hands were blistered like overcooked fish. When the whistle blew, he heard the foreman's bellow echoing through the caverns.

"Go on up, boys."

Matthew planted the tip of his shovel into the ground and slowly pushed himself upright against it. Nope, his hands wouldn't be the only part of him sore tonight.

Much to his dismay, leaving wasn't just a matter of walking out. Matthew had to get his ore bucket on the rails so it would be hauled to the surface and weighed. He was relieved to learn that he didn't have to stand around and wait for them to take an accounting of it. If he trusted them, and he did, he could leave it and head back to town.

Once aboveground, he squinted even though the clouds softened the light. Would he ever have lungs full of clean air again? That cough, so prevalent in mining towns, would be his cross to bear if God didn't spare him. The men working their own leases enjoyed better health. That was, if they found enough zinc and lead to keep food in their bellies.

"I just delivered my last bucket for the day, Parson."

Matthew turned to see Silas approaching. He pulled a grimy

handkerchief out of his back pocket and swiped it against his forehead. Silas managed to do well enough on his lease even though he started work late and quit while the sun was still up. The fickleness of the ore mines on display. When someone as industrious as Dan Campbell couldn't dig up enough zinc to make ends meet, but a frolicking playboy like Silas pulled up baskets of it by the shovelful, one better understood some of the psalmist's laments on the unfairness of life.

Still, Silas was working, and Matthew didn't begrudge him his reward.

"Are you headed to town?" Matthew asked.

"I'll keep you company, if you don't mind," Silas answered and fell into step with him.

Matthew enjoyed knowing someone who wasn't wallowing in need like Irvin or dripping in riches like Clydell Blount. Going to town with Silas made him feel like less of an outcast. More like he had a peer, and today he could use the companionship, because he didn't have any good answers about Calista.

"How was the mine?" Silas asked.

"Not bad." Matthew rolled his shoulders and stifled a groan. "The mine was fine, but I feel like I've been dragged behind a horse."

"I hate to tell ya, but that's how it's going to be," said Silas. "Now, those blisters, you need to get something on those. Go to the dry goods store and ask for the cokey's ointment. They'll set you up. C'mon. I'll take you."

They'd reached Broadway and were turning toward the mercantile when Matthew noticed something new. Plastered on the brick wall of the alley next to the DeGraff Building was a poster that hadn't been there that morning.

Support the Joplin Children's Home
Baby Raffle Under Way
Tickets Available at the Carnegie Library

Silas whistled. "A baby raffle? Who ever thought?"

"I'll get that ointment later. I need to pay a visit to the library."

"Count me in. I never pass up a curiosity."

Despite his earlier good humor, Matthew could feel his face settling into grim lines. By the time they'd followed the trolley tracks to the library, he felt like Moses rumbling down the mountain with the stone tablets, but instead of rioting Israelites prostrating themselves before a golden calf, he saw an assortment of Joplin's citizens waiting at a table.

Atop a sky-blue silk tablecloth sat a wooden box with the words *Joplin's Baby Raffle* stenciled on it in gold. A woman wearing a modest coat over a waitress's uniform opened a brown paper sack and counted out a stack of coins to a clerk behind the table.

"Five dollars. Thank you, ma'am."

"My husband and I have talked about getting a child for years but didn't know if we should. I guess if we win, then we'll know it was time."

"Yes, ma'am. Did you complete the entry form?" The clerk held out his hand and took it from her. Scanning the form, he took his pen, asked for her address, then dropped the form through a slot on the side of the box and put her money into some contrivance beneath the table. "Your ticket has been registered. Good luck."

"Thank you." She smoothed the empty sack, folded it, and tucked it inside her coat.

"Looks like the contest is under way," Silas muttered as another woman approached the table.

"May I see the little one again before I buy my ticket?" The fur collar of this woman's jacket wasn't rabbit or fox or any animal Matthew had ever seen. Behind her, her maid stood, holding some recent purchases.

"Didn't you see him yesterday?"

"Yes, but I want another look. I don't buy things on impulse." The woman's eyes swept over the copious bags her maid was holding before returning to the clerk. "I might have missed something on the first inspection. He could be absolutely unsuitable, and then where would I be?"

"If you win and decide you don't want the child, we'll pick another winner. You'll have the consolation of knowing that your money is still helping the rest of the children at the home."

The lady checked with her maid to see if she shared her annoyance. The maid kept her eyes on the ground.

"I'll tell you this, if I'd known there were such beautiful children at the Children's Home, I would've gotten one before now." The woman reached into her purse. "It's only five dollars. It's worth a chance."

"Here's a form for you to fill out, if you don't mind."

"I do mind. You know who I am. If you have any questions, you can contact my solicitor. Good day." She lifted the front of her skirt to make a tight turn and exit the building. She dipped her head in acknowledgment of the man who'd just entered and was strutting across the lobby.

"Mr. Blount." The clerk tugged his starched cuff down over his wrist. "So glad to see you. We've done a brisk business. This shows every sign of being a huge success."

"It should, by golly." Mr. Blount scratched at his fitted suit like it was infested with fleas. "Tell you what. I'd be a poor sport if I didn't purchase some tickets myself. Here's fifty dollars. Put my name in ten times."

"Ten times?" The clerk took the money with a deferential smile. "Does Mrs. Blount want a youngster?"

"Lands no, but the old gal needs something to liven her up. Getting long in the tooth, she is." Mr. Blount scanned the room to see who appreciated his humor, but his grin only proved that his dentist wasn't as particular as his tailor.

"Yes, sir. That would be one lucky child to be raised in your household. Good luck to you, sir."

Matthew couldn't help himself, even if Mr. Blount owned the

mine he worked at. "Excuse me," he said. "You probably don't remember me, but I spoke to you at the Children's Home. I'm disappointed to see that you're going through with this."

Mr. Blount's eyebrows lifted, and he smiled broadly. "Ah, I remember you. Yes, well, unless you know of a better way of raising money, I'd recommend you take your moral outrage to the bank and see how many of the Children's Home's bills it will cover."

"Surely you see what's going on here. People are treating this child like a commodity. They are discussing its worth, its qualities, as if it were a piece of merchandise."

"And while they are talking about the babe, they are putting money in that box. That's the bottom line, and I know a thing or two about bottom lines."

Matthew hadn't expected a rich man dressed so fine to act so coarse. Or maybe he hadn't thought that a coarse man could become this rich.

"The child doesn't deserve to be sent to whatever home was drawn out of a box," Matthew said.

"Who of us gets to pick which family we're born into? This child has a better chance than most. At least we know the parents wanted the child and they had enough fortitude to put together five dollars. And it's putting several in a mind to adopt that would've never considered it before." Mr. Blount stepped back and scratched again at the bothersome spot. "Young man, I reckon you're not a bad sort. What do you want?" He reached for his wallet. "If I remember correctly, you're trying to help the miners?"

Matthew wasn't sure of his response. Mr. Blount seemed sincere, but it could be that he sincerely wanted to buy Matthew's complicity. It also seemed that he was unaware that Matthew worked for him. Better to keep it that way.

"No, thank you," Matthew said. "I'd rather know that our charity doesn't include selling children."

"No one is forcing anyone to be involved."

"Besides the child. You are forcing his participation."

Blount's good humor was fading. Matthew seemed to have that effect on people. "You've made your point. Now get, before I have you arrested."

Matthew stood toe-to-toe with him, but in this instance, Silas had better sense.

He grabbed Matthew's arm. "Don't get a trespassing charge, Parson. I'm not going to bail you out of the pokey."

Common sense slowly began to filter back in. It was frightening how close Matthew had come to ruining his reputation. He rubbed the back of his neck. "My apologies," he said. "I have no right to do more beyond expressing my opinion."

Mr. Blount snorted, then held out his hand.

And because he could think of no way the man had caused him personal offense, Matthew accepted the handshake, returning it wordlessly.

He'd lost again. The satisfaction of keeping his cool was weak tea, but he could reflect on the fact that he wouldn't have to come back and make amends. His only accomplishment was in not making a fool of himself.

Not yet.

"Mr. Cook." Mr. Blount's voice echoed in the cavernous library. "If you're curious about how to help, you ought to have another visit with my pastor. He's having a charitable meeting even as we speak."

Matthew's teeth ground together with a satisfying groaning noise. His last meeting with Reverend Dixon hadn't been helpful, but maybe this time he could make some progress. He'd give it a shot.

So with his thanks and with a good-bye to Silas, he turned his feet and his mind to the Tabernacle Church.

Matthew waited in the hallway of the Tabernacle Church and wondered what his preacher at the one-room church back home would think about having a secretary. He reckoned a pastor needed some help in a building this big, lest people get lost and endlessly wander the halls, unable to find their way out.

He'd only worked his hands around the brim of his straw hat once before the door opened and Reverend Dixon stepped out. "Mr. Cook, I'm afraid I don't have time right now. I'm in the middle of a meeting."

"I'll be brief. Mr. Blount told me to call."

Reverend Dixon's face stretched in surprise. "Well, then, I'd better hear what you have to say."

No use in beating around the bush. "The baby raffle hasn't been canceled, and some of your church members are promoting it. As their spiritual adviser, it's your duty to call them into account."

Reverend Dixon studied him for a moment. "Why don't you come inside?" He cleared the doorway and turned toward a raw-boned man with blueprints in hand. "No need for you to leave, Oscar. Let me hear Mr. Cook out, and then I'll get back to you."

Matthew recognized the manager of his mine, Oscar Kentworth.

"Not to worry. I know Mr. Cook." Mr. Kentworth watched Matthew with a keen interest as he entered the room.

Reverend Dixon's office wasn't what Matthew expected. He'd never seen walls painted that purply-pink of a cow's tongue before. With the white paneling and gold fixtures, he reckoned his mother would say it was elegant, but he couldn't understand how any man could spend more than a passing moment in it. He could feel the pink draining the strength straight from his body.

Instead of going behind the desk, the pastor sat in a chair angled toward Matthew. "Thank you for coming with your concerns over the baby raffle. I've thought over your objections, but I've decided I won't oppose the charity efforts."

His calm answer made Matthew feel uncouth and graceless, but it didn't weaken his resolve.

"Is your decision swayed by the donations of Mr. Blount?" Matthew asked.

To his surprise, Reverend Dixon considered the question carefully. "I don't believe so, no. Even if no one I knew was proposing the idea, I don't think there's enough harm in it to warrant protest. Rather than spend my time stopping people who are trying to help, I'm listening for what God is leading me to do."

"You think Blount's trying to help? Instead of selling babies, why doesn't he refuse to lease his buildings to saloons? Why doesn't he improve ventilation in his mines, so the miners don't get sick? Why doesn't he set a better example to all his workers who see his success and want to imitate it?"

Reverend Dixon leaned forward. "The church is for sinners, rich and poor. Some come to us already trained and discipled, while others have only begun their journey. If we turned away everyone who hadn't surrendered their will, where else would they hear the challenge to do so?"

Matthew squirmed beneath the pastor's piercing gaze. "It's unseemly," he said at last. "There should be some accounting."

"I agree, and I pray every day for the wisdom to apply that accounting when needed. In the meantime, we take the resources that God has granted us and do what we can. Right now, Oscar and I are looking at plans for a learning center at the Fox-Berry Mine. It'd be a place the employees could go to further their education and get medical help. Mr. Blount is donating the money to build and outfit the building, and if we provide the volunteers, then we're free to conduct Bible studies on the premises as well."

Matthew looked at the blueprint greedily. Something like that might have made a difference for Uncle Manuel. Just a place to go after work instead of heading to the saloon. A doctor, a pastor, people who cared who could've seen the danger he was in and intervened. It was just the kind of work Matthew had hoped to start himself.

"How was your first day?" Mr. Kentworth asked.

With the raffle and now the blueprints on his mind, Matthew had forgotten about his grimy skin and britches. Even though he'd donned a clean shirt and changed boots in the doghouse, he didn't look sharp enough to be meeting his boss and a rich pastor.

"I'm grateful for the work," he said. "It'll be tough to keep up one's spirits down there day after day, but I'm going to do my best."

"We're working to improve that, but I'm glad you noticed." Kentworth shared a smile with the pastor before adding, "You know, it's frustrating to be the one who sees what should be, young man. To see what no one else wants to see. But maybe that frustration is only telling you that you're in place to do the most good."

"Amen," said Reverend Dixon.

Matthew looked from one to the other. How could it be that they had disagreed with him, but still seemed to be on his side? He rose, and because he was learning that in the city harsh words didn't have to mean the beginning of a feud, he offered his hand to each man in turn before commenting to Mr. Kentworth, "If you're looking for someone to design that learning center of yours, you could offer the job to your niece Miss York."

"Calista?" Mr. Kentworth drummed his large, bony fingers against the table with a laugh. "My daughter Olive has been working on the sketches, but I can't imagine Calista having an interest. Beware, Mr. Cook. Whatever Calista is cooking up, someone is going to get fried."

Matthew's forehead wrinkled. This man trusted Mr. Blount but warned him against his own niece. What was she up to?

CHAPTER

13

"I'm going to have another guest in my room," Calista said to the smooth-faced hotel clerk at the front desk. She motioned to Maisie, who was standing on the opposite side of the fish tank with her nose against the glass as a blue-and-yellow striped fish glided in front of her. Her eyes, already magnified and distorted, crossed as she followed its path. Calista coughed to clear her throat. "She's my cousin."

The clerk nodded in sympathy. "No need to explain. I have cousins too. Would you like another key, Miss York?"

"Another key would be helpful, thank you."

He went to a wall of dividers and fished a key out of the cubby that corresponded to her room. "Also, you had a telephone call while you were out. The caller said he would call again tomorrow morning. Is there anything else I can do for you?"

Calista took the brass key with its satin tassel. "That's all for now. Thank you."

Mr. Pinkerton was anxious for a report. What did she have to offer him? Only a list of the places Lila was not.

Despite Calista's best efforts, it was as if Lila had vanished without a trace. Again. She couldn't fathom the distress the missing girl was in.

Calista walked around the fish tank and handed Maisie her key. Thank goodness Granny hadn't insisted on Calista telling Maisie about her job. Her head was already spinning with the prospect of getting to stay in town.

"My own key?" Maisie whistled, drawing the attention of two well-heeled businessmen. "I don't think Pa and Ma even have a lock on our door at the farm."

Calista took her arm. "Keep it with you at all times, and always lock the door behind you when you leave our room. This isn't Granny's ranch. They call it Wicked Joplin for a reason."

"Excuse me, miss." The clerk had stepped out from behind the counter. "I forgot to ask your guest to sign the register."

"Let's do it." Maisie clapped her hands. "And when Evangelina doesn't believe I stayed here, I can pull out this register and show her my signature. Take that, Evangelina!"

Why Maisie thought Calista's sister back in Kansas City would care about her name being in a hotel register was beyond Calista. Then again, the two of them did tend to get competitive with each other. Perhaps it *would* rankle Evangelina.

"Try to stay in the lines," she said as Maisie pushed back her sleeve and gripped the pen. Calista saw her own name at the top of the page with the date, but many people had come and gone since then. Everyone who had stayed in the hotel . . .

Maisie bent to blow on the drying ink of her signature just as Calista began flipping the pages of the book. "Careful," she said in her too-loud voice. "Don't paper-cut my face."

"Sorry. I'm looking for something."

It had been nine months since Lila Seaton had gone missing. She had to stay somewhere, and while it was unlikely that she had the funds to stay at the Keystone, Calista would start here. You never knew when a familiar name would show up in an unexpected

place. Or when names, read repeatedly, might become familiar
and give you insights that you hadn't known would be helpful.
Already she'd heard spoken around town the name of one of the
men in the record of fathers whose children had been left at the
home. It was the man who drove the milk wagon, and she couldn't
guess if he knew he had a child there or not, but it was a piece of
information that she valued. So even if she didn't see Lila's name,
there might be another that filled in a gap.

With her finger running down the column of dates, she scanned
the names. All were strangers—travelers passing through that she
would never meet—but the idea had merit. As soon as Maisie was
settled, they'd visit every hotel in town, especially those whose
names graced the children's forms at the home.

"C'mon." Calista hurried across the lobby, rustling discarded
newspapers on marble-topped tables as she passed.

She'd nearly forgotten Maisie by the time they reached their
rooms, but at the door, Maisie pushed her aside.

"Let me use my key. I have to figure this out." Maisie knelt at
the door, held the key in front of her face, and closed one eye like
she was sighting a rifle.

"The keyhole isn't moving. You don't have to aim."

Maisie leaned forward with her whole body as she inserted the
key. She wiggled it both ways before finding the right direction
and hearing a click. She grinned at Calista as she stood, turned
the knob, then flung open the door.

"Would you look at that?" Her eyes flashed as she took in the
room. Calista couldn't help but share her joy. She'd taken the expensive hotel for granted, and that was a shame. She'd be a better
person if she could appreciate the beauty of it—something she
was learning from Matthew.

Maisie walked inside as if in a daze, her head tilted up to the
high ceilings and white molding. She rocked on her feet, testing
the thickness of the carpet, then dropped to her knees to run her

hand over it. "It's thicker than the rag rugs that Ma and I make. Almost as cushy as a seat cushion."

"You've seen rugs like this." Calista dropped Maisie's bag on a blue-and-white fauteuil chair. "Please act like you've been to town before."

"I've seen them, but I was never at liberty to feel one . . . and it feels wonderful."

"Wait until you see your bed."

"*My* bed? Do I get my own?" Maisie sprang toward the door that divided the living area from the private rooms. "Do I get to pick which room I want? Or are we sharing? One person alone would get lost in this bed. Maybe we should share."

"You take the purple room," Calista said. "My things are already in the wardrobe in the gold room. Now, I have some errands to run. . . ."

But Maisie wasn't finished. Like a moth, she fluttered to the open window. "Look at the view. I bet I can see home from up here."

If one was going to be delayed, looking out the window wasn't a bad way to waste time. Calista joined her at the windowsill.

"The people down there look little. And the streetcar! Watch it go. They don't even know they're being watched, do they? The tops of the buildings are dismal, though. Just tar paper and pipes, but the rest is wonderful."

"It's my favorite place to sit," Calista said. "I could just watch all day."

"I'm sure you could. It's a wonderful view of God's creation."

God's creation? Here in the middle of town?

She followed Maisie's gaze to a crowded flower garden, where two men were repairing the fence. It took a moment before she recognized the thin man with wavy blond hair as Silas, but at the sight of Matthew, her face warmed. He'd stripped down to his undershirt and was hoisting a fence post on his shoulder. Even from the sixth floor, she could see that his arms stretched in all the right places as his muscles played. He lifted the post and lowered it into a hole, then held it while Silas shoveled dirt in around it. Holding the post steady with one hand, he wiped his forehead while laughing at something Silas said.

Calista didn't realize that she'd leaned forward until her forehead thunked against the glass pane.

"Just like I said, a wonderful view of God's creation." Maisie winked. "I bet you spend hours here every day."

Calista stepped back. "I've got some errands to run, but I'll be back before dark. Make yourself at home—"

"I'm going with you."

"I'd rather you not."

"Why else did Granny send me? It was to keep an eye on you. If I let you go without me, then I've let them all down."

Of all the investigating that Calista needed to do, looking through the guest books of hotels would be the least dangerous. If Maisie had to come with her, this evening's tasks weren't too scandalous. "Fine, but don't pester me with questions. You might not understand what I'm doing or why I'm doing it, but I have my reasons."

"And you can't tell me those reasons?"

"No, I can't. Granny approves. That's all you need to know."

"She approves to such an extent that she sent me to watch over you. That doesn't sound like the highest form of approval."

"But it's enough."

The girls put away Maisie's bag, availed themselves of the water closet—which Maisie couldn't help but exclaim over—and then headed back out to the street. Before she'd begun this mission, Calista had spent time with maps of Joplin and had familiarized herself with the general grid. Now she applied that knowledge to the streets that had become familiar to her to make her plan. It was unlikely that Lila, no matter what her reasons for coming, would have stayed at an expensive hotel. Calista would have better luck with the smaller inns mentioned on the forms at the Children's Home.

When they reached the ground floor, she started toward the front doors, but Maisie grabbed her arm.

"I haven't seen the other side of the lobby. Let's go out those doors."

Calista rolled her eyes. They hadn't made it out of the building, and already Maisie was getting her off track. "What could possibly be so exciting about those doors?"

Maisie jutted her jaw forward. "What's it hurt if we go out those doors? It'll just take a moment to walk around to the front."

Calista was used to being spoiled, not to spoiling, but Maisie had already developed a pout. "Fine. Let's go."

Instead of being deposited on the well-traveled Fourth Street, they were dumped into an alley. Turning the corner, they intercepted two workmen. Only they weren't workmen. They were Matthew and Silas.

Calista's steps stuttered as Matthew looked up from where he was digging another posthole. If she'd thought that getting caught in his undershirt and covered in dirt would embarrass him, she was wrong. He seemed to expand, daring to take up more room than before as he stretched into their path and blocked her way. If her feet were still working, she would have walked away offended.

"Calista, what are you doing in the alley?" He lifted the shovel and dug its blade into the ground to punctuate his question.

The noise demanded that she look down, and then, despite her best efforts, her eyes took their time getting back to his face.

She forced a painful swallow. "I only came this way because Maisie said to."

"While you're here, you might as well take a look around."

"She's looked plenty," Maisie said. "Her room looks right down

on top of here. It's her favorite view." In case they didn't understand, she pointed helpfully up to Calista's window.

Now Matthew looked a smidgen perturbed. "Is that so? And
what is it that she enjoys watching?"

"Silas, is that you?" Calista interrupted. "How rude of us. You
haven't been introduced to my cousin. This is Maisie Kentworth.
She's come to stay with me while I'm in town."

"Miss Kentworth." Silas stuck his shovel beneath his arm and
wiped his hand on his pant leg before offering it to Maisie. "It's
my pleasure. Is this your first time in Joplin? It must be, because
I'd remember you if I'd seen you before."

Maisie fluttered at his clumsy attempt at flirtation, but when
Matthew stepped closer, Calista had her own problems to worry
about.

"Is Maisie here by invitation, or because your venerable grandmother insisted?"

He smelled of clean soil and sweat—a scent that reminded her
of the ranch and made her yearn for bare feet in the creek. The
thought of playing in the creek with Matthew made her pause
before she could answer.

"Granny insisted. She didn't think it wise for me to stay here
alone."

"Your granny and I are of the same mind. But why didn't you
stay at her ranch instead? If I had an errant loved one, I'd insist
on keeping them at the hearth."

Calista couldn't ignore how he'd put himself in the shoes of a
much-loved family member. Some warmth, some sweet emotion
wanted to reach her heart, but intellectually she knew that having
another guardian would do nothing but slow her progress.

"I am not your responsibility." She kept her smile, despite the
growl in her voice.

"You're my something," he said.

Her throat caught as he captured her gaze. She couldn't look away. She'd seen his fierceness directed at others, but this was different. It wasn't anger, it was resolve. He was making a resolution, and it was about her. She'd known from the beginning that he cared for her, but this was more than what a Christian felt for their fellow man. He was making a claim on her personally, and to her surprise, Calista welcomed it.

But could she? With a quick prayer for discernment, Calista said, "We mustn't take more of your time. Maisie and I were taking a stroll."

Maisie seemed to have hit it off with Silas. He whispered in her ear, and she shrieked, then slugged him in the arm. In typical Maisie fashion, she hit him harder than he expected, but he rubbed it off with a grin.

"Why don't the fellas come with us?" Maisie looked from Silas to Calista, then back again. "We could wait for them to get their clothes on, couldn't we?"

Oh no. This wasn't good. "Time is of the essence." Calista took a step backward toward the alley. "And we mustn't interrupt their work. We'll do better on our own."

Matthew reached for the shirt hanging over the fence. "It'll just take me a moment to wash up. What do you say, Silas? Feel like an evening stroll?"

Silas locked gazes with Maisie. Maisie didn't know what to do, so she slugged him on the arm again.

"I've been hankering for a break." Silas winked, and Maisie crammed her hands deep into her pockets.

"Then it's decided. You might as well come in the garden and wait here instead of this alley. I'll only be a second."

The girls followed them through the gate and down a path of pavers between the exuberant flower beds. Calista paused beneath a rose-covered arch, drawing in the fragrances she couldn't appreciate from her perch in the hotel. When she'd come to visit his cabin before, she hadn't stopped to see the garden between it and the greenhouse. She turned to face the wall of foliage and trailed her fingers over the braided vines.

"They might need help at the Children's Home on Saturday." Matthew stepped beneath the arch with her. Even though she'd dallied, Matthew hadn't left her, and she wasn't surprised. "You think you can go?"

He was giving her another chance? This grace he preached wasn't all fake, was it?

"I do." She spun around to face him, only then realizing how close they were. She looked down at her hands. "Where did Maisie and Silas go?"

"Follow me." Holding out his hand, Matthew directed her through the garden. What was the cause of this sudden change of heart? Where she'd thought he would be more distant than ever, he seemed to be in heedless pursuit.

Calista joined Maisie outside the door of Matthew's apartment while the men tidied up. Using her charms to soften up a mark was a skill she should practice, but to her knowledge, no one had warned her about it being used against her. The fleeting thought crossed her mind that Matthew could be an adversary. She hadn't considered the possibility that he could be a villain, trying to draw her off track.

The thought was ridiculous, but if someone were trying to influence her, Matthew would be a dangerous weapon. Already he was changing her plans for the evening. Calista rubbed her forehead. Mr. Pinkerton was calling in the morning, and she needed some progress to report. There was no way around it. She would have to come up with an excuse for looking at all the hotel registries right under Matthew's nose.

"What do you know about Silas, and why haven't you mentioned him?" Maisie picked at her stubby fingernails, trying to look nonchalant, but Calista wasn't fooled.

"He's a miner. Seems like a decent guy. He does Bible study."

"Then Pa would approve."

"Your pa would require more than cracking open a Bible before he approved. Not to mention that Finn and Amos will have opinions."

"Finn isn't home, and what's Amos have to say about it?" Maisie caught a rough fingernail between her teeth, tore it off, then spit it in the flower bed. "And I ain't planning to marry him. Just thinking he'll make sure company while I'm watchdogging you."

Sure company? Silas seemed more than agreeable for that. Too agreeable, actually. It could be that her family had miscalculated. Sending Maisie to watch Calista was one thing, but who was going to watch Maisie?

CHAPTER 14

Matthew had come to Joplin with the intention of interrupting the cycle that caught the miners—from the promise of easy riches, to poverty, to pain, to numbing the pain by utilizing the ever-present alcohol. Matthew wished they could think past the next day, the next drink, the next meal. On some things, he had definite ideas of his purpose and what would constitute success—like his new coworkers who had come to his Wednesday night study. On other quandaries, like Calista, he was searching in the dark.

But she was here now, and despite the grueling toil of his day, he had the energy to go wherever she wanted.

They left the flower store. He and Silas walked behind the ladies as Calista led the way. What exactly they were hoping to accomplish, he couldn't say. From the time he'd realized that he was to leave Pine Gap, Matthew had prayed diligently for God's guidance. For most of the situations he'd faced, he was confident that he was representing Christ well. His desire to help these people hadn't wavered. He had managed to hold the loneliness and homesickness at bay. So far, he'd had no doubts concerning God's calling. But no matter how many times he brought up Calista's name to God, he never got a satisfactory answer.

Calista's steps were quick and light as a deer's, while Maisie's showed more strength and surprising grace, considering her general manners. The two girls couldn't be more different, but there were rare flashes of family resemblance—gestures that called to mind the other, like the way they tilted their head to the side when listening to a story, or the subtle alertness that made them difficult to surprise. And, of course, the easily discernible widow's peak that even Oscar Kentworth had. Come to think of it, Matthew should be suspect of anyone in town who had that trait, since he already knew her family to be in the area. The last thing he needed was more of Calista's relatives confounding him.

Although Matthew thought he had ample reasons to end his acquaintance with Calista, he could never pull the trigger. It was as if all the half-truths, unexplainable quirks, and outrageous behavior were to be ignored. Every time he opened his mouth to call her to account, he felt the restraint of the Holy Spirit. *Mercy, patience, forgiveness.* He'd come to town with the understanding that he would encounter people who lacked good raising. He'd scolded himself to remember that he couldn't expect holiness out of lost sheep who'd yet to meet the Shepherd. But he felt an urgency with Calista that he couldn't justify with a clean conscience.

For some reason, Matthew didn't feel the same frustration with Irvin, no matter how many of his paydays went to the whiskey shops. Irvin was a work in progress, and if he made it into heaven with a deathbed conversion, Matthew would celebrate with the angels. But he didn't have the same patience with Calista. Every misstep of hers affected him deeply. He couldn't endure the inconsistencies. They grieved him. Should he feel the same sorrow for everyone who strayed, or was there another element present?

Calista stopped before a dingy building. Her broad-brimmed hat hid her face as she talked to Maisie. Silas stepped forward to join the conversation, leaving Matthew to ruminate. It was time to be truthful to God and to himself. It wasn't an overwhelming sorrow about the state of her soul that had him crying out to God about her. The urgency he felt wasn't holiness, it was selfishness. It wasn't an offense to righteousness that concerned him, but the offense done to his heart. But God didn't care about protecting his heart, so Matthew had to continue this tightrope of admiring a woman who showed virtue and character but who applied it so poorly as to be criminal.

Calista turned to address him, trepidation evident in her eyes. Why did she have to be so transparent? Even before she opened her mouth, Matthew knew she wasn't going to tell him the truth.

"I just caught a glimpse of an old friend from Kansas City through the window." Her face was alight with joy, but her eyes told him all he needed to know. "If you'll excuse me, I'll rejoin you shortly."

Maisie stepped closer to Silas, pleased to beg off the errand, but Matthew was caught. Should he ignore the lie and do as she asked, or call her into account? But a third option compelled him. Protect her, even in her deceit.

He looked at the lettering over the lacquered door. A hotel? That settled it. She wasn't going in alone.

"I'll be right back," he said to Silas.

Calista didn't look pleased that he was joining her, but neither did she look surprised as he held the door open, then followed her inside.

His first thought upon entering was how different this shabby room was from the opulent hotel Calista was staying in. The rug was worn through and pocked with burn holes, especially by the cold hearth that currently held a collection of spider webs. While the tiny room held three spittoons, it didn't hold a single person. Missing was the friend that Calista claimed to have seen.

Also missing was a clerk at the desk. Matthew strode to the desk and popped his hand down on the bell. Besides a dull clink, there was no sound from it. Not one. The lobby was absolutely empty. He started toward a door, figuring it was an office, but Calista placed a hand on his arm.

"Let's not disturb them."

"But don't you want to see your friend?"

Instead of answering, she bent over the guest book on the desk. Flipping back a few pages, she paused, checked the dates, then flipped back even further.

He had to tamper his frustration. Maybe she really was looking for a friend. If she'd thought she saw someone, then checking the guest registry would be a good place to verify it. He'd cut her some slack.

She straightened and dusted off her fingertips. "She's not here. Let's continue."

They exited the building to find Maisie leaning against a light post with her arms crossed. "Where's your friend?" she asked.

"Where's yours?" Calista returned.

"Silas? He went on ahead, saw some shopping he wanted to do. Said he didn't like loitering in front of places like this."

"So he left you to wait alone?" Matthew felt like a herder of crickets, none of them with any more sense than the last, hopping all about.

"Nobody is going to tangle with me," Maisie said, "and someone had to stick around and tell you where he'd gone."

"I didn't find my friend," Calista said. "It must've been her double, but there's no use loitering here."

"Then where do we go next?" Maisie asked.

Matthew was about to suggest a trip to Lakeside Park when Calista skidded to a stop. "Across the street," she said. "Let's go across the street."

He shot her a sideways glance, but Calista was already scooting through a break in the traffic, leaving him and Maisie jogging to catch up with her on the other side.

"What I'd really like to do is go inside here," Calista said. "It looks quaint. If you all would like to shop next door . . ."

Matthew glanced up to see that they were at another inn, this one scarcely nicer than the last. He was too jaded to even ask why. Instead he said, "I'm staying with you."

"Miss Kentworth!" Silas waved them down as he hurried to catch them. "Miss Kentworth, may I take you to the"—he leaned back to read the title painted on the window of the next building—"undertaker?"

"That sounds dandy." Maisie laughed as she walked away with arms swinging high. "We'll see y'all later."

Calista had the grace to look uncomfortable. "You're probably wondering why I'm going in here," she said. "This place surely could use some sprucing up. If I'm ever going to get my business going, then I must cultivate relationships with establishments like this." She patted the sandwich board next to the door that advertised a free cup of coffee and bath with any room.

As if a classy lady like Calista would have anything to do with this hole-in-the-wall. But Matthew had decided not to question. Instead he followed her inside and humored her as she hemmed and hawed over the threadbare sofa, the dead plant stuck in a barrel, and a broken lamp that hadn't had a drop of kerosene in it for years. He watched her work her way around the lobby, noticed that once again she didn't seem to want any clerk to be called, and finally found herself at the guest register.

What was it about the guest register? Was she looking for someone? She continued to name colors and fabrics that she would splash around to make the place presentable, but while she talked, she flipped the pages of the registry back and ran a finger down the date column again.

Interesting. What had happened nine months ago? Those were the dates she was checking. Come to think of it, although she claimed that a friend was staying at the other hotel, she hadn't bothered looking at the current guests, but instead flipped back to see what had happened in the past. Different excuses, but the same behavior. Whatever she was doing, it was calculated.

She bit her lip as she flipped the same page back and forth, then, with a sigh, smoothed it and turned toward him. "They don't have many paying guests, so it's not likely they'd be able to afford my services. We can go."

She steamed ahead, not even noticing when her skirt brushed against a dried, leafless potted plant and toppled it over. Matthew lunged to keep it from spilling on the carpet. He set it upright and hurried out after her.

This wasn't the stroll he'd hoped for. He'd thought she might linger in his company, sympathize as he bemoaned the baby raffle that would take place on Thursday, and listen as he acquainted her with his plans and progress in Joplin. He'd thought that spending more time together would mean that she would learn to appreciate him more. That they would grow closer.

Instead, she was like a bloodhound on the scent, darting through people, crossing streets, sniffing the air to see which way to turn. Barely aware that he existed.

"Hey, Matthew." Silas waved a hand over his head to get his attention. "I'm going to take Miss Kentworth to the ice cream parlor. The undertaker's wasn't much fun."

"You don't say." Matthew turned to his distracted companion. "Calista, how does ice cream sound?"

"No thank you," she said, "but you go ahead. I don't mind walking alone."

Out of the question. Matthew shook his head at Silas. "Go on. We'll look for you later."

Silas wasted no time escorting Calista's eager cousin away.

"Your granny should've sent Amos to look after you. It didn't take Maisie long to get her head turned."

"Mm-hm." Calista stopped at the intersection and looked up

and down the street. He wondered if her tail would wag like a hound's when she smelled what she was looking for. He choked down a groan at the thought.

"Let's go this way," she said, and took off without looking to see if he'd agreed.

"If I were to guess, I'd say that we're going to stop at another hotel." He clasped his hands behind his back and stretched out his chest as they stopped before the wooden Indian in front of the Grosman's Inn. "What a surprise! Another hotel. Shall we?"

The look she gave him showed that his response was inconsequential. Calista was going to do what Calista wanted to do. He could go along peacefully, bellyache, or leave—nothing was going to stop her.

Why was he putting himself through this? What was her aim?

He opened the door for her, pleased that this place looked more respectable than the last two. The plaster walls had been painted recently, and someone was keeping the cheap brass lantern on the clerk's desk polished. The clerk was in attendance and looked at the two of them eagerly.

"Welcome to Grosman's. How may I help you?"

Naturally, the clerk referred his question to Matthew, but Matthew deferred to Calista. What would she say? Something about the decorating?

Instead of the confident lady who navigated busy city streets, she suddenly acted like a girl. She twisted on her toes and picked at her fingernails. "I was here a few months ago, and I left a hatbox behind. I wouldn't have bothered coming back, but it had my mother's hairbrush in it, and it was silver-plated. When I arrived home without it, she sent me back straightaway. I do hope you have it."

If the clerk looked confused, Matthew was sure he looked even more so. "I would've remembered you, ma'am."

She blinked in wide-eyed wonder. "Am I at the right place? Oh dear. I thought this was the hotel where I stayed." Holding her hand against her chest she fluttered until she spied what she was looking for. "There's your guest registry. If you don't mind . . ." Bunching her shoulders up tight, she was the perfect picture of apologetic favor-asking.

"Certainly. I can find it." He pulled the book to himself. "What name am I looking for?"

"No need to trouble yourself." With a wrinkled nose and another submissive shrug, Calista pulled the book around to herself. "It was back a few months. I should easily spot my own signature. It'll only be the work of a moment." Her mouth moved as fast and as easily as her eyes. Just as before, she flipped the pages back until she found the dates she was looking for, but this time, Matthew stepped to her side and watched.

Whatever she was hunting for, it had happened in October of last year, and she wasn't sure of the exact date, because she touched every line as she read through the list of names.

He sensed the tightening of her body before he noticed that she'd landed on one particular line. She'd found it, but what was the name? She snatched her finger away, and before he could make sense of the heavy loops of the signature, she'd snapped the book closed.

"You're correct," she said to the clerk. "I'm at the wrong establishment. My apologies."

The clerk exhaled in relief. "Good to hear. I didn't know anything about a hatbox or a silver hairbrush, but I'd feel terrible if I'd lost it. Good luck," he said.

She tucked her chin and batted her eyes at the besotted man. His glance collided with Matthew's, then flashed with alarm. Excusing himself, the clerk bustled into the office as they left.

They found themselves back on the road to the Keystone and Trochet's. If Matthew wasn't mistaken, she'd accomplished something, although what, he had no idea. She stopped, tilted her head back, and squinted into the sun and then at him, as if just remembering that he was along.

"You found it," he said.

Gone was the simpering girl. The self-assured woman was back, and she looked him in the eye. "Found what?"

"What you were looking for."

"I still haven't found a job, if that's what you're saying. But I've done enough searching for one day. We can rejoin Maisie and Silas."

"Wait here," he said. "I'm going back inside. I'm going to turn that registry to October of last year and take note of exactly what name it is that you're looking for. I'll be just a second."

"No." She grabbed him by the arm. "Don't."

"You'd better have a good reason why not." He steeled himself against the allure of her soft brown eyes. He couldn't allow his judgment to be clouded by her beauty.

She bit her lip as she weighed her options, but finally the words came tumbling out. "You can't go in there. It could put me in danger."

"Why should I believe you?"

"If the wrong person knows I lied, they'll come after me." She loosened her fingers but kept the contact with his arm as she looked nervously over her shoulder. "Don't let anyone see us arguing, please. Let's walk."

He clenched his teeth so hard that his jaw popped. No one he knew could get him twisted up like this woman. "Thanks for finally admitting it—the lying—but I can't let it slide that you're telling me someone is looking to harm you." He glared at the miner whose eyes lingered too long on Calista as he passed. "Who's after you?"

Her hand slid forward from his arm to his wrist, as if she was seeking contact with his skin, and boy, did he ever notice when she found it. She hooked her little finger in his cuff, rubbing her pinkie against the inside of his wrist.

"It's hard for me to say this, and it's going to be even harder for you to hear, Matthew, but I can't tell you what I'm doing. You have to trust me."

They had stopped in front of the ice cream parlor. Through the gilt-painted lettering on the window, Calista could see Maisie wiping at Silas's face with a handkerchief. She'd do well to keep an eye on those two. Granny would tan Calista's hide if anything happened to Maisie.

All this family and Matthew to boot. Too many people to keep count of, and all Calista wanted to do was go back to the hotel and make a triumphant call to Mr. Pinkerton. Lila had been to Joplin, and she'd checked into the Grosman's Inn. Calista had proof now. And she had the names of people who'd signed the register next to her—Della Rush and Gerald Mason. Either of them might be a lead. She couldn't wait to talk to Pinkerton tomorrow morning.

But she also had an irate man on her hands.

"How can I trust you if I don't know everything?" Matthew asked. His head was bowed. He was watching as she traced his skin along the cuff of his sleeve.

"If you knew everything, then it wouldn't be trust," she said.

"Miss, oh, miss!" A young woman in a scandalously provocative getup was hailing her from the streetcar.

Calista could feel Matthew tense beside her. The woman bounded off the car when it slowed to go around the corner, and she ran toward Calista like her life depended on it. Only when she clutched Calista's arm did Calista recognize her as the gap-toothed girl she'd met at Dr. Stevenson's—the one she'd shown Lila's picture.

"Have you seen her?" Calista whispered, trying to get her away from Matthew. "The girl in the picture? Have you seen her?"

The girl's face fell. "No, miss. I'm sorry, but that's not why

I'm here. I was thinking about what you said about my family—thinking about going home. I told myself if I saw you again, then it was meant to be. I should just run away and go back home. I'm like to get in a heap of trouble if I'm caught, but they won't know I'm missing for an hour at least. Maybe I'm making a mistake, but when I saw you . . ." The words hung with uncertainty.

With a pained look over her shoulder that revealed Matthew's obvious interest in the conversation, Calista dug in her handbag for some bills. "You're doing the right thing," she said, and taking a pencil, she wrote on one of the bills. "Present this at the Atchison, Topeka, and Santa Fe Railway office and tell them if they have any questions to contact Graham Buchanan. They can read my signature here, and he'll know what to do. You should get a free trip home, and along the way, you can use this money for food and some decent clothes. Don't stop until you get away from here, though, you hear?"

The girl nodded, her eyes filling with tears of relief. "Thank you, miss. I won't forget you."

"It's God you should thank," Calista said. "He's the one who will see you through this. Now go, before someone else gets off that streetcar."

With a quick hug, the girl darted into an alley and headed toward the depot. Calista watched her depart, praying for her safety, and praying that she herself would be able to dodge misfortune as well.

"Another incident I'm supposed to ignore?" Matthew asked.

"It doesn't involve you," Calista replied.

"If you can't tell me what you're doing, can you tell me why?" His gaze pierced her. "Please, Calista. Give me something I can hold on to."

She'd met some nice people on her other cases, people she hadn't wanted to deceive, but no one had made it difficult like Matthew. Had Mrs. Warne, the Pinkerton agent who had worked for Calista's parents, felt alone? Did she have anyone to confide in besides the other operatives at the agency? When Calista had applied for this job, she'd known she would be sacrificing safety and comfort. She hadn't realized she'd be asked to forfeit love as well.

"The why is easy," she said. "I do it because it's the right thing to do."

"Lying is the right thing to do? Pretending to be a nurse? Whatever you were doing in the office at the Children's Home . . . that was the right thing to do? And how do you know that girl? Where would you even meet someone like her?" Taking her chin in his hand, he lifted her face to his. "Are you doing anything illegal?"

Calista felt bound by his gaze. She shook her head, aware of the heat radiating from his hand.

"Are you doing anything that would bring shame on yourself?"

This was harder to answer. She lowered her eyes, but with a tug, he forced her chin back up. There was no avoiding the question.

"The only shame involved is if people don't understand what I'm doing," she said.

"And how can they understand if you won't tell them? Why wouldn't they think you're behaving shamefully?" It was a test—not an insult, not a stab. He wasn't giving up on her, but he was demanding an answer.

"I need to think. If there was a way . . ."

She'd decided that she would tell her family once she was an official member of the agency, but what Matthew demanded was different. Even if she could tell him, to what avail? He could declare his love for her, but she wouldn't be in Joplin long. She'd be traveling around the country, never home, never free to be the wife he was undoubtedly looking for. It was better to squash this feeling before it grew.

"You know the Scripture, Parson." She took a calming breath to bolster her resolve and override the warmth of his fingers against her skin. "'A talebearer revealeth secrets: but he that is of a faithful spirit concealeth the matter.'"

The air between them sparked. She felt weightless, flimsy, and like she was being pulled toward the solidity of him.

But he didn't draw her in. Instead he responded, "'With her much fair speech she caused him to yield,'" he quoted, "'with the flattering of her lips she forced him.'"

"Forced him to do what?" she asked. The clanging of the trolley bell and other street noises were coming back into focus. How had the whole world gone silent a moment ago?

He released her. "Forced me to buy you ice cream."

"Ice cream?"

"I need something to cool me down," he said. After a long look at her, he stepped away. "On the other hand, I forgot how enthusiastically you go after an ice cream cone. If you have a hankering to do that again, it might not help me at all."

CHAPTER 15

The cousins had talked long into the night, with Maisie asking a hundred questions about Calista's siblings and wanting to hear about Calista's expensive finishing school. As much as she was able, Calista turned the conversation back to Maisie's family to avoid tripping up in her stories, and Maisie seemed eager to share. Just when Calista would think Maisie was winding down, she would pop back into Calista's room with a quilted blanket around her shoulders, spouting another clever quote from Silas that she thought would amuse Calista. Duty-bound to respond positively, Calista would lift her head from the feather pillow just long enough to emit a convincing chuckle, then let her head fall back down and wonder how much longer Maisie could go without sleep.

Finally the room was quiet, leaving Calista with her thoughts. For every smile Maisie had collected, Calista had earned a frown from Matthew. She shouldn't care. She couldn't. He was only a complication. Yes, he'd been helpful with his connections at the Children's Home, but that hadn't produced anything. If she had more time, she could accompany Mrs. Bowman to the hotels to give reports on the children, but the sand was slipping through the glass. She'd be better off chasing down her fresh discovery—actual evidence that Lila Seaton had stayed at the Grosman's Inn. And since the young lady was not traveling of her own volition, the names Della Rush and Gerald Mason needed to be investigated immediately.

Calista flipped onto her back and punched the mattress beneath her. Matthew was new to town. He wouldn't know these people. There was no reason to keep him around. No reason except the fact that she was falling in love with him.

Why couldn't he see that Calista was poor company? Why wasn't he content to let their relationship fade before it caused them both pain? She couldn't be truthful. Not to him. If he knew who she was and what she was doing, would he be able to hide, pretend, and mislead to protect her story? No, he wouldn't. Granny Laura was wily. Calista trusted her to keep their secret. It also helped that Granny was out at her ranch. But guileless Matthew wouldn't be able to sit by and let Calista do what she'd been trained to do. He would interfere and jeopardize Calista's career and Lila's safety.

The thought of being in danger with Matthew did have a romantic quality to it. She buried her head deeper into the pillow and imagined him rescuing her from the evil men who'd taken Lila. He'd rescue Lila too, but Jinxy would magically appear to take care of his daughter, leaving Calista and Matthew to share the victory alone. Matthew would take her in his arms, his heart full of how much she meant to him and how it terrified him that he might have lost her. Calista would reassure him that nothing would come between them anymore. Then they'd kiss, as Matthew finally put his restraint aside, and . . .

She must have dozed off at that part, because when Calista opened her eyes from the best and longest kiss of her imagination, sunlight was peeking through the heavy drapes. Kicking her feet out of bed, she wrestled the blankets off and hit the ground at a trot. What time was it? Mr. Pinkerton was expecting a telephone call first thing this morning.

Not thinking past the joyous news she had to report, she reached for her own wardrobe pieces. Now that she had a few names to track down, she didn't need her working girl uniform. The important thing was to get dressed quickly, and her hand fell to her white blazer suit with yellow and blue trim. She hadn't worn it yet in Joplin, but it was festive, and she felt like celebrating.

She'd slept in her stays, so a few tugs pulled them tight enough for the fitted suit. She surveyed her face as her fingers flew up the row of buttons on the blouse. Lines marred her cheek, evidence of her pillow. Puffing up her face, she tried to smooth the creases while working her foot into her boot. A few more tugs and hops, and she had everything in place. She tiptoed to her bureau and found her brush. Maisie's soft snoring continued unabated as Calista ripped the brush through her hair, only to back brush it so it would have the soft, pillowy pouf that completed her look. She patted the bouffant, then let her hand glide down her neck as she remembered Matthew touching her face.

Was he thinking of her right now? Probably not. It was the day of the baby raffle. He had more important things on his mind, and so did she.

Flipping open the lid to her jewelry case, she fished out the sapphire earrings her father had given her. They matched the blue buttons and were modest enough for day wear. No matter what the day brought, she felt more prepared and more comfortable dressed as fitted her station.

After her telephone call, she'd probably return to her room, but one never knew, so she grabbed her handbag on the way out of the room and headed toward the lobby.

The clerk's face lit up at the sight of her. "Good morning, Miss York. What are you celebrating today?"

Oh dear. Perhaps she'd misjudged the difference between her undercover clothing and her usual wardrobe. She hadn't meant to be remarkable.

"No celebration, Wilton. I just aired out some of the outfits at the bottom of my trunk, that's all."

"Saving the best for last, eh?"

"If you say so. May I trouble you for the use of your telephone? My father is expecting a call from me this morning."

"Be my guest." He stepped out of the way, clearing the path for her to access the office.

Calista rattled the receiver and waited to hear the operator's voice. Robert Pinkerton had long ago registered his phone in the name of Robert Bluingship, knowing that his operatives wouldn't be able to call him otherwise. One whiff that someone in Joplin was calling the Pinkerton office in Chicago, and that telephone operator would have the juiciest gossip short of the mayor's renegade son.

"Connecting to Robert Bluingship in Chicago . . . please hold."

Calista looked over her shoulder to check the doorway, but no one was around. Mr. Pinkerton's eager answer told her that he'd been anticipating news from her.

"Daughter, so good to hear from you. Everything is well, I hope."

"Yes, sir. Very good. I was surprised to see that a friend of mine has been in town."

There was a pause. "That's excellent. Have you seen her?"

"No, but I found her on a guest registry at a hotel. She checked into the Grosman's Inn on October twenty-fourth. I don't know where she went after that, but it's a start."

"That's fantastic. The rest of the family will be interested to know."

It wasn't fantastic, but it was something. Mr. Pinkerton over the wire was much more the enthusiast than Mr. Pinkerton in the office. When conversing over the line, everyone had a role they played.

"Do you know if she was traveling with anyone?" he asked.

"There were names above and below hers. You should tell her father and see if he knows them. The first name is—"

"Wait," Pinkerton interrupted. "Why don't you wait to share that news in person?"

Calista looked over her shoulder at the empty doorway. "Are you expecting me back in Chicago?" she whispered.

"Your friend here has asked me to give you one more week for your vacation. You have that much time, and then you can share what information you have with your . . . brother, when he comes to fetch you."

Her stomach dropped. One week? He wasn't giving her more time?

"Yes, sir. I should have everything we need by then. I'm working diligently on it." And she was. Having Matthew and Maisie around was like trying to run while shackled, but Calista was doing her best.

"Let's talk tomorrow morning," he said. "Be careful, and your mother says hello."

That was always the last thing he said, just in case someone had forgotten the fiction that they were family. Calista's mother hadn't said hello in weeks. Not over the telephone. She'd always addressed her telegraphs and letters to a dummy office that Mr. Pinkerton had set up in St. Louis. Then the letters were forwarded to Calista to hide her location from her parents. That, along with the falsehood that the sick friend she was nursing didn't own a telephone and there wasn't one in the vicinity, had kept her activities well hidden. Now that Granny had told them that Calista was in Joplin and under her care, they had no further concerns. Her mother could turn her attention fully to Corban and Evangelina. Then again, her mother's attention tended to flit around. But just as you thought she wasn't attending, you'd find out you'd been under surveillance all along.

Her cousins were much the same way. Calista had just replaced the receiver when Amos spoke up.

"The clerk told me you were in here. Who were you talking to?"

Calista spun around before answering, "My friend." She crossed her fingers behind her back, a habit she'd developed at Granny's. "It's been a misery leaving her to convalesce alone, but her recovery is progressing." She stepped around Amos to escape to the lobby. "What are you doing in town? Is Maisie going back to the ranch?"

"Pa said he could spare me today, and Ma admired the idea of me checking in on you girls. She said Aunt Polly would do the same for us if we were up in Kansas City."

And that was the problem with loving, responsible, extended family members. A Kentworth didn't have only one set of parents, but a whole tribe of elders looking out after them. And when the elders weren't doing the job, the cousins were more than happy to make nuisances of themselves.

"You're welcome to go upstairs and get Maisie." Calista was glad she'd brought her handbag down already. "I was just going out to get some breakfast."

But the elevator doors chose that moment to part and reveal Maisie. She clutched her skirt and took an exaggerated step over the threshold. The elevator operator smirked until Calista shot him a dirty look. He hurriedly pressed the button and closed the doors, causing Maisie to dart forward and tuck her hips beneath her.

"Did you see that?" she crowed. "Those doors nearly caught my tail feathers."

"You don't have to jump out of it," Calista said. "It stops for you."

Maisie's round eyes grew even rounder. "Have you looked down the crack between the floor and the elevator? It goes down deeper than a well."

Her brother laughed. "You aren't going to fall through that crack. You wouldn't fit even if we pushed and shoved. You're more substantial than that."

"Maybe, but I don't want to chance it. No use lingering." For being dead asleep and snoring less than half an hour ago, Maisie was remarkably chipper.

"Couldn't agree more," Amos said. "Calista was on her way to breakfast. Do we want to join her?"

"I haven't had a decent breakfast since coming to town." Maisie pinched her waistband and stretched it away from her stomach. "No eggs, sausage, or Ma's biscuits and gravy. It's no wonder I'm afeared of falling through cracks."

"Actually, I was going to the bakery," Calista said. "Their croissants are so light and fluffy—"

Maisie snorted. "Heavy and solid beats light and fluffy every day. It's time you took me to a real restaurant."

But Amos wasn't sold. "Do they have cinnamon rolls? I've got a hankering for a cinnamon roll."

"Follow me," Calista said, and before Maisie had stopped pouting, they each had a warm baked good in hand and were back on the sidewalk.

"Where to now, ladies?" Amos ripped off a steamy layer of his buttery roll.

"We're going to the Carnegie Library," said Maisie. "That's where Silas is going to be. You just have to meet him, Amos."

The Carnegie Library? What business did Maisie have there? But then dread settled in Calista's stomach as she remembered. The baby raffle. That was at the library. If left up to her, she wouldn't want to be within a hundred miles of that place, but something compelled her. This event burdened Matthew. The decision today would weigh on him, and she didn't want him to suffer alone. Although he'd been an inconvenience—underfoot and overbearing at every turn—he had good intentions. He'd been the best friend she had in Joplin, and something told her that he felt the same way about her. Against his better judgment.

"Who is Silas?" Amos asked.

"He's a miner," Maisie answered. "Gonna be rich ere long. Already has a house built and a lease of his own. Just waiting for the right time to settle down."

Calista arched an eyebrow. They'd had some productive conversations, if Silas had already spilled the beans on his plans. Not that Calista should be surprised. Maisie was as guileless and enthusiastic as a puppy. When the right man came along, she'd waste no time making him beg, but Calista wasn't sure that Silas was the right man. He didn't hold a candle to Matthew. Matthew was Silas's superior in every area, except maybe for agreeableness. But what did it matter? She had too much sense to dwell on him. Didn't she?

According to the advertisement nailed on the notice board, the raffle was being held at ten o'clock, but when they reached the Carnegie Library at half past nine, there were already people flocking toward the building.

"What's going on?" Amos pushed the brim of his hat back so he could get a better look at the variety of people gathering.

"They're raffling off a baby from the Children's Home," Calista said. "Someone is going home with a child."

Amos gawked at the nervous crowd as Maisie giggled. "Can you imagine?" she said. "Wouldn't that be the worst surprise ever? 'Congratulations, ma'am. Here's the baby you won today.'"

"As Granny Laura would say, '*I never did hear tell the like*,'" Amos said. "What is the world coming to?"

Rather than go through the explanation of what made it unsavory and the financial benefits that it would bring regardless, Calista looked for Matthew. She really didn't have time for this. More than anything, she wanted to sleuth out the two names on either side of Lila Seaton's entry in the registry. That was what she should be doing, but once this was behind her, she could spend the rest of the day looking after her case.

Her cousins followed her inside the library but wandered toward the ticket table, where Silas was standing. Calista spotted Matthew alone, leaning on a sandstone column, looking glum.

She hurried to him, wishing it was permissible to give him a big hug. Well, in Joplin nearly anything was permissible, but not to Matthew. Instead, she rubbed his arm like she might a hurt child . . . as long as it wasn't bleeding.

"How are you doing?" she asked.

"Miserably," he answered. "Only started work this week, and I had to ask off to be here. I just had to see it with my own eyes."

"Remember Moses. God had a plan for him, even when he was ripped from his home."

"But these aren't pagan Egyptians. These people claim to be Christians, but they don't see anything wrong in supporting this travesty."

Mr. Blount hammered against the side of a bell at the ticket table, silencing the room. "Ladies and gentlemen, only ten minutes left to purchase your tickets. No more tickets will be sold at five till. Don't wait. This is a once-in-a-lifetime opportunity." He set down the bell, then stepped away from the table to shake hands with Mr. Holly, the owner of the paint factory. From their smiles and puffed chests, it was obvious they felt the campaign had been a success. Calista dearly hoped so. Since Matthew could do nothing to prevent it, it might as well help the kids and the home.

"Thanks," Matthew said.

"For what?"

"For being nice. I know you don't understand my complaint, yet you're acting like you care."

"I understand," she said. "I understand your heart and how much you care, and that's what makes me care. If you'd seen the things I've seen over the last few months, you might not think a baby being won by a family that wants it is the worst thing that could happen to it."

"The things that you've seen?" He pushed off the column to stand before her. "You know, last night I did some thinking. I went through all the things you've said and done that you didn't have any reason for. All the things you said that ended up not being true, all the decisions you made that seemed random, and spontaneous, and senseless. I went over it all, and I came up with a limited number of possibilities."

Calista forced a smile. "I'm flattered that you were thinking of me."

"I decided either you are insane and honestly have no control over yourself, or you're involved in criminal enterprise and can't disclose what you're up to."

"Insane or a criminal?" She threaded her fingers together. "My goodness. I'm flattered."

"The only other option, and it's so unlikely that I sound crazy suggesting it, is that you're involved in some secret law enforcement activity. Could it be for a private citizen who's hired you to investigate someone? It could be that the Joplin police department is involved, or maybe you're one of those operatives from that famous agency in Illinois."

Calista's mouth went dry. The blood had drained from her face, and her heart was pumping furiously to keep from drowning in it. She'd never been exposed before. How had he figured it out?

"It's time, folks. The moment is here," Mr. Blount called. "Bring the child to me, and let's see who the lucky winner is."

"You must be kidding me," Calista said. "A female agent? Who ever heard of such a thing . . ."

But Matthew was looking over her head. His jaw tightened, and he started breathing as hard as she was. Mrs. Fairfield from the Children's Home stepped forward holding a happy baby boy. He was in a ribboned white gown, sucking on his fist. He stared back at the audience, wondering at all the attention he was receiving. When one well-heeled lady smiled and waved at him, his face split into a smile, and his legs began pumping, eliciting sighs of approval from the crowd.

"We have a winner! Some lucky lady is going to be a mother today."

But Calista couldn't care less, because as soon as this event was over, she had to face Matthew's questions or avoid him completely. If he persisted, she'd have to admit to Mr. Pinkerton that she'd been discovered, and that would be the last straw. He'd recall her and probably end her employment.

Unless she could solicit Matthew's cooperation and get him to promise not to interfere. She couldn't let him or anyone else get in her way.

Interrupting her thoughts was Mr. Blount's announcement. He held the paper before him. "And the winner is . . . Miss Calista York."

CHAPTER
16

Calista's jaw dropped. There must be some mistake. She hadn't bought a ticket.

Across the room, she could see Amos doubled over, holding his stomach. Maisie was wiping tears from her eyes as she made her way toward Calista. No one else in the room had spotted her yet, or maybe they didn't know who she was. Instead, the people were talking, scanning the crowd, waiting for someone to step forward.

Maisie grabbed Calista's arm and fell across it, breathless with laughter. "I can't believe it worked. Amos bought the ticket, saying it'd be a hoot if you were stuck with the baby, but I never in a hundred years thought that you'd win it."

"You put my name in the drawing?"

The Elks were huddled over the slip of paper, probably debating what they'd do if the winner wasn't present.

Maisie laughed. "Remember when Pa told you that you'd bought that duck at the auction? You were fiddling with your hair, and he told you that you'd bid without knowing it, and that you were left with a duck to take care of? Wait until he hears about this! We outdid him, for sure."

"This is not a duck," Calista growled. "They must draw another name. I have to tell them." She pushed Maisie's hands off her arms, but before she could get away, Matthew pulled her back.

"You can't do that, Calista. Think about it." His face was drawn, intense.

"I am thinking about it. I don't want a baby. I said that from the beginning."

"If you don't take him, they'll draw another name."

"Good. That's what they need to do." She tugged against him, but his grip held firm.

"But who will they draw? Will it be the right family? This could be the Moses story. It could be that God wants this child with you, and that's why He had your cousin put your name in the drawing." His words were coming fast, trying to convince her even as the crowd was starting to grumble.

"You can't blame God for what Amos did. Amos isn't getting off scot-free."

"Listen. Listen to me, listen to God. Stop thinking about your cousin. Stop doubting that God can fix this. Just ask what the right thing to do is."

Through the hubbub, Calista stilled. She felt annoyance, anger, assurance that this wasn't fair to her and that she'd done nothing to deserve this complication, but also resignation. Matthew was right. She always prayed that God would guide her steps. In her heart, she knew she couldn't walk away.

Her eyes flicked up to Matthew's. This was a disastrous complication. It would delay her search. It would frustrate her progress. It would keep Lila in the hands of her abductors for even longer. Calista had to save Lila, but maybe she was saving this child as well.

"Thank you," she said. *Thanks for making me do what I didn't want to do. Thanks for making me be a better person than I want to be today.* It was a hard thanks to give, but it was the kind of thanks that was best given while one still had the grace to give it.

She took a deep breath, straightened her shoulders, and turned.

"I'm Calista York," she said, and strode toward the woman holding the baby.

⁓⁓⁓⁓

Matthew's bad day had just gotten worse. He'd failed to stop this outrage from taking place. He'd braced himself for the defeat. He'd prepared himself for the sorrow but had determined that he'd see it through, knowing that once it was behind him, he could pray for the child, then turn his attention to other issues.

Finding out that the child was now in the hands of a mysterious young lady with no parenting experience and questionable morals wasn't the worst. The worst was that he was the one responsible for making her keep the child. Far from having the distasteful incident behind him as he'd expected, now he was going to be tangled up in it for . . . how long could this go on?

"You're Miss York?" Blount's scarred brow wrinkled as he looked her over. "I suppose you have the means to raise this child?"

Where had she gotten that dress? It was fancier than anything Matthew had seen her in before. But from her carelessness with money and her residence at the Keystone, Matthew had always assumed she was well-funded. People who had to check their pockets and count their change before buying something didn't spend like Calista.

"I have funds, yes," she answered.

Mr. Blount looked at the other Elks before asking, "Are you married? Do you have any references?"

"I'm not married, but as for references, I'm the granddaughter of Albert and Laura Kentworth."

Instant respect appeared on their faces. If that wasn't enough, Mrs. Fairfield said, "And she's volunteered at the Children's Home in the past weeks." Nothing was said about her locking herself in an office, but perhaps Matthew was the only one who knew about that.

199

"That settles it." Mr. Blount motioned for Mrs. Bowman to bring the baby closer. "Attention, citizens of Joplin. We have our winner here. Miss Calista York. We congratulate her on winning, and thank you all for participating in our little contest. Keep in mind that we have other children available for adoption, so if you didn't win today, you could still be parents. Help the Children's Home feed and care for Joplin's disadvantaged."

Everyone waited expectantly as Mrs. Bowman put the baby into Calista's arms. Calista's face went tight, but she managed a pained smile. The baby boy drew back his head to look at her in puzzlement, then searched for a familiar face, reaching out when he saw Mrs. Bowman. Calista juggled him awkwardly to keep him from bounding out of her arms, crushing the pleated collar of her suit in the process.

"We have paper work here for you to sign, which we'll file to finalize the adoption." Mrs. Fairfield directed Calista to the table. "And the Elks would like to get a picture of you and the child. Their national organization always likes to hear about their efforts to improve our community, and this will be of great interest to them."

Matthew's thoughts were broiling as Calista took the child, then dutifully lined up with the preening men. With chests puffed out, they faced the photographer as if they'd accomplished a great and mighty feat, but all they'd done was take money from lonely families, and now those families were all disappointed. The person who'd won was the most disappointed of all.

Why were people staying? They seemed to want to be acknowledged by Calista or the child. They waited as if there was going to be a demonstration of her fitness for them. Or maybe they were loath to say good-bye? Maybe some had already considered the child their own and couldn't stand to leave him.

Another reason Matthew had hated the idea of the contest from the beginning.

"This is quite a surprise, Matthew." Reverend Dixon patted him on the back. "I thought you were against anyone participating in this carnival, but here your friend Miss York won."

And now he was tainted by association. Matthew's annoyance notched up another spoke. No one had prepared him for the messes that one could get into while trying to do ministry.

"I was taken by surprise, I promise."

"But, see, some good has come of this. A child might help our friend Miss York settle down. As far as the child is concerned, it could've found itself in a worse situation."

Help Calista settle down? What was her pastor implying? "What do you know about Miss York's activities?" Matthew asked.

Reverend Dixon took a step backward. "I'm not speculating. She's a fine young lady and never has given me any reason to doubt her sincerity."

"But . . ." Matthew prodded.

"But nothing." The reverend tucked his hands beneath his arms. "I think her heart is in the right place. Beyond that, I can't judge."

Matthew's guess was that Calista's pastor assumed her to be as flighty as she'd first appeared to him. He probably hadn't thought about it any further. It was only Matthew who was kept up at night wondering about her.

"If you mean to suggest that the raffle was a success because a member of your congregation won," Matthew said, "I have to disagree. From the beginning I was promised that they would carefully screen all applicants and wouldn't let the baby go to an unfit home. As much as I enjoy Miss York's company, I think this proves that they've failed in their duty. Miss York doesn't have a home, a husband, or any experience with children. The charitable inclinations of this town have been misguided. The outcome is a disaster."

"Do you think it's out of the question that Miss York might have a home and husband ere long?"

The heat flooding Matthew's face wasn't welcome. "That's not your concern." And because there was nothing stronger he could say without having to apologize for it later, he left to join Calista.

The newspaper men and the photographer had finished their tasks. Calista's face had lost all its cheer. The lines around her mouth made her look a decade older. Women surrounded her, some giving her a friendly hug, but most wanting a chance to evaluate her.

"She doesn't have the first clue what to do with the baby," a woman with the beginning of silver streaks at her temples said to her friend. "It'll be back at the Children's Home before long."

"Did you see her friends laughing at her? They think it's a joke," her friend replied. "It makes me ill to consider the child's future. I can't bear it." To emphasize her point, she headed to the door, but not without walking slowly by Calista to make sure her disapproval was recognized.

Even with a dozen hands pulling on her and the child she was holding, Calista didn't miss the judgment in the eyes of the women leaving. She repositioned the baby on her hip and glared right back—proud and strong even though she was lost and afloat.

She'd endured enough. Matthew cleared a path to her and held his arms out for the child. Coming in as a party to this disgraceful event might forever taint his reputation, but he wasn't going to leave her to the wolves.

Lifting the baby high on his chest, he pulled it out of reach of the crowd. The women stepped back, affording him more distance than they'd given Calista.

"Let's go," he said and marched to the door, ignoring the questioning looks from all the men he'd challenged over the raffle.

Maisie and Amos fell in line next to Calista.

"What are you going to do?" It was finally dawning on Maisie that the consequences for their prank wouldn't be easily corrected.

"I'm going to take him to my room and collect my thoughts," said Calista. "But no mistake, I'll deal with you later."

"You have to admit, this is the best prank ever," Amos said. "You'll be hard-pressed to come up with a better."

Matthew's head was going to explode. Fortunately, Calista intervened before he lost his temper.

"Amos Kentworth, I have half a mind to head straight to your parents and leave this little bundle of joy with your ma to raise. What do you think she'd say about that?"

Funny how her refined city accent roughed up when her cousins needed a talking-to.

"No call for that," Amos said. "We didn't know you were going to win. Just your bad luck."

Seeing the growing tension, smooth-talking Silas stepped forward. "Have y'all been to Lakeside Park? Why don't we get some food and go out there? It's likely to be hot in town, but the breezes coming off the water . . ."

Maisie and Amos quickly agreed, leaving with injured looks in Calista's direction.

"That's a fine how-de-do. They buy me a baby, then run off to play at the lake," she fumed.

"I'm not running off, Calista. I'm here."

Her head snapped his direction, but her gaze softened as it traveled from the baby to him.

"What's its name?" She stopped on the sidewalk, oblivious to the attention they were attracting from the crowd leaving the library.

"His name is Howard. Howie, if you like." Matthew looked both ways. "Let's go somewhere private and decide what to do."

"Miss York?" The young nursemaid from the Children's Home ran down the steps to reach them, bouncing a modest bundle against her side. "Here are a few of his things. Mrs. Fairfield told me to include one outfit, but with all the money this little chap raised for the home, I figured we could spare some diapers and food as well."

Calista's eyes grew big. Matthew looked away, knowing who she would blame with each and every diaper she changed.

"Thank you, Mrs. Bowman," she said. "What sort of food is he accustomed to?"

"Oatmeal, milk, mashed potatoes, cooked carrots. He has a good start on teeth, so he'll be wanting more solid food soon. I'm sure you already know all this . . ."

"Let's pretend I don't. What else can you tell me?" Calista said.

"He's a quick one. Scampers around like a kitten. Puts everything in his mouth. Is used to going to sleep without rocking, so don't spoil him if you want it easy. That's about it. I don't know if you'll find time to come back to the Children's Home now—"

"Yes, I will—"

"—but if you have any more questions, come find me." Mrs. Bowman smiled up at Howie. "I'm glad he's going to have some good parents now." She looked from Calista to Matthew, then her face turned pink. "At least, I hope he will soon."

Matthew avoided Calista's gaze, already knowing this would be the assumption of many in town. "Thank you for your help, Mrs. Bowman. Don't you worry, we'll be looking for you soon."

Her youthful face beamed. "I hope so. Good luck."

Calista pulled the brim of her hat lower against all the curious stares until they passed through the ornate brass double doors of the Keystone. Howie spotted the fish tank and watched it as Matthew carried him past. The elevator operator looked just as curious as Howie when his doors opened on Calista and Matthew fussing with the child.

"Back so soon, Miss York?" His eyes asked questions he'd been warned never to voice to customers.

Her tight-lipped smile was the only answer she gave. Matthew felt a growl wanting to let loose from his chest. What could she say? *This isn't my baby. I won him in a contest that I never entered.* He wanted to grab all those self-satisfied benefactors by the neckcloths and show them the trouble they'd brought about with this ridiculous idea. He'd been the only one to see the danger in this stunt, but he and Calista were still caught by the consequences.

They'd reached her room, but they hadn't reached the end to this madness.

Calista rushed inside and pulled off her white-ruffled suit coat. Dropping it on a table, she pulled the pearl-tipped hatpin out of her hair and tossed her hat on the sofa. She tilted her head back to release the tension in her neck, but finding that it was useless, she turned her frustration on Matthew as she still gripped the hatpin.

"I went along with your plan. Now, how do we get out of this?"

Matthew frowned at the pin in his face. He bent and put Howie on the ground before addressing her. "I'm thinking about it."

The baby immediately flipped on its stomach. Grabbing a handful of the tassels that lined the edge of the rug, he stretched them to his mouth.

"Surely you have someone back home who has room for the kid," Calista said. "Your mother? A married sister?"

"Nobody comes to mind. People in my neck of the woods already have enough kids underfoot. They aren't looking for another mouth to feed."

"Neither was I."

"This is exactly why the raffle was a bad idea."

"Now you're giving me an I-told-you-so? It was your idea for me to accept him!" Calista reached for her hat. "I'm taking him back. That's all there is to it. I have a job to do—"

"Ah, yes. And what would that job be?"

Blast that cocky tilt of his head. He had her over a barrel, and he knew it.

He took a seat on her blue-and-white sofa like he had no plans to leave. "You never told me which of my guesses was right."

"Your guesses . . ." She was buying time, and he seemed to know it.

"Either you are a compulsive liar, insane, doing something illegal, or you are involved in some kind of investigation. Is it one of those, or is there another possibility that I missed?"

From the frying pan to the fire. With a tug to adjust her fitted skirt, Calista dropped to the floor with her back to Matthew and dangled a bracelet in front of Howie. "If you *are* right, what possible good can come of you knowing?"

From the corner of her eye, she saw his foot slide forward until it was next to her. "It would do a great deal of good. It would help me decide once and for all whether you are someone I can trust."

"I trust you."

"But not enough to handle the truth?"

Howie crawled into her lap. He really was a beautiful child, even if he was gumming the thick beads of her bracelet. He lurched, throwing his weight into her and causing her to bump against Matthew's leg. Remembering his Scripture on seductive women, she started to straighten, but Matthew caught her shoulder and drew her against him. With a strong hand, he kneaded the base of her neck.

"I'm demanding. I have high expectations for myself and for others." His low, country voice was as soothing as his touch. "In most cases, I'd bide my time, wait and see what you were all about. Time would show whether you were playing me false or if you were answering to a higher purpose. But I don't have time. I need to know now."

Her eyes were closed as she surrendered to his treatment. "Why now?"

"Because I'm falling in love with you."

He'd stopped massaging her neck, but his hand remained on her shoulder. Every movement, every sound in the room had amplified—from her coursing heartbeat pounding in her ears, to the slurping baby.

Matthew loved her. It was simple, pure, and what she'd wanted from first knowing him. But could she accept his love?

Calista laid her head on his knee. Sensing the change in the room, Howie quieted as Matthew stroked her hair. Having the baby to hold was the only thing keeping her from crawling into Matthew's lap. Drat the kid.

Her emotions warred with her ambition. Telling him the truth was taking another step away from her instructions, another infraction that could cost her this job. Or maybe Mr. Pinkerton would understand that she'd already been discovered, and it was better to bring Matthew in as an ally instead of keeping him at arm's length.

He wasn't at arm's length. He was much closer than that.

"You were right. I work for the Pinkerton Agency," she said, "and it's against the rules to tell you anything. I only said it because you figured it out on your own. But you can't get involved. You haven't been trained."

Operatives had to improvise on the field. Telling Matthew something he'd already figured out for himself didn't mean anything. It didn't mean she was choosing him over her calling. It didn't mean she was professing any affection that she'd have to later deny.

"I have an honest-to-goodness Pinkerton Agent here?" His hand was warm on her shoulder.

Calista would be lying if she didn't admit that she liked the awe the title inspired. "I've just started and am still on probation. That's why you can't say anything. My job is precarious."

"They sent a beginner on a dangerous case like this?"

"It's not dangerous. Not really. The only danger is that a friend would get caught up in it."

"I don't believe you. I've seen you at work. I've seen you in the liquor shops. Don't forget, I've saved your hide on occasion. You are in danger."

She sat up and twisted around to look up at him. "Do you know Lila Seaton? Gerald Mason or Della Rush?"

"No. I'm as new to town as you are."

"Have you seen this girl?" She stretched to reach her handbag and handed him the picture.

"I don't have a good memory for faces, but she doesn't look familiar."

"Then you can't help me. Besides, you have your own work. It'd be a waste of your time to follow me around."

"A pity."

"But a reality. The best thing for you to do is to put away your concerns. Don't fret over my daily activities. Pretend I'm spending my time shopping and socializing, and then in the evening, we can have time to ourselves."

"You're forgetting someone."

Calista played with wisps of Howie's hair. "You have a goal, a future you're working toward, but I do too. It's important, and that's why I can't keep him. You have to watch him."

"I'm at the mine tomorrow. I can't take him there."

Her eyes narrowed. "You didn't plan this just to keep me from doing my job, did you?"

"I didn't buy the ticket, did I?"

"My stinkin' cousins. I should have Maisie watch him during the day. That would serve her right."

"Do you trust Maisie with a baby?"

"Good point. Then who?" she asked.

"I'll find someone. I'll ask around for names of those who entered the contest. Give me a week. I promise, if you can provide for him until then, I'll fix this for you. Trust me, Calista. There's more to this than we know. Just think how many tickets were sold, and your name was only on one. God is doing something here. Just be patient."

God was doing something. He'd brought her to a man she could spend the rest of her life with, had she had a different life. Was God testing her resolve? But now that Matthew knew about her job, would he still want to share her company?

Doubtful, because already Calista was thinking of how she could use a baby to enhance her disguises and find Lila Seaton. Matthew would never approve.

CHAPTER
17

Her time was limited. When the newspaper published the picture of her and Howie, Calista would lose her chance to pose as an unwed mother. Everyone in town would recognize her as the winner of the raffle. But she had today, and all it would take was one productive conversation to lead her to Lila Seaton.

Today was the first time she'd put on a disguise in Joplin. Yes, she'd dressed in varying degrees of respectability, but she had never tried to hide her features. Today was a different story. After leaving the Keystone lobby, she borrowed the washroom at the library to turn her skirt inside out to the rough, stained fabric she'd kept hidden until now. She rubbed vermilion powder into her hairline to redden it, then set a battered cap atop to hide her untouched dark locks.

Disguising Howie was simple. He dirtied his clothes automatically, so staining them wasn't necessary. Hiding his shoes and socks in her bag, she brushed some charcoal powder on his bare feet and legs. Howie wiggled his toes and laughed at the feel of the brush on his soles. Of course, he looked too well fed and happy to be starving, but he would have to do. She didn't have time to find a more miserable child.

Tucking her tools into a moth-eaten bag, Calista kept her head down as she dodged her way out of the library, praying that no one who saw her go in would see the difference when she came out. Keeping her shoulders hunched around the child, she hurried toward the first set of hotels she wanted to target. Since it was Friday morning, there wouldn't be many girls out, but their customers wouldn't be interfering either. Talking to the girls unobserved was her best chance.

She slowed as she walked past the Grosman's Inn. This was her second visit, and she'd yet to see anyone who looked like they were in the trade, but it was where Lila's signature was, so she had to start here.

Howie kicked his feet excitedly as a horse huffed from where it was tied at the post.

"You see the pony?" Calista cooed, then wondered what had come over her. Howie was a nuisance, not a pet. But then he gurgled a chuckle, and Calista's day felt brighter because of his smile.

Calista edged her way around the front of the hotel to the side alley, where two girls were huddled over a lit match. The tallest one looked her way before getting back to lighting her cigarillo. The shorter one smiled through smeared makeup, then hurriedly took her turn with the match. They looked friendly enough.

Calista stepped unsteadily forward, not finding it hard to adopt a vulnerable attitude. "Do you have one to spare?" she asked, knowing that if her family caught her in that alley, it wouldn't matter if she was smoking. She'd still be hung out to dry.

Calista saw the hesitation in their eyes. She dropped her bag and hoisted Howie higher on her hip. "It's okay. I need a place to stay more than I need a smoke."

As expected, the girls couldn't keep their eyes off Howie. The shorter one offered him a grimy finger, which he grasped with delight. "How old?" she asked.

Calista had forgotten to make note of that. "Ten months . . ."

she ventured. "I came looking for his no-account father, but he's hit the trail. I don't know how I'm going to feed the baby now."

The shorter girl looked her up and down. "A filthy gin-drinker, I'd wager. Told you he'd take care of everything, didn't he?" She spat before popping the cigarillo into her mouth and grumbling around it. "Ain't that the way of it?"

Very likely it was the truth of Howie's story. Calista held his head to her shoulder with a sudden affection she hadn't expected. "I have a friend," she said. "If I could find her, she said she might could get me some work. Would you happen to know her? Her name is Lila."

Unless they were very skilled at deception, they were telling the truth when they shook their heads.

The taller girl exhaled a thin plume of smoke. "Never heard of a Lila. Sometimes the girls change their names, though."

The short girl nodded. "But ask around if you need work. You'd have to find somewhere for the baby to stay, but there's work to be found. No gal as pretty as you is going to starve in this town."

Calista noted their lanky frames and the unhealthy pallor of their skin. They were so much more valuable than their next meal, but they didn't know that. If only she had work she could offer them that didn't destroy their hearts. But she couldn't do that. She was on a mission, and it didn't involve saving every lost girl—just Jinxy's daughter.

"Thanks," Calista said. "I'll keep looking."

She picked up her bag, but she couldn't walk away. It was breaking the rules, both the agency's and her own, but it couldn't be helped.

"If you're ever hungry on a Saturday night, I know where there's a free meal," she said. "Go around behind Trochet's Flowers by the greenhouse. It's a safe place for girls like us. You'll be well fed."

Now that she thought about it, she should contribute some

money to Matthew's funds, in case the girls came. They'd want more than the dreadful pickle sandwiches.

But they shook their heads. "Not on Saturday night." The tall girl kept her eyes on the ground. "That's when we get the best pay."

It had been worth the effort. With a sad smile, Calista nodded her understanding and wondered how Howie felt twenty pounds heavier as she walked away.

Matthew walked in the shadow of the chat piles and past the miner's camp he'd begun to think of as a second home. It was Friday, and he'd come to work carrying foodstuffs to distribute on his way back to town. By now, many of the miners would be running low on supplies. The sack of bread and beans he lugged over his shoulder would help them make it through the end of the week. Then tomorrow was payday, and maybe with some skill and self-control, they'd be able to stretch out their funds for longer than seven days.

He also wanted to check with some of the miners' wives about looking after Howie. Mrs. Campbell was his first thought. She'd been dragging lately, and Matthew thought the upkeep of a child might brighten her day. Who knew? Women seemed to set store by such things.

As much as he'd like for Calista to stay safely in her hotel, he recognized the zeal in her eyes. It was the same fervor he felt about his vocation. He couldn't oppose her. He might not approve of every decision she made in pursuing her case, but he understood her motives.

All he could think about was seeing her again. He'd told her how he felt—or how he could feel, if she gave him a chance—and she hadn't turned from him. In fact, the pull between them had grown even stronger.

The first friendly stake Matthew reached after work was Silas's.

He called his friend's name, but the shack only echoed back his empty call. Matthew looked around, but Silas wasn't at his lease. It didn't look like he'd been there all day, in fact. When a miner took a claim, he couldn't predict how it would produce. Silas had been one of the lucky ones. Knowing him, he'd probably already made enough money for the week and had quit, never considering that he could put some by for a rainy day. Yep, that sounded like Silas.

Continuing on, Matthew headed toward Dan and Loretta's claim. He looked in vain for their tent, then saw them kneeling on the ground, wrapping the canvas around their belongings.

"What's this?" Matthew asked. "You'uns pulling up stakes?"

"We are." Dan kept his eyes down as he pulled the rope tight around the bundle. "Our lease is up, and we're going to move farther afield. Try our luck at another spot. This one has given us nothing but sorrow."

Loretta turned her tear-splotched face away from Matthew. He had comforting words ready, but from the looks of it, she'd rather do her mourning alone. Matthew picked up a spade and pickax and put them in the Campbell's pull cart. He didn't know what to say, but his hands could help with the heavy work. Loretta wandered away, straightening some smaller housewares while he helped Dan lift the tent and poles into the cart.

"I guess they had that raffle yesterday," Dan said. He was bent beneath the side of the cart, tying his ore bucket onto the side.

"Yes, they did. It was surprising—"

"Then the babe won't be going back to the Children's Home?" Dan grunted as he pulled one rope tight, then bent for another bucket.

"Um, no. It doesn't look like it." Matthew's eyes flickered over to Loretta. She wasn't even pretending to work but stood staring at the gray piles of chat dotting the horizon. He wouldn't ask her to look after the child. Not now. Remembering his errand, he reached for his bag. "I happen to have some vittles along. If you would help me lighten my load—I don't want to carry them all back to town."

Dan wiped his nose with the back of his hand. "Mighty kind of you. And when we get back on our feet, we won't forget what you've done for us."

"I want to see where your new claim is. I might as well help move this stuff over." Instead of waiting for permission, Matthew lifted the handles of the cart and waited for Dan to point the way.

"I'm optimistic that this next claim will earn out," Dan said. "Gotta keep up my spirits for Loretta. She's made of stern stuff, but we've had a rough go of it. Many hungry days and miserable nights we've suffered already."

"By God's grace, those are behind you."

"Pray so. We don't need much. We're simple folks, but we can't put rocks in our bellies. We gotta have food."

It was exactly what Mr. Blount had said at the Children's Home. Matthew looked again at Dan and tried to picture him cleaned up, fleshed out, and wearing a tailored suit. It seemed impossible that Mr. Blount had been in the same situation less than ten years ago. Now he owned a mine, employed dozens, and lacked for nothing. The speediness with which his life had changed must have made Mr. Blount's head spin. No wonder he didn't have all the niceties down. No wonder he tended toward coarseness and vulgarity. He was still learning his way.

Much like Matthew was still learning his.

"Don't forget, tomorrow night after the settlement, you and Loretta come on over, and we'll break bread."

Dan nodded. "We'll be there. Could use the prayer. The cloud of discouragement has been hanging over our heads for quite a spell."

Matthew understood. Sometimes the way the world worked didn't make any sense at all.

After parting with the Campbells, Matthew walked to the flower store, reflecting on how quickly he could get discouraged as well. Unlike Silas and Dan, every workday he was at the beck and call of the company whistle summoning him to work. He turned his face up to the sun. How would he manage day after day, two hundred feet below the surface? It wouldn't get any easier, but if that was where the people were, that was where he needed to be.

Whither shall I go from thy spirit? or whither shall I flee from thy presence? If I ascend up into heaven, thou art there: if I make my bed in hell, behold, thou art there. If I take the wings of the morning, and dwell in the uttermost parts of the sea; even there shall thy hand lead me, and thy right hand shall hold me.

It was natural to have misgivings about the job that had taken his uncle's health, but if that was what God required, Matthew had better count on obeying. How was it, though, that giving up his life seemed an easier sacrifice than giving up on Calista? The woman loitering by the Delilah Inn had brought Calista to mind, though she was far rougher and more common than Calista. If her twice-turned-out skirt and crushed hat didn't tell her story, the way her head drooped forward as if expecting to be boxed declared to the world that she'd met her share of trouble, as had the three women she was talking with. And her with a baby too.

Matthew stopped on the sidewalk. It wasn't possible. The clothing, the posture, the hair color—every outer sign said it was a stranger, but Matthew knew that child. With a quick look for wagons, he stalked across the street to the cluster of women.

The woman with cropped, dirty-blond hair saw him first. She stepped out of the grouping and gave him such a speculative smile that he wanted to hurl his dinner. Matthew remembered when he'd thought prostitutes must be the most beautiful women in the world to succeed. How naive he'd been. The ones he'd seen on the streets were more likely to elicit pity than temptation. And here Calista was trying to blend in with them. Why?

Too late, Matthew remembered Calista's warning that he could put her in danger. Too late did he consider that his appearance might cause her trouble instead of rescuing her. She'd trusted him. He couldn't mess this up.

"Hiya, sweetie. Are you looking for a friend?" the blond woman asked. From her haircut, he could only assume that she'd had a recent illness or infestation that required the shearing. Neither option made him want to come any closer.

"I think I found her." At his voice, Calista turned, and it *was* Calista, although she'd done something dreadful to her hair. Howie didn't seem to mind, though. Barely stopping himself from giving away her name, Matthew coughed out his greeting. "I'm glad I found you, love. I just wanted to see that you're alright, then I'll be going."

A girl wearing a faded cotton dress with missing buttons eyed him cautiously. "Is this the man who left you with the babe?" she asked Calista.

Calista opened her mouth but hesitated. Matthew had been taught to own up to his mistakes. He had no qualms about taking responsibility.

"It was me, and I've apologized to her—"

"Apologized?" The word exploded as all three women turned on him. "You leave her with child, and you think an apology will suffice?"

They came at him, talking over each other in a cyclone of female indignation.

"Ruined her, and then left."

"Footloose and fancy free for the fella."

"Fatherless child . . ."

All Matthew could do was hold up his hands and back away as his stammered explanations went unheeded.

Suddenly, the short-haired woman gasped. "I recognize you. Aren't you that preacher?"

The looks the girls exchanged were murderous. "A preacher?"

asked the one with the missing buttons. "You call yourself a preacher, and you got this girl with child?"

Matthew's throat burned. They had the facts wrong, but the facts were so complicated that there was no explaining. And more than the embarrassment he felt was the horror that they would forever believe that a man of God had done this despicable thing.

"Girls, he's here to make amends." The face was Calista's, even if the mousy voice and the unnatural hair belonged elsewhere. "If I find it in my heart to forgive him, then my child will have a future." Her eyes drilled through him, daring him to open his mouth again. "Thank you for your help. We'll be going now." She lifted Howie toward him.

Matthew scooped up the baby and followed her around the corner, where she darted inside a furniture store to get them out of the public eye.

"You can't do that to me," he whispered. "This is my reputation."

"You stepped into that on your own. I didn't invite you into the conversation." She wiped the soot off her cheek with a clean handkerchief from a dirty bag. "Before you interrupted my investigation, I did come up with an idea. Have you ever thought of having a get-together for the girls? It wouldn't do to take them out to the ore fields for Bible study—they'll attract too much attention from the miners—so it'd have to be at your place. And they can't meet on Saturday night because that's when they work, but there should be some way to start a friendship with them."

Matthew's head spun. "You're asking me to invite prostitutes to my apartment? Calista York, that is outrageous."

"If you keep following me around, no one will be the least bit surprised at you consorting with prostitutes."

"How can I help you?" The salesman walked out of his office, leaning heavily on a cane with an eagle adorning the handle. He took one look at Calista's tattered clothing, and his welcoming smile melted.

"We'd like to browse alone, if you don't mind," said Calista, her entitled manner at odds with her rumpled appearance. "If we need assistance, we'll be sure and ask."

The man nodded and spun around his cane. The eagle head seemed to grimace as he leaned on it in his hobble back to the office. Calista walked down the ramp to the showroom. Wardrobes, sofas, and tables lined the aisles. Ladderback chairs stood atop every flat surface, the merchandise piled to the ceiling.

"Exactly what were you telling those girls?" Matthew asked as soon as they had lost themselves in the stacks of furniture. "And this . . . costume. Who are you trying to be?"

"I told you it could be dangerous to get involved. I can change clothes, and they won't recognize me, but you . . . they'll forever think that you have an illegitimate son."

"If I did have a son, I'd be honor-bound to marry his mother." Matthew could tell she was listening closely, wondering what he was going to say next. Matthew wondered too. He dipped his head to Howie's forehead. "That would be one way to clear my name, if it came to that."

Her smudged face and unkempt hair made her look so vulnerable. He had to remind himself that she wasn't a lost street urchin. She was a privileged socialite who'd decided to throw herself into harm's way. But it didn't matter what he knew about her profession. He couldn't fight the urge to protect her.

She'd rested her hand against the back of a rocker. The chair swayed beneath her touch. She sighed. "That would be counterproductive."

Of course it would. Matthew knew he couldn't marry a Pinkerton detective who would always be traveling, but that didn't keep him from ruminating on the idea. "I already stuck you with a baby. It'd be unchivalrous to stick you with a husband to boot, but if it was a choice between leaving Howie in a precarious situation and—"

A look of tenderness passed over her face, but it was toward the child, not him.

"Keeping Howie might save him," she said, "but who else would be lost without my help? We've got to find somewhere safe for him so I'm free. God didn't bring me this far for me to quit now."

Matthew had caught Calista in enough falsehoods to know when she was lying and when she was being sincere. As much as he hated it, he could tell that she believed what she was saying. It was truth as far as she knew, even if it wasn't a truth he wanted to hear.

Calista paced the flower store, the stiff fans of the irises rustling as she passed by with Howie on her hip. Howie had taken to her, that was a fact. And she guessed she had taken to him too. He leaned forward to put his face in front of hers. Calista smiled in spite of herself.

"If I didn't have anything else to do, watching you would be a treat," she said. But there was plenty to do, and that meant Maisie was on the hook. While Maisie was usually ready to roll up her sleeves and work, ever since meeting Silas, her sense of responsibility had been waylaid. She took every opportunity to disappear when she was needed most, but Calista had found her and wasn't letting her slip away again.

"Come out here, Maisie Kentworth. I know you're in there!" Calista stopped to beat her fist against the door again. "I'm not leaving."

Howie pounded his soft fist against the door and grinned at Calista.

"Miss York, that's the broom closet. No one is hiding in there." Mr. Trochet wiped his hands on the half apron he wore around his waist with a pair of shears in the pocket.

"Do you have a key?" Calista rattled the doorknob.

"It doesn't lock."

"Then someone is in there." She pushed her face against the door and raised her voice. "Holding the door closed!"

Calista had barely registered what time it was when Maisie had crept home last night. When she'd woken at dawn to find Maisie had already left again, she was outraged. It didn't take her long to track Maisie and Silas to Matthew's cabin, but when she'd tried to sneak through the garden gate to surprise them, they'd made their exit through the flower store. At least, they'd tried to make their exit.

Mr. Trochet knocked on the door. "Is someone in there? I'll get the police."

"Fine!" The knob twisted, and the door flew open. A broom handle clattered to the floor as Maisie and Silas stepped out.

"Hiding wasn't my idea." Silas held his hands in front of him as if ready to fend off Calista's blows. "I told her it wasn't smart."

"A broom closet? You wait until your pa hears about this," Calista said. Uncle Bill let his kids run wild on the Kentworth ranch, but when they crossed a boundary, he reined them in with an iron hand.

"Why can't you leave me alone?" Maisie whined. "I'm leaving you alone."

"Leaving me alone with a baby you won me!"

"And this is the thanks I get?"

Mr. Trochet looked nervously toward his front door. "I'm trying to run a business here. What if a customer comes in?"

"Look, Maisie," Silas said. "Those blue flowers match your eyes. What are they called?"

"Those are delphinium," Mr. Trochet said. "They must have had a good season this year, because the color isn't usually that true. Now, if you're looking for—"

"If you're not helping me, Maisie, then go home," Calista interrupted. "Your folks would rather you be home than here, buzzing around like a honeybee getting pollen from any bloom that catches its eye."

"That's not true." Maisie pushed her sleeves up. "It's just Silas. It's only been Silas, and he's a complete gentleman. I might be spending an inordinate amount of time with him, but we're making plans, Calista. Plans for our future. Why would you want to get in the way of that?" She licked her lips, then called over her shoulder, "I'd prefer roses over those blue things. Roses are more romantic."

"The only way I'm going to let you off the hook is if you take the baby." Calista hoisted Howie higher on her hip. "He's a good boy. You should enjoy him."

"How would that look, Calista? I can't go carrying a baby down the streets of Joplin with Silas. What will people say?"

"The same thing they say about me." The same thing they were saying about Matthew. Why hadn't he listened to her?

"But you don't know anyone here. I have a reputation."

Calista tilted her head and frowned. "What time did you get in last night? Were you worried about your reputation then?"

Silas stepped forward and stuck a rose beneath Maisie's chin. "It doesn't match your eyes, but it looks like the blooms on your cheeks."

"Oh, Silas." She giggled as she took it from him. "You say the prettiest things." The bud bent as Maisie buried her nose in it. "We're going, Calista. We thought we'd see Matthew this morning, but he hasn't come back yet. Tell him we'll be at his party tonight."

She hooked her arm through Silas's, then stumbled sideways as if he'd pulled her away, but Calista wasn't fooled. She was left in the flower store with Howie and no one to watch him.

Only someone who knew Maisie and Amos could understand how Calista had gotten into this predicament. And if anyone would understand, it would be another cousin.

With fresh resolve, Calista headed toward the streetcar stop at the corner. She'd go to Olive. If Aunt Myra was having a good day, then maybe Olive would like a break to watch a rambunctious child instead of her ailing mother. Why Calista thought Olive would want to use her free time to sit with a child, she didn't examine. Olive was the one they went to when there was a sacrifice to be made. That was just the way things worked in the Kentworth family.

Uncle Oscar's house stood on the edge of a modest neighborhood, the last street of what could be deemed respectable. Uncle Oscar's job as a supervisor at the Fox-Berry paid enough for the family to be comfortable, had it not been for Aunt Myra's chronic illness. As it was, most of their funds went to doctor visits, medicines, and outlandish treatments, hoping for a cure. Those expenses had made this Kentworth family the recipients of family charity, but only when it was possible to give without hurting their pride. Recently their fortunes had changed, though, with the marriage of their eldest daughter, Willow.

When Willow had left to work as a Harvey Girl at the Harvey House restaurants, Calista didn't blame her a bit. Not only had it made it possible to send funds home to the family, it also gave her room to spread her wings and breathe air that wasn't of the sickroom. Poor Olive, the younger sister, might never get that chance.

Calista walked up the dirt path to the faded front door. The flower beds were well kept, if well kept meant no weeds, a lot of dirt, and very few flowers. It looked like someone, probably Olive, was doing all she could with what she had. Calista thought of Trochet's garden behind his shop and wondered if he'd let her take any starts from it. It was worth an ask.

A cat lying on the windowsill watched her approach. Howie pointed at it and gurgled something, but it jumped down before Calista had a chance to knock on the front door.

She could hear voices inside, more spirited than she'd expected.

What was going on? Uncle Oscar was sure to be at work. Was Olive having a party? Were all the Kentworth cousins except her having fun today?

The door swung open, but it wasn't Olive. It was her sister.

"Willow! What a surprise! I didn't know you were in town." Calista grabbed her cousin for an awkward one-armed embrace to keep from squishing the baby.

"And the surprises aren't only on my part," Willow said. "Who is this?"

"It's a long story."

"Come on in, and let's hear it. But first, would you like some refreshments? I have a pot of tea on and some finger sandwiches." Willow hadn't forgotten her training at the Harvey House restaurants.

"Yes, please," Calista said. "Is Graham here, as well?"

"Yes, he was asking about you. Come on inside."

Calista followed the new Mrs. Buchanan to the parlor. It wasn't every girl who left home to work as a waitress and instead caught the eye of the son of a wealthy railroad tycoon. Because of Willow's good fortune, her family no longer had to worry about finances, but old habits died hard, and Calista would wager that Olive still didn't think spending money on garden flowers was a necessary expense. Good thing Willow hadn't listened to Olive's concerns when it came to the interior of the house. The fresh drapes matched the new sofa, showing that Willow was doing what she could for her family, even if her new life kept her from home.

Inside the parlor, Olive and Graham sat opposite each other in reupholstered chairs. Olive wore a castoff dress of Calista's that she hadn't seen in two seasons, and had a sketchbook on her lap.

Seeing Calista, Graham leapt to his feet. "Miss York!" He came forward with arms extended and planted a kiss on her cheek. "You're looking well. How's that sick friend you're tending?"

Calista had met Graham when his father's railroad company

hired her to catch some smugglers. When Willow got entangled with Graham in the midst of the investigation, she learned about Calista's job, but she hadn't ratted her out to the rest of the family. Willow, Graham, Granny Laura . . . and now Matthew. Had ever a secret been so well-known?

"My friend is doing well. Well enough that I might be able to finish out my education. The school is going to allow me to complete my certification by performing a variety of jobs. Something about being well rounded." Calista shrugged lightly. "I thought Joplin was as good a place as any to find employment."

Graham looked askance at Olive, then raised one brow. Calista answered with a slight shake of her head. No, Olive didn't know. They weren't safe talking. Not yet.

"If I may ask, whose child is that?" he asked with a wide grin.

Calista couldn't help but smile at the drowsy boy. "He's more like an unanticipated complication," she said as she took a seat next to Willow on the sofa. "Did you hear about the baby raffle?"

"Yes. What a dreadful stunt," Olive replied.

"Well, our cousins Amos and Maisie thought it was so horrid that they purchased a ticket in my name. As luck would have it . . ."

"No!" Willow put a hand to her chest as her mouth dropped open.

Graham unbuttoned his suit coat as he took a seat. "You warned me about your family, dear, but I never thought they could be that dangerous. Yet, isn't there a remedy? Can't you return him?"

"As I said, it's a long story," said Calista. "What I'm hoping is that I might find someone interested in helping me with him. My situation is hardly conducive to parenting."

All eyes turned to Olive, the designated martyr of the group.

"I wouldn't want him to be in the same room with Mother," Olive said, "but with Willow here for a few days, I'm free. . . ."

Calista shook her head. "No, you have company. Enjoy your time with your sister. If I'd known she was in town—"

"But maybe for a few hours a day," Willow said. "I'd already determined to tend to Mother. There's no reason for Olive to sit here and watch."

Because there was nothing else Olive would rather do with her free time than babysit? But the prospect seemed to agree with her.

"A change of scenery would be delightful, even if it is your hotel room," Olive said. "I could work on my sketches while watching him."

"Show Calista the blueprints you're working on," Graham said. "Mr. Kentworth is proposing a community center for the workers at the Fox-Berry Mine, and Olive here has turned out to be quite the architect."

Olive ducked her head. "It's nothing. Just something I've picked up along the way."

"I'm not surprised one bit," Calista said. "You're the most clever of us all. I'd love to see them."

But Olive drew the book against her chest. "They aren't quite right yet. Mr. Blount wants some changes, and it's not ready. If I get it corrected tonight, maybe I can show you then. As long as Willow doesn't mind me leaving her."

Willow patted her on the arm. "You've done more than your share, little sister. Let me and Graham step in for once."

Calista felt like a log had just rolled off her chest. "Thank you, Olive. You're my hero. I'll get you a key to my room and some money, if you'd like to step out with him during the day. Oh, and if Maisie comes back to the room for anything, you give her a piece of your mind for putting us in this situation."

"Let me talk to Ma, then I'll get ready." Olive stood and made her exit.

Graham perched on the edge of his seat, barely able to wait until Olive left the room before speaking. "What's going on, Calista?" His eyes twinkled with anticipation. "Is there danger here in town?"

"In Joplin?" Willow snorted as she stood and gathered the cups and saucers. "Every Saturday night there's danger."

"It's a missing person." Calista set Howie on the floor. "The girl is in danger, but we don't know from whom."

"Is there anything I can do?" Graham asked.

"Graham, really?" Willow came back from the kitchen. "Last time you nearly got run over by a train. Wasn't that enough?"

Of course he would ask. When Calista was assigned to the railroad case in Emporia, Kansas, Graham had also gone undercover to investigate. The railroad magnate's son pretending to be a busboy—he hadn't earned any praise for how he washed dishes, but at least one waitress found him charming.

"I only involved you last time because you worked for the company that hired me," Calista said.

"Owned the company," he amended.

"Along with the rest of your family," Willow said.

"Blood ties that come with privileges." He winked at his wife.

"Since you have no ties to this case, let's just pretend I'm pumping you for information and you have no idea what's occurring," Calista said.

"Have it your way. What's the question?"

"Is there any way to check your passenger lists for names without drawing any attention?"

"Easiest thing in the world. Who are you looking for?"

"Primarily, Lila Seaton. Other people of interest are Gerald Mason or Della Rush."

Graham reached inside an inner pocket of his suit coat and produced a short pencil and envelope. Folding the envelope over, he wrote on the back. "I'll send a message up the rail to headquarters in Kansas City. That way we keep these names off the wire. If they traveled coach, we probably won't know unless they reserved tickets in their names before their journey. There's a chance."

"We're assuming she boarded a train in Chicago, but we don't know with whom."

"Always thorough in your work." He beamed his approval. "But I can't for the life of me figure out how you managed to get left with the care of this baby. I've seen you get out of some sticky situations. Why couldn't you get out of this one?"

Aware that everyone was looking at him, Howie lifted his head and grinned. He was a good-natured child, but finding himself in unfamiliar surroundings with no familiar faces had been hard on him. After a restless night, unenthusiastic eating, and a fussy morning, he was starting to feel like himself again. And maybe Calista was learning what women found so appealing about the little strangers.

"When they announced my name, I couldn't believe it. I hadn't bought a ticket. I was on my way to the table to protest when someone stopped me. There were concerns that this baby raffle was immoral and not in the best interest of the child. Seeing that I'd won, we decided that rather than put him back at the whim of random selection, we should wait a bit and see if a more suitable home could be found for him."

"We?" Willow sat with perfect grace, a vision of loveliness in the most stylish gown Calista had ever seen her wear. "Is there a gentleman involved in this decision?"

All Calista could do was glare.

"She doesn't deny it." Graham took his wife's hand. "And from the trouble she's having choosing her words, I'd say it's a significant gentleman."

Willow rocked on the thin cushion. "Goodness, but this is fun. No wonder they tormented me so much when I brought you to Granny's for the first time."

"Has *he* been to Granny's yet?" Graham asked Calista. "I don't know what our travel schedule looks like, but I could make arrangements for us to be there."

"I have a job to do with no room for entanglements," Calista said. "Don't tease me. Just thinking about it makes me cross."

"Thinking about what?" Olive said as she reentered the room with both arms behind her as she untied her apron.

"Calista's fellow," Graham said.

"Why is her fellow making her cross?"

"I'm not the only one," Calista feinted. "Maisie is seeing a man named Silas. If there's anyone who needs harassing, it's them."

"Nice try, cousin," Willow said. "Don't think that we're distracted so easily."

"But we shouldn't waste more of her time." Olive bent and picked up Howie. "She's been trying to find work as a nurse for a few weeks now. She needs our help."

"A nurse?" Willow and Graham exchanged significant glances before Willow continued. "Yes, Calista. Good luck getting hired on as a nurse. All that experience with your sick friend will stand you in good stead."

As they very well knew, there had never been a sick friend.

The hardest part of her job—remembering who knew what story—was only getting harder.

CHAPTER

19

Saturday night and all it implied. Excitement rose as the sun set on the flat roofs of Joplin's whiskey dens, gaming halls, and bordellos. The miners tossed their shovels down for the last time that week. With tired hands, they scrubbed the mud and dust from their faces and necks. If they owned more than one shirt, the cleanest one was donned, and then they headed to town.

Also headed to town were the landowners, the prospectors, the mine owners, and the smelters. The money would start at the top of the chain, work its way through all the middlemen, and then touch the fingers of the miners, before it reached the velvet-lined cash register drawer behind every saloon bar. And if the poor man didn't have a terrible thirst, some of the coin might actually make it home to his wife and children.

And somewhere in all that hubbub was a young lady named Lila who probably didn't favor Saturday nights any more than Calista did.

Calista stood at the window in her room and watched Matthew in his garden below. He'd already carried the two garden chairs inside his apartment in preparation for his Saturday night gathering. Maisie was getting ready in her room, and after a robust protest,

231

she'd agreed to take Howie with her. Because Howie couldn't go where Calista was going tonight.

She paused to kiss the sleeping babe on her bed as she went to her wardrobe and selected her outfit.

No fine clothes. Looking pretty would help, but she couldn't look upper-class, not without attracting attention she didn't need. In a stroke of luck, Graham had found that Della Rush had claimed two second-class tickets from Chicago the week Lila had gone missing. Whether she played a hand in Lila's disappearance or was a victim as well, Calista didn't know, but she hadn't been able to find any trace of Lila or Della since their one-night stay at the hotel.

Gerald Mason was a different story. He was a frequent visitor to Joplin. A second visit to the hotel to look at the register had revealed that he stayed there regularly. He was from St. Louis and hadn't come in on the same train Lila and Della had, but there were women's names next to his on the registry every time. Was he meeting them there, then taking them elsewhere? Was he a middleman? Or perhaps he didn't play any part at all. All Calista knew was that the man driving the gin wagon had said she'd be most likely to find him at Black Jack's on a Saturday night if he was in town. So that was where she'd be.

A crash in the powder room, an exclamation from Maisie, and then the door opened. Maisie's braid was only half finished, and she held Calista's silver-plated hand mirror flat like she was trying to balance an egg on it.

"Shush!" Calista warned with a look at Howie. "Don't wake him."

"I dropped the mirror." Maisie wrinkled her nose as she passed over the shattered mirror. "Guess that's seven years bad luck for you. Sorry."

"For me? I didn't break it." Calista carried it to the waste bin and shook out the sharp pieces of glass. She hated that she would miss Matthew's Saturday night gathering, but she'd hate it even more if he learned where she was. "What are you going to tell Matthew again?"

"I'm to tell him that you would've been there if you could, but you'd had a busy day."

"That's right." She didn't want to outright lie to him, but if he thought she was staying in her room, that'd be best. "And under no circumstances will you bring him back here."

Maisie rolled her eyes. "You'd think I was thick as a block from the way you have to keep explaining things to me." Her dress sleeves strained across her shoulders as she pinned up her hair. "I'm here to help you, remember."

And she was helping. Once Maisie settled down a bit, she was a good hand.

"Be sure and feed Howie before you go," Calista said. "Matthew might not have anything he can eat." She spritzed an extra spray of perfume and, with a last pat on Howie's rump, walked out the door.

Surely with Matthew's friends, Dan and Loretta, Silas, and even Irvin, Howie would be looked after. Since the side exit to the hotel went right past Matthew's garden, she waited in the lobby for a crush of people leaving. Before they even reached the sidewalk, the ladies of the party were exclaiming about the riffraff on the streets. They must have been new to town. Calista ducked her head, matching their steps as if she were included in their group, until she'd passed the flower shop and was safely out of sight.

Black Jack's was a small brick building smashed between the cobbler's shop and a hardware store. Boots, shovels, and gin—everything the miners needed, right in a row. The typical Saturday gaiety seemed missing in this part of town. No lively piano music or shouts of laughter—just a grim determination to make one's money stretch until they could reach oblivion.

Black Jack's was painted on the windows in thick block letters that nearly obscured the view of anything going on inside. Calista's skin tingled. She was on her own. No one here to save her. She had to think ahead, but all she wanted to think about was Matthew back in his apartment and how she wished she could be with him instead.

"Lila," she muttered to herself. "It's about Lila."

After the girl was found, then perhaps Calista would have the luxury of a few days with Matthew—at least until Mr. Pinkerton sent her on her next assignment.

A woman approached in flimsy slippers and an expensive gown. At least, it had once been an expensive gown, but it had been altered to accentuate her wares in a way no respectable dressmaker would allow. A quick look at her face told Calista it wasn't Lila, but it very well could be someone Gerald Mason was responsible for. She walked past Calista and went wearily into the saloon. Everything in Calista wanted to stop her, to intervene with plans for a different life, but to do so would expose her role. She had to pretend that she approved of whatever was happening inside.

She unbuttoned two buttons of her blouse and tucked it more tightly into her waistband. Her dress wasn't flashy enough to catch any eyes, but she couldn't look respectable, or her errand would be pointless.

She'd barely darkened the door when she was grabbed around the waist and spun into a corner. Calista hooked her leg behind the knee of her assaulter and shoved him for all she was worth. Losing his balance, he flailed his arms as he went down like a redwood, sending chairs scraping across the floor and into tables.

Calista covered her mouth and widened her eyes. "Oh my, I'm so sorry." She stepped closer to a man playing billiards, hoping he had enough money wagered on his game that he wouldn't pursue her as well. "Is that your friend? I hope he isn't hurt. He must've tripped."

With his emerald satin vest and rolled-up shirt sleeves, the billiards player might be her best bet for decent treatment in this place. He took a pull from his thick cigar before answering. "He tends to trip when a pretty lady comes around, but he's not my friend." He took aim and sent the cue ball spinning.

Calista knew positioning her body the right way would send a message so that actual words weren't necessary, so she angled toward the billiards player long enough for the waist-grabber to scowl her direction, then move on to another victim. As his opponent took aim, the billiards player removed his cigar, gave her a frank appraisal, then introduced himself.

"I'm Teddy. And who are you?"

Well, he half introduced himself. This was one of those times when Calista wished her mother hadn't given her such a unique name. Between being too formal and taking the chance that he'd heard of her before, she chose the formal. It was too late to start using a pseudonym. "I'm Miss York, and I think I might be lost."

"Where are you supposed to be?"

She waited as he took his turn at the table before answering. "I'm supposed to meet a gentleman named Gerald Mason. Do you know him?"

He rested the end of his pool stick on the floor and regarded her more thoughtfully. "I haven't seen him today."

"But you know him?" Her nostrils burned as she inhaled cigar smoke.

"Gerald Mason from St. Louis? Yeah, I know him. He's a salesman for a brewery there. He won't be here tonight, but he's in town."

Calista let her shoulders slump to hide her excitement. This was new information when she'd thought she'd hit a dead-end. She pouted and twisted her toe. "Do you know where he is?"

Teddy took his turn. "Get yourself a drink, and I'll take you as soon as I finish this game."

"Thank you. I appreciate it! I do." She went to the bar with confidence, having established a protector in the saloon. She ordered herself a seltzer water, but before it arrived, she spotted a friend. "Irvin? I'm surprised to see you."

The glee faded from his face. "What are you doing here?"

A question she couldn't answer. In fact, she probably shouldn't have let him see her at all. "Why aren't you at Matthew's tonight?"

"I'm going. I just stopped in here for . . ." The bartender pushed a shot glass toward him at the same time he delivered her seltzer water. Irvin's eyes were glued to his glass. His whole head turned toward her before his eyes could be pried away from the liquid in the cup. "Nothing. I'm going to Matthew's." He stood, dug a coin out of his pocket, and dropped it on the bar. "There. Are you pleased with yourself?"

"I didn't mean to make you angry," she said as he passed, but she couldn't help feeling a tiny iota of triumph. Matthew wouldn't be happy to know she was out on Saturday night, but at least it had done some good for someone.

The seltzer tickled her nose but gave her somewhere to focus her attention as she waited for Teddy to finish his game. And when he did, he made it clear that he wasn't waiting on her.

"There's another game starting," he said. "If you aren't ready . . ."

"Let's go." She swept her handbag off the bar and weaved her way through the morose patrons to the door.

Back in the stream of people outside, Calista could breathe again. There might be another uncomfortable venue ahead, but for now, walking in a crowd of witnesses was safe, even if that crowd was as rowdy as Bourbon Street on Fat Tuesday.

Teddy kept his pace, making it difficult for her to keep up, especially with men stopping in her path to leer. Amazing what a difference two buttons could make.

"How do you know Gerald?" Teddy walked with his hands in his pockets. Matthew would've taken her arm and cleared a path for her.

"I don't, really. My father told me to meet him when I got to town." They'd turned on Seventh Street, where the prosperous restaurants were full of people divvying up funds. On this street were families waiting for the husband to get his wages so they could do their shopping.

"Your father isn't in town with you? You're out here on your own?"

Calista giggled, but she didn't miss the change in his demeanor. "My pa knows I can take care of myself. But I'm not alone here. I have friends."

Had she hesitated too long before adding the part about friends? Because Teddy seemed to be entertaining a new idea. He turned on a side road toward Kentucky Street and the railroad tracks. Any comfort she'd taken from the crowds vanished as they moved ahead. The people on this street seemed less celebratory and more furtive.

"But what about you?" Calista asked. "My friend Mr. Blount knows a lot of people. Where do you work?"

"I'm not at work today," Teddy said. He put a hand on her shoulder and steered her past a group of loitering tramps. These men had nothing to celebrate, even if it was payday. "Let's not talk about work."

There were no light posts here to hold back the darkness. None of the buildings ahead looked open. No lights, no doors thrown wide to welcome customers. Just dark warehouses and storefronts locked up for the night.

"Mr. Mason is expecting me tonight," Calista said as she stopped walking. "Otherwise I would've waited until morning. Then again, it's late. I'll come back tomorrow."

With a sneer, Teddy's grip on her shoulder tightened as he

forced her onward. "No reason to wait. If he's as impatient as I am, he won't appreciate the delay."

And Calista knew she'd made a mistake.

Matthew had bought the food, and he'd arranged the chairs. His Saturday night gatherings were another fleece, another test to see if what he was doing in Joplin had merit. Was he where he was supposed to be? Was he needed here, or should he head back home?

The squeak of the garden gate alerted Matthew that someone was on their way to the cabin.

"I brought the chicken." Silas walked through the open door and dropped the basket on the table.

Matthew took the money he'd set aside for the evening's needs and gave it to Silas. "Go easy on it. I don't know how many will be hungry."

"I'll just take a leg." The paper rustled inside the basket as he unwrapped the food and tore off his portion. "Who do you think will come?"

"Two of the men on my shift seemed interested. They're coming to town to collect their wages anyway." Matthew looked at the door. "I expected you'd bring Maisie and Calista."

"Oh, I've got to head over and get them. Maisie said she'd wait on me to come and walk her over."

Matthew watched him reach for another piece of chicken. Why didn't Silas hurry? But Matthew shouldn't be overanxious to see Calista. Tonight wasn't a night for the two of them. It was for everyone. He had to change his expectations. For one thing, he had to pay particular attention to Dan and Loretta.

Loretta came inside cradling a jar of stout tea with the tea bags still floating. "If you have a pitcher, I'll dilute it," she said. "Made no sense to mix it at the tent and carry it over heavy." She set the jar next to the chicken, then stepped out of the way, seemingly content to wait unobserved.

Dan slapped Silas on the back, forcing Silas to move his chicken leg to the other hand before greeting Dan with a handshake.

"We made it through the week. We're moved and have already struck a good chunk of ore. It's time to look to the future. Put the past sorrows behind us." Dan's eyes slid sideways toward Loretta. "We're here, determined to be thankful for what we have."

His bravery tightened Matthew's throat. Sometimes he thought these people beyond redemption, but when he faced folks like the Campbells, he was reminded of his own inadequacies and how shallow his struggles were.

Overall, the group was cheerful, greeting each other robustly after another hard week of work. Some new people came. Cokey John pestered Matthew about how slowly he filled his ore bucket at work, but he'd brought two friends with him to meet the new hand at the mine, regardless. Matthew hadn't planned on all these people crammed into his little cabin. He should have had Silas buy more chicken.

Silas appeared at his elbow. "I'll get the ladies. Be right back." He ducked out as Matthew began introductions.

First they went around and told how long they'd been in Joplin. Matthew was surprised to hear that Mr. Green was a landowner. He'd come at the invitation of Dan and Loretta. When he passed Matthew some folded bills to cover the expense of the meeting, Matthew stood staring at the money until he could recover his senses.

"What's this for again?"

"Because you are giving these miners an example to follow." His work boots were just as dirty and old as Dan's, but his clothes were newer. "They need to be reminded that there's a lot of luck involved in this business, but the decisions they make still guide their lives. I see you teaching them that. Next week I'll bring my wife and son. We want to be a part of what you're trying to do."

Matthew looked at the door, wishing Calista had seen what had just transpired, but it was empty. How long did it take Silas to get there and back, anyway?

He thanked Mr. Green and opened his Bible to share a word with his guests, paying particular care to Loretta and Dan. Tears seemed always on the verge of spilling out. They'd had a rough week, but they were good people. Their faith in God would get them through this downturn if they'd let it.

Where was Silas? Was there a problem with Howie? What else could be keeping them?

As Matthew finished his teaching, Irvin entered the cabin, walking as if every step was an affront to his dignity. He pegged Matthew with a hard stare before taking Silas's seat and crossing his arms over his chest.

Matthew asked, "Something wrong?"

"You tell me," Irvin groused.

Matthew didn't have the patience for this. Irvin was sober, and that might be enough to explain his ire. Time to wrap up the lesson.

Dan, Loretta, and Mr. Green left after the Bible study. Cokey John and his friends stayed for a spell but then claimed they had shopping to do before the shops closed. Irvin was the last to leave.

"I was here, and I didn't touch a drop." The chip on his shoulder was almost visible.

"Have I done something against you?" Matthew asked. "You're out of sorts."

"What's it mean when a man can't be trusted? What's it mean when a man can't go about his business without looking over his shoulder? What's it mean when someone pretends to be your friend, then sends a spy to follow you?"

A spy? Matthew's heart jumped into his throat. There was only one spy he knew of. "What are you talking about?"

"That lady. She pretends to be so fine, puts on airs, and then she goes lurking around in the most miserable of places, trying to keep a body from availing himself of the fruits of his labor. One look from her, and I knew what she was doing. You'd sent her there to catch me in the act. Her and that nasty bloke she was with." He shook his head. "I thought you had decency. Just decency is what I thought. But I didn't touch a drop. Came straight here. I hope you're happy."

"Who was Calista with? Where was she?" Matthew's blood started roaring. He knew she didn't want him to interfere, but he couldn't help himself. He had to find her, even if it meant watching from a distance.

"She was at Black Jack's," Irvin said, "and as mad as I am that you were looking for me, I can't believe you'd send that lady to a den of iniquity."

"Who was she with?"

"The guy is there a lot, name of Teddy. I don't know what he does, but he owns a warehouse on Kentucky. 'Tis a pity you'd stoop so low as to put her in danger. Seeing her there with the likes of Teddy, it's enough to make me swear off spirits for the rest of my life."

Matthew's stomach churned. "I'm going."

It was Saturday night, the most dangerous night of the week, and the worst part of town. He fumed as he ran out of the cabin and busted out into the alleyway. When he dove into the crowd on the sidewalk, some pushed back, but he hardly felt them in his rush to get to the gin shop. Despite what Calista thought, she needed protection. If he could forget about her and let her face the consequences . . . but that was as impossible as forgetting his own name.

He strode through the crowd, little caring who got in his way.

He didn't know exactly where the bar was, but Irvin had pointed him toward the east part of town, so he had a good idea of the neighborhood. He strained to see the saloon signs ahead by the gaslight. If only he knew for sure—

The sign at the corner said Kentucky Street. Wasn't that where this man was supposed to have a warehouse? Matthew stepped away from the streetlight, hoping to see something among the shadows, and what he saw was enough to bring his blood to a boil.

CHAPTER
20

"I don't want to go with you. Let go of me," Calista huffed.

Teddy kept his grip on her while opening a side door to a dark warehouse. "Come on inside. I'll get you a drink, and we can visit while we wait for Mr. Mason." He smiled like her efforts to escape amused him. "I'm a nice guy. Give me a try, and you'll see."

He wasn't a nice guy, and if he thought Calista was just a nice girl, he was going to be surprised. No matter how simple or how elaborate Calista's wardrobe, all of her skirts had one feature in common: pockets. And in that pocket, she kept her spring-loaded baton. Twisting to get herself some room, Calista pulled the canister out of her pocket and activated the button. Old Teddy never saw the baton until it whacked him across the arm.

"Ughf!" He released her, and then, seeing what she held, his nostrils flared. He lunged forward, reaching for her arm to control the baton, but she met him coming with a strong strike to the side of the face.

Blood poured from the corner of his eye. Calista's head went light at the sight of the injury, but she tightened her grip on the baton and forced herself to focus. She'd never had to defend herself physically before. It served to clarify issues.

"No one gets away with hitting me," he growled.

She stepped backward. This time he wasn't blindly striking out. He tried to circle around her, but she turned to keep him before her. She had to keep him in sight without looking at the blood dripping down his face. Her knees wobbled. She hadn't thought he'd be this determined. Why not let her go?

Teddy held up an arm to block the baton, and then moved in. Her eyes flickered on the darkness over his shoulder as she tried to clear his injury from her mind. He stepped in, and even though she swung as hard as she could, he deflected it while grabbing her by the neck with his other hand.

She was caught, but she wasn't finished fighting. Calista struck again, this time only hitting his thigh, before he captured her arm. With only her wrist free, she jabbed the pointed end of the baton at his eye. If he thought he had her beat, he didn't know who he was dealing with. He turned his face away as he tightened the fingers around her neck. Her options were narrowing. Maybe another jab at his face—

Something crashed against them. Calista's legs gave way as Teddy was dragged off her. She landed on her rump on the ground and filled her lungs with cool, damp air. This was her chance. Still dizzy, she crouched and swung the baton with all her might at the side of Teddy's knee. It buckled, and he crashed to the ground next to her, unconscious.

Pushing away, Calista used the warehouse door to pull herself up and only then saw boots that she recognized.

It was Matthew.

This was awkward.

Before she could think of an excuse, he snatched her away from the door and into his arms. He pulled her away from the unconscious Teddy and, with a strong hand, lifted her chin.

His eyes swallowed her whole, taking in every detail as he moved her head to catch the scant light from the stars. She must look a mess with her hair tumbling down and the red marks on her neck. She knew the second he saw them. Something in him snapped. The arm behind her tightened as he pressed his lips against her forehead.

So that was how it was going to be? Calista had had enough of being jerked around by men for one night. She should have a say in how she was handled, so she did. Grabbing Matthew by the back of the neck, she pulled his face down to hers. He wasn't the only one who could steal a kiss. She could too, and she would if she liked. A kiss to show this preacher boy that he couldn't control her.

But faster than lightning, things whirled out of control. Matthew crushed her against him, then possessed her mouth with a thoroughness that stunned her. There was nothing proper about his response, or how her traitorous heart surrendered. Somehow, everything strong about her had gone weak. Everything she'd repressed ran free. She wasn't going to love him. She'd already decided that. So why was her only thought how to give him more?

Matthew growled. He swept his lips across hers one last time, then said, "You're an imbecile." He released her.

"What?" Calista's eyes opened. "What did you say to me?" She steadied herself against a wall and repeated her question. "What did you say?"

With three big steps, Matthew reached Teddy, took his wrist, then dropped it in disgust. "He's still alive. Let's get out of here."

"You said I'm a what?" Calista retrieved her baton from the ground, keeping an eye on both men.

"An imbecile, but I'm just as bad." He grasped her hand and took out, dragging her in his wake. "I knew you had no sense, but here I am, carrying on like you should know better."

"I did the only sensible thing. I was defending myself."

"If I hadn't come along . . ." Matthew swallowed hard.

"He had just about given up." Calista didn't like being wrong, and she refused to consider how much danger she'd been in.

"I shouldn't have hit him so hard the first time," Matthew said. "It would've done me good to beat on him some more."

"But after I took out his knee—"

"I knocked him out cold. His knee had nothing to do with it." They'd reached the main street. Matthew's agitation was obvious from the way he kept looking behind them. "What are we supposed to do now? I guess we're in the city. City folks go to the law."

"The law?" Calista was still reliving that kiss. After that, she was dealing with the disappointment that Gerald Mason would not be met that night. Too much to think about. She couldn't keep up with what Matthew was saying. "I don't want—"

"Officer!" Matthew had spotted a man in blue when they reached the corner. "Officer, this lady was attacked."

No. Bringing in the law would only complicate matters. There'd be too many questions, and if Mr. Pinkerton thought that she'd been reckless, he'd recall her, quick as a wink.

But after taking a look at her disheveled condition, the policeman was obviously getting involved. He blew a whistle, and before she knew it, she and Matthew were being escorted to the station.

Every painful swallow reminded Calista how dire her situation had been, but there was no use in lingering on what could have happened. Besides that, she was a tiny bit awed at Matthew's behavior. Had he lost control of his faculties to kiss her like that? Was he sorry? Would he apologize? For a conscientious man, he had passion lurking beneath the surface that she hadn't suspected.

As she'd expect on a Saturday night, the police station was crowded, and the officer they were assigned to seemed more at home behind the desk covered in files than he would have been wrangling rowdy revelers on the street. He chose a form, took her name, then took a long look at her before writing for a solid three minutes. Seated in a chair next to Matthew, Calista cast him a questioning look. What could the officer possibly have to write? He hadn't asked them any questions yet.

Matthew raised an eyebrow and let his eyes drift to her neckline. "Button your shirt," he whispered.

With trembling fingers, she did up the two buttons, suddenly remembering that she'd dressed to present herself as a light-skirts. The police would make assumptions from there. She had to turn the tide.

"If you don't mind, I've just endured a shocking attack. I'd like to get the interview behind me."

The officer put his elbows on the desk and rested his chin in his hands. "I'll finish recording my observations later, if you insist. Now, let's start from the beginning. Where did you meet this Teddy?"

"I was at Black Jack's." She refused to look away, even as he smirked. "I was looking for a man named Gerald Mason, and Teddy said he would take me to him."

"Who's Gerald Mason? What business do you have with him?"

Calista could feel Matthew's stare. She kept her voice curt. "I've never met him before. He's a friend of a friend. Regardless, Teddy had offered to escort me to meet Mr. Mason. Something I assumed was a gentlemanly gesture."

The sergeant nodded to Matthew. "And who are you?"

"I'm her . . . I'm her pastor." He cleared his throat and shot a sheepish grimace at her. "Matthew Cook."

"You have a pastor?" the sergeant asked, though he didn't expect a reply.

How badly she wanted to tell him that she wasn't the type to frequent a gin house of her own accord, but to do so would disclose her mission.

Instead, she'd focus on what she could tell him. "Teddy led me to Kentucky Street, to the warehouse there. He told me we were going inside. When I protested, he attempted to force me inside. I fought back and managed—"

"When I got there, he was choking her," Matthew interrupted. "Had her by the neck, defenseless."

"I wasn't defenseless," she said. "I was definitely defending."

"He would've killed her had I not come along."

The sergeant straightened to write some more on his form. "How did you happen to be in the vicinity, Mr. Cook?"

"I had a Bible study tonight, and one of the men at it told me he'd seen her at Black Jack's. He knew the man she was with and told me where to find her."

"Two of your Bible students were at Black Jack's? You have a very interesting congregation, Mr. Cook."

"That's putting it lightly," Matthew replied.

The sergeant chewed on the end of his pencil before swinging forward and pulling two more papers from a pile. "If you'd both be so kind as to fill these out. Just write your story . . . you can write, can't you?"

The withering look Calista sent him answered for her.

"Capital. Write what happened, and we'll file it with the report. We have officers looking for the man. If he's still there, as you claim, we'll have no problem identifying him. Now, if you'll excuse me."

In Calista's training, they'd never covered how to write a police report. In most cases, it would behoove the operative to tell the police who they worked for. In her case, she didn't want Mr. Pinkerton to know what had happened. She'd have to handle this like a civilian.

"Keep it to the facts of what happened tonight," she whispered to Matthew. "Don't write anything beyond that."

"You mean, let them think you're a light-skirts drifting around dark alleys on Saturday night?"

"It's better than the truth."

Matthew snorted in disapproval, but he stopped arguing.

Calista wrote furiously, skipping the shady preliminaries and going straight to when she'd been assaulted. She assumed that Matthew was just as eagerly recording his account until he spoke.

"It's a disgrace how that officer treated you. Can you imagine being a young woman, uneducated and without recourse, and being treated like that?"

If Lila needed help, would they have listened to her? "He made assumptions about me based on how I was dressed."

"Even so, you deserve courtesy."

"Another issue for you to campaign against?"

His eyes were sad. "What was I thinking, coming here? I had all the answers back in the mountains of Pine Gap."

"But you moved somewhere that needed you."

"And you did need me tonight."

"That's open to interpretation."

The sergeant breezed back to his desk with another police officer in tow. "They found the man you reported. Because of his injuries, they took him to the hospital."

"Injuries? Which injuries?" Calista asked.

The sergeant motioned the second police officer forward to answer. "Lacerated brow, broken kneecap, possible broken ribs."

"Was there a knot on the side of his head?" Matthew asked. "Have they determined which blow felled him?"

"I didn't note any knots on his head," the officer said. "The other injuries were more severe."

"Told you so," Calista said, suppressing her smile.

"Thank you for the report, Officer Rush." The sergeant's pen moved swiftly over his form, but Calista bolted out of her chair.

"Officer Rush?" She wiped her hands on her skirt. "Do you know someone named Della, by chance?"

Officer Rush was a redhead, and his complexion showed his agitation. "Why?"

This might be a mistake, or it might be a breakthrough. She was already at the police station. Nothing bad could happen to her here.

"I'm an old friend of hers."

Officer Rush looked at the sergeant, who held up his form and read, "Miss Calista York."

"She's never mentioned you," Officer Rush said. "Where do you know her from?"

"We have a mutual friend who introduced us. Her name is Lila Seaton."

The officer's eyes flickered over Calista, then Matthew. His mouth formed a tight line, and he clasped his hands behind his back. "Lila Seaton? I've never heard of her."

Calista looked at the sleeves of his navy jacket so he couldn't see the skepticism in her eyes. He was lying. This policeman was lying to her. What did it mean? Were there officers on the force involved in kidnapping? Was he covering for someone who was?

"Maybe I have the wrong Rush family," Calista said. "My apologies."

"Sergeant," Officer Rush said, "may I speak to you?"

The sergeant stood and followed him to the other end of the large room.

Matthew was getting restless. "They have your attacker," he said. "Why don't they let us go?"

Calista shrugged. "We could be asked to identify him. I wouldn't be surprised if they escort us to the hospital."

But what happened next did surprise her.

The sergeant returned and took her by the arm. "Miss York, please hold your hands behind your back. You are under arrest."

CHAPTER

21

Matthew jumped to his feet. "What did she do?"

"You don't know your friend very well, do you?" The sergeant used his key to secure the handcuffs. Calista's shoulders dropped with the weight. "Come this way. One of our prison matrons will deal with you."

"Matthew!" She turned, the paleness of her face bringing into sharp focus the bruises on her neck.

Matthew had never considered attacking a lawman, but his resolution was being tested. "Why are you taking her? She was the one attacked."

"Are you her husband?" the sergeant asked. "Or any kin?"

"No."

"Then you have no interest in this."

Somehow, despite her efforts to keep the officer from carting her out, Calista maintained her dignity. Already tousled and bruised from her earlier fight, she managed to stay composed, but the sight of her bound was unraveling Matthew's control. There was fear in her brown eyes, more fear than there had been while she was being choked to death by a thug.

What was wrong? What was going on? But he didn't have a chance to ask, because she was dragged around the corner and hidden from view.

"You can't just take her." Matthew pounded his fist against the officer's desk. "She came to you for help."

"You won't be any help to her if we lock you up too. I suggest you move along." The officer leaned back in his chair and watched Matthew warily.

He was right. For whatever reason, Matthew would find no sympathy here. He had to get away. Go for help. He rushed outside with no plan. Where could he go? Who could help? Family. That was where she turned every time. It was only another block to the Keystone Hotel.

The streets were a blur as he imagined what Calista was enduring. He barely noticed when he passed through the doors of the hotel. Instead of waiting for the elevator, he took the stairs—all six flights—then beat on the door with his heart hammering in his chest.

"Something better be burning down," Maisie groused as she opened the door. She already had one arm in her robe and was holding her shoes beneath the other arm.

"It's Calista. She's been arrested."

Maisie's eyes widened. She dropped her shoes and jammed her bare feet into them as she pulled her robe around her. "Calista is a good person. They can't do that to her. We gotta save her. Spring her from the pokey. You run to the farm and tell Granny. I'll drum up a following to confront the police."

Maybe he should have gone to her uncle instead.

"Going to Granny's will take too much time," he said. "Is there someone in town?"

"Graham!" Maisie slapped her hands together. "Graham's in town, and he's a particular friend of Calista's. He's at the train station. He'll set this aright. C'mon." She pushed past Matthew, then skidded to a stop. "Wait. What about Howie? I can't leave him." She yanked at a frizzy lock of hair in frustration.

Her concern did her credit, but Matthew had to go. "Graham's at the train station at this time of night? How can I find him?"

"Graham?" She snorted. "You can't miss him. But give me a second. I'll wake Howie and go with you."

"Sorry, gotta go." He turned and jogged back to the staircase.

"Tell Calista I love her," Maisie called, heedless of the sleeping residents of the hall.

Matthew nodded as he took off toward the train tracks. He'd always thought that he felt an urgency for saving the lost souls of Joplin, but never had he prayed with the same desperation as he prayed now. It wasn't right, what they'd done to Calista. Matthew could fight a thug on the streets, but he was powerless against the law. Only God could intervene, and to Him Matthew breathed prayers with every step.

He needed help, but it wasn't until the yardman at the train depot pointed him toward an elaborate personal railcar parked off the main tracks that Matthew realized the Graham he was going to find was none other than Graham Buchanan, the railroad magnate.

What business did Calista have with him?

Any fool could tell Calista was quality. Any fool knew she was better than a poor miner from the hills of the Ozarks, but it came like a dousing of ice water to consider that she had friends like Mr. Buchanan.

Despite the hour, Mr. Buchanan graciously received Matthew as a friend of Calista's. Matthew tried not to gawk at the electric lights in the railcar or the intricate wood paneling in the sitting room on wheels. Because of the urgency, Matthew spent the time telling Mr. Buchanan what had happened to her, but what he really wanted to know was the nature of their relationship.

"She involved the police?" The gentleman raised a teacup and sipped a long draw. When Matthew had realized that he was going to meet a Mr. Buchanan, he'd expected an elderly gentleman, not this young, competent man. "That's an unusual choice, considering her profession."

Matthew stared at his untouched cup, wanting to throw it against the silk-lined walls. He was the one who'd waved down the officer, not Calista, so the blame fell on him. And it rubbed him wrong that Calista had seen fit to share her secrets with this sophisticated man. But if Mr. Buchanan knew her profession, maybe he should know everything.

"She's looking for someone named Lila Seaton," Matthew said. "The names Della Rush and Gerald Mason have also been spoken, but I don't know what any of it's about. She didn't tell me the details of the case."

Buchanan's smooth brow wrinkled. "So she asked Officer Rush if he knew Della Rush, and that was why she was arrested?"

"He didn't appreciate the question, but it wasn't until she asked about Lila Seaton that he decided she couldn't walk free."

"Interesting. I suppose we'd better make a phone call and see what we're to do about it." He picked up his cup and saucer. "Follow me to my office."

They hurried down a carpeted corridor to an adjoining car. Of course Graham Buchanan didn't use the depot office. He had an office with a telephone on his train. Would wonders never cease?

"Operator? Connect me with Chicago, if you please." Keeping one foot on the floor, Buchanan sat on his desk and motioned Matthew to a leather wingback chair.

Matthew shook his head, too anxious to sit.

"Thank you," Buchanan said. "The Pinkerton Agency, please. Robert Pinkerton, if he's available."

Pinkerton? Matthew's eyes bugged. They were going to call Mr. Pinkerton at this time of night? Again, Matthew marveled at the turn his life had taken. Growing up, he'd heard about the exploits of the Pinkertons, but he'd never thought he might meet one. Much less kiss one.

"Mr. Pinkerton? Sorry to wake you. This is Graham Buchanan here. I'm in Joplin, Missouri, and a mutual friend of ours has run into some trouble."

Matthew crossed his arms over his chest, but that didn't feel right. He hooked his thumbs into his waistband but still couldn't stop fidgeting as he tried to imagine what was being said on the other end of the line.

Buchanan darted a look at him, then nodded. "I have a man here she trusted. I don't think he knows your side of it, but he witnessed what happened at the station. I'm going to put him on the line." He offered the receiver to Matthew. "Here you go."

Matthew balked. He was going to speak to the infamous Pinkerton? But it was for Calista. My, but she got him doing things he never thought he'd do.

"This is Matthew Cook. How can I help you?"

The voice was rough and clipped. "Tell me exactly what happened—every word she said, and why you were at the police station in the first place."

"Yes, sir." Matthew related the attack that he'd walked into. He gave substantial details concerning Calista's injuries, but the director seemed impatient with his recital, so Matthew moved on to what had happened in the police station.

"The trouble started when she asked the officer about someone named Lila—"

"Don't say that name," the director snapped. "There are ears everywhere, and if this incident is any indication, the local justice might not be our ally." There was a long pause. "My office won't be able to help her from here. It would only bring her more trouble. Put Mr. Buchanan back on."

Matthew handed the receiver back, still unsatisfied that he

didn't have any answers, and Buchanan's stilted conversation wasn't enlightening. Finally, he hung up.

"To the police station we go." The rail magnate drained his teacup and pulled on a hat.

"It's fortunate that you have all this at your disposal," Matthew said as they left the office behind.

"I am fortunate, no doubt about it," Buchanan replied without a touch of humility.

"And also fortunate that you aren't worried about Calista's straits." Buchanan's buoyancy made Matthew's agony all the harder to bear.

"Listen, brother." Buchanan stopped at the corner and turned to Matthew. "If Miss York is determined to follow this path, she'll face worse situations than this. She has to learn how to cope."

What was worse? That Buchanan didn't seem to be worried about Calista, or that he knew her better than Matthew did?

"What's the plan?" Matthew asked.

"We are not to invoke Pinkerton's name. It appears that the police are holding her fraudulently. The only reason they could have for that is if they are involved in Lila Seaton's disappearance. We should stick to Miss York's original story that she was friends with the ladies and continue to hide her connection with the Pinkertons. If these corrupt officers know that she's part of a detective operation and she's searching for the girl, it could have dire consequences for Lila Seaton. It could be just as bad for Calista."

"Then, how do we get her out?"

"As you've pointed out, I have many tools at my disposal. People want to be agreeable to me. It might be that I have some influence with the officers." Had he ever used his influence on Calista? Mr. Buchanan must have felt Matthew's glare, but he shrugged it off. "If they don't cooperate, I have other means available."

Matthew should have been grateful for his help, but instead he was wishing he'd never laid eyes on the man. Buchanan made

Matthew truly take a look at himself. Even as they walked toward the police station, Matthew compared Buchanan's custom-made shoes to his worn boots. Buchanan's elegant hands to his rough and broken fingernails. It would be obvious to everyone that Calista belonged to Buchanan, not Matthew.

As disheartened as he was, Matthew had to appreciate Buchanan's confidence as he walked right past the police desk and straight to an office with a nameplate reading *Captain Dirk* on the door.

"I demand to see Calista York."

Only the portly man's eyes moved as they lifted to see who dared address him like that.

Buchanan leaned both hands on Captain Dirk's desk and repeated, "Where is Calista York?"

"Steinham, get this jackanapes out of my office." Captain Dirk rocked as if he could settle even further into his hard wooden chair.

"Miss York was unlawfully detained, and I demand to speak to her," Buchanan persisted.

"I don't know this Miss York or where she's off to, but it's Saturday night, and we have more to worry about."

"She was attacked," Matthew said. "I was with her. We came in to report the attack, and the next thing I knew, she was being arrested. Officer Rush took her in. Ask him."

The bored-looking officer at the door must have been Steinham. "This office is not for the public," he said. "Let's go, Mister . . ."

"Buchanan. Graham Buchanan."

Matthew had to admire how Steinham stepped away. A nervous look at his captain said everything.

"Graham Buchanan, huh?" The captain leaned back in his chair to get a better look at his accoster. "And what's your interest in this lady?"

"She's family."

Matthew's eyes darted to the side. Was that the truth? What

kind of people was he befriending when he didn't know whether to believe them or not?

Turning to Steinham, the captain asked, "Do you know what he's talking about?"

"Yes, sir. I was there when she was arrested."

That answer didn't sit well with the captain. With a huff, he stood and said with begrudging respect, "Make yourself comfortable while I see what is going on here." He brushed against the desk on his way past, rustling the pile of papers.

Matthew didn't feel like sitting, but Graham eased into a chair and swung his crossed leg nonchalantly. "They'll straighten this out."

"Family?" Matthew said. "Is that true?"

Graham's mouth quirked. "Absolutely. I married her cousin Willow Kentworth. I believe you know Willow's father, Oscar."

"You married a Kentworth cousin?" Matthew could hardly believe his ears. How could Graham Buchanan have joined the same family that produced the likes of Amos and Maisie? "How did that happen?"

Graham lowered his voice. "Our railroad hired the Pinkertons to work a case. Miss York was the operative. Willow got caught in the middle."

Matthew felt a knot releasing in his chest. Calista had been hired by Buchanan. Now, instead of jealousy, he felt pride for Calista's family. Both he and her granny were Missouri ranchers, but it didn't keep them from aiming high.

Even though Matthew had more questions, his concern for Calista made him too ill-tempered for chitchat. "What's taking them so long?" he asked.

"There'll be paper work to do before they release her."

"That and the captain might ought to take time to give Officer Rush a stern talking-to," Matthew added.

With a dip of his head, Buchanan acknowledged the point. Matthew stretched his legs in front of him and cradled his clenched fist. Only now was he beginning to feel the knuckles that had pounded that cad. They wouldn't hurt long, though. Teddy's head would take more time to heal.

Waiting was misery, made even more miserable by the railroad magnate's ease. Matthew wanted to shake him until he was as fired-up as he was, but he was in a police station, and he'd probably get in trouble for that. Besides, Buchanan was a friend, even if they'd got off on the wrong foot.

Finally, their wait was over. The captain came in like a bull was running behind him and he was wearing red. Having to take orders from Mr. Buchanan had put him in a foul mood.

He sat and scooted a few papers around before he addressed them. "Your friend will not be released tonight. She is under arrest."

Buchanan's face paled even as Matthew's burned.

"You can't do that," Matthew said.

"On what grounds?" Buchanan asked.

"On suspicion of conspiracy to kidnap. It's our belief that organized crime is involved as well."

"Organized crime?" Matthew moved to the edge of his chair.

Captain Dirk glared at Matthew. "Either you're a criminal, or you don't know your friend very well. And, Mr. Buchanan, you might have sway in New York or Chicago, but this is Joplin. We're not impressed with your fine airs. Just because you have money doesn't mean you can buy a criminal freedom."

"It's not about my money." Buchanan's voice grew cold and precise, just as Matthew was feeling like he was losing control. "It's about the law. She hasn't done anything wrong, and you can't hold her."

"She refuses to answer our questions," the captain said. "She's already written a report about her attack, but she refuses to answer questions about her other activities."

"Has she requested a lawyer?" Buchanan asked.

The captain gave the merest shake of his head.

"Well, she's going to get one." Buchanan pounded his knee. "As soon as he can pull his suspenders on and lace up his shoes, I'll have a lawyer here to end this crisis."

"Unless that lawyer can explain what she's been doing here in town, I don't know what good he'll do you, but be my guest."

Was it morning yet? Matthew felt the weariness of the night, but the fight in him was far from giving up. Mr. Buchanan, for all his confidence, wasn't swaying the captain. If Calista was going to be held all night, someone needed to know.

"You get the lawyer," Matthew said. "I'll have Maisie take me to Calista's Grandma Kentworth. Her family will be worried about her."

"Wait." The captain turned his head to the side and watched Matthew from the corner of his eye, as if he was afraid of what he was going to see. "Are you talking about Laura Kentworth?"

Matthew tensed. "Yes. Miss York is Mrs. Kentworth's granddaughter."

"I thought I knew all the Kentworth clan," Captain Dirk said.

"Miss York is from Kansas City. Her mother married a man there."

The captain wiped his hand across his jaw. "I'd forgotten that. And then with a different last name . . ." His chin wobbled. "Has Miss York been in touch with her grandmother since she's been in town?"

"Of course. She's been in touch with all the family." Here Matthew was only guessing. He'd met Maisie and Amos and knew that Olive had watched Howie, but he had no idea how many more cousins were prowling around.

Captain Dirk darted a glance over his shoulder as if he hoped to find a new route of escape in the corner of his office. Evidently, Mr. Buchanan didn't pull the weight that Calista's little granny did.

The captain picked up a pencil. "If she would've told us she was here visiting family, we wouldn't have detained her." He scribbled on a pad of paper. "I apologize for the inconvenience. Please make that clear to Miss York and send Mrs. Kentworth my regards." He ripped off the top sheet and handed Matthew the paper. "Present this to the officer on duty at the jail behind the building. I'll explain my decision to Officer Rush, but I wouldn't want a repeat of tonight. Impress upon Miss York the importance of staying in the respectable parts of town."

"Yes, sir." As if Matthew hadn't been trying. He took the paper, barely grumbling a thanks as he rushed out of the office.

He'd made it out of the police station and to the jail before he thought to look for Buchanan, but Buchanan was on his heels.

"You didn't need me after all. One mention of Granny Laura's name—"

"If I'd known that, I would've said something sooner." The electric streetlights had gone dark. The streets were nearly empty, and those still on the street would probably sleep where they lay.

"Isn't it interesting that Calista didn't say anything? If her grandmother has that much influence, why wouldn't she drop her name sooner?"

Matthew didn't like that question. "She's probably protecting them. It'd be just like Calista to shield her family while claiming there's no real danger."

Graham nodded. "The important thing is that she's not being held in a cell with criminals all night." He looked toward the light coming up in the east. "Or all morning."

The clock had never moved so slowly, but finally they were at the desk and Calista was brought forward to sign out.

Her bristling outrage had dissolved into something more cautious. She thanked the clerk who handed over her handbag and baton, and then signed a form. Matthew couldn't image how she was maintaining her dignity. Then again, there was a lot about

Calista that he didn't know. But when she turned and gazed at him, he reckoned he knew enough.

He held out his arms, and she folded into his chest. Wrapping her arms around his waist, she sighed against him.

"I knew you wouldn't leave me." She winced at her raspy voice and touched her throat.

Thinking of her injuries, he handled her gently. "Actually, I did leave, but only to get Mr. Buchanan."

He felt her body straighten, and then she stepped away.

"Graham, my apologies. I didn't see you standing there."

"Evidently not." Buchanan's eyes twinkled. "Seeing that you're in good . . . hands, I'm going back to the car. Willow will be fraught with worry until she hears that you're alright." He cocked an eyebrow. "You are alright, aren't you?"

She shot a look at the clerk at the desk. "For the time being, but something is wrong. I'll call the office."

"Yes, they have concerns." He gave a small bow to Calista and offered Matthew his hand. "Watch out for her. At least, as much as she allows you to."

"I intend to."

Matthew couldn't get her out of there fast enough. Neither of them spoke as they made their way through the wasted streets. A milk wagon crossed the intersection in front of them as they reached the hotel. All the lights in the lobby were out except a lone lamp on the clerk's stand. They quietly passed, not wanting to be spotted sneaking in early Sunday morning, disheveled and tired.

When they reached her door, Calista handed him the key.

"My eyes are so blurry, I don't think I can see to unlock it," she said.

All he wanted was to get her somewhere safe. Someplace where he could take care of her. He motioned Calista inside and looked up and down the hallway before closing the door of the apartment.

Maisie rushed forward. "Are you alright? What happened?"

First she held out Calista's ripped skirt, then took her hands to look for bruises. "At least you got a few strikes of your own in."

"I was attacked," Calista said, "and now that the police have figured that out, things will be fine."

So, Maisie didn't know about Calista's job? Matthew had wondered who in the family she'd taken into her confidence.

"You look a mess," Maisie said. "Let's get you cleaned up." Taking Calista by the arm, she started toward the washroom.

"I don't want you to go," Calista said to Matthew. "Will you wait for me?"

"As long as you need."

He rearranged pillows on a sofa, trying to imagine how she would be most comfortable. He might have dozed a bit, listening to the girls' low voices in the next room. When Calista returned, her sleeves were rolled up and her forearms glistened.

Matthew stood, took her by the fingertips, and pulled her to the sofa. "You must be exhausted." He bent and lifted her foot to unbutton her boots.

The ghost of a smile graced her lips. "Maisie heard Howie stirring, so she went back to soothe him. She won't hear us talking."

"Good, because I'd like to know how the man who attacked you is involved in your case."

"The attack, that was just bad luck. Perhaps Teddy is involved in kidnapping, or he could just be an opportunistic cad who thought he'd found a vulnerable woman he could meddle with."

"Kidnapping? You're going after a kidnapper?" Forgetting the buttons on her boots, Matthew lifted his head. "You were going alone to find a kidnapper?"

"I wasn't trying to arrest him, just get information. But now that the police know about me, Mr. Pinkerton is bound to replace me. He's not going to be happy about this."

"I'm not happy about it. Do you know how close you came to disappearing?"

"I don't want to think about that. If I think about that, how will I do my job? How am I going to help Lila? I can't forget that picture of her." She blinked up at him, begging his indulgence.

"I've seen that same haunted look on most of the girls out there," he said. "They all need help."

"You can help the many. I've got to find the one."

"At what cost? What makes her life more valuable than yours?"

Calista closed her eyes and rested her head on the back of the sofa. "What made you leave your family and come to a desperate town? What made you take the most dismal position at the mines? The same God who compels you to declare freedom to the captives has given me the task of freeing a very specific captive. There's no difference."

He bent back over her boot and unfastened the last button. The pieces began to fall into place—her persistence, her knowledge of Scripture, the glimpses of worship he caught at their studies, her bravery, her family's influence. Calista wasn't a flighty woman looking for adventure. She was the woman he'd hoped she was, and so much more. The answer to his most pressing question had been given, and he'd almost been too irate to catch it.

"Tell me more about Lila," he said at last and pulled her boot off her foot.

"Her family hired the agency to find her. They think she was spotted at the House of Lords, but she isn't there any longer. We know she was brought on a train from Chicago, and Della Rush purchased her ticket with Lila's. You can see why I suspect Officer Rush. He became suspicious when I asked about Della, but when I mentioned Lila Seaton . . ."

"That's when he decided to stop you." Matthew lifted her other foot, dropped it on his knee, and started on those buttons.

"Which means he's hiding something and isn't afraid to abuse the law to succeed," Calista said. "I've got to wonder if more officers are involved. This might be bigger than I can handle."

"And more dangerous. There." He removed her second shoe and dropped it to the floor. "Is that better?"

She extended her bottom lip in a pout. "So much better." Drawing her feet beneath her, she reached for a white woven blanket.

Matthew took the blanket and spread it out so it covered her better. In the poorly lit room, he shouldn't have been able to see the marring on her neck, but the bruises had gotten darker since the attack. A knot bound his throat, making words impossible. He thought of the man's hands, how his fingers had been right there, crushing her beautiful neck, choking out the air that filled her lungs. He wished he could wipe away every trace of that man, all the grime, all the dirt, but the marks would remain.

His heart pounded as he gathered Calista against him, fitting her shoulder into his side and resting her head on his chest. He'd do anything for her, including taking her pain if it was possible, but he couldn't bear to see the ugly marks on her neck in the new day's light.

"Thank you for everything." She lifted her head. "We've both been so sorely tested tonight that it's no wonder we're behaving rashly."

She didn't know about him running all over town. She couldn't know about his jealousy of Buchanan. What had he done rashly?

The deep richness of her eyes and hair contrasted with the white blanket. Despite her exhaustion, her color had returned, pinking her cheeks and tinting her lips.

Oh . . . that was what he'd done.

Matthew shifted against her. "Is this about the kiss?"

The pink on her cheeks deepened. "It was out of character."

"You don't know me as well as you think." Matthew found her waist beneath the blanket and lifted her to him. "Let me acquaint you."

He didn't need the excuse of fury and fear this time. The warmth that floated through his veins as their lips met was comforting.

The night had been agony—loving her, aching for her, wishing he could do more, be more for her. But here she was, and she was accepting what love he could give.

But after all she'd been through, he wanted her to rest. He raked his lips across hers one last time, despairing of her sweetness, then drew away.

Holding on to his shirt, Calista pulled herself against him and snuggled into his arms. At the end of her sigh, she trembled and then burrowed even closer.

"I've got you," he said. "Nothing can happen here."

"I didn't mean to involve you." Her voice was muffled by his chest. "You know everything now."

"The most important thing I know is that you're not just a nice lady I'm trying to help. You're my heart, and anything that threatens you threatens my future." He lifted her face and went to kiss her again, but she turned away.

"'I charge you, O daughters of Jerusalem, that ye stir not up, nor awake my love,'" she quoted. "Until its time." Her eyes fluttered as she looked up at him with gentle merriment, waiting for his response.

"The time is coming, O daughter of Jerusalem," he said, his voice husky. "The time is nigh."

"That's not Scripture."

"It's a prophecy." After pressing a quick kiss to her knuckles, he got slowly to his feet, trying not to disturb her. "I have to prepare for our church meeting this morning. Is there anything I can tell the group?"

"No. I'm going to get some sleep, but if I wake, I'll go to the Tabernacle. Reverend Dixon is convinced he's making progress on my sanctification." She stood, and with her first step, she faltered. He held out his hand, but she waved him off and took a few more steps, testing her balance. "I'm going to be sore, but I think I'll sleep well, at least until Howie and Maisie wake me."

"Sun's up. It won't be long." He shifted his feet. Leaving was turning out to be a lot more work than he'd thought it would be. "Will I see you tonight?"

"I hope so. I don't know if these bruises will leave me presentable."

"As long as you promise you won't go anywhere alone."

So intent was Matthew on getting a last kiss, he didn't realize until later that she'd never responded to his request.

CHAPTER
22

Whatever was bouncing against her face, Calista didn't bother pushing it away. Her sleep was so restless and troubled that the barrage barely registered. She was too busy trying to stay out of the clutches of a crazed man who was chasing her around a barred cell while Officer Rush egged him on. The pats on her face were the least of her worries.

But they were more persistent than her dreams. Flopping onto her back, away from the edge of the bed, Calista blinked the midmorning light into perspective. Her throat hurt, her head throbbed, and her joints ached. Having heard about her close call, Mr. Pinkerton would be adamant about replacing her. She'd do her best to persuade him otherwise, but beneath all the difficulty, she had the assurance that she wasn't in the struggle alone. Finally, Matthew knew everything, and he approved. At least, she assumed he didn't make it a practice to kiss people he disapproved of.

But what did his approval mean? Did it matter? Not unless she was going to turn her back on her duty.

A squeal in her ear brought her eyes wide open. What in the world? She turned toward the noise. Leaning against the side of her bed, Howie was slapping the mattress with an open palm.

Only after Calista offered him a finger to hold did she see Maisie standing in the doorway of her bedroom.

"How are you feeling?" she asked. Her bare arms looked as sinewy as a miner's. "Any worse for wear?"

"No worse than getting scratched up in the blackberry patch," Calista said.

Maisie's smile showed that she didn't believe Calista but was willing to let it pass.

"I'm going to Matthew's church with Silas. You want to go? Matthew asked me to come and visit with Loretta Campbell. She could use a friend right now."

Calista covered her eyes against the light. "What's wrong with Loretta?"

"She strikes me as being very solemn, don't you think? I'm hoping I can cheer her. If Dan's mine doesn't prove out, I might see if Pa could hire him onto the ranch for a bit. Just trying to help."

Calista smiled at her cousin. It was good to see Maisie thinking of someone besides herself. Other than their ages, she and Loretta Campbell didn't seem to have much in common, but perhaps she was right. Maybe Loretta could use some of Maisie's tomfoolery to lighten her mood.

Once Calista agreed to keep Howie, Maisie lost no time in slipping on her boots and getting out the door, leaving her hat behind in the process.

"It's just us today," Calista said to Howie. "I hope you feel like a nap this afternoon."

Her first order of business was to call the office. Matthew had explained how Graham had called Mr. Pinkerton the night before, and Calista knew, being the professional that he was, Mr. Pinkerton wouldn't rest easy until he heard that she was safe, Sunday or not.

Instead of asking at the front desk, she smiled and pointed inside the office. The clerk waved her on through with a curious look at Howie. Closing the door behind her, she took a deep breath as she waited for her connection.

"Father, I hope everything is well," she said at the sound of his greeting.

"Good to hear from you. Your cousin's husband called last night and said that you ran into some people who thought they knew you."

"I'm not sure what the nature of our acquaintance is," she said, "but complete strangers don't usually hand out such a welcome without a cause."

"That's very troublesome," he said. "My friend here has never suggested that anyone working for that institution was involved."

"They are most credibly involved," she said. "When I asked about certain names, the effect was immediate."

The only sound was the clicking that Calista knew to be Mr. Pinkerton's pen against his desk as he thought. From the speed of the clicking, it must be a tough decision he was pondering.

"I'm recalling you," he said.

Calista's stomach dropped. "There's no need." She moved Howie to her other hip, breathing hard into the receiver. "I'm so close."

"You've done marvelously, but your identity has been compromised. With all you've learned, it won't take any time for this to come to a satisfactory conclusion. I regret that the satisfaction will come from another of our teammates, but I'm concerned about your safety."

"No, please." While she never forgot the urgency of her mission, she had pushed away all thought of what would happen when it was over—when she had to leave. She was at home in Joplin, but home had taken on a whole new meaning with Matthew. "Give me more time."

"Buy train tickets to Kansas City. Leave as soon as you can tie up loose ends. Make sure you aren't followed, and you can meet your replacement in Kansas City to share whatever information you've gathered."

Knowing that her portion had ended, Mr. Pinkerton wasn't even bothering to keep up the familial ruse on the telephone, and he didn't need to explain the Kansas City meeting. If the agency suspected that one operative had been compromised, they could only meet their replacement in a secure place. She must leave Joplin before the next operative arrived. There was no question of them meeting under the nose of the criminals they were trying to catch.

The pen had stopped clicking. He'd made a decision, and there was no changing his mind. Calista hugged Howie against her, surprised at the hitch in her breathing. She'd been naive not to see this day coming. She had no control over where she was going next, or when. She was totally at the agency's mercy, and this decision felt particularly merciless.

How had she come to rely on Matthew so much? How had she blinded herself to the certainty that this day would come? Calista had a mission, one that was very important to her. A calling that she believed was from God. Matthew was also called, but to a different field, and she would think less of him if he abandoned it. There was only one choice for both of them—obedience. Only Calista hadn't expected it to cost them so dearly.

But if she could find Lila herself before the other operative was due to arrive, maybe she could bargain for a few days' leave. Maybe she could have the time to make a decent good-bye to Matthew and thanks to Willow and Granny for keeping her secret. Maybe she'd have a better chance of getting the permanent position as an operative.

"Yes, sir," she said. "The depot might not sell tickets on a Sunday, but I'll do it first chance."

She hoped that excuse would buy her a little time, because first thing tomorrow, she was making a telephone call to Carthage and asking for records from the county courthouse. Records on Della

Rush, in hopes of learning what her relationship was to Officer Rush.

⁂

Sunday had been a frantic day of combing the streets, looking for any signs of Lila. In most places, Calista wouldn't have a chance to carry on the investigation on a Sunday. All business would be suspended in honor of the Lord's Day. Joplin wasn't most places, but Calista's attempts hadn't been profitable. She'd learned nothing that would reverse Mr. Pinkerton's decision.

Monday morning found her in the hotel office, watching the clock, waiting for the hour that the county courthouse would open. A decent, quiet town like Carthage was as reliable as they came, and the clerk at the courthouse picked up on the first ring at 9:00 a.m., ready to search for the record she requested.

"Miss York? You're in luck. I found a marriage record with that name on it," the voice on the telephone line reported after several minutes. "Della and Gregory Rush were married in Jasper County two years ago. Gregory Rush's profession is listed as a police officer."

Della Rush, who'd dragged Lila from Chicago, was Officer Rush's wife? She'd been involved in Lila's disappearance from the start.

"That's very helpful," Calista said. "Thank you."

"My pleasure," the clerk replied. "Gregory Rush and Della Bowman, it says it right here on the paper."

"Bowman?" Calista's eyes widened. Could proper little Mrs. Bowman from the Children's Home be involved? It sickened Calista to consider it, but she'd stopped believing in coincidences. "Thank you," she said. "You've been an incredible help."

She hung the receiver in the cradle, then picked up Howie. She'd been closer to the truth than she'd realized. Whatever Mrs. Bowman's role, it was notable that she worked with the product of their unholy commerce. Was she there to whitewash the records so that names like Lila Seaton's were never recorded? How deep did this ring go?

Calista was running out of time to find out. Maisie had tiptoed out of the hotel room while Calista was in the washroom that morning, leaving Howie behind again. She had to admit, when the baby was with someone else, she missed his sweet babbling. If she never had to worry about dangerous assignments, he'd be a pleasant distraction.

She left the hotel's office with the baby on her hip and headed toward the streetcar stop. What would happen to Howie when she finished her case? Matthew had promised to find a solution, but they hadn't realized she would be relocated so soon.

Calista looked at the two men and the lady who boarded the streetcar with her, watching for signs that they had devious intentions. None of them seemed interested in her. Just in case, it was helpful to have Howie with her. Howie gave her an excuse to go to the Children's Home. She'd ask about him teething or something if she was challenged for her reason for visiting. How she'd introduce the subject of Lila Seaton with Mrs. Bowman, she wasn't sure yet, but inspiration often sprang from unseeded pots.

One by one, the passengers who'd boarded with her disembarked. Calista allowed herself a breath. Things were dire enough, but at least she didn't have to worry about being waylaid on the road between the streetcar stop and the Children's Home. The walk had never seemed so far, but it had everything to do with her anxiousness to solve the case before Matthew got off work.

"Do you recognize this place?" she asked Howie as his eyes followed the high gate of the home to its top. But Howie kicked his feet and babbled some meaningless answer that she had no interpretation for.

Would Howie return here? It wasn't such a bad place. The people who worked here did what they could for the children, but it wasn't a home. Calista would feel that she'd failed if he was sent back, but she wouldn't feel it as strongly as Matthew would. She kissed Howie on the head as she walked through the front door.

Mrs. Fairfield came out of her office. Her eyes alighted on Howie, and she smiled. "Oh, here's the little man. Just look at him, fat and sassy as he should be. Come on back. Most of our staff is busy, but they'll want to see him."

She led Calista back to a waiting room, and Calista took a seat on a bench, pleased that her visit was welcome. Her presence wasn't disconcerting to anyone. What *was* disconcerting was that Calista couldn't see past the hanging sheets that divided the room into private alcoves.

"I thought you all would want to see how well he's doing," she said. "You must miss him terribly."

Mrs. Fairfield smiled. "He's a doll-baby, but we'd be selfish to wish him back. His crib has already been filled by another."

"I really thought that Mrs. Bowman would want to see him. They seemed to share a special bond."

The first crack in the facade appeared. "Mrs. Bowman? She should be here, but now that you mention it, I don't think I saw her this morning. Let me ask. I'll be right back."

Calista remembered not to let her disappointment show. "Yes, please. That'd be delightful."

She bounced Howie on her knee and looked around the room. It was obviously some sort of interview area. The sheet dividing the room would shield someone from sight but wouldn't keep their conversation private—as was evident when two people entered and began an interview on the other side of the room.

Normally, decorum would dictate that she make her presence known, but Calista was learning to set aside etiquette in pursuit of the truth. She slowed her bouncing and prayed that Howie wouldn't give away their location.

"I have a few questions, Miss Vanek. We like to have a complete file on the children when possible. We have no desire to shame you. This is in the hopes that should you find yourself in happier circumstances, you might decide to return and reclaim your child."

"Does that happen often?"

Calista smoothed Howie's hair and wondered how often his mother thought of him.

"All the time," the volunteer replied, "but it wouldn't be possible if we didn't keep records on the children. Now, I have your name. What's the child's birth date?"

"It was this April, the eighteenth. I remember because my own birthday was also on the eighteenth of October—or that's what my ma always told me."

Through the gap in the curtain, Calista saw the girl, and her heart twisted for the young mother. Matthew was right. Maybe a Children's Home would always be necessary, but wouldn't it be better if the families could manage to keep the children themselves?

"And what is the father's name?" The nurse's voice was tentative, as if this question had received a poor reception before.

"I'll tell you who it is, although you don't have to worry about him coming after this baby. It's Silas Marsh. He's the baby's father, and he won't do a blamed thing for her."

CHAPTER
23

Matthew had learned the rhythm of the shovel—thrust, scrape, lift, and dump. He knew the timing of the explosions that knocked tonnage down when they'd cleared the ground and were ready for more. He knew the harsh music of the jaw crusher aboveground that crushed the rock into smaller bits so it could be carried by conveyor belts to the hand-jigging area. And he knew the movements of the workers at the jig cells, washing the pieces and separating the jack from the chat.

No longer did they call him an apple knocker. He might have started out as a farm boy, but he knew mining now, and with new men starting every week, no one thought of him as inexperienced anymore. In fact, he'd noticed his foreman paying special mind to his work. If Matthew were to guess, someone had been talking about him.

"Cook." The foreman's light grew brighter as he approached over the piles of debris. "You're wanted in the office."

The men on either side of Matthew didn't falter in their cadence. Their shovels continued to chip away at the pile, even as they looked at him, worry apparent on their dark faces.

"It's fine," Matthew said. "I'll be right back." But just in case, he secured his paddle marker in his bucket to claim the load of ore that he'd started.

He walked past the mules tethered to ore cans. Those mules walked in a circle, raising the full ore cans and lowering the empty. Once the mules were brought down into the mine, they would spend the rest of their lives in the cave, never to see sunlight again. Hearing that fact from an old cokey with swollen joints had nearly crushed Matthew. He wouldn't wish it on any beast, but some of the men weren't much better off.

He entered the elevator that ran next to the ore can lift. It clanged as it went up the two hundred feet. At shift change, it was always full of men. Without the other miners, all the odd creaks and clangs took on a more insidious tone. Usually, coming up to daylight meant his work was over, but ending the day early meant that he had other concerns.

First Matthew headed to the doghouse to hang up his tools and hat and wash up, then he went to the office by the scales. When he gave his name, he was directed to the main office, where he was pointed to a folding chair and sat next to a man holding a rag against his bleeding forehead.

The miner lowered the rag, frowned at the blood, then reapplied it. "Does it look as bad as it feels?" he asked Matthew.

"It's a lot of blood, but foreheads are apt to do that. You'll be fine."

A mine employee came out of a back room and called the injured man's name. "Wish me luck with the sawbones," he said. "Let's hope he stitches straight."

"Godspeed," Matthew replied and wondered again why he'd been called up.

He didn't have to wait much longer. The raw-boned man who came to fetch him had cuffs that didn't quite reach his wrists and was none other than Calista's uncle, Oscar Kentworth.

"Mr. Cook, it's a pleasure to see you again." He escorted

Matthew into his office. "According to Graham, you were able to clear up the misunderstanding at the police station. How they could mistake my niece for a criminal is inexplicable."

Mathew knew it wasn't his place to explain, so he grunted in agreement.

"What I wanted to see you about is a new position here at the Fox-Berry." Mr. Kentworth's smile was sincere even if his eyes bore a sadness. "As you might remember from the meeting I had with Reverend Dixon, Mr. Blount has decided to create a new position here at the works. As our plans have progressed, your name continues to come to mind."

Matthew sat up a little straighter. He'd taken this job to help him reach the miners. Would another position give him the same access? "I'm all ears," he said.

"It's been brought to Mr. Blount's notice that his miners often miss work because they are sick or injured. Even more often, their sickness is self-induced by the choices they make on Saturday night. He thinks it would benefit his company if the miners showed more restraint."

"It's true. The mine would be more profitable, if that's his primary concern."

"But it's not yours." Kentworth steepled his fingers. "I've heard about the guidance you've offered the miners and how you've even intervened to see that they had money at the end of the week. I've also noticed that my family members think highly of you." He pinned Matthew with a look that was indecipherable. "You have good intentions, and I'd like to give you a chance to multiply them. You would be paid to act as a resource for our men and their families at the new workers' center we're building . . . when you're not squiring my niece about."

"What kind of a resource?"

"Counseling the men, training them to be good stewards of their money, giving them a place away from the whiskey and gin to visit and congregate, being an ambassador between them and the management. Of course, we wouldn't interfere with your Sunday services. In fact, I think this would be a way for your ministry to continue during the week."

Matthew looked at his hands, still damp from being washed. It was a dream come true, and it was going to be made possible with help from two people he'd judged unfairly—Mr. Blount and Reverend Dixon.

"What does this new position pay?" he asked.

"More than a cokey. Everything pays more than a cokey. You'll be paid at a manager's rate. Perhaps not at the highest level, but with time . . ."

A manager's pay? Enough to move out of the florist's cabin? Enough to buy a home? And he'd get to do work that he'd come to do. Could it be possible?

"It sounds good. . . ."

"Think it over," Calista's uncle said. "Talk it over with Reverend Dixon, as he and his church would like to provide volunteers to help you. If you don't want the job, your position as a cokey is still available."

Matthew stood and extended his hand. He didn't need to ponder it any longer. "I'll do it." He couldn't wait to tell Calista.

"Excellent. I'll tell Mr. Blount. Despite your disagreements, he respects your opinion and will be pleased that you've accepted. Tomorrow we'll meet with him and Reverend Dixon. Unless you want to finish the day's work, I'll have them weigh up your ore can and pay you for what you've done already this morning. That'll give you time to make arrangements before it's too late." His sad eyes warmed a bit, making Matthew wonder if Calista's Uncle Kentworth already thought of him as family.

Matthew barely noticed the walk to his cabin. His mind was reeling. What sorts of projects would they start? What resources would Mr. Blount and Reverend Dixon make available to him?

Could he have Bible studies there? Meetings? Suddenly all the vague, wistful ideas he'd thought of to make life better for the families of Joplin seemed possible. Once he knew that Calista was safe, the whole future was ahead of them.

As he walked up Main Street, his eyes went to her window on the sixth floor of the Keystone. On Sunday, he'd stayed at the minefields until too late to call on her. Dan and Loretta had wanted him to come to their claim and see the ore they'd discovered. The only way he would have rejoiced more was if Calista had been with them, but she needed to recover, and he had his duties to fulfill. Today she wouldn't expect him until evening, so instead of visiting her unannounced, he'd use the time to make himself presentable.

Instead of tracking his dirty boots through Mr. Trochet's shop, Matthew walked around the brick building and came through the garden gate. As much as he liked this crowded, overgrown square of beauty, he hoped for more, and he hoped for it with Calista.

Yet he wasn't expecting to find her inside his cabin.

When he opened the door, she froze, bent over the table with a pencil against a piece of paper.

"I'm writing you a note," she said. Her face was drawn tight, her eyes weary. Whatever was going in that note, Matthew knew he didn't want to read it.

From the floor, Howie fussed as he crammed his fist into his mouth. Calista spared him a glance, then dropped the pencil. "I've got to find Maisie. I think she's with Silas, but I don't know where his claim is."

"I can take you," Matthew said, "but I have some news first—a lot of news. Before I tell you what is happening at the mine, I want you to know that on Sunday we arranged to start a Bible study for the working girls. Loretta Campbell is leading it here in my cabin while I'm at work on Fridays. You can invite whomever you like."

"That's wonderful. It really is."

"It was your idea, but now for the real surprise. I've got a new job at the mine. It's not in the mine, but it'll still be working with the miners. I talked to your uncle—Olive's father. He said I'd be like a manager."

She blinked like he was speaking Greek. "I'm happy for you," she said finally, but she didn't act like it.

"Do you know what this means?" he asked. "I'll be doing something that matters. I'll have permission and access to the people I want to help. And what's more, I'll be more independent. My salary—"

Howie screeched as he rolled to his knees and crawled to Calista. He pulled on her skirt to no avail.

"I'm sorry," she said. "I'm glad you're happy. It's good news. It's just that . . ." Her gaze went down to the fussy baby tugging on her hem. "I spoke with my boss. He's sending another operative."

Matthew felt like a weight had been lifted off his chest. "About time. I know it's important that the girl is found, but I'll rest easier knowing you aren't in danger. Let someone else deal with the corrupt police. Now you'll have time to take me out to the ranch. I really want to meet the rest of this family you've talked about."

The day was getting better and better, if only Howie wasn't having such a bad time. Matthew scooped him up and bounced to soothe him. He'd been looking for a good home for Howie. Could it be that they'd have a house to raise him in shortly?

But Calista seemed immune to all the good news.

"I went to the Children's Home," she said.

"Alone? Calista, you know better. What if you were arrested again?"

"I was there, and I heard a girl who was leaving a baby. She said that the father of the child . . ." Her hands trembled. "There's so much to do here. I can't leave. Not now. But I'm being reassigned. I'll have another client somewhere else. A new town, a new state. I can't stay."

Her words hit him like an anvil. "You're going? Away?"

She nodded. "Tonight. Tomorrow, at the latest. I found out that Mrs. Rush used to be a Bowman. Somehow she and Mrs. Bowman are tied, so I went to find Mrs. Bowman at the Children's Home, but she was gone. Didn't show up for work today. There's a connection. I can feel it."

She was telling him things that were important, but he couldn't understand. All he knew was that it was impossible that Calista could be going away. She didn't mean it. She would explain soon. She'd tell him how she'd figured out how to stay.

"And while I was there, I heard the girl. What she said, Matthew, I hate to repeat, but you must know. She said the father of her baby is Silas Marsh."

Her words cut through the fog. "Silas?" He shook his head. "No, there's a mistake."

"It's not a mistake. Unless she's lying to the nurse, but why would she do that?"

Silas? He'd thought Silas was a decent sort. Silas had been a friend to him.

"If I'd known, I never would've introduced him to your cousin." Matthew had to make amends. He motioned to the door. "Let's go. Maisie is lucky that she hasn't known him long enough for an attachment to grow."

"How long have we known each other?"

Her question stopped him in his tracks. "I don't see what that has to do with anything."

"I'm leaving. I don't know when I'll see you again, but how long we've known each other matters. One shouldn't change their course because of a short acquaintance."

"I disagree. Maybe under some circumstances, but not this one." Calista looked nearly spent. Matthew drew in a long breath. "I don't want to argue," he said at last. "We'll find Maisie and decide our next move."

She held out her hands for Howie. "Once I know Maisie's safe, maybe I can think past the next hour."

Matthew wanted to think about forever with Calista, but unless he'd misunderstood, she wasn't thinking along the same lines.

Silas's claim was on land that belonged to Mr. Green. In a few blocks, they left behind the paved streets of Joplin and were on the chat roads leading out to the minefields. Matthew carried Howie, who wasted no time falling asleep. He wanted to think about his meeting with Mr. Kentworth. He wanted to go back to basking in the happiness that his new position gave him, but he couldn't get past the fact that Calista was leaving. He couldn't see around that. Add to his hurt his concern that Silas wasn't honorable, and that Matthew had introduced him to the ladies, and Matthew was about to snap.

Dan and Loretta's little shack was on their path. Normally, he'd stop to visit, especially with the Campbells' good news, but they didn't have time. Not today.

But Loretta had seen them coming.

She came out with a sock in her hand and a darning needle hanging by a string of yarn. "What are you doing?" she gasped. Her eyes bugged like she was seeing a ghost.

"We're looking for Silas. Do you reckon he's at his claim?" Matthew looked around, but there was no sight of Dan. The intensity of Loretta's eyes concerned him.

"I reckon. Why do you have the child?" she asked.

Calista said, "I've been caring for him since the raffle. Sometimes my cousin helps, but today it's just me."

"You have him? How did that happen? How do you have him?" She reached out to brush Howie's arm. Something about her actions made Matthew uneasy, but Calista felt differently.

"Can he stay with you for a bit? We'll return in less than an hour, but he needs a nap."

Loretta dropped the sock she was darning in the grass. "Please." Her eyes shone as she waited for Matthew to hand him over.

Matthew gave Calista another uneasy look, but she nodded her consent as Loretta gathered the baby into her arms.

"I'll take good care of him," Loretta whispered. "Don't worry about a thing."

Howie drowsily waved an arm before settling against Loretta's chest and snoozing away.

"Something's wrong," Matthew said as they continued toward Silas's.

"She seems thrilled to have him," Calista replied. "Perhaps she and Mr. Campbell would like to raise him."

"You think that the first time they get a little money, they want a baby?"

She shoved her hands into her pockets. "What do you think is going to happen to him? I can't take him with me."

"I'm trying to forget that part of our conversation."

"It never was supposed to be forever." She shot him a pained look.

She had only been in town a month, but she'd changed his life. And he wasn't going to let her go without a fight.

But that fight was still ahead of them.

"This is Silas's place," he said, "but I don't think he's here." He pointed at a ditch in the ground with black bricks of galena visible in the rip and a shovel against the pile of dirt. "If he was, he'd be working right here."

But Calista wasn't listening. Instead she marched past him to the neat clapboard shack that Silas had built with his first year's earnings and banged on the door. "Maisie, are you in there? If so, you'd best come out right now."

The house looked empty, but when a floorboard creaked, Calista banged again. "Silas, it's Miss York and Matthew. We need to speak to you."

"Coming," he said from inside.

"How hard is it to reach the door?" Calista groused. "This house is the size of a breadbox."

"I'll do the talking," Matthew said. "Silas needs to explain man to man."

"If Maisie is here, I'll keep her outside until you can get an accounting—"

The door opened. Silas frowned. "Aren't you supposed to be at work, Matthew? Is everything okay?"

"Send Maisie outside, please." Calista reached in her pocket, and only then did Matthew remember the collapsible baton she'd used on her attacker.

"You're welcome to come in. It's a mite crowded, but—"

"Come on in." Maisie tugged on Silas's arm so she could peer over his shoulder. "You've never been here before."

"And you have?" Calista said coolly as she stepped inside.

According to her own reckoning, Calista had failed. She'd failed Jinxy, she'd failed Mr. Pinkerton, but most of all, she'd failed Lila. Even though he had no part in this case, she also felt that she'd failed Matthew. But there was one person she wouldn't fail to rescue, and that was her cousin.

The threadbare house smelled of coffee and wet dirt, and Maisie looked way too comfortable being there.

"Come in," Maisie said as if she were the mistress of the home. "Isn't this quaint? There's not much room, but Silas already has plans to expand."

"Silas, I want a word with you. Outside," Matthew said.

Silas eyed him warily. Instead of moving to the door, he stepped toward Maisie and clutched her to his side. "I want a word about Maisie. This lady is the absolutely best woman in the world. There's nothing I wouldn't do for her, and I want to make her my wife." Calista's stomach rolled as he gazed at Maisie. "I'm sorry for not saying it sooner, but would you marry me?"

"No," Matthew said.

"Yes," said Maisie. "Yes, I'll marry you."

"We're not here to plan a wedding," Calista said. "We're here to ask Silas about a girl I met today. She was at the Children's Home."

If Silas had any idea what she was talking about, he hid it well.

"No other woman matters. It's just Maisie," he said.

"I feel the same way, Silas," Maisie replied. "Let's go home. I'll get Ma and Pa and Granny and all the cousins together, and we'll tell them then. I'll be the second cousin married. Won't that be something?"

Had Matthew not been standing in the way, Silas and Maisie would have trotted off without a backward glance.

"Silas, this conversation will be embarrassing," Matthew said, "but Calista thinks she heard something."

"I did hear something," Calista corrected.

"Right. This is your last chance for us to talk without the ladies," Matthew warned.

"Say what you want to say. I don't have anything to hide from my love." Silas gave Maisie a wide grin.

"The ladies are who it concerns," Calista said. The clock was ticking. There was a train with her name on it already headed toward Joplin. She couldn't leave this to be sorted out later. "The girl at the Children's Home was leaving a baby, and she reported the name of that baby's father. It was Silas Marsh."

So intently was Calista watching Silas that she didn't see Maisie coming until she'd shoved her in the arm.

"That's not true," Maisie said, her face florid. "That couldn't be true. Silas is a gentleman. Some men might lollygag around and never tell you how they feel"—she looked down her nose at Matthew—"but Silas is true to his heart, and you shouldn't hold it against him."

"I didn't concoct this story out of thin air—"

"Are you sure? The truth and you don't always share a yoke," Maisie said.

"I was there. I heard it myself."

"Then the girl is lying." Maisie squared her shoulders. "Why would we trust her? We don't know her."

Considering that it was his honor being discussed, Silas remained calm. "Was she a bigger girl? Redhead?" he asked.

"No," Calista answered. "She'd just had a baby, but she looked petite. Had a birthmark on her cheek. Miss Vanek."

"Yep," he said. "I know her. Didn't know she was going to have a baby, though. Now, Dahlia, she'd told me already, and I thought her older sister was going to raise the kid, but this one is a surprise."

Calista couldn't believe her ears. "You admit that you fathered this child?" she gasped.

"I admit it's possible." He raised his shoulders to his ears and gave that winsome smile that had worked its magic on Maisie. "But that was before I met Maisie. Those girls don't matter anymore."

It sounded like a bull's bellow mixed with a pig's squeal. Calista had always known her Kentworth farm cousins were uncommonly strong, but she hadn't accounted for them being so fast. Maisie launched herself against Silas and shoved him with all her strength. He wasn't prepared. No one was prepared. And when he tumbled toward the window, all they could do was watch as he toppled through and fell over the sill, head over heels, crashing on the grass outside.

"Nicely done," Matthew said.

Calista caught Maisie by the arm to keep her from climbing out the window and inflicting further damage. Maisie leaned out the window and yelled, "You lowdown beast. You're so low a pig would scrape you off his hoof before he got in the sty." She hiked her leg over the windowsill. "Let me go, Calista. Did you hear what he said? Those girls don't matter? Those girls he ruined? Those girls who had his children? I'm not finished with him. Let me go."

"I have half a mind to do it," Calista said.

Then Maisie spun on Matthew. "You're his friend. You should've known. How well do you know Matthew, Calista? Have you thought about that? We shouldn't trust these men at all."

Calista feared looking Matthew's direction. She had no questions about his character, but had she been just as impulsive as Maisie in allowing him to mean so much to her? Had she opened her heart before she'd thought through the consequences?

"Take her back to the hotel," Matthew said. "I'll finish up here."

"I'll get Howie on my way," said Calista. "C'mon, Maisie."

Maisie followed with teary-eyed fury. Calista kept a sharp eye on her cousin when they exited, fearful that she might run around the house to attack Silas again, but she'd recovered her dignity and marched through the mine claims with the posture of a soldier.

"I thought he really loved me," Maisie said, wiping away tears. "I thought I was special."

Calista took her arm. "You've got to be kidding me, Maisie Kentworth. You *are* special. Everyone you meet knows it. Just because a cad took an interest in you doesn't mean that's all you're good for."

"I want to go home. This dirty city isn't any fun anymore."

"Now's a good time for you to go. I'm leaving Joplin tonight. Going home to Kansas City."

"You're giving up on getting a job here?"

Calista had never told her about being a Pinkerton. There was no reason she needed to know now. "Yes. I can find somewhere else to finish my class requirements."

"It's for the best," Maisie said. "I wouldn't want you to get too besot with Matthew. These city boys aren't what they advertise. Go back to Kansas City. But those would be city boys too." She kicked a clod of dirt. "There's nowhere safe, I reckon."

They'd reached the Campbells' house. "Let's stop and get Howie," Calista said.

"You do what you need to. I'm going back to the ranch. Do you want me to tell Granny that your visit is over? That you're leaving?"

Granny would want the full story, but Calista answered to the office first. "Yes, please. Tell her that everything is just fine, but my stay ended. I'll write her with the full story soon."

Calista turned to walk down the bare path to Loretta's, but Maisie wasn't finished.

"Calista." Maisie swung her arms listlessly. "It really stinks that Silas was a rotten apple, but thank you for watching out for me. And if you don't mind, let's not mention any of this business to the family. If Amos hears, he might put a hurt on Silas that would get him in trouble with the law."

True. And it'd be even worse if Maisie and Amos's oldest brother found out. Finn was a known rounder. Where he was, no one knew for sure, but they didn't doubt that he was up to his eyeballs in trouble.

"As far as I'm concerned, Silas never existed," Calista said.

Maisie threw herself into Calista's arms, forcing her to regain her footing before they both fell, but the gesture made her smile nonetheless.

"Now, go on home," said Calista, "and behave yourself."

She stopped for a quick prayer of thanksgiving as Maisie left. She'd been sick with worry over Maisie's pain, but even more, over Maisie's reaction. Praise God, Maisie's good sense overrode any romantic instinct that had developed. But when it came to balancing romance and common sense, Calista wasn't sure she was one to judge.

Leave Joplin she must, but she couldn't bring herself to buy the tickets. She couldn't bring herself to make arrangements. She told herself that it was because Lila Seaton hadn't been found and she hated to give up on an unsolved case, but as the time approached, she had to admit that Matthew's draw was just as powerful. With him, she felt stronger. She felt that together they could accomplish something. In fact, she felt certain that he would accomplish something, and Uncle Kentworth saw the same promise. But while Matthew was saving the world, she had the family of a missing girl counting on her.

The thin boards and sparse roofing materials were the bare minimum one could have and still claim the title of house, but Calista knew not to pity the Campbells anymore. On their walk to Silas's claim, Matthew had told her that their fortunes had changed. Dan hoped they would soon be able to construct a home, maybe even one in town. Such were the fortunes of the miners in the area. Starving one day, rich as Midas the next. If only there was a story where a king turned everything he touched to zinc and lead instead of gold, it would be more fitting.

Calista knocked on the door, then stepped back to wait. A miner's wife and two children strolled by happily, carrying groceries for the week. What a blessing to live simply, to know your neighbors, to bring home food to prepare for your family. Calista had left Kansas City because she didn't feel needed. Her job with the Pinkertons gave her purpose, but would she still have her position once all the facts were known?

Loretta opened the door. Without a word, she stepped aside, opening the way for Calista to enter. Calista looked around but didn't see Howie. Unease crept into her chest. *Calm*, she reminded herself. *You're just on edge because of Silas.* Moving gracefully and deliberately, she took a seat on a rickety cloth-covered chair.

"Where's Howie?" she asked.

Loretta sat next to her in a posture almost of supplication. Despite her shaking hands, she looked more hopeful than Calista had ever known her to be. "He's asleep on the bed, but I wanted to talk to you about him. Now, don't feel ill-at-ease. No matter what you tell me, it's your choice. I have no rights in the issue. I just want you to listen."

"I'm always happy to listen." Calista tried to look past the sheet that divided the room, but she couldn't see the child. Now would be a good time for Matthew to arrive. She didn't know Loretta well, and she could tell something important was about to be shared.

"You know about Dan's injury last year, don't you? He lost his job at the mine when he broke his leg. We were destitute. We lost everything and didn't know where our next meal was coming from."

Calista nodded. "You shared that at our gathering. It was a dark time."

"But there's something I didn't share. It was too painful, and I was afraid no one would understand. Last year, when that happened, I was pregnant." Her mouth twitched in a smile of remembrance. "Dan kept telling me that it would be alright, but when the baby was born, we had no money. Nothing in the cupboard. Dan couldn't walk, much less shovel ore. We were new to town. Every once in a while, people tried to help, maybe share a meal, but our future was grim. I was so hungry, and I didn't want the baby to feel that way. When I couldn't feed him any longer, I had to put his needs first."

"You put him in the Children's Home." Calista's eyes stung. With the pain of an upcoming sacrifice looming, she felt a kinship with Loretta.

"It was only for a little while. Just until we got back on our feet. Then we figured we'd go and adopt him back. They allowed for that with other mothers, they told us. But we waited too long. Dan thought that after his leg healed, the mine would hire him again, but they didn't want him. They said he was accident-prone. So then he was left doing odd jobs until we could get enough together to lease a claim. The last claim failed, and then we heard the news. They were going to sell raffle tickets to decide who got Howie."

Calista's eyes darted to the hanging sheet as understanding dawned. "Howie is your baby?" With a yelp, she slid off her chair onto her knees. Loretta startled, but Calista caught her hands. "Tell me, is Howie your baby?"

Loretta nodded, sending Calista into unladylike laughter.

"All this time, I was worried sick over how I was going to take care of him."

"And I've been distraught that he was gone. I couldn't even bring myself to look at the paper and see who had him. It seemed easier not to know. After Matthew failed to get the raffle canceled, I told myself that was that, I had to forget him. I'm just surprised you bought tickets, knowing how opposed Matthew was."

"I didn't. It was a prank by my cousins, but Matthew insisted that it was God's provision. He said for me to take Howie and have faith that everything would be settled in the end. And it is. I will gladly return your son to you. You made a sacrifice to keep him well, despite the judgment and sorrow it brought. That was the most selfless act you could've undertaken. And now, just a few months later, you're able to provide for him."

"Truly, you'll let us have him?" Loretta stood, yanking Calista to her feet and wrapping her in a hug. "I didn't know if it was legal, since you'd filed paper work."

"There's no law on the books that can keep him from you," Calista said. "I can't tell you how happy I am to see him returned. I was worried, with me leaving, but this is the perfect news at the perfect time."

Loretta stepped out of the embrace. "You're leaving? But I thought you and Matthew . . . ?"

Why did everyone think stuff about her and Matthew? There was a lot of speculating going on in this town, and it had nothing to do with minerals. And what would it take to convince Matthew that she didn't love him? The longer she thought about it, the more convinced she was that rejecting him was the kindest way, but it would be the most trying performance of her life.

"Do I need to take Howie for now?" Calista asked. "If you aren't prepared . . ."

Loretta's eyes widened. "Don't you dare. I put him to sleep in the other room because I thought it safer to keep him out of your reach. If you left with him, I'm afraid I'd be right at your heels."

Calista held out her arms, and Loretta gave her another hug that made her backbone crack.

"Thank you for watching over my boy," Loretta said. "We'll never lose him again."

"Thank Matthew. This was all his doing." Calista went to the door. "I have some clothes for Howie and a bottle or two. I'll send them this way."

Loretta started to answer, then covered her mouth and with shining eyes headed toward her room to wake the boy she'd thought she would never see again.

Calista would long remember how thrilled Loretta was to have her baby back. She could imagine how Loretta would fuss over him, bathe him in tears and prayers of thanksgiving, and how eagerly she would wait for Dan to come home and share their news. It would be the happiest day of their lives.

If only Jinxy Seaton could have the same reunion.

CHAPTER
24

Matthew clipped another daisy from the raised patch of flowers in his garden and set it aside. He'd miss this little square of beauty when he got his own place, but there was nothing written that forbade him from planting his own garden once he got a house for himself. Or for himself and Calista.

The sun had gone down behind the Keystone Hotel, but there was still an hour of daylight left. The air had begun to cool, and bugs were buzzing around the more fragrant bushes. How could Calista leave? She couldn't. She had to stay, and Matthew would convince her of it. But the later in the day it got, the more he worried that trouble had befallen her. Perhaps another man like Teddy or a crooked policeman had attacked her, or Silas had come looking for her to even the score. It might be something as simple as her going to Granny Laura's to say good-bye and after that catching the train. Whatever it meant, he didn't like it.

From the alley, he heard the rustle of cloth. The blooms of tiger lilies shivered as someone hurried past on the other side of the fence. It was Calista. His throat tightened when she opened the gate and came in.

"For you." He held out the untidy bouquet.

She dropped the small, soft bundle she was holding and reached to take the flowers. "There's so much. I don't know where to start. Has Silas been dealt with?"

"I'm flummoxed," Matthew said. "How could he stand there and show no remorse?"

"Those poor women. And the children . . ." Her eyes shone. "But I have unbelievable news. Guess where Howie is."

"With Maisie?"

"With Loretta Campbell. He's their baby."

Matthew frowned. "You're not making any sense."

"He was born during Dan's injury. Remember them talking about how hungry they were? How they had no money even for food? They took him to the Children's Home. They hoped to get him back when they got some money. You can imagine how distraught they were when the raffle was announced."

Matthew shook his head. He couldn't think of anything more painful. And ever since then, Loretta had mourned bravely, never telling them the reason. "They didn't know you had him?"

"She said the pain was too great to bear. They avoided the newspapers. They didn't want to read about how happy he was to be going with another family. She just prayed that he would be cared for."

"But now she has him?"

"These are his things." She pointed to the bundle. "I told Loretta you would bring them. You'll want to see them. They're so happy. It turns out you were right. God used Maisie and Amos's prank for good. I'm glad I listened to you."

The bruises on her neck hadn't faded yet. Her face was flushed with excitement and animated by her good news. She was beautiful, and he had something important to tell her.

"I have news too."

"Did you find Mrs. Bowman?" she asked.

"No, but I found Mrs. Cook." When Calista made no remark, he continued. "Calista, I'm not a humble man. I think I can improve the world. I think I can help people. And I think I can make you happy. Your parents might be wealthier than I ever aspire to be, but you've told me that it doesn't mean much without a purpose. If you're willing to get by on less money, you'll never lack for a purpose here. You'll be with me, looking after the miners and working girls in Joplin and making it a city to be proud of."

He felt the release of days of frustration. His speech had been easier to deliver than he'd expected. Once he got rolling, it had been the most natural thing in the world.

Calista dropped her arms. The flowers dangled from her hand. She reminded Matthew of a weary miner who'd just dropped his shovel, only to learn that he had to take it up again.

"You have some nerve." She sounded more wounded than outraged. "You think you can make an offer that will tempt me to give up everything I've worked for?"

Was it surprise or wounded pride that made him sputter? "You want to stay. I can tell you want to stay."

"I want a lot of things. I want a nap. I want a new locket to go with my damask corsage. I want ice cream—no jokes about me eating it. But what kind of woman would I be if I neglected my duty for any of that?" She'd started this as a recital of facts, but she was growing more passionate. "Have you considered how fortunate I was that the Pinkerton Agency allowed me to join them despite my age? Did you take any time to look at my accomplishments and think if it was fair for you to ask me to give up my job?"

What was she saying? It was like she'd flipped the whole world on its head and was reading a script backward.

"I have to accept this position at the mine," he said. "The timing, the offer—it's God's moving. If I quit, what would that accomplish?"

Calista blinked back tears. Matthew wanted to comfort her,

but he recognized it was her struggle. She looked up, eyes full of sorrow.

"I don't want to leave you, Matthew. I don't. There's so much more that I thought we'd get to do together. So much more that I thought we'd get to be to each other, but I failed. I didn't find Lila, and I can't see past this failure. It's not my pride. It's that a girl is out there, somewhere, separated from her family and friends, enduring Lord knows what, and I didn't find her." She reached into her pocket and pulled out a folded picture. "This is her. This is my duty right now. That's all I can think about."

Bless Calista and her single-mindedness. Matthew nodded his understanding as she folded the picture away. Although he felt her rejection all the way to his marrow, he'd take it on the chin. They both had their callings. The woman he'd assumed was thoughtless, heedless, and fickle had turned out to be principled—and those principles were keeping them apart.

Instead of admitting that it wasn't going to happen, Matthew would tell himself that it wasn't going to happen *yet*. He would set his disappointment aside and do what he could to ease her mind.

"You furthered the investigation," he said. "You found the connection between the Rushes and the Bowmans. When they find Lila, it'll be because of the work you did."

She raised her head and took his hand. "You're kind. Kinder than I deserve. Don't think that I want to say no to you. Don't think that it's easy for me. I wasn't expecting it. I thought that I'd love my job so much that there wouldn't be room for anyone else." Her chest rose with a deep breath. "I love you, but there's a chance that the next assignment might be just as important. I might catch a killer, or prove someone's innocence, or locate another missing child. I don't know what God has in store, but I'm determined to follow Him, no matter the cost." She pressed his hand to her lips. "Please don't hate me."

No, there was no hate. Just unbelievable sadness.

"What time do you leave?" he asked.

"First light in the morning. Graham is making the arrangements for me. I'll meet the new agent in Kansas City, tell him what we know, and then go back to the office in Chicago and see what awaits me."

"Will you tell Mr. Pinkerton about me?"

She stood. "Not everything. I couldn't tell him everything." She looked up shyly. "You're too special to share."

He'd been a gentleman. He'd been considerate of the rough handling she'd endured. But here was the woman he loved telling him that she was leaving. Leaving with no words of when she'd return, when she'd see him again, when her conscience would release her to be his.

He moved slowly, deliberately. He slid a hand around to her back and held her against him. She didn't object, but her hands remained hanging at her sides. He wanted something more than resignation. He bent his head to catch her lips. A kiss—sure and sweet, but a good-bye, nonetheless, with no promises implied.

He sighed and rested his forehead against hers. "You can't give me anything more?"

"I'd be better off forgetting."

He'd always been able to tell when she was lying, even when she was lying to herself. "If I thought you could forget, I'd be miserable right now, but I'm not. As soon as you get settled somewhere else, you're going to realize that you miss me, and you'll work particularly hard to figure out a way for us to be together."

"I've got to go, Matthew. The way things stand right now, it's all I can do."

His confidence wavered. What if she were right? What if she'd always walked away from a case and never thought about it again? Where would that leave him? How long could he pretend that she was coming back?

"God be with you," he said. "It's in His hands. If it's His will that you come back, then I pray that it happens in good time."

"Amen." She looked him over, and he'd be lying if it didn't feel like she was memorizing him for the future. A future without him. "Good-bye, Matthew. Thank you for all you've done."

He hadn't done enough, or she'd be staying. But he let her leave with a friendly wave. Her skirt swished and rasped as it brushed against the tiger lilies that lined the walkway in the garden, and then she was gone.

Calista closed the door of her hotel room behind her, then, on shaking knees, stumbled to the window. Gripping the sill, she peered at Matthew down below, still looking at the closed gate that she'd passed through. She'd barely managed to tear herself away from him before she'd crumbled, threw out all her resolve, and accepted his offer of marriage. Pulling away without some word to soften the separation was like a knife's slice across her heart. After stumbling through the lobby, she'd counted the floors in the elevator, willing herself to think on anything besides the despair and regret flooding through her. But now, with the door closed behind her, she could finally release the emotions she'd hidden from him.

She had to leave. She'd made a commitment to Mr. Pinkerton, and until she satisfied her agreement with him, she couldn't entertain another contract, however attractive. In the depths of her heart, she told herself that she'd come back. That she'd check in at the office, see what the next assignment was, and then make her decision on whether to return, but she knew it was unlikely. Calista wasn't very old, but already she'd learned that paths, once taken, rarely allowed you to go back and change direction without some penalty. Once the decision was made at the fork in the road, it was incredibly hard to change course.

She couldn't allow Matthew to wait in hope, because sooner or later there'd come a day when she'd have to tell him that he should extinguish that hope. She'd have to write, or visit, and tell him again that she wasn't coming back. It had been better not to procrastinate. Better to tell him now and end it cleanly.

But this didn't feel like a clean break—more like a jagged tearing. How she wished there was something she could have said to ease the sorrow. She laid her chin on the sill and let the tears fall freely as she watched him go to the gate and look down the alley where she'd been.

The pain was too great. Calista turned from the window and gathered her things. Graham and Willow were going to let her use the guest bunk in their private car for the trip to Kansas City. She would go there now and get some sleep while waiting for the train to leave. Better now than to wait until morning and have to be up at the crack of dawn. Better to barricade herself in the private car tonight than to wait at the hotel alone and fight the temptation to go next door and say *yes*.

It was an hour's work to pack her bags and alert the bellboy that she was vacating. He sent for a wagon to haul her trunks and a driver to take her to the train station. Calista turned her head as they passed the flower shop, knowing that she'd jump out of the buggy at the first sign of Matthew, and that was not what she needed to do.

With a few hurried instructions from the subdued staff on Graham's private car, her bags were taken care of. All that was left was to get to her bunk and hide until the morning when they were under way and her eyes no longer bore the marks of heartbreak.

But it wasn't to be.

"I'm glad you decided to come in tonight," Willow said as she met Calista in the passageway. "It has worried me sick, the way you were treated at the police station."

"I'm exhausted. If you'll show me to my room . . ." Calista kept her eyes down, but it was no use.

"What's the matter? Are you crying?" Willow dipped her head to get a better look. "You poor thing. Graham told me what you've been through. I've been so worried about you. But you're fine now. By morning light, Joplin will be far behind you. No one can touch you then."

More tears threatened as Willow patted Calista on the back, making soothing sounds of comfort.

It wasn't the police she feared. It was the fear that she'd just made the biggest mistake of her life, yet she couldn't go back to correct it. Not without going forward first.

A throat cleared, and Calista looked up to see Graham standing in the doorway. His mouth was turned down in sympathy. "Is this about that miner friend of yours?"

"Of course not," Willow huffed. "He didn't do anything to hurt her."

"I didn't say he did." Graham slid his hands into his pockets. "Does he know how you feel?"

"He knows that I . . . not the extent. He doesn't know how much." Calista sniffed, then took the handkerchief Graham offered. "I have to leave for my job. I have no choice. A girl's life might depend on it."

"But after?" Willow asked.

"You told him you'd come back once it was solved," Graham added, trying to settle the matter.

Calista shook her head. "I won't make any promises when I don't know what's ahead. I left him with nothing but a good-bye."

Willow bit her lip and looked away in disappointment. *Go ahead*, Calista wanted to say. *Judge me. You can't make me feel any worse.*

Graham motioned to Willow with a tilt of his head. "She needs rest. It's been a trying day. Everything will look up in the morning."

It was her cue to go. He was giving her an escape. Taking her arm, Willow led her silently to her room and bade her good night, leaving Calista in the little berth alone.

She was doing the right thing. She knew that, but it had caught her unaware how badly she wanted to do something different.

CHAPTER
25

"Miss York checked out of her room last night." The clerk fought a yawn, as if his news was of no consequence. "Sorry. I've been on duty since last evening."

Matthew tapped the counter once by way of reply, then set his sights on the train station. He had nothing new to say, and he wouldn't pester her for a promise, but he wanted to be there. Mostly, he wanted to be there because she was hurting, and he couldn't stand to think of her hurting alone. He'd stay at her side as long as she let him . . . maybe until they pried him off the railroad car and it started down the tracks.

The train's whistle told him that he wouldn't be able to offer even that.

The Joplin depot was crowded with gondola railcars hauling lead and zinc to factories around the country and the world. By the time Matthew got to the right track, the train to Kansas City was already moving. Matthew watched for the very last car, and when he saw the gilt lettering and large viewing windows, he knew it was Buchanan's car and that it was carrying his love away.

But not all of his loves.

Funny how yesterday he'd been given the job of his dreams.

Even better, a job he hadn't dreamed about because before yesterday it hadn't existed. But today his arms yearned for a pickax and shovel. He could chip a tunnel all the way to Kansas if they'd turn him loose.

But that wasn't what God had ordained for him. After all his prayers, all his efforts, God had given him the desire of his heart—to be able to minister to the people surrounding him. This was what he'd been brought to Joplin for, to intercede for folks like his uncle Manuel before their despair and hard living caught up with them. This was the door that had opened. He couldn't keep standing in front of a locked door, wishing for a key.

He had an appointment with Reverend Dixon and Oscar Kentworth. He had plans to make, a ministry to commence, people to enlist. Maybe later he'd think about what he wanted to say to Calista. Maybe he'd write her and then miraculously learn where to send her letters. It wasn't likely, but it was all he had to hold on to.

Matthew arrived at the church too early and had to wait for Reverend Dixon to arrive. He bought a breakfast of sausage and biscuits to eat while he sat on the church steps, but he'd barely gotten settled when he heard a groundskeeper unlocking the church doors behind him.

Whoever had unlocked the door hadn't seen him sitting there. Matthew rose and pulled the door open.

Although the lights hadn't been turned on yet, the entryway was lit by the morning sun coming through the windows. His entrance startled the young lady passing through, and then he recognized her and *he* was the one startled.

"Mrs. Bowman? What are you doing here?"

She stifled a cry as she pushed her spectacles up her nose. Her shoes scuffed against the smooth marble floor as she turned and ran toward a door at the end of the hallway.

"Why are you running?" Matthew called. "You know me."

And he knew her. Despite the fact that she wasn't dressed in the uniform from the Children's Home, there was no mistaking her. And because of her and Officer Rush, Calista had been arrested and had to flee town.

Matthew ran after her, stopping only as she slammed an office door in his face. "You owe me some answers." His voice echoed in the long hallway.

"Matthew Cook!" Reverend Dixon barked as he entered the building. "What are you doing?"

"Mrs. Bowman. What's she doing here?"

The pastor's face wrinkled in confusion. "She's a member of this congregation."

"But why was she here overnight?" Matthew looked around. "There are no services going on. There's no reason for her to be behind a locked door."

Reverend Dixon studied him for a long moment. "As you're going to be working in conjunction with the church, you'll be expected to abide by the same rules we do, and that includes holding stories in confidence."

"What do you know about her? Do you know her contacts?" Matthew asked.

"I do."

"And you trust them?"

"Absolutely not. That's why she's here."

It was too early in the morning for such riddles. Matthew frowned. Being demoted back to cokey was looking like the inevitable result of this morning's work.

Stepping carefully around him, Reverend Dixon knocked on the door. "Mrs. Bowman, would you mind coming out here and talking with us?"

The scratching sound was her shoes moving across the floor. "He's one of them," she said. "The ones I told you about."

Matthew filled his lungs, but Dixon thumped him in the chest to halt his protests. "It's Matthew Cook. I trust him, and you should too."

"He's with that lady. They're the reason I can't go home."

The pastor looked up at Matthew. "Do you know what she's talking about?"

Matthew's eyes darted away from the pastor's piercing gaze. If Mrs. Bowman was involved in a kidnapping ring, then she was a danger to Calista. How to explain without exposing Calista?

"I do. All I can tell you is that before God, Miss York has the courage and integrity of the prophets. She is doing the Lord's work. If Mrs. Bowman or you can tell me something that shows me I'm wrong, then I'll submit to your wisdom."

Reverend Dixon leaned his head near the door. "Did you hear that? Don't you think that sounds fair, Lila?"

"Lila?" Matthew's eyes stuck open wide. "Lila Seaton?"

He'd found her? If this was Lila, then Calista's mission was finished. She hadn't failed.

Reverend Dixon spun around. "How do you know that name?"

"We're looking for her. Her family is looking for her. They want to know she's safe."

The reverend didn't budge.

Matthew raised his voice and spoke to the door. "They're worried about you, Lila. They'll be so happy to know where you are."

Reverend Dixon started walking forward, crowding Matthew down the hall and away from the door. If he hadn't been a pastor who was offering to help on this new job, Matthew would have taken offense.

"You know her family? I have to ask you to leave, Matthew. I'll talk to Mr. Kentworth, but I'm not sure this arrangement is going to work."

"What's going on?" Matthew had never been so confused. "I've never met her parents, but they claim that she was abducted. What does that have to do with me?"

A bolt clicked, and the door behind Reverend Dixon opened a crack. They both watched as a slight, determined face peered out at them.

"He already knows I'm here," Lila Seaton Bowman said. "As long as my plans for escape aren't compromised . . ."

"We'll get you away from Joplin without anyone the wiser." The preacher held the door open, removing the barrier between her and them. "But maybe it would be best if you explained to Mr. Cook what you're running away from."

Matthew must have passed twenty heartbeats in the time it took her to decide. Finally she nodded and allowed herself to be escorted to the pastor's office. Mrs. Bowman clasped her shaking hands and took one of the polished chairs.

The pastor sat in a wingback chair between them. "Let's start with you, Matthew. What do you intend to do, now that you've found Lila?"

Matthew squirmed on the backless stool. "That depends on her. What does she want to do?"

"I want to stay in Joplin, but you've made that impossible." She removed her spectacles and set them on the table before her.

"Me? What did I do?"

"Miss York, then. She's going to alert my family to where I am, and my husband and I will have to flee again."

"No, no, no." Matthew waved his hands in front of his face. "That wasn't what we wanted to do at all. All we wanted was to bring your family back together."

"What if that's the last thing I want?"

Matthew shot the pastor a nervous look. "Can I ask why?"

"It's a fair request, Lila," said the pastor.

"My father is a criminal," she said. "For years he conducted business right under my nose. I didn't understand most of it, but as I grew older, I began to realize that the things he was telling people to do weren't legal. When I began questioning him, the trouble started. He wouldn't let me meet people at parties. He became very selective of who my friends were. It was like living in a fishbowl with a big cat just waiting for me to swim the wrong way."

"You're an adult," Matthew said. "What power does he have?"

"You don't know Chicago. My father says he's protecting me, but he couldn't protect my sister from his boss, Baxter Perkins. When she was killed, I knew that sooner or later I would be faced with a choice—either lie to protect the business or become a target of the big bosses. That's why I can't go home. I can't go to the police. Half the police in Chicago report to Baxter."

"Like the police in Joplin?"

Lila's eyes flashed. "Officer Rush is a fine man. When Miss York asked for me by name, he knew she'd been sent by my family. He had to act. It gave me time to seek sanctuary while my husband Bart gets us packed up. Tomorrow we'll quit town and go somewhere else, because now that Miss York has found us, we know we aren't safe here."

Matthew traced the wood grain on the tabletop. "Miss York is mistaken. She was told that you were kidnapped."

"You can see for yourself that I'm not in distress. I met Bart and his sister Della in Chicago years ago. Our correspondence advanced our relationship, and knowing my dilemma, he offered to rescue me. It wasn't long before we were married. Della and her husband have been most helpful in keeping my identity a secret. I've gone to great lengths to hide from my family."

The lady before him so little resembled Calista's picture that Matthew would have never guessed. Even now, with her spectacles removed, Lila Seaton didn't have the same haunted look of the girl in the photo. The porcelain complexion and the upturned nose were the same, but her months of freedom had completely altered her appearance.

"Calista doesn't know that you're hiding. If I could get word to her before she reports to . . ." He paused, still aware that Calista's occupation was better left undefined. She was on her way to Kansas City to meet with another detective. Once that detective had the names of Della Rush and Mrs. Bowman, it would take him no time at all to find out that Mrs. Bowman was Lila Seaton. And no matter where they traveled, they would still be pursued. "We need to call off the hunt. If I can get word to Calista before she talks to her replacement, you could stay here."

"Do you think she'd give up on the job, just on that?"

Would she? While the story made perfect sense to Matthew, Calista was more wary. And she was devoted to her job. More devoted to it than she was to him, evidently. Would she oppose the mighty Pinkerton Agency on behalf of a young lady who wanted to cut ties with her family? If she believed him, believed Lila, then she would. He had to have faith in her. Hadn't she kept Howie, even though it inconvenienced her something terrible? She might vacillate, but in the end, she would make the right decision. All his future rested on that hope.

He had to get to her before she passed on her information. Time was slipping away from him.

"Don't go anywhere," he said. "If we can convince Miss York of your plight, you might be able to stay in Joplin. I have to catch her."

He stood, banging his knee against the leg of the round table, but he barely felt it in his hurry. He accepted Reverend Dixon's well-wishes and assurance that he would explain his absence to Mr. Kentworth and Mr. Blount, and then Matthew raced to the depot to buy a ticket. But where in Kansas City was she? It was even bigger than Joplin. He doubted he could just ask for directions from someone at the depot. He'd lose valuable time.

"Matthew Cook! Just who I was looking for."

Turning, Matthew saw another Kentworth, and this one was angry.

"What do you mean, introducing my sister to the likes of Silas?"

Amos had the same fighting stance as his sister, but Matthew reckoned he could throw more weight behind a swing.

"I didn't know, or I wouldn't have."

"There's one thing you can do to make it right. Show me where he lives. He's due a visit from me." Amos spat on the ground to punctuate his threat.

But the pieces were falling into place for Matthew. "Sure, but one thing first. Have you got a minute? Come with me to the depot."

Amos's face lightened. "What are we doing at the depot?"

"If I got you to Kansas City, could you find Calista's house?"

"Yep. Only been there twice, but it's not the kind of place you forget."

"Then c'mon. We're hitting the rails. You can go see your uncle and aunt York."

Amos, always ready for an adventure, jumped into step with Matthew. "I should wash up before I take a trip. That's what Ma and Granny taught me, but since we're in a hurry . . ."

"You can wash up on the train. Your aunt will be happy to see you regardless."

But would Calista? She hadn't told Matthew good-bye only to have him show up on her doorstep the next day. She'd talked about having time to think things over, seeing if she could live her life without him. If she wanted space, he wasn't giving her much at all. But there was more than his desires at stake. Lila's safety mattered too. He had to reach Calista before the other detectives did. He had to stop her from sharing what she'd learned if they really wanted to save Lila Seaton.

CHAPTER
26

It had been months since Calista had passed through the clematis-lined arch that led to the Yorks' private gardens at their house on Scarritt Point. Although their green expanse in the city had never offered the freedom that Granny Laura's ranch provided, it was enough room for the raucous activity that was part of any Kentworth's birthright.

The sound of breaking glass was Calista's first clue as to where her family might be. She crossed the Japanese bridge over the lily pads and found her mother and two siblings involved in some sort of contest.

"You stepped over the line," Evangelina cried. "Before you re-leased your shot, you stepped over the line." Her frock of gauzy silk crepe floated like wisps of scented smoke on the air. Her dark hair framed her face amid all the pastels and drew attention to her striking coloring.

"What line? All you said was that I'm supposed to stand here. I didn't know there was a line." This from her brother, Corban. The elegant suit he wore showed he should be working in one of the high-rise offices their father owned. Instead, he'd traded his account book for a slingshot and was standing opposite a line of china plates propped inside a bookcase that had been carried outside from the study.

With an explosion, a plate shattered. Calista's mother, Pauline, lowered her slingshot. "Did you observe your mummy? My toes didn't go over the line, and that puts me in the lead."

"Calista!" Evangelina squealed and ran toward her, catching her in an aggressive embrace. "We didn't know you were coming."

Her mother hugged her as well, while Corban tested the elasticity of his slingshot bands.

"Are you back for good?" her mother asked.

"How is . . . what is your sick friend's name?" Evangelina asked.

Calista didn't miss the arch look that passed between her mother and brother. Disbelief. "The doctors think she's completely recovered."

"Would you swear on a Bible?" Corban asked.

"Don't be vulgar," Calista replied.

"I received a letter from your school that says you are finishing up the final requirements," her mother said. "Is that correct?"

Once she'd secured a permanent spot in the agency, Calista would gladly tell them the truth. Until then, it was better to stay with the story they'd invented.

"Just be glad I'm here," Calista said. "When did we start destroying fine china?"

The beauty of the York family was that when a conversation became inconvenient, there was usually a ready distraction.

"Father's investment group bought the Fremont Hotel, but they're going to reopen it under a new name. He told me to dispose of anything with the old designation on it." Corban tilted his head toward the plates. "Just doing my duty."

"We're all helping," Evangelina said. "Mother even thought to put down a tarp before we started, lest the ground become sown in shards."

"I so enjoy the grass on my bare feet." Pauline Kentworth York had never succumbed to the niceties of her social class, a fact that both Calista and her father found charming.

"Willow and Graham asked if they could pay a call this morning," said Calista, "and then this afternoon I will be receiving a call from a man I know from Chicago. Light refreshments may be required."

"Willow's coming?" Evangelina took another jawbreaker and loaded her slingshot. "We'll save some plates for her."

But Corban had second thoughts. "Graham Buchanan has better things to do than break dishes in the garden. Come to think of it, so do I. I'd better get back to the office. Father is probably looking for me."

Their mother smiled. "Good idea, son. We wouldn't want an important man like Mr. Buchanan to catch you shirking your duties."

Corban relinquished his slingshot on the tray next to the jawbreakers, took up his suit coat, and hurried out.

Evangelina handed his slingshot to Calista. "Join us."

"No, thank you. I'll go inside."

"Your room is fresh, if you'd like to retire," her mother said. "You look like you could use a revival."

Calista agreed as she departed. Since daybreak, Willow had kept her company, asking about the case in Joplin and what Calista thought lay ahead. Willow claimed to understand the difficulty Calista was having in saying good-bye to Matthew, but Calista knew she couldn't fathom the depths of her pain. How could Calista explain that she knew she was doing the right thing but wished it was anything but the right thing? In time, she should feel God's peace and pleasure over her obedience, but right now all she felt was the loss. She could only ask if it was worth it. And it wasn't only her own pain that grieved her, but knowing that Matthew was hurting as well.

The sacrifice is an offering, she whispered as she climbed the stairs to her room. *I'm offering my pain to you, Lord. Please accept it as the most precious gift I can give you right now.*

She was doing what was right, and she'd thought that when she left Joplin, she'd feel freer. That once the decision was behind her, she could rest in the assurance that it was the only decision she could have made. But instead, she ached more with every mile. This wasn't going to be the decision of a moment but a decision she had to live with every moment, perhaps for the rest of her life.

Reaching her lilac and lace bedroom, Calista flopped on the bed and allowed herself to drift to a troubled sleep. After her sleepless night on the train, she shouldn't have been surprised that she slept so hard, but when her mother woke her, she was astonished to hear that she'd slept through Willow and Graham's visit.

"They told me not to wake you," her mother said. "Since you rode with them, I assumed you wouldn't feel cheated to miss out on their visit. But your Chicago friend has arrived, along with your cousin. They're waiting downstairs."

Cousin? Who was with the detective?

The bedclothes wrinkled beneath Calista as she rolled to the edge of the mattress and sat up. It would take a moment to get her wits about her. Her hair felt lopsided, and she could feel the seams of her quilt imprinted on her cheek. "I'll be right down," she said and reached for the carafe of water to pour herself a drink.

She'd never had to admit to this kind of failure before. But not only had she failed, she'd been recalled. She'd endangered the investigation and perhaps endangered the victim. She could only hope that her replacement could use the information she'd gathered to find Lila and lift the burden of her mistakes from her.

Spritzing some perfume on herself, Calista took a final look in the mirror. Her cheeks were flushed from her nap, but her mouth had a determined set. No simpering or playing the ingénue for whomever the operative would be. This was business.

Who had the office sent? She made her way down the stairs to the parlor. Jinxy Seaton would insist on the best, especially after her failure. Would it be Leon? Sampson?

Upon entering the parlor, her mother gave her a quizzical smile. "There you are, dear. Amos and I had begun to wonder if you were going to make it."

Amos?

"Surprise!" her cousin called, bounding off the sofa. "Bet you didn't expect to see me. I sure didn't expect to see you today, but Matthew prevailed upon me—"

"Matthew?" How her heart twisted at the sound of his name. Why was Amos here? To agitate her wound before it had time to heal?

Then she saw movement from the corner of the room. A figure pulled away from the drapes where he'd been looking out at the garden. Her lungs filled as Matthew came forward, holding her gaze. His collarless shirt and suspenders represented something solid and unaffected in a room full of gilt and veneer. He came near but kept both hands on his straw hat, clutched in front of him.

"Hello, Miss York. I should've warned you I was coming, but there wasn't time."

Her hands trembled. What was this about? When they'd parted, she thought they both understood the impossibility of a relationship between them. If he'd come with plans to persuade her to go back, he was just inflicting more pain. Both cruel and pointless. Why make her do this again?

She could feel the blood draining from her face.

"Amos," her mother said, "let's find Evangelina. She's got a game in the garden that you'll tear up. Come see if you can beat Corban's score." Pauline laid a hand on Calista's arm as she passed with Amos, stopping only to shut the doors behind her as they left.

"This isn't right." Calista couldn't bear to look at him. She gripped the back of a chair like it was a shield against her weakness. "Nothing has changed."

315

"Nothing between us has changed, but everything else has." Matthew took a deep breath. "I found Lila."

Calista gaped. "Where? How?"

"Have you already talked to Mr. Pinkerton? Does he know the names Rush and Bowman?"

"It wasn't safe over the phone. That's why we're meeting here."

"Good. You can't tell him anything." Matthew said it so matter-of-factly, like it was the easiest decision in the world.

"I can't tell him? What are you talking about?"

"You've met Lila Seaton. You've known her all along. She ran away from home after her sister was killed. Lila knows more about the mob than is good for her. She knows that her father's boss is responsible for her sister's death, and she knows that sooner or later she'll meet the same fate."

"Baxter Perkins killed Florence Seaton? Jinxy doesn't know?"

"She doesn't think so. But he wants to control her every move, just in case. Lila was under constant surveillance. Her father thinks he's keeping her safe from his criminal activity, but he can't protect her."

"So she faked her own kidnapping?"

"And she doesn't want to be found. She wants to be free from the criminals he exposed her to. She wants to have her own life away from crime. A few years ago, she met Della and her brother in Chicago and started a correspondence with them. When she decided to flee, they offered her sanctuary. Not surprisingly, she married Mr. Bowman soon after. Since then—"

"Bowman? Mrs. Bowman from the Children's Home?" Calista paced the floor. "I was talking to Lila Seaton the whole time?"

"And if she had known you were looking for her, she would've disappeared sooner. When Officer Rush arrested you, he suspected you were hired by her family. He was giving Lila and her husband time to leave town. For all they knew, you were with the gangsters trying to do Lila harm."

"And in a way, I was. However innocent my intentions, the end result would have been the same." Calista was starting to breathe easier. Talking about her problems with Matthew was as natural as humming as she walked. "I'll call Mr. Pinkerton and explain that we can't give Jinxy the answer he's looking for. I don't know what we can do to keep him from hiring someone else, though."

"But Lila won't have to run again. That's all she's asking—that I bring home your assurance that the search will be called off and she's free to stay in Joplin. As for you, you won't lose any more sleep worrying about her misery." He was keeping his distance, but his care for her was as intoxicating as any caress.

"That's why I do this job," Calista said. "I could be here, shooting jawbreakers at china plates, but that wouldn't be fulfilling."

He looked confused by her example but nodded with her conclusion. "Here's to work that we love," he said.

It was starting again. The regret, the wishing, flooding over her. Pure torture, but now that she knew why he'd come, she didn't hold it against him. And from the look of it, he was suffering as much as she was.

"Well, I've said what I've come to say. There's nothing else." For the first time, he looked around the room, taking in its extravagance.

"It's ridiculous, isn't it?" Calista laughed. "Father hires a decorator to keep us in fashion because Mother has no interest in it."

"You left all this for your job? That makes me feel less slighted." His grin was bittersweet.

"Miss York." It was the butler. "Mr. Pinkerton and Mr. Sampson are inquiring if you are home."

Pinkerton himself had come? Ever since his father's passing, Robert Pinkerton had done his best to live up to his example. If the circumstances had been different, Calista would have been flattered by the attention.

Matthew cleared his throat. "I'll be going."

"There's not another train south for an hour." She had to say good-bye, but not yet.

He lowered his chin. "You've got a job to do. Take care, Calista. You're forever in my prayers."

And he walked out the door.

She could only pray that the searing of her heart wouldn't pain her for long.

Matthew's visit had been unexpected, and so had his news. Calista also hadn't expected Mr. Pinkerton to come, but it was for the best. Arthur Sampson didn't have the authority to change the mission without Mr. Pinkerton's permission.

Mr. Pinkerton came to the threshold of the door, then paused as he scanned the room.

"There's no danger here," Calista said, although she knew danger wasn't the only thing he searched for. He also looked for information that might come in handy later. Clues that would reveal something of her family's character, her own upbringing. Perhaps having the meeting at her house wasn't a good idea after all. "Please have a seat."

"We don't have much time." Mr. Pinkerton removed his hat and sat at the edge of the chair, his weight still over his toes. "Your next assignment awaits."

Even though Calista had slipped up by involving the police, he wasn't terminating her contract. "Thank you for giving me another chance," she said.

Who knew what the next case would be? Another family looking for resolution? Recovering funds that had meant opportunity to a business? Calista glanced at the window from which the sound of shattering china could be heard. Getting back to work would be for the best. She needed the reminder of why she was doing this. She'd go to a new location, and this time she'd have a new identity, and the new person she was pretending to be wouldn't be in love with someone impossible.

318

"We only have a few minutes for you to brief Arthur, then I'll take you as far as Phoenix while we create your documents and story." Mr. Pinkerton removed a handkerchief from his pocket and patted his forehead. "Now, what can you tell Arthur to help him find Lila Seaton?"

"She doesn't need finding," Calista said.

Her boss's head jolted. "You found her?"

"I found out about her. She wasn't kidnapped, and she isn't in danger, at least not from any strangers. Lila Seaton ran away from her father and from Baxter Perkins. She doesn't want to be found."

Why did he look more annoyed than relieved? "Did you find her in Joplin?" he asked, as if Lila's safety wasn't the first priority.

Calista blinked. Her fellow operatives had always been the only people entitled to hear the full story. They were a team who understood the stress of the falsehoods and the elation of the victories. She had never hidden anything from them.

Until now.

If Robert Pinkerton thought he was going to force Lila's location from her—well, Calista answered to a higher authority. If the two were in conflict, she knew where her loyalty must lie.

"No, despite all my searching, I didn't find her in Joplin." Her eager-to-please, naive persona had served her well with suspects. Now she was using it on her boss. She would have thought Mr. Pinkerton would see right through it, but even the cleverest of men were liable to see what they wanted to see.

"Then, where is she?" Arthur asked.

"What's it matter? She isn't in danger. She never was," Calista answered.

Mr. Pinkerton folded his handkerchief carefully as he studied her. She knew what he was doing—deciding which approach would give him the information he sought. She'd been trained by him. She knew his methods.

"Sometimes we get so involved with the cases," he said, "that

319

we begin to sympathize with the objects of our investigations. When we set aside our identities and make new ones, those moral safeguards don't always appear when we need them. At times like those, we go back to the foundations of the case. What was the purpose of this job? Who is the customer? When we look at those facts—not feelings, but facts—we see that we owe Jinxy Seaton an answer."

"We owe Jinxy Seaton a return of his fees." Calista sat up taller to meet the gazes of the two men straight on. "That's all we owe him." Her heart raced. If he would only listen to her . . .

Mr. Pinkerton shook his head. "Don't do this, Miss York. You were paid to do a job. If you refuse to turn over the evidence you uncovered during your tenure, you'll have to return your wages."

"Gladly."

"Don't forget the expenses," Arthur said. "A month in that swanky hotel? You can't afford to pay that back, not on your salary."

"You don't think so?" Calista raised a fine eyebrow.

Mr. Pinkerton took another look around the elaborate room and then heaved a sigh. "You've been an asset to the firm, and I'm prepared to offer you an official spot on our roster. Don't ruin your career over this one unorthodox case. We'll come to some compromise." He pounded his knee as he pounced on the solution. "We can arrange a meeting between Jinxy and his daughter. They can work out the details. It's probably just a family spat. . . ."

As he continued, Calista could feel the rending taking place, and unlike the last separation, this one was filled with light and joy. This, then, was her answer. She'd known God had provided this job for her when she was searching for purpose. Her dissatisfaction with her life in Kansas City had been a gift that had led her to more challenging tasks. Every day, in every way, she'd known that working for Pinkerton was the right thing to do. She hadn't doubted that until she'd met Matthew. But now she saw that God had called her to set things aright, to bring healing to people's deepest pains. Her purpose hadn't changed, but the way she followed it would.

Calista wasn't one to fold up shop at the first hardship, though. She would have endured. She would have sacrificed. But suddenly the path she'd known God was leading her on veered sharply, and she couldn't have felt a greater relief.

She stood, and Mr. Pinkerton and Sampson's conversation halted.

"I'm grateful for everything you've done for me," she said. "I'm grateful that I was able to work on the side of justice and disclosure, but this is something else altogether. I will not aid you in disclosing the whereabouts of Miss Seaton if it jeopardizes her safety."

"We were just discussing our options," Pinkerton said. "There's no need for you to act against your conscience. You'll move on to the next case, and Sampson will pick up where you left off. Since you never left Jasper County, we can assume that Miss Seaton is somewhere nearby. I'll track down the clues you left, and we'll continue from there. I can appreciate your dilemma and will do my best to work around it while still fulfilling our duty to our client."

"That's not acceptable," Calista said. "I'm not going to leave Miss Seaton"—how hard it was not to call her Mrs. Bowman!—"at the mercy of the agency. If she needs any further obstructions to stay out of her father's clutches, I'll be happy to provide them."

Arthur scoffed. "That's pure contrariness. What could you possibly gain from such a course?"

"Knowing that I did the right thing." Calista breathed deeply, feeling the weight of her worries lifting. "If I may advise you, Mr. Pinkerton, the best course of action from here would be for Mr. Sampson to accompany you to Phoenix and begin working on the next case. As soon as you have him settled and you return to Chicago, you can inform Mr. Seaton that his daughter is well and good and wants no further contact from him. Should he try to find her, I'll arrange for her to serve as a witness against him concerning his business dealings with Baxter Perkins.

"After you finish with that matter," she continued, "tabulate what my change of heart has cost the agency, and send the bill to this address. You might as well address it to my father, Mr. Richard York, as that's who will sign the check. Is there anything I'm missing?"

Mr. Pinkerton didn't like having no recourse, that was evident. But he was too smart to waste time on things that were out of his control. "You've made yourself clear. I hope you don't regret your decision."

To this, Calista could only smile. Perhaps this was why she had been assigned to this case. Instead of a good detective, God had needed someone who wouldn't find the girl . . . not until she found the courage to say no to her boss.

But there was someone she could say yes to, and Calista would waste no time in doing so.

CHAPTER
27

Matthew had had a good day. He hummed to himself as he and Dan left the newly named Lighthouse on the Fox-Berry property. They had already started meeting with the miners even as the building was being constructed around them. Oddly enough, Olive Kentworth was frequently there, consulting on the construction plans and talking to the builders, but when Mr. Blount arrived, she'd slip away and leave her father to do the directing.

Mr. Blount was a wonder. It was he who had named the center, figuring that the men spent enough time in the dark during their working hours. Despite his rough edges, he had a kind heart. Even rarer, he held the riches that he'd earned in low esteem, claiming that he'd been blessed, so it was his job to spread that blessing. While he and Matthew didn't see eye to eye on every matter, God used imperfect vessels. And Matthew was learning just how imperfect he himself was.

Today had been Matthew's first full day at the center. After the shift bell had clanged, Matthew had led a Bible study with a dozen miners, including some of the independent prospectors from nearby plots. After the study, he'd invited Dan Campbell to introduce a topic that was near to both of their hearts—starting

a bereavement fund for injured miners. Dan shared what a difference that would have made for his wife and himself, and donations
were taken on the spot. Most of the men attending didn't have a
prospect as lucrative as Dan's, but their gifts were a start. Besides,
if these men could learn the joy of giving, their community would
reap the benefits for generations.

Matthew had done the right thing by staying. He swallowed the
lump in his throat that appeared despite his peace. He was needed
here. What kind of life could he have with Calista as long as she
was a Pinkerton? He could hardly follow her from assignment to
assignment. He'd made the right choice, and someday it wouldn't
hurt to think about it.

"I'll see you on Sunday," Dan said as they reached the fork in
the road. "I'll tell Howie you said hello."

Matthew had to laugh. He'd tried so hard to prevent that baby
raffle, and look where it had landed him. "Is he sleeping better
now?"

"He's settled right in. It's almost like he knows he belongs with
us." Dan tipped his hat. "Good night."

Night was coming on fast. By the time Matthew reached the tall
buildings of downtown, the sky had darkened to a bruise color,
pretty nonetheless. He'd wash up, then go back out for dinner and
his evening stroll. His work didn't end at the shift bell. He was a
fisher of men, and in Joplin, the fish were biting at all hours in a
pond that was growing by the day. The borders of Joplin were expanding just as quickly as the riches were hauled out of the earth.

Reaching Mr. Trochet's shop, Matthew cut through the store
to his cabin in the back but immediately realized something was
wrong. Keeping his eyes on the gate to the street, he pulled the
shop door closed behind him. He hadn't left the gate open. Perhaps
Mr. Trochet had used the exit? But it wasn't like him to leave the
shop unlocked if he was out.

If it hadn't been for the fight with Calista's attacker, he wouldn't have thought twice about someone hiding in the greenhouse, but now he watched his back. The green scent of the garden hadn't changed. Early evening lightning bugs glowed in the thick stalks of the cannas. Nothing was out of place except the lady pacing the flagstones.

Words failed him. He could only stand and watch. She sensed him and slowed. Gone was her smile, her cheer. In fact, she looked like she'd swallowed a caterpillar whole and it was trying to climb back up. He knew, because he had the same bothersome feeling in his gut.

It was about Lila, he reminded himself. She had come to finish her business.

"Is something wrong?" he asked. How he despised the uncertainty in her eyes. If he had his way, she'd only be secure and confident.

"I told Mr. Pinkerton that I wouldn't disclose Lila's location. He wasn't satisfied with that answer. He thinks that we owe first responsibility to our clients, not to justice."

Matthew's neck tightened. "You can't. We both know Mrs. Bowman. She isn't lying. She isn't playing us false."

"And she went to great lengths to hide, even preparing to run again. If Reverend Dixon hadn't blurted her name in front of you, we still wouldn't know."

"We have to warn her. We have to tell her that her father will be sending men. She has to leave." He tore his eyes from her elegant form wrapped in a violet gown. "You shouldn't have come. The less you know, the less you have to report back to your boss. It'd be better if I handled this alone." He turned to go.

"Matthew, wait." She stepped forward, her skirt swaying over the paver stones. "Mr. Pinkerton insisted that I give up Lila's whereabouts, but I refused. When I saw his intention, I decided that I couldn't tell him anything. Not the names Bowman or Rush, and not that she was anywhere near Joplin. Only that she was safe, hadn't been kidnapped, and did not want to be found by her father."

"Calista, you're amazing." Her eyes shone at his praise. "Only you could tell the mighty Pinkerton Agency no without any repercussions. I'd like to have seen his face—"

"But there were repercussions," she said. "I had to resign. I can't work for him any longer."

The air whooshed out of his lungs like a candle being snuffed in the shaft. He'd thought finding Lila would help Calista, not ruin the course of her life.

He shuffled his feet, trying to find hopeful words for her. "Pinkerton can't be the only detective agency. There's got to be others who could hire you." Because that was what she wanted. She'd told him in no uncertain terms. And honoring her wishes was what he'd committed to doing.

"I told my family what I've been doing. They were flabbergasted. I don't think they'll approve of me working in that business again."

He wanted to be sorry for her—he really did—but when he looked up again, he saw a glimmer of hope in her eyes that hadn't been there before.

"Should I be sad for you?" he asked.

"I don't know. It could be bad, if . . ." She lowered her eyes. "I haven't decided what's next. I guess I'll just have to wait and see what opportunities present themselves."

Like a rising sun, he was gradually seeing the light. There was no new assignment drawing her away. She didn't have to leave. Not tomorrow, maybe not ever. Could it be that was what she wanted?

Matthew moved toward her. It had taken all of his strength to let her go the first time. Even worse the second. Now here she was again.

"Marry me," he said.

Her eyes crinkled. "Is that offer still available?"

"It doesn't matter. I'm making it again, but only if you know for certain that this is what you want. You can't do it to fill your lack of employment until something better comes along." She lowered her head, but he grabbed her by the shoulders. "Don't hide your face, Calista. Give me an answer. You knew before you got on the train that I'd ask, and you knew what you'd say before you rolled into town. Say it."

"Yes." Her face glowed with her slow smile. "That's why I'm here."

"Because you knew you'd be miserable anywhere else?"

"I was willing to be miserable if needed, but that path ended, and it ended right at your doorstep."

Matthew paused, unsure what to do, then quick as a wink he pulled her to himself and kissed her. At first their smiles were too big to kiss properly, but after a few chuckles, her lips softened, and their humor was replaced by joy.

"You were never second choice," she whispered. "You were the impossible dream."

"Impossible would be a rich detective falling in love with a poor miner."

"My specific gift is doing the impossible." She gazed into his eyes. "And just because I marry doesn't mean my heart has changed. There's plenty of injustice that needs addressing in Joplin, but instead of pretending to be a nurse or a decorator, I think having your help will open the necessary doors."

"With me rooting for you, and the entire Kentworth family behind you," Matthew said, "you're bound to succeed."

They were still the same people with the same dreams and same goals, but the paths to those goals had merged. So many plans, so many possibilities, and they would be explored together.

A Note from the Author

Dear Reader,

Pinkertons, mining towns, and baby raffles! There's so much to cover in this brief historical note.

I was born in Joplin and grew up frequenting it on trips from Oklahoma, but until I started my research, I had no idea what a rambunctious town it once was. Wow, Joplin! You surprised me!

The rags-to-riches examples in this book are based on historical accounts. There were many penniless men who took a lease, dug just two feet deeper than the last man, and found themselves wealthy beyond their imagination. Others were stuck in poverty.

Speaking of poverty, the Joplin Children's Home had difficulty keeping up with the needs of the community. In 1910, the Elks planned a charity fair for the Children's Home, and M. B. Peltz, the new manager of the Electric Light Park, offered his services to promote the amusements.

When Mr. Peltz announced his plans for a baby raffle, Joplin was thrown into chaos. The Elks were divided on the idea, but Mayor Humes said he'd call out the militia to prevent a baby from being raffled. Despite the threat, Mr. Peltz continued to share the tragic (and often contradictory) history of the orphaned child, along with promoting the other amusements of the charitable fair. He was arrested, and even after he posted bail, he couldn't help but drop hints to the newspapers about the poor child that would be rescued by someone willing to buy a ticket. We know that babies were raffled off by a foundling hospital in Paris in 1911, so a baby raffle wasn't unheard of in that era.

The day of the Joplin fair arrived with its parade, carnival, and games. There was no baby among the raffled items, but the controversy seemed to have achieved its purpose. One thousand two hundred dollars were raised for the Children's Home, and Mr. Peltz undoubtedly credited himself and the scandal for the success.

One liberty I need to confess involves the inclusion of the Joplin Carnegie Library. It's such a lovely building that I placed it in the story even though it wasn't built until 1902. (Guess what material they used for the roof. Zinc shingles! What else?) That building is still standing today.

And what about those Pinkertons? They were so much fun to research! In the early years, the operatives relied on psychological manipulation to get confessions when evidence was scarce. Kate Warne, the first female operative, was a master at it. But after studying a few of her fascinating cases, I decided that Calista might have an issue with those methods. Still, I recommend reading more about Mrs. Warne. You'll be amazed at her skill and courage.

Thank you again for reading my stories and giving me a reason to dive into our fascinating history. To see what I'm working on next or where to find more of my books, please visit me online at www.reginajennings.com or find me on Facebook.

Sincerely,
Regina

Regina Jennings is a graduate of Oklahoma Baptist University with a degree in English and a minor in history. She's the winner of the National Readers' Choice Award, a two-time Golden Quill finalist, and a finalist for the Oklahoma Book of the Year Award. Regina has worked at the *Mustang News* and at First Baptist Church of Mustang, along with time at the Oklahoma National Stockyards and various livestock shows. She lives outside of Oklahoma City with her husband and four children and can be found online at www.reginajennings.com.

Sign Up for Regina's Newsletter

Keep up to date with Regina's news on book releases and events by signing up for her email list at www.reginajennings.com.

More from Regina Jennings

Caroline Adams returns to Indian Territory craving adventure after tiring of society life. When she comes across swaggering outlaw Frisco Smith, his plan to obtain property in the Unassigned Lands sparks her own dreams for the future. When the land rush begins, they find themselves battling over a claim—and both dig in their heels.

The Major's Daughter
THE FORT RENO SERIES #3